Deeper

Than

Red

A NOVEL

D1216852

SUE DUFFY

Kregel
Publications

Deeper Than Red: A Novel
© 2014 by Sue Duffy

Published by Kregel Publications, a division of Kregel, Inc., 2450 Oak Industrial Drive NE, Grand Rapids, MI 49505.

All rights reserved. No part of this book may be reproduced, stored in a retrieval system, or transmitted in any form or by any means—electronic, mechanical, photocopy, recording, or otherwise—without written permission of the publisher, except for brief quotations in reviews.

The persons and events portrayed in this work are the creations of the author, and any resemblance to persons living or dead is purely coincidental.

Scripture taken from the *Holy Bible*, New International Version®, NIV®. Copyright © 1973, 1978, 1984 by Biblica, Inc.™ Used by permission of Zondervan. All rights reserved worldwide. www.zondervan.com

ISBN: 978-0-8254-4267-4

Printed in the United States of America
14 15 16 17 18 19 20 21 / 5 4 3 2 1

To my grandchildren, the storytellers to come

Acknowledgments

I am grateful to the following for their enormous help in crafting the Red Returning trilogy . . .

To concert pianist Marina Lomazov—on whom the character of Liesl Bower was loosely based—for the exquisiteness of her music and her willingness to guide me in selections featured in this trilogy.

To my son, BM1 Brian M. Duffy of the U.S. Coast Guard, for his hands-on knowledge of weaponry, boarding procedures, and Homeland Security protocol.

To my husband, Mike Duffy, for his expertise in boats and navigation.

To my brother, Scott Railey, a former charter captain, for his knowledge of fishing the Florida Keys.

To the works of authors Josh McDowell, Don Stewart, and Texe Marrs for their coverage of cults and the occult in such books as *The Deceivers* and *New Age Cults & Religions.* Other research materials included books and brochures gathered on-site at the medium colony on which Anhinga Bay Spiritualist Camp was based. Yes, I went inside their bookstore where Mr. Fremont would have worked. Yes, I dared to wear a cross around my neck. And yes, what happened to Tally in this story happened to me.

To the global intelligence gatherers and analysts at Stratfor, to which I subscribe because they know things the rest of us don't.

To my family who allowed me such long stretches of isolation to complete this and all my novels. I love you more.

Chapter 1

Moments after the Russian president's motorcade pulled away from the Kremlin, one of the phones in Evgeny Kozlov's bag vibrated. He turned from the window overlooking a dingy Moscow street and glared at the canvas appendage to a life on the run, always ready for the grab and escape.

With one last visual sweep of the street, he crossed to the unmade bed and retrieved the phone. Noting the familiar code that flashed onto the screen, he answered with only a clipped "Yes."

"Something is not right," Viktor Petrov alerted. "President Gorev just left for his village near the Volga to meet his wife and children for the weekend. He left with his usual security detail in three cars, except for the drivers. At the last minute, they were all replaced."

Evgeny went still. "Replaced with whom?"

"New recruits. I don't know their names. Part of their training, I was told." Viktor had worked for the Federal Security Service, a Russian intelligence network, since its former days as the Soviet KGB.

Evgeny could hear his old friend begin to wheeze and the discord of traffic in the background. "Where are you?"

"Near the office." That would be Lubyanka Square across town, now pulsing with rush hour traffic that Thursday afternoon.

Evgeny grimaced. Surely Viktor was out of range of his agency's hawk-eyed surveillance systems, always monitoring their own. Surely time hadn't dulled the old agent's serrated wits. "Are you safe?" Evgeny asked, hearing a horn bleat somewhere on the square.

"More than you. Are you in the same place?"

Evgeny glanced around the decomposing room in what the Americans would have called a flophouse. But no one searched for him there. Not this moment. "I will leave immediately."

"Evgeny, Gorev is a good man. Ineffective, but honest."

"Honest always loses." With his free hand, Evgeny shoved clothes and toiletries into another bag on the bed. "I will signal you from the road. Hurry back to your office."

He dropped the phone into his jacket pocket before closing the door behind him and picking his way down a stair littered with refuse and one drunken human form crumpled into a corner of the landing. Evgeny had known far better than this in his life, at least in material matters, though the old days of ready cash and heady power had also carried the stench of betrayal to everything he'd once known to be good and just. The penniless orphan who'd escaped his lot and landed solidly within the fraternal clutch of the Cold War KGB wouldn't have dared question its integrity or authority. His survival had depended on blind devotion and unwavering obedience . . . until his great unraveling in the realm of Liesl Bower.

He paid his bill to the woman at the front desk and hesitated at the door before entering the street. Through the glass, it seemed a normal summer afternoon in the sluggish bowels of the city. He looked back at the cashier. Her black-lined eyes were still fixed on the lurid magazine photos she'd barely turned from to take Evgeny's money. He was glad to see they weren't the frightened, darting eyes of one who'd just been instructed to act normal until the man in room 14 had exited the door, then duck.

He stepped confidently from the hotel and hurried to the faded-blue Fiat parked around the corner, knowing he was already fifteen minutes behind the motorcade. He was glad for the sight of the boxy little car wedged between two sanitation trucks. The money he'd deposited in various banks while still a well-compensated KGB agent was dwindling rapidly. Viktor had supplied the little car and new plates.

Evgeny wound his way toward one of the ring roads skirting the Kremlin. Between buildings he glimpsed the towers in the great wall and the golden domes of cathedrals enclosed by it. He sensed the heartbeat of his motherland, feeling its erratic pulse. But he feared the things underfoot in the back rooms of power, things that threatened the country he loved, though it had never loved him back.

Leaving the ring artery, Evgeny turned onto a freeway leading northwest out of the city, his accelerator foot slammed to the floor.

President Dimitri Gorev had long preferred retreating to his modest family farm rather than the stately dachas provided him and Russian presidents before him. He'd always been a man of the soil whose deepest regret had been his inability to deliver a better life to those who'd toiled the earth through Soviet oppression and into the hope of a new day, which never seemed to dawn for them.

He was a man of the common people, despite the luxurious, and heavily armored, Mercedes sedan in which he now rode. His usual complement of security agents was with him on this routine weekend transport—except his customary driver, who'd been pulled that morning. So, too, had the drivers in the other two cars. Gorev chose not to concern himself with the abrupt switch after his security chief assured him it was a necessary training exercise for the young men.

He'd survived one assassination plot, thanks to a young American pianist. Liesl Bower had discovered the code that exposed the coup conspiracy of Gorev's countrymen Vadim Fedorovsky and Pavel Andreyev. Both had been executed.

That had left one—Ivan Volynski, the mastermind of the conspiracy, who would have launched a wave of terrorist strikes against the United States . . . if he hadn't been incinerated over the East River in New York six months ago. That had created something of an implosion in the shadow world of the Kremlin, where Gorev knew Ivan's people still bred. The man's death had not ended those back-corridor murmurings of subversion that still threatened the present administration. After the foiled assassination plot, Gorev had purged the ranks as best he could. He'd held exhaustive interrogations and surveillances that had employed old Soviet KGB tactics. In the end, he'd rooted out only a handful of insurgents, and the taunts to him persisted, one coming that very morning in his own village, which was normally a stronghold for him. Someone had displayed a public notice referring to "the late Dimitri Gorev."

Was he reading too much into the threats? Imagining others? Was it not true that his own prime minister had averted his eyes from Gorev too many times? That Arkady Glinka had gradually withdrawn from all but required interaction with his president?

There was no doubt that something was still festering in the underground of his government. It was time to draw a sword and attack. But first, this brief respite in the village of his birth. He leaned back against the seat and watched regiments of birch trees parade by. Just a few more miles and his gentle wife would wrap him in her arms. His children would run barefoot through the yards to greet him, and the Kremlin would fade away, for a while.

He watched the lay of the land begin its descent to the river ahead, a lethargic tributary of the Volga where Gorev had fished as a child. He turned to the guard seated beside him. He was a middle-aged man employed by the Federal Security Service and recently assigned to the president's personal detail.

"Yuri, where did you grow up?" Gorev asked.

"In Moscow, sir." The man glanced past Gorev at the view through the window. "I am afraid I have never known the country life, though I intend to when I retire in a few years. Then I can fish every day."

Gorev waved a hand toward the river. "I will show you where I caught my first fish. Just ahead, the road will bend sharply to the south to follow the riverbank. Then it will wind through the woods, a remote stretch of road with fish pools along the way."

Now past the turn, Gorev leaned forward in his seat to catch the first spark of sunlight off the water. Just then, the driver suddenly stomped on the brake and sent the unbelted Gorev lurching forward, impacting the back of the seat before him. Its occupant, one of Gorev's most trusted aides, emitted a painful cry as his head slammed into the dash. Instantly righting from his own fall, Yuri grabbed his gun from the holster beneath his coat.

Gorev turned on the driver. "What are you doing?" he demanded angrily. But the young man didn't answer. Instead, he flung open his door while simultaneously lowering the bulletproof windows. Gorev spun in his seat toward the tail car and saw its driver also leap from the vehicle.

Feeling the rush of air from the now-open windows, Gorev turned back to see his driver running hard toward the tree line. From those same trees emerged a swarm of gunmen bearing down on the motorcade, their weapons raised.

"No!" Gorev shrieked as more gunmen advanced from the opposite side of the road. Before Yuri could open fire, the president grabbed the gun from the man's hand and squeezed off only one round. It hit the fleeing driver in the back and dropped him just short of the trees. It was judgment, a death sentence carried out by a man just seconds from his own execution.

Chapter 2

*E*vgeny ran the Fiat wide open, risking interference from a highway law enforcer with no right to know the things Evgeny did. And there was certainly no time to explain them. He would have to close the fifteen-minute gap between him and the motorcade in a car that threatened to blow some critical part if he didn't slow down, which he refused to do.

Evgeny knew what a last-minute switch of drivers meant. He'd long been programmed to know such things. It was part of the core curriculum for assassins. To interpret the signs, plot, infiltrate, anticipate, kill, and to trust those who said it was all for Mother Russia and the ultimate good of her people. He'd gladly swallowed every bit of it through all the years he'd served the Communist juggernaut, until it burned and sank in 1991. He'd jumped clear just in time, though for a while he'd floundered in a sea of disillusioned fellow agents. Most of them had climbed aboard the next ship to stop and pick them up—the new Russian Federation with its tastes-like-KGB intelligence machine, the Federal Security Service, known as FSB.

But Evgeny and a few others chose not to follow. They longed to return Russia to its former position of world power. Two of the KGB's most powerful and inspired leaders, Pavel Andreyev and Vadim Fedorovsky, promised to do that for them. So Evgeny leapt into the fold, pledging allegiance to their renegade order. What he didn't know was that someone unseen had long been working Andreyev and Fedorovsky like puppets. Evgeny had likened it to discovering an unknown planet in the solar system. How had he missed it? But once the phantom fist of Ivan Volynski materialized, Evgeny realized that the man's feverish quest for power, wealth, and brutish dominance over the United States would eventually destroy Russia.

Ivan Volynski, a self-exiled Kremlin power broker, ruled over a secret brotherhood strategically embedded throughout the new government and military, waiting for the moment to snuff out the Federation, seize control, and return Russia to its former might. Ivan Volynski was to rule as a modern-day czar. Until one pleasant afternoon six months ago when Evgeny fingered a small remote and blew Volynski out of the New York sky.

The Fiat screamed northwest along the busy highway until the turnoff to Gorev's hometown. There, Evgeny left the highway and slid along a tranquil road leading to a tributary of the Volga River. He checked his watch. Almost four. He'd made remarkable time and hoped to catch up with the motorcade before it reached the small village where the president's family had farmed for six generations.

From a bag on the passenger seat, he pulled out a personal-size arsenal with enough firepower to counter whatever he might face ahead. Three handguns, an Uzi, grenades, and tear gas. What did he think he was doing? He'd once been party to a conspiracy to kill President Gorev. Now, Evgeny was risking everything to save the man. But from whom? Ivan Volynski was dead. But his power-lusting compatriots, the ones who hadn't already been executed for treason, surely had climbed back to their camouflaged hiding places along the rungs of national power. They were still there, Evgeny was sure, looking for a new leader to deliver them. But it was too soon for one to have risen in Volynski's wake, in time to stage the thing Evgeny feared lay ahead. *Who's pulling the puppet strings now?*

The road curled through forests so deep and dark that their boundaries seemed like the edge of night. The innocent beauty of the trees, their graceful bowing, the wind now chiming symphonically through his open window all conjured the image of Liesl Bower. He glanced at the cold weaponry on the seat beside him. How had she landed in such a world as his? Or he in hers? She'd once been his prey, now his conscience. He willed her image to flee from this peril, back to the fine old home on Tidewater Lane, under the sultry Charleston skies.

He inhaled the wild scent of the Volga and wished himself to flee as well, yet knowing he would never be free of the thing that had drawn him back to Russia, the primal need to cleanse himself of the blood on his hands.

He cocked his head toward the open window, hoping for the sound of clean, rushing waters, but what he heard triggered a spasm through his body. Gunfire. A distant fury of automatic weapons. He was too late.

And then it stopped. There was only the shriek of the Fiat's now-futile race down the winding road to the river. Downshifting around one more curve, Evgeny suddenly braked into a sideways skid and came to rest before the riddled remains of the president's three-car entourage.

Almost bumper to bumper, they lay like a single butchered serpent, its last breath just released. No after-death twitching from nerves still firing. Not this time.

Evgeny grabbed the Uzi and dashed from the car to an outcrop of boulders just off the road and listened. He knew the sound of an escaping hit team, and he heard it now. The garbled signals to each other, the swift and careful footfalls over raw ground. The blinding quiet left behind.

The assailants were gone. No need to follow. Evgeny knew the escape tactics that had been his. He glanced down the road in both directions. He didn't have long. Though the ill-kept road was remote, some unsuspecting motorist was sure to come along soon.

Evgeny turned back to the ruin. He hurried to the middle car, knowing that's where he'd find the president. As he passed the last car in the line, he looked inside. The condition of the two bodies there triggered the taste of bile in even this veteran killer. He hurried to the big Mercedes and stopped at the backseat window. As in the car behind, the bulletproof shield had been fully lowered.

The president stared at him with unseeing eyes. Evgeny stared back at them. It was too hard to look at the rest of him.

Careful not to leave a print, he reached through the open window and checked for a pulse in the president's neck. Then he slid the back of his finger along the man's bloodied hand. "I am as guilty of this as they are," he told the corpse, its blood still warm against Evgeny's skin. "But I will find them and make them pay, just as I too must be brought to justice one day." The eyes held Evgeny fast, though their clear sheen was fading quickly. "So go, and be at peace. I envy you."

Evgeny stepped away from the Mercedes and went quickly to the lead car, finding its occupants as shattered as the others. There was no one at the wheel of any car. He believed the order to substitute drivers had come from too far up the chain of command to trace, certainly not by him. Surely an intricate cover-up was already in place.

He'd just started back for his own car when he heard the faint whine of an approaching vehicle. Seconds later, the Fiat hurtled away from the scene, though Evgeny would revisit it many times. It would be captured by the first photographer to arrive at the grisly discovery, then blitzed throughout the world. But its images, like Gorev's blood, were already indelible inside the broken vessel that was Evgeny Kozlov.

Who did this? Evgeny's mind zoomed as fast as the Fiat's climb from the river valley. Coming just months after Volynski's murder, was it his people's revenge? Did they believe their own president had ordered the hit, and not the Americans, on whose lands Volynski would have mounted a campaign of terror? Why would Volynski's people not suspect the American president had conveniently rid himself of the ruthless half brother who hated him? Everyone knew of that kinship now. Travis Noland himself had announced it to the world. In doing so, had he sealed his own fate? Was Noland next? If the avengers couldn't be sure who'd killed their hero, maybe they were just brash enough to cast judgment and sentence on all the candidates.

Volynski's followers couldn't know that Evgeny was the executioner. He didn't exist anymore, not even to the hunters inside Russia's voracious intelligence community. They had their warrens and he had his, the two never intersecting. And now, he was driving hard to reach the nearest drop-hole into his netherworld. From there he would pick up the scent of those who'd just fled through the woods.

Chapter 3

*I*n the unopened hours before sunrise that Thursday morning, Travis Noland had stood before his bathroom mirror, the only sound the scraping of a blade against the gray stubble on his face.

Confronting him in the mirror was a conflicted man whose struggle for equilibrium had begun to emit something like the hot-wire hum of a transformer. Intrusive and incessant. Wiping the remaining foam from his face, he'd once again observed the influence of both maternal and paternal genes. From his mother, a high forehead, and now, at age sixty-one, slight jowls settling on either side of his chin. What dominated, though, was the short, broad nose that rose to a high bridge and wide-set, blue eyes. His father's nose and eyes, most everyone had noted when Travis was growing up.

F. Reginald Noland III had been a force to contend with, both in the Noland household and at the U.S. State Department. The brilliant negotiator who'd helped steer the country through the world's diplomatic minefields for more than three decades had succumbed to his own arrogance and lust. He'd much preferred the heady challenge of his far-flung assignments and the power they afforded him to his home turf. He particularly craved his choice of female companionship. In time, coming home to his wife and only child in Joplin, Missouri, was barely tolerable, until the day the *New York Times* ran a front-page story exposing the distinguished elder statesman's covey of mistresses lodged in diplomatic ports from Istanbul to Moscow. Particularly incriminating were the photographs of him with two women the CIA had identified as foreign intelligence agents assigned to lure classified information from him. Though an investigation found insufficient evidence to indict him, Travis's father resigned and came home to Joplin, where he lived alone until he died. His wife had received all the evidence she needed to secure a divorce and flee the scandal with her teenage son, Travis.

The president had looked hard at his image in the mirror. At the Noland nose and eyes. How had he not recognized them on the face of Ivan Volynski? How preposterous if he had. Why would he have thought such a thing on first meeting the Soviet Army officer nine years his senior, an adversary of the first class, a hostile man whose own blue eyes shot fiery darts from some secret reserve.

But once the president confronted the truth of their kinship, the Noland resemblance sprang at him from the face of the man who would have blown a hole in the United States, if someone hadn't executed him.

Noland had mourned the loss of his tortured half brother. How different it might have been if they'd discovered each other as children. Or would it? Would one have remained privileged and the other impoverished? One snug in the security of his mother's protection, the other left to fend for himself while his chambermaid mother scrubbed away her youth and lay down her self-respect. One sent to ivy league schools, the other cast off to fight for scraps of knowledge that would free him. But he was never free of his hatred for Travis Noland, the pedigree son.

It was now almost ten that June morning, and the West Wing was at full stride, despite the encumbering heat outside. The president knew the day's docket was too full to suit his secretary, Rona Arant. But he'd insisted on plugging the only gap in the schedule with a goodwill visit from a couple of legislators from his home state of Missouri.

While he awaited their arrival, he downed a couple of decongestant tablets, having detected the signs of a summer cold. Setting the glass down on his desk, he focused on a photograph of his wife and two sons beaming at him from a tortoise-shell frame on his desk. He'd visited the DNA of a murdering revolutionist upon his sons' bloodline and they'd treated the news as if Ivan Volynski were just a kooky uncle to contend with—until they, and the whole nation, saw the footage of the man's private helicopter splinter into flaming wreckage. For the last six months, they'd had to deflect the barbs of their father's political adversaries who'd taken a near fiendish delight in exploiting the "Noland family shame," as one senator had called it. Still, others had rallied around the president and admonished those who'd slung their scorn at him, daring them to peel back the layers of their own families and look hard at what lurked beneath.

The arrival of his guests broke into Noland's reverie. He was just showing them to their seats when Rona reappeared at the door.

"Sir." She summoned him with a slight lift of the hand. Theirs had been a long and comfortable partnership, begun during his tenure at the State Department. She'd made the move with him to his congressional office, then on to the White House. At nearly seventy, she had no intention of retiring, for which he was grateful.

"Excuse me," he told the legislators and moved quickly to the door. "What is it, Rona?"

"The CIA director is here, sir. He says it's urgent that he see you immediately."

Noland tried to read her face, though he was certain Don Bragg wouldn't have confided anything to her. "Okay, Rona. Take these gentlemen to one of the conference rooms and get them something to eat, please."

The president apologized to his guests for dismissing them so abruptly, but expressed hope that the interruption wouldn't last long. He was wrong.

Moments later, Director Bragg rushed into the Oval Office. Noland was standing behind his desk.

"Good morning, Mr. President."

"Have a seat, Don."

"I'd rather stand, sir."

Noland nodded and remained on his feet.

"We just received an alert from one of our field agents that President Dimitri Gorev has been assassinated."

Travis Noland felt as if the floor beneath him had just shifted. He leaned hard against his desk and placed both hands flat on top of it. "Go on," he said tightly, his eyes riveted on the director.

"It's unconfirmed, though my team is working to pin it down. There's been no official announcement."

"This source is reliable?"

"Yes, sir. Our agent has a contact inside FSB."

"When did this happen?"

"About an hour and a half ago, sir. About five PM Moscow time, on a country road near his family farm. He was going home for the weekend."

"Do we have specifics?"

"Gunmen were waiting for him in the woods. They surrounded the motorcade and opened fire. We're not sure of much else."

"And your best guess who these gunmen were?"

Bragg drew a long sigh. "Indulge me, sir." Noland nodded a go-ahead. The director brought a hand to his chin and started to pace in front of the desk. "Six months ago, Volynski and his closest aides vaporize over the East River. Only a handful of us know that Evgeny Kozlov planted the bomb. He'd seen Volynski for the madman he was. So Kozlov decides to save Russia from the guy and, acting completely on his own, plans and carries out the hit.

"The media goes ape, digs up everything they can on Volynski and the terrorist on the tug who tried to blow up the Brooklyn Bridge at the same time the chopper exploded. They can't find too much on Volynski and we, of course, aren't talking. But then the TV-network contributors—the retired crew-cut generals and other Beltway pundits who are paid to wax authoritative with insider knowledge they don't always have—suggest Gorev might have ordered the hit, though we know he didn't."

"Keep going, Don."

"What our people are sure of, though, is that Volynski had a sophisticated network of followers in Russia, dug in along the halls of power from government to the military. And in the youth population, where a growing number of subversive coalitions were beginning to clamor for Volynski to come back from self-exile and make Russia the powerhouse it used to be."

Noland eyed him with certainty at what was coming. "Draw your conclusion, though I see it already."

Bragg nodded. "In my opinion, sir, Volynski's loyals didn't need our press to suggest that Gorev ordered the assassination. They were sure of it. So they killed him. Though the death isn't confirmed yet."

Noland stared down at his desk. "God help us," he said aloud, then walked to a window. He stared into the garden beyond, at the faces of roses tilted up in innocence. But hidden beneath their fine costumes were the thorns that would mercilessly pierce a man's flesh. He returned to the desk. "I'll get your confirmation." He pushed a button on his phone and summoned his secretary.

"Yes, sir," she answered instantly.

"Rona, get Arkady Glinka on the phone for me, please."

"The Russian prime minister, sir," she clarified, a note of surprise in her voice.

"As quickly as possible. Thank you." He looked up at Bragg and saw the apprehension on the veteran spy's face.

"Sir, I'm not sure that's what you want to do," Bragg said tactfully.

"I assure you it is. I have my reasons."

"Forgive my asking, but would you mind sharing them with me?"

"At this moment, I would. Now, please, make yourself comfortable." He motioned to one of the chairs opposite his desk, and Bragg complied.

Noland settled into his chair and carefully regarded the venerable CIA director. "I know what you're thinking, Don, and yes, I ignored your warning not to announce to the nation that Ivan Volynski was my half brother. Here I go again. Right?" Bragg started to respond, but Noland raised a polite hand and continued. "But there are things I know that you don't. You couldn't." Noland gauged the man's bearing, his guarded expression, yet his transparent devotion to his role as keeper of the nation's darkest secrets. Such a trust could gut a man in time. The president hoped his old colleague would retreat before that happened. He liked Don Bragg for the wounds he already bore from his own tours as an undercover field agent, but mostly from the weapons fired at him by senate subcommittees aghast at the things he sometimes allowed his agency to do to protect the country. Sometimes they were the right things, sometimes not, Noland knew. But always, Bragg was a patriot.

Noland cleared his throat and leaned back in his chair, choosing now to bring the director closer to the truth. "Arkady Glinka is more than just second in line to the Russian presidency and a long-time figurehead in Russian politics." Noland caught a glint of anticipation in Bragg's eyes. "You seem sure of what I'm about to tell you."

"Pretty sure," Bragg replied. "That Glinka was once Volynski's childhood friend and later, KGB boss. That Glinka mysteriously disappeared from Russia about ten years ago, then resurfaced as a converted conservative. A believer in and passionate supporter of all things Gorev, at least on the outside. In fact, Glinka so enamored himself with Gorev, the rising president tapped him as his prime minister. We know everything about his career, his family, and his appetite for fast Italian cars and even faster women."

A half smile creased Noland's weary face. "Go on. There's more."

Bragg's confidence stumbled. "I'm not sure what you're referring to, sir."

Noland straightened in his chair. He hadn't meant to parlay his privileged information into a one-up game with Bragg. "I'm sorry. Your team would have uncovered this soon enough. So I'll tell you what I know." He shifted again in his seat, hastily assembling in his mind what he would and would not reveal. "A few months ago, a young Israeli intelligence agent started tracking the rise of Arkady Glinka to prime minister. You might call it an excavation. The agent was particularly interested in Glinka's possible connection to Volynski's earlier scheme to assassinate Gorev and the Syrian president, and he produced forged documents to prove that Israel had pulled the trigger on both. A plot laid bare by the code Liesl Bower found in her music, as you well recall." Noland smiled. "I wonder if Volynski ever faced a more comely and threatening adversary than Liesl, who surfaced yet again to help dismantle his terror campaign inside the U.S."

Bragg nodded acknowledgment of the pianist's unlikely role in that, but kept pressing for more information. "And did this young Israeli discover a connection between Glinka and Volynski's ongoing conspiracy?" Bragg didn't seem to mind not knowing.

"More like an umbilical cord, but one that was invisible to Gorev and most of the Kremlin."

"But not enough evidence to arrest Glinka?"

"Not yet. Maybe never."

"Who is this Israeli agent, sir?"

Noland eyed the man cautiously. Something told him it wasn't the time to identify the one whose exhaustive work now promised a straighter shot to the matrix of Russian power. The one whose own DNA was as inextricably linked to a murdering anarchist as Noland's was. When Maxum Morozov fled Israel after Liesl Bower's code exposed him as a Russian mole inside the Israeli Defense Department, he left behind a son reeling from that discovery. Now, the son hunted the father. Young Max had temporarily laid down his violin and picked up his father's trail. Along the way, operating as an unofficial agent of Israel's legendary Mossad, Max had uncovered the secret life of Arkady Glinka.

"What's more important is what he discovered," Noland said with the conviction that protecting young Max Morozov's deep-cover quest was more crucial to American security than sending the CIA alongside. At least for now. "By the time Mr. Glinka dropped from Russian radar a decade ago, he had plunged headlong into the occult."

Bragg was clearly stunned.

"It started out as a mere dalliance," the president continued. "A séance here and there, psychic readings by practitioners, from a young blind woman in the Ural Mountains to a set of male twins in Istanbul. Our young Israeli even tracked Glinka to a hut in Bali where he'd once lived on the beach for almost a year, floundering around in some cosmic haze possibly induced by a bit of substance sampling."

"How long did Glinka's, uh, spiritual quest last?"

"Four or five years. But only a couple of those were spent hopping from blacked-out parlor to parlor, crystal ball to who knows what. Then something changed. He fell under the spell, so to speak, of a colony of mediums in Germany, who later moved en mass to a remote mountain range in Montana." Bragg arched one eyebrow. "You know something about that?" Noland asked.

"About four years ago, the FBI backtracked a shipment of meth leaving Montana for points unknown. It came from a mountain commune that had a strict code against substance abuse among its so-called family. They'd just turned the meth-maker in to the nearest sheriff's office when the feds busted into their camp."

"Glinka wouldn't have been there. He returned to Russia six years ago."

"From Montana?" Bragg asked.

"No. He left Montana a few months after he arrived. And that's where the trail goes cold, except for one little blip on the screen. Two years ago, a sheriff's deputy stopped a speeder in the Florida Keys. The violator's name was Arkady Durov, who produced a legitimate Ukraine passport and claimed to be a tourist."

Bragg listened expectantly as the president added, "Durov was Glinka's mother's maiden name."

"No other documents were produced?" Bragg asked.

"It was a one-light-town officer with no apparent inclination to do more than issue a warning and send the man on his way. End of trail. We don't know where he'd been or was going, or how long he was there. But we do know that when Glinka—if that was him—was stopped, there was a man in the car with him."

"How do you know that?"

"Our Israeli friend hunted down the officer, who is now retired and still living in the area. He happens to remember that particular traffic stop because the two men spoke Russian to each other. The officer knew this because his grandmother was Russian. So he engaged them in conversation about the motherland and the one summer he'd spent there as a boy. Evidently, the exchange made a lasting impression on the officer, who described the driver as dark complected, not so handsome, and heavyset, which certainly fits Glinka. He remembers the passenger as nice looking, slim, and less interested in conversation."

"Could he identify either man from a photograph?"

"Photos of Glinka are being sent now," Noland said. "But even if he is positively identified, it tells us nothing at this point."

"And the other man?"

"The agent is sending a photo of Volynski as well."

Bragg cocked his head. "An excellent move. But what makes this agent suspect Volynski was the other man?"

Noland smiled. "Just a hunch, I'm told."

"A hunch can be a powerful thing. Let's hope it leads to something more substantial than fortune-telling and . . . wait a minute." Bragg paused and squinted as if searching some distant mental file. "I once heard about a place down there that's known for that clairvoyant, hocus-pocus stuff." He thought a minute more, then snapped his fingers. "Anhinga Bay. An Army buddy who lived in Miami told me about the place."

Bragg seemed to pull himself up a little straighter, his expression shifting to official bearing. "Sir, there's no need to pretend I don't know who this Israeli intelligence agent is. You of all people shouldn't underestimate our reach. We've had young Max Morozov in our sights ever since his father went into hiding. And we've worked too many tandem ops with Mossad not to know their personnel."

Noland nodded his head in concession. He'd drawn too close to the young virtuoso violinist and his American friend Liesl Bower. He'd helped shield them from their enemies during and after their perilous hunt for the code and those who plotted disaster. Why had he thought they were his personal domain and not of continuing interest to national security forces?

"Then you must know how critical it is for him to work alone," Noland said, "without interference and added risk to him. He has a vested interest unlike any of your agents. Let him navigate the turns by himself. I know he's searching for someone of great interest to you. But the fact that you haven't found Maxum Morozov the father, or even determined if he's alive, justifies his son's own efforts, however unconventional they may be."

"And if he finds his father before we do?"

Before Noland could answer, the phone on his desk buzzed.

"I have Prime Minister Glinka on the line, sir," his secretary said. "I was told he isn't in Moscow. I was patched through to a mobile number." Noland dragged in a breath. Did Glinka know of the assassination or not? Was he guilty or not? What diplomatic furor might this call ignite?

Noland nodded toward Bragg, who then leaned forward in his chair, his eyes bearing down on the phone.

"Put him on, Rona." The president pressed the speaker button and began his performance.

"Prime minister. It's good of you to return my call."

"What can I do for you, Mr. President?" The clipped straight-to-business tone sent a signal Noland couldn't yet interpret. He would have to fire his opening round.

"On behalf of the American people, I wish to express our shock and deepest regrets for the loss of your president."

The silence on the other end spoke volumes to Noland. If the report of Gorev's death was false, Glinka would promptly have asked what Noland was talking about. If the Russian president had, indeed, been killed, surely the second-in-command would have been notified by this point and would acknowledge condolences with no hesitation. Why was Glinka so taken aback? Noland's mind whirled through too many unsavory reasons.

"Prime minister, are you there?" Noland asked, his eyes on Bragg.

"Of course," Glinka finally rallied. "So, you have already heard of our president's death. I am impressed by the speed of your spy craft inside our country. It is even too soon for our own people to know of this tragedy." Noland's condolences had been met with accusation. Why?

"Too soon?" the president questioned. Too soon for what? For the hit teams to escape the vicinity of the crime? For the mechanics of a cover-up to engage? Noland wished it not to be true.

Glinka's voice slit like a blade. "Surely you understand these things, Mr. President. We must gather the evidence at the scene and respectfully tend to the victims of this horrible crime before releasing the news to the public."

"I apologize if my inquiries offended you, Prime Minister. I only wished to offer our sympathies and our willingness to help in any way we can." Then he fired his next round. "Do you have any idea who is responsible for this?"

The reply came too quickly. "Do you, Mr. President?"

The hostile insinuation struck Noland broadside, the suggestion of U.S. complicity barefisted. But Noland didn't miss a beat in answering. "I choose to ignore the audacity of that question and hope you soon regain your diplomatic balance. You will need the support of all of us in the global community through the difficult days ahead."

Seemingly unfazed by the rebuke, Glinka said, "And I trust I will have it. Thank you for your call, Mr. President." He hung up.

Noland replaced the receiver, barely containing his outrage, though knowing he had deliberately provoked the encounter. He looked up at Bragg. "There's your confirmation. Gorev, the polished diplomat with an honorable vision for his country, is dead. A very different era has begun. Glinka will assume the presidency until a new election is held. But that's time enough for him to usher in whatever's lurking in the wings. I can't put a face on it. Not a living one, now that Ivan's dead."

"But he left his clones in place."

"Is Glinka one of them?" the president posed.

"Possibly. I'll need to move into his world to know for sure."

The president thought that over. "Okay, Don. I'm going to ask Max to step up his investigation of Glinka, and suggest that he welcome a CIA assist." He paused. "But there's something else. You said one of your field agents learned of the assassination from a contact at FSB? What does that mean? Do you think the attack came from FSB?"

"Not necessarily. I'm waiting for the details, but I understand that the FSB source was alerted by someone at the scene."

"Who?"

Noland watched the CIA director hesitate one second too long.

"Answer me, Don. Who was there?"

"Evgeny Kozlov."

Noland stared at him in disbelief. But Bragg was quick to add, "We understand from our Russian contact that Kozlov was there to warn or otherwise aid the president."

"Where is he now?"

"We don't know."

"You don't know how to reach him?"

"No one reaches Kozlov unless he wants them to, sir."

Noland knew it was true. "Right. Just keep me informed of every development. And thanks for coming."

Bragg seemed eager to leave. "Thank you, Mr. President."

As soon as Bragg left the Oval Office, Noland's thoughts turned to the only person he knew who'd broken through the armored plate encasing the whole of Evgeny Kozlov. An unlikely pairing if ever there was one—the ruthless Russian spy and the classical pianist from Charleston. As much as the president wished Liesl Bower asylum from Kozlov's world, she was about to reenter it.

Chapter 4

Every morning should be infused with Beethoven, Liesl thought as she lifted her hands from the Steinway grand. Performing the German master's music was more invigorating than a wake-up run along the Charleston Harbor, more cleansing than even the salt-scrubbed winds off the Atlantic. Like that one skewering note of a tuning fork that takes dead aim at perfect pitch, Beethoven pierced through all the layers to strike at the very heart of Liesl Bower and to make it whole and well again. God, she believed, had given her the gift of regenerative music when she was a small child because he knew what was to come.

She looked around the airy studio with its twin grand pianos, one for her and the other for the students she taught at the College of Charleston. There would be no lessons today, though, nor the rest of the summer. Besides the upcoming concerts in Israel and Germany, she wished nothing else to intrude on her repose against the cushion of her graceful old home and the arms of her new husband. Cade O'Brien had nurtured her, rescued her from herself, and she loved him unconditionally and completely, allowing him to love her back.

Still, she had struggled to properly shelve the scarring events of the last two years. There had been little rest between the frantic hunt for the sonata code and the blind chase to find the terrorist who might have ruled

Russia. Now, almost six months after the man's death, she was still trying to heal from the emotional scourging. The family she had gathered about her, the old house on Tidewater Lane, and the soothing harmonies of vintage Charleston promised to do what surely God himself had called them to do. That and the concerto she would soon play with her old friend and violinist Max Morozov during their program at the Nuremberg Music Festival. That's why she'd been hard at practice since six thirty that morning. Rather than disturb the peace on Tidewater Lane, she had opted for her soundproof studio on campus.

She'd just launched into a lilting passage of the concerto when the landline phone next to her rang, yanking her from her reverie. She glared at the insistent instrument then glanced at the clock. Just after nine. The office would be open by now on this Thursday morning, but rarely did the music department's secretary disturb her with calls to her studio.

She sighed and picked up the receiver. "This is Liesl," she said distractedly, her eyes still scanning the sheet music before her.

"Miss Bower, uh, I mean O'Brien—sorry, I keep forgetting . . ." the secretary began.

"Either one is fine, Tina. How can I help you?" She was afraid her impatience was showing.

"I have a gentleman on hold who says it's extremely important that he talk with you. Do you want me to put him through?"

Liesl sorted quickly through any possible urgencies. Cade or anyone else at the house would have used her cell number. But *extremely important*? "Yes, Tina. Thank you." She heard the holding line click open. "Hello, this is Liesl Bower."

No one spoke.

"Hello, who is this?"

Still nothing. Liesl heard the sound of a car passing nearby, the chatter of birds, and a slow, fairly exaggerated intake of breath. She tried once more. "Hello." Then the line went dead. She pulled the receiver away from her ear and stared at it as if it owed her an explanation. Perhaps something in the school's rather antiquated phone system had failed to transmit her voice. Probably a student anxious over a grade. She'd handed out a few failing ones at the end of the Maymester. She replaced the receiver with hardly another thought about the aborted call.

There was far more to think about that morning. She would need to prepare her wardrobe for the trip and phone Ben. He and Anna were supposed to join them in Tel Aviv. She wanted to make sure of it. Since barely surviving the attack that killed his brother-in-law in January, Ben had resigned his White House position and joined the rest of his family in Israel. "I think I'm finally home," he'd told her. She was eager to see him and how well he'd healed.

Her mind continued to drift. She fingered the keys before her, plunking out nothing in particular, thinking only about Cade now, and how she longed to rest in his embrace, protected and loved. He'd decided to work from home today, as his downtown office was being recarpeted. Charleston's new metro magazine had hit the stands with a flourish and the tempo hadn't diminished. Advertisers had liked what they saw inside the glossy pages filled with more than just Lowcountry interiors and recipes. Managing editor Cade O'Brien had pumped a growing number of pages full of "talkers"—features that plumbed beneath the surface streets of Charleston, stories no one had ever heard before and were eager to pass along.

Liesl realized her session that day was over. She would make up for the lost practice the following day. But for now, her mind was already home. She might as well follow.

When she stepped from the contemporary, cubic-faced School of the Arts, the morning threw its warm June wrap around her and made her long to stroll barefoot with Cade through the cool grass of their garden. She walked single-mindedly along the sidewalk to the old white Volvo she'd kept far too long. She could afford a new car, but the thought of abandoning the trusty chariot that had carried her through the highs and lows of the last ten years wasn't on her agenda.

Only when she stopped to insert the key in the door, did she look behind her. Students in flip-flops and shorts crisscrossed the street in the slouching choreography of the summer term, moving slower toward class than away. Cranking the Volvo, she pulled away from the curb and navigated down the narrow street, lined on both sides with cars. It was one of the pretty streets skirting the campus. Old Victorians and single houses were bedded down with lush gardenias, hydrangeas, and heirloom altheas rising to touch the lower limbs of crepe myrtles already ripe with great panicles of sherbet pinks. Distracted by their frothy canopy, she almost didn't see the cat that suddenly streaked in front of the Volvo, whose brakes Liesl now stomped to avoid hitting the creature. Fearing a rear-ender, Liesl winced toward the rearview mirror. The car behind, a bright green Volkswagen, screeched to a halt just off her back bumper. A small SUV behind that, something brown with a roof rack, also managed to stop in time. The cat safely on the other side, Liesl moved on to the corner and took a right turn.

In Charleston, it can take just a single turn to leave one world for another. Now, the sidewalks scrolled past a row of shabby storefronts. As she gazed into the windows of one, she saw the reflection of the brown SUV behind her and glanced at her rearview mirror. The man at the wheel waited calmly for the light to change.

At the next corner, she turned right again and headed south toward the tip of the peninsula and Tidewater Lane. At the next light, she glanced at the rearview mirror and spotted the same SUV, two cars back. Just ahead was the hub of town where all roads led. The traffic had grown to a torrent and Liesl was anxious to clear the congestion and wind her way back toward the harbor. That meant bypassing town. She signaled a left toward the Cooper River and a less traveled route. But halfway into the turn, she caught sight of the brown SUV in her side mirror. It was now directly behind her. Somewhere inside, a familiar alarm sounded. She hadn't heard it in six months, and wished never to hear it again. But it persisted. With it came the same acidic spasm in her stomach, the sweat beads on the forehead. Was it just the body's unfailing memory, its involuntary response to the alarm she'd failed to disengage? An alarm no longer necessary. Right now, she would prove it true.

Liesl eased off the accelerator and began a series of turns. The SUV stayed with her through all of them. But just as the alarm grew louder, as more drastic measures sprang to mind—like stopping in the middle of the street and brazenly confronting her pursuer, which she'd done before—the brown vehicle peeled away at the next intersection and headed in the opposite direction.

Shaken, Liesl pulled over and parked at the curb. She needed time to think. There was something familiar about this scenario. It had happened when she and Evgeny had been tailed in New York. The car that had followed them from City Island all the way to Manhattan suddenly turned off and vanished, only to reappear later. That it proved to be CIA agent Ava Mullins, now one of Liesl's most trusted friends, didn't matter. She'd used tactics surely nonexclusive to U.S. agents.

Is that what this was? Or was six months simply not long enough to smother old fears?

Liesl looked around, checked all the mirrors, and waited. No brown SUV. Only tourists with cameras strapped about them. A woman in running clothes holding a leash to a massive Harlequin dane crossed the street in front of the Volvo, her countenance bright and confident. As Liesl's should be.

She had to restore herself before returning home. As she reached for the ignition key, a seagull squawked overhead and Liesl turned to watch its dance upon the capricious thermals that whipped about the city. "Yes, I'm coming," she said aloud to the bird. The one place that had long fused itself to the core of her now called with the voice of the gull.

Exodus. She envisioned the old boat slumbering in soggy contentment at its slip, not quite mothballed but seldom called into service since the breathy runs to and from the cabin had ended. As if some overriding homing device had suddenly engaged, Liesl started the Volvo and headed straight for the Ashley River, whose waters stroked the peninsula's west side.

Driving headlong to her respite, she couldn't help but flick a searching glance here and there for the brown SUV, smiling each time she didn't see it. Already, her peace had resurfaced.

She looped around Charleston's waterline and eventually turned north toward the Metro Marina. She rolled down her window and heard the river exhale, its briny breath running hot through the forest of masts sprouting from the marina ahead. She turned into the parking lot, still scanning for the brown vehicle and wondering, with a twinge of amusement, if its driver had any inkling of the start he'd given her. Surely he hadn't.

She parked and got out. Now focused only on the long dock before her, she grabbed her backpack and hurried over the rough, splintering boards. Here and there a fellow mariner tending his vessel looked up and waved. They knew her here; some since she'd been a young girl drawing gape-mouthed surprise at her masterful, solo handling of the thirty-six-foot, twin-screw Grady-White.

"Hey, Liesl," one bronzed old man called from his live-on sloop. "Sure good to see you here. *Exodus* has been awful lonely."

Something about that made Liesl flush with guilt over fleeing her past and the boat that had sailed her through it, through seas that had both calmed and slashed. "I hope you're doing well, Gus." She smiled brightly at him as she passed, remembering the sure countenance of the woman walking the dane.

"Better than I deserve," the man called after her. "You take care of yourself."

This time a chorus of sea gulls summoned Liesl on until she caught sight of *Exodus*, the light merciful on her fading beauty. She was still regal, though, still willing to shelter those who'd lost their footing on solid ground. Liesl had rescued the boat too many times from the hands of her drunken father, only to thrust it into the midst of her own desperate battle. But that was over now.

As she stepped over the gunwale into the broad open stern of the boat, nothing could have stopped her from looking at the one place that would never let go of her, at the stain that would never fade. Perhaps she didn't want it to. It was the lifeblood of her beloved aunt Bess, spilled from a spear wound to her abdomen, pooled indelibly against white fiberglass. It was both a reminder of her father's careless, whiskey-driven hand and the imprint of hope for his ongoing struggle to find his peace.

As Liesl had done so many times before, she knelt to touch the remnant of the woman who had played a penny whistle until the dolphins surfaced behind her island cabin. Then she'd slide into the tidal creek to swim with them. The same woman who'd erected a towering, roughly hewn cross on the island and ushered Liesl to the foot of it, assuring her that one day she would understand what had happened on another cross just like it and why it had to be.

The gulls flashed again overhead, and Liesl watched them assemble into a V-formation. She looked farther down the dock where two women chatted between their boats as if over a backyard fence. A dinghy from a sailing ship anchored in the harbor bounced through a light chop, its lone occupant clutching a basket of clothes headed, no doubt, for the marina laundry. Liesl looked up at the puffs of clouds, and closed her eyes. All was well.

She unlocked the cabin door and shoved it open. A stale gust escaped from inside as she descended the steps into the snug chamber. She opened the windows on both sides for a fresh cross breeze. Stretching her long limbs, she released a luxurious moan, then settled onto the forward berth. Soon, a silky sweep of air caressed her body and her breathing slowed to a mindless rhythm. The rocking berth cradled her and her eyes drooped in sleep.

Almost an hour later, the chime of her phone woke her. She pulled it from her bag and saw the image of the caller filling the screen. The face of her new husband smiled at her with that beguiling composite of manly strength and boyish vulnerability. Each seemed to surface at just the right time. Right now, Cade O'Brien was sure of himself.

"It's time for you to come home," he told her when she answered. "If anyone around here complains about having to listen to one of the world's greatest pianists, I'll deal with them personally."

Phone in hand, Liesl climbed to the helm and sank into the captain's seat, swiveling to take in the river view and reveling at the sound of the voice in her ear. "I'm on my way." In her mind, she was. She hadn't needed to come, she assured herself, but she was glad she did. It was good to be back on the water. She glanced toward the imposing bow of the powerful boat. Soon, she silently promised *Exodus*, the whole family would return for a long-overdue romp at sea.

After the call, Liesl shouldered her backpack and headed back to the car, her step lighter. She was more eager than ever to get home, to the ones who'd pieced her world back together. She'd neglected them lately, plunging headlong into the regimen she always imposed upon herself in the weeks before a concert. Besides the grueling practice sessions, she had stepped up her fitness, often running alone before breakfast and lifting weights before Cade arrived home for dinner. By then, there was too little left of her to give. That would have to change. She had been jettisoned from her insular, self-absorbed domain and, despite its persistent call, she would have no more of it. Cade O'Brien and the God of new beginnings had freed her.

When Liesl pulled away from the marina, a hand turned the ignition key in the brown SUV concealed behind a palm thicket across the street. The driver eased from his hiding place only after the Volvo was well out of sight. There was no need to follow closely. The man could now track Liesl Bower with the device he'd just fastened to the underside of her car.

Chapter 5

L iesl lowered all the windows in the car as she drove along the Ashley River, allowing its wild zephyrs to run invisible fingers through her hair. At some point, a honeysuckle vine hurled its sachet into the car and she slowed to capture all of it. Just beyond her open right window, the outbound river currents swept the late-morning stragglers toward the Atlantic, urging tuna-tower rigs to catch up with the earlier flotilla of fishermen hot after whatever was running in the Gulf Stream. She caught the eye of one captain and he issued a rakish salute to the fetching young woman with the golden, wind-tossed hair.

Near the tip of the peninsula, she turned east into a neighborhood whose streets were strung with homes as lovely as pearls, each as luminous as the next. They were Old World, Neo-classical, Tudor, Georgian, Craftsman bungalow—and all of them Charleston bred, especially the distinctive single house. And there was no finer example of that than the Bower home on Tidewater Lane. Though it never intended to be anything but a refuge for a once-broken family, the old house couldn't help being grand in architectural line and proportion. Like the centerpiece of an elaborate bouquet, it rose above gardens allowed to ramble at will. It stood tall, not in defiance of its age, but in celebration of it.

Turning into the driveway, Liesl let moist, grateful eyes take in her home's blustery sweep of porches stacked one above another, black wrought-iron gates as intricate as lace, and tall windows that reflected the canopy of oaks. Then her sights fell upon two things wholly incongruent to the rest. Two bright orange bikes had come to rest beside the heirloom camellias, and all that remained of the morning's tension uncoiled in a burst of laughter she couldn't contain. "Ava, you did it!" she cried to herself. "You said you'd get him on a bike. And I missed it? Ian O'Brien in a helmet and Spandex?" She grinned and slapped at the steering wheel. "We might not survive that."

She locked the car and hurried through the garden gate, slowing only to inspect the audacious bikes. She pumped her long legs two steps at a time up to the main-level porch, and before she could reach for the door, it opened. "Too late," Cade announced with a mischievous eye. "The ride's over and, well, you can hear for yourself." He motioned toward the kitchen where Ian's exasperated voice rose above Ava's more disciplined tone.

Liesl embraced her husband and lingered over his warm, sugary kiss. But the noise from the kitchen was too distracting. They released each other and slipped in unnoticed by the old man in long, baggy dungarees wiping sweat off the back of his neck and declaring loudly, "That is the last time you'll catch me on that thing. Or in that ridiculous helmet."

Looking over Ian's shoulder, Ava made swift eye contact with Liesl and returned to the matter at hand. "If the doctor told you that roller skating backwards down Broad Street was good for your heart, you'd be wearing a helmet with a rearview mirror and a pillow strapped to your backside about now," Ava insisted. "Instead, he told you to ride a bike. How hard is that?"

"Gee, Pop," Cade snickered. "I thought the helmet was kind of cute."

Ian rounded on his grandson. To Liesl, though, he stretched out his arm. "Come here, darlin', and tell these people that I'm too old to be teetering around on a bicycle they can probably see from the space station." He turned back to Ava. "What possessed you to rent psychedelic orange?"

"It was all they had." Ava shrugged and bit at her bottom lip.

"Uh, Pop. Want to tell me about the ropes around your ankles?"

Ian looked toward his feet, then reached into a plastic shopping bag on the counter beside him and whipped out a pair of black biking shorts. "Ava bought these things for me to actually wear out in public. They're called biking shorts, but they're obviously women's panty hose cut off at the knee. Poor woman didn't know the difference."

"Okay, I think I'm beginning to follow," Cade offered. "You couldn't bring yourself to wear the panty hose so you tied up your pants legs with rope."

"Nothing wrong with that." Ian frowned as he spread the legs of the new shorts apart. "Now look at this, son. See this little bitty pad they got stitched to the crotch of these things? Like that's going to do any good." He looked at Cade with all earnestness. "Have you ever sat down on one of those needle-nose bike seats?" Cade shook his head and glanced nervously at the women in the room. "Well let me tell you, it's nothing short of a surgical procedure."

Liesl clapped a hand to her mouth to stifle the giggle. Ian seemed not to notice. "So why on earth don't they just make the seat wider?"

"And while they're at it," Cade added dryly, "they could strap a little bell to the handlebars, and run up a long pole with a red flag on top so nobody in Charleston would miss seeing you with your leg ropes and tractor seat." Ian was about to sputter a reply, but Cade persevered. "But better yet. Forget the bike and just walk the block a few times every day."

"My hips don't work."

Cade kept coming. "There's nothing wrong with your hips. It's your lips that get you into trouble. So quit complaining. It's nothing but an excuse to avoid exercise." Cade motioned toward Ava, who leaned against the counter with her arms folded and surrender on her face. "This good woman cared enough about your health to bring home a bike and wrestle you onto it. But if that won't work for you, do her the honor of breaking a sweat at something else. And fishing doesn't count."

Ian remained impassive throughout Cade's whole delivery. But when it was over, the faintest upturn appeared at the corners of his mouth, parting the gray hedge of his beard. He turned calmly to Liesl and said, "He's pretty good at that, don't you think?"

She leaned into the old man for a hug, then drew up sharp. "Eww." She fanned the air in front of her. "Someone's deodorant has failed."

"Well, it's not mine," Ian sniffed. "I'm not wearing any." With that, he turned back to Ava. "Well, secret agent, I guess I didn't even thank you for going to all that trouble with the bikes. I'm sorry. But if it's okay with you, I'll just walk." He turned crinkled eyes on Cade, then Liesl, and headed out of the kitchen, tossing something half-mumbled over his shoulder. "And I plan to smell real good doing it."

When he'd left, Ava pushed off the counter and gathered up the biker shorts and discarded helmet, shaking her head. "There are no words." She grinned, then looked up. "Why don't you all come to dinner at my place tonight?"

Cade and Liesl looked at each other and nodded agreement. "You're on," Cade said. "And I'll bring fresh grouper from Pop's last charter. One of the customers left his whole catch behind. Said he'd rather kill 'em than eat 'em."

"Don't forget the size of my kitchen, though," Ava noted. "Carriage house apartments have lots of charm but no room to team cook."

"So we'll prepare it here and—"

A ringtone sounded in the kitchen, and the conversation went dead. All eyes turned toward the bag where Liesl kept two cell phones, the one least used calling to her now with a preset code of beeps no one in that room had heard for six months. It was the secure phone Ava's CIA team had programmed especially for the concert pianist on the Russian underground's most-wanted list.

But Liesl heard more than the insistent beeps as she moved to retrieve the phone from her bag. She heard the breath of the caller to her studio that morning, the wordless void at the other end. In her mind, she could see the brown SUV close behind. Was the CIA calling to warn her? She slid anxious eyes toward Ava, the now-retired agent who'd hustled Liesl through a gauntlet of global terrorism, then answered the call.

"Who is this?" She couldn't stop her hand from trembling. Cade moved closer.

"Miss Bower, this is the White House." Liesl blanched and looked sharply at Ava, then hit the speaker button on the phone. She didn't want to handle whatever was coming alone.

"Yes, go ahead," Liesl answered weakly.

"You'll have to speak up, Miss Bower."

Liesl breathed deeply. "I'm sorry. Is that better?"

"Yes. Now please hold for the president." Just like that. No hint of purpose for the call. No soothing tones. The three of them stared at each other until Travis Noland's baritone amplified into the speaker. "Liesl, thank you for taking my call."

"Mr. President, this is a surprise."

"I'll just bet it is. Are you alone?" Only then did she catch the hard pitch of his voice.

"Uh, not really."

"Are we on speaker?"

Something was terribly wrong. "Well, yes." She cringed.

"Who's listening?" he asked.

"My husband, Cade, and Ava Mullins."

"Ava? You there?"

"Yes, sir."

"Okay. Keep it on speaker. Liesl may need your backup. And you may as well hear this too, Cade." He paused. "I'm sorry to be so abrupt. I should begin with pleasantries, but I'm afraid urgency overrides that. My apologies."

Urgency? Liesl thought. *No! I'm through with that! Lord, make them leave me alone.* Noland proceeded, his voice out of sync with the egg-smeared dishes still on the kitchen table, with the faded calico curtains at a window far removed from the Oval Office. "I won't belabor the need for confidentiality regarding this phone call."

"This is a secure line and everything said here will remain so," Ava assured him. She looked to the others with confirming certainty.

"Good," Noland said. "I'll come quickly to the point. The media will soon burst open with the news that President Dimitri Gorev was just assassinated, in his car outside of Moscow."

Liesl leaned hard against Cade, her mind scrambling to understand.

"That wasn't supposed to happen, sir." She felt suddenly light-headed. Was she making sense? "We stopped that plot two years ago. Who did this?" She tried to contain the fear clawing its way up her throat, drawing it tight.

"I can't comment on who might be responsible, Liesl. I truly don't know. But I need your help."

"My . . . help?" she asked incredulously. "How could I possibly—"

But the president was a step ahead. "We have reason to believe that there was a witness to the shooting. Evgeny Kozlov."

Liesl reeled with the implication. Surely the man she'd come to trust with her life—after he'd threatened to take it—hadn't done this thing.

"We believe someone had alerted Kozlov to the possibility of an attack, and that he was en route to warn Gorev."

Liesl drew a sharp breath of relief. "How do you know this, sir?"

"I can't tell you that. You understand, of course. But what I need from you, Liesl, is your assurance that if Kozlov makes any contact at all with you, you will alert us immediately. I'm asking you—and you, Ava—to work with us to bring him in, for his sake and ours. It was a hit squad, Ava. An ambush. They massacred the whole security detail Gorev was traveling with."

Liesl shook her head in disbelief. Would it ever stop? Then she thought of Evgeny. The last time she'd seen him, he'd been at ease with himself. A smile flickered inside her as she remembered the new clothes he'd sported that day, at the gentleness of the hand that stroked her cheek before he slipped into the alley, running toward the nearest hole into his vast warren.

"I haven't heard from him since January, Mr. President," Liesl said more calmly. "I don't know why he would contact me now."

"I don't either, Liesl. He may simply need a friend, and I'm told he'd grown quite fond of you. But there's something else." The president paused. "As before, he knows things we don't, things that are critical for us to know. Do you understand?"

All too well, Liesl thought. Hadn't the hunt for such critical things swept her from the vortex of one storm after another for too many years of her life? "Certainly, sir. And if he should contact me, I'll . . . uh . . ."

What *would* she do? Would she betray him? Lure him to some CIA trap? Or could she convince him to cooperate? What if he refused? Then something Ava once told her returned quickly: "There is something more powerful than guns and missiles . . . that would have prevented the deaths of thousands on that morning of September eleventh. Information. It's the most critical weapon we have against our enemies."

Liesl turned to see Ava's resolute nod, the go-ahead for Liesl to do what she must. "I'll do everything I can, sir." Though she didn't know what that might be.

"That's all I can ask, Liesl. And that you keep the phone you're using right now within arm's reach at all times. Ava, you'll be hearing from Don Bragg regarding this. I trust you and Liesl will work in tandem. And Cade, my apologies for however this matter might intrude. Now I must go. My blessings to you all."

"Goodbye, sir," came the collective end to the call. The three gazed silently at each other, almost stooped beneath the ponderous weight of the president's news. Then, one by one, each moved in a different direction. Ava grabbed her phone and headed toward the door. "I'm not waiting for Bragg to call. I'll talk to him from home, though. See you for dinner at six."

"And we proceed with life as usual," Cade responded, his sarcasm aimed at no one in particular.

Liesl turned mournful eyes on him. They'd tried so hard to escape the tentacles of Evgeny Kozlov's world. Just six months ago, they'd placed their marriage in God's hands and reveled in the finely knit order he'd brought to it, in their love so quenching, in the peace of family woven together in the harmony of the old vine-clad house beneath the oaks. What discord had just hurled itself at them? Unforeseen and unwelcome. Liesl could adequately steel herself against it. She'd had far more practice at it than Cade. But there was something else they both had, something she wasn't used to calling on because it was still too new to her. Though she'd finally placed her life in God's hands, too often, she'd taken it back and proceeded as if she were still alone against the world. But now she remembered.

When Ava had left, Liesl took Cade's hands in hers and looked deep into his troubled eyes. "Don't you remember what you told me on the dock at the cabin that night? That God never forsakes, never abandons. That he is our future."

Cade pulled his hands from hers and wrapped his arms snuggly around her. "And I have every reason to believe it's going to be a humdinger, isn't it?" he said over the top of her head. Precluding an answer, he leaned down and swept her lips with his, then lingered there until familiar footsteps approached.

Before he and Liesl could untangle themselves, Ian stepped lively into the kitchen and stopped. "It's a little early in the day to start that, don't you think?" Then he looked around the kitchen. "Where's Ava?"

Cade and Liesl exchanged glances. There was no immediate reason to bring Ian into confidences the president had so clearly insisted on. "On her way home. She's invited us all to dinner tonight."

"Oh, yeah? That's real nice of her." But the words seemed to tumble automatically. It was Ian's eyes that held the most expression as he observed their faces. "What's going on?"

"What do you mean?" Liesl asked too warily.

"You both look funny. Different than when I left. What's up?"

Cade relaxed his hold on Liesl and shook his head. "Just a loose board on the sidewalk steps. Want to help me fix it?"

Ian eyed him suspiciously. "Okay, young man. If you and Liesl have a secret, it's all yours. You're entitled. But I hope nobody around here's pregnant. Not yet anyway." He turned to Liesl. "You need a good long time to yourselves before we have to start changing diapers."

Liesl walked over to Ian and hugged him gently, feeling her ill-timed tears overflow their bounds. She brushed his stubbly cheek with a kiss and left the kitchen without a word.

"What'd I do?" Ian asked blankly.

"Not a thing, Pop. You know how jittery she gets before a concert."

Cade heard the creak of worn stair treads and knew Liesl had retreated to their bedroom.

Ian looked at the empty doorway then back at Cade. "Nuremberg, huh? Why does she have to go so far from home?"

"It's a favor for Max. I understand the tickets for both their Nuremberg and Tel Aviv concerts are almost sold out."

"Yeah, well. It's too soon."

Cade knew what he meant. As much as anyone, Ian knew the toll Volynski's conspiracy of terror had taken on Liesl and others who'd helped bring him down. Such as Evgeny Kozlov. Where was he now? Cade wondered. Headed back to Tidewater Lane?

Cade watched the lines fold deep along Ian's brow and was glad his grandfather hadn't heard the president's news that morning, or sensed the gathering storm behind his words.

Chapter 6

Liesl closed the bedroom door behind her and sat on the bed. Her hand went to the phone she'd just dropped into her pants pocket, the CIA-issued phone on which the president of the United States had just reenlisted her to active duty. The commander-in-chief of a nation—one recently spared horrific attacks by the man who'd once lined her up in his crosshairs—had now cautioned her once again. Not in so many words. Not wishing to alarm her. But he'd used the word *urgent* alongside the name Evgeny Kozlov. Alongside his directive to keep the phone with her at all times. Every bit of it spoke of caution, of a clear and present danger somewhere out there. Liesl jerked her hand from the phone as if it might bite her and redirected her attention.

She turned to look at the gowns laid out on the bed beside her. She would take them to Israel and Germany the following week. Beside each one was the scant jewelry she allowed herself during a performance, certainly nothing to trip up her hands' sprint across the keyboard. She also had meticulously searched all apparel for loose hooks, snaps, buttons, seams, hemlines, and any other conceivable hazard. Though such things were of little concern right now. Something had just pried open the steel lid she'd bolted over the last two years, even though somewhere in that sad saga had risen the great love of her life.

She closed her eyes now, and despite the fearful morning, thanked God for his mercies.

Just then, the sound of one of those mercies rose to her window, and she got up to see. Nestled in one corner of the back yard was the playhouse Henry Bower had built for his only child, determined that at least *she* would have a refuge from a wound-inflicting world. The only retreat he'd known was the golden liquid he drained from a bottle each night before joining his wife in the bedroom next to Liesl's. It had been the bottle that carried him off to a faraway "death" on a rocky Mexican beach. Then homeless, Henry Bower had seized the chance to fake that death and free his mother, wife, and daughter of the miseries he'd dealt them for too long.

It wasn't until years later, when he'd learned of threats to Liesl's life, that Henry Bower returned from the crypt, stripped of all but his love for her, and so cleverly disguised that she didn't recognize him in passing. She never knew that through all the years since she'd witnessed the murder of Schell Devoe—her Harvard professor and mentor who'd been living a double life as a Russian agent—Henry Bower had kept watch over her. Then one day less than two years ago, she discovered him, a scarred and broken refugee of his war against himself, sustained only by the visceral need to protect the only good thing left of his life, his child.

She pulled back the curtains and looked down through the filigree pattern of limbs and leaves suspended over the yard, and saw him. His rangy, slightly bent frame leaning against the side of the playhouse, he was whittling something from a length of wood. As she often did, she studied him, wondering what simmered beneath the surface. The father who'd returned to her wasn't the same one she'd known. No, he didn't drink anymore. But something had gouged out a chasm inside him and from its depths came voices Liesl couldn't hear, only feel as their vibrations disturbed the air around him. Too many times, they'd summoned him and he would abandon a conversation without moving, with only a flicker of something pulling at him inside. Though others had witnessed it, it had frightened no one but Liesl. Looking down at him now, she wondered if the voices were calling to him.

Turning from the window, she ignored the demanding clutter of her room, now hers and Cade's, and hurried down the stairs. She was grateful that no one stood between her and the back door, guessing that Cade and Ian were gathering tools to work on the sidewalk steps. Liesl took one more flight of steps down to the yard and crossed toward the playhouse, brushing bare feet through the grass her father kept neatly clipped.

Could there possibly be another structure like the one ahead? A child's playhouse that sprouted a steeple, a replica of the one atop the majestic St. Philip's Church just blocks away. How ironic that her father would emulate the place where Liesl had often run to escape him. It was from the church's bell tower that she'd seen him stuffed into the back seat of a police cruiser and taken away. She hadn't seen him again for twenty years.

Once again, her heart spilled gratitude for his homecoming as she walked slowly toward him, only now catching his eye. It was the way his head jerked toward the closeness of her that signaled he'd been far away. His worn and crusty face, nearly charred from exposure when she first found him, now creased with delight. "Hey, Punkin." His pet name for her also had returned.

"How are you, Dad?" She walked into the arms he opened for her and returned the embrace. His denim shirt smelled freshly laundered. It seemed to Liesl that he was trying to scour away the years that had trailed him from Mexico. Fastidious didn't begin to describe his relentless pursuit of cleanliness. More like redemption.

"The better question is, how is the lady of the manor?" He winked. "And . . . is she really leaving us old folks behind next week?"

Liesl released him gently and sighed. "Dad, I know you disapprove. You all do."

"Got that right. It hasn't been that long since I chased off a bunch of foreign-speaking thugs ransacking your house."

"Thugs led by a man who later saved my life. Don't forget that, Dad."

"Evgeny Kozlov is a treacherous man who'd turn on you again if someone ordered him to." Now wasn't the time to tell her dad about the president's phone call. Like the rest of the country, he'd hear the news of Gorev's assassination before long. And that, she was sure, would springboard into another of his forays through the what-ifs of any situation even remotely associated with her tenure as a Russian target. No, this wasn't the time.

Liesl sniffed the breeze and affected a winsome smile. "Gee, I thought I'd just spend a few tranquil moments in the garden with my gentle dad. Hmm. Where did the moment go?"

Henry reached over and released the large clip securing the knot of hair to the top of her head. "That looks better," he said. Liesl caught the disguised apology and smiled up at him. "Now, you look like your mother." And suddenly his eyes hooded and Liesl felt a familiar tremor in the air. She wasn't going to let him slip away again.

"Dad, let's go into the playhouse." She began pulling him onto the small porch whose white paint had mostly peeled away.

He looked at her curiously. "Why would I want to do that?"

"Because you have no choice." She beamed and tugged harder.

Inside the one-room little house, where neither of them could straighten to full height, there were a couple of folding chairs. Rusted, their webbing shredded here and there, they protested the weight now imposed on them as Liesl and her dad sat down.

Henry looked around. "Remember the party we had when I finally finished this place?"

Liesl gauged him warily, but saw no outward signs of despair. "I'll never forget it, Dad. Or the feast we had on Lottie's best china."

She had always used her grandmother's first name, which Lottie Bower had preferred to Granny or any other such moniker. "I'm relic enough without being called one," her grandmother had said. Now it was Liesl's turn to slip off just a moment, thinking of the woman who'd held the world together for the child of tragedy. When Alzheimer's finally snuffed out Lottie's remaining life a few months ago, Liesl and her dad mourned from a depth only they could know.

Henry reached for Liesl's hand, but said nothing.

"Hey, speaking of feasts," she hurriedly offered, veering from yet another brooding subject, "Ava has invited us all for dinner tonight."

"Oh, I don't know, I just—"

"Look, Dad, you and Ian work so hard on that charter boat of his.

When you're not at sea, you're sanding or painting the boat and getting it ready to take you there. Loosen up one night and come with us."

"Ian going?"

"To see his best girl and chow down on her amazing food? What do you think?"

Henry snickered. "The old coot. Do you think he's in love?"

"Nothing else explains his following her every lead. You heard about the bike?"

"Who do you think helped him climb onto it?" Henry chuckled with ease and Liesl marveled again at the effect Ian had on him. Soon after Henry had rejoined the Bower household, Ian bought a used sport-fishing boat and started a charter business like the one he'd run in the Florida Keys. Liesl was quite sure it was more for Henry's good than the old sea dog's. She believed it had saved her dad from a precarious future. He had needed a purpose to get up every morning. A boatload of paying customers and the harvest of the Gulf Stream had provided abundantly.

"For someone who'd spent his whole life on a boat, Ian had next to no balance on that bike." Henry shook his head and grinned. "Watching him wobble off on that flaming orange two-wheeler with that crazy helmet strapped through his beard—man, it just doesn't get any better than that."

"Yeah, it could have—if he'd worn the Spandex pants Ava bought him."

Henry looked at her in surprise, slapped his knee, and howled. "I didn't know about that." Now he was laughing so hard he had to lean over in his chair to catch his breath.

The phone in Liesl's pocket beeped the code, again.

Chapter 7

Max Morozov shoved his feet into the warm sand and gazed at the setting sun. The Mediterranean lay before him like a slate-gray tablet awaiting a scrawled message. He wished it were that easy, that some authoritative hand would clearly pen the directions for him, for he didn't know what to do next. Only where he—and Liesl—shouldn't go.

Scanning this remote stretch of beach in Haifa, Israel, he could see only a few swimmers to the south and nothing moving north to the bend. Down the coast was Tel Aviv, where he'd recently crafted a double life for himself: violinist with the Israel Philharmonic and Mossad undercover agent. Ludicrous! All because his father had chosen to be a Russian spy. Why not a veterinarian or a soft-drink salesman?

Max turned to look behind him at the plain, cement-block house shielded by a few palm trees and a squad of security agents, compliments of the Israeli government. It was the recently inherited home of President Travis Noland's former domestic policy chief, Ben Hafner, who now awaited news of Max's phone call to Liesl. But he hadn't placed the call yet.

The last person Max wanted to trouble was the woman he'd loved since they were young conservatory students romping carefree together through Moscow, blind to what was heading their way. No, she'd never returned the kind of love he had for her. Yes, she was married to someone else, but that didn't change the way he felt about her. If he ever loved that way again, he guessed there would be two equal chambers of his heart devoted to two different women. It wasn't a healthy prospect and he knew it.

He thought of Erica and wondered if she might one day fill that other chamber. The young woman who'd recently moved into Max's building had immediately caught his interest. She was lovely, in an unadorned way, yet seemingly unconvinced by what her mirror told her. Or just didn't care that she turned heads. She was a serious photographer with a flippant notion about her person, shunning all things fashionably pretentious. Max had become enthralled.

But quickly, the image of Erica faded into the surf sliding toward him, reminding him of the advancing hour. His hand squeezed around the phone and he finally lifted it before him. He tapped in the coded number and waited. He hadn't spoken to Liesl since they'd settled on the programs they would perform in Tel Aviv and Nuremberg. That was almost two months ago. Since her January wedding, Max had restricted his calls to her, wishing not to intrude on what was now Cade O'Brien's private domain.

It was taking too long for her to answer. Max was about to hang up when the line clicked open. "Hello?" came the halting voice in his ear.

Could that be Liesl? "Say something else. I don't believe this is really Liesl Bower."

But the voice was still hesitant, almost fearful. "Max, is that you?"

Now he was worried. "Liesl, what's wrong?"

"Why are you calling me on this phone?"

He hadn't expected such a reaction. His mistake. Liesl knew the easygoing Max Morozov of her youth had crossed into Mossad's subterranean world of intelligence gathering, but she didn't know how far he'd roamed through its treacherous labyrinths. Perhaps he should have told her, but blowing your cover to anyone was severely frowned upon by his superiors. Still, the woman had been shot at just six months ago by some of his father's colleagues. That's why he was calling. That's why she was about to hear more than she wanted to.

"I just received clearance to access your secure line, Liesl. And before you ask, I had to leap through a blazing CIA hoop to get it." Hearing her sudden intake of breath, he knew he had to lighten his approach. "Because me and the Blues Brothers are, you know, 'on a mission from God' and God doesn't like people who shoot at piano players. Or fiddlers, for that matter."

The line was dead silent. Then, "You're CIA now?" she asked.

"Better than DOA, which someone in Israeli intelligence feared I might be if I didn't help find my murdering, vengeful father. But, no, I'm not CIA. I just get to supplement my limited intelligence with theirs and use their gadgetry. Impressed?"

Finally, he heard the music of laughter from his old friend. "The Blues Brothers?"

"Hey, Belushi's gone and Aykroyd's too old for this. God picked me to carry on."

"Hmm. Maybe he did. But what is it you're supposed to do?"

The cold-sober question ended the repartee. There was work to be done. "Liesl, I'm just going to dive straight to the bottom of this, so listen up. I've been told that you already know about President Gorev's assassination."

"How did you know that?"

"I read it in my tea leaves this morning. Come on now, stay with me." He drew a quick breath and was about to proceed when he shifted direction a moment. "By the way, where are you?"

"In Charleston, in the yard. Why?"

"Anyone with you?"

"I was talking to Dad when the code sounded on this phone. He's back there stewing over what's going on."

"He doesn't know about the assassination?"

"Not yet."

"Well, there's more, so here it is." He heard her sigh. "I think you know that Evgeny Kozlov witnessed some part of the attack on Gorev."

"Yes, I was told."

"But what you don't know is that just before daylight this morning in Gorev's little hometown on the Volga—almost twelve hours *before* the attack—one of the locals saw a man, a stranger, tape something to the door of the post office on the village square, then run away." Max paused. "It was a copy of the flyer that's been circulating throughout Germany, the one announcing *our* appearance onstage at the Nuremberg Music Festival. Only someone had crossed out the name of the festival and written in bold letters: *A Memorial Concert for the Late Dimitri Gorev*."

The moments grew leaden before she answered. "The killer." Her voice was chilled.

"At least one of them. There were others." Max paused. "Now why do you think they chose our concert ad—a German ad at that—to deliver their message?"

No response. Then, "Maybe one or more of them were German."

"Interesting thought. So one of them just happened to have a flyer from home folded into the breast pocket of his favorite assassination shirt and thought it was as good as anything to write on. Is that what you're saying?"

"I don't like your tone or where this conversation is headed. Are you getting close to suggesting we abort our concerts over this incident?"

"I'm suggesting we do exactly that."

"No, Max. I quit running when Ivan Volynski went down in that helicopter. Long before, actually, but others insisted I keep ducking my head. Yes, it saved my life a couple of times. And yes, I was foolish to resist protection other times. But now? I can't run away because of something that proves nothing."

Max knew it was rational thinking. Perhaps the flyer really had been the handiest thing for some local crackpot with a grievance against Gorev to write on. Could it be mere coincidence that it involved the one pianist and the one violinist who'd stopped the music long enough to dismantle a launch-ready revolution in Russia? Twice? Who could be sure?

"Promise me this, Liesl. If anything else surfaces anywhere in your hemisphere that doesn't look or sound right to you, you'll notify me, Ava, or the president himself if need be. I never knew he was such a hands-on kind of guy."

"He was embedded deep in this even before he discovered that Volynski was his half brother."

"And that was a nine on the Richter Scale. The global intelligence community is still quaking from that one. Didn't see it coming."

"Least of all the president. But Max, you and I aren't going to react to a false reading on that scale. And that's what I believe this is. Now, tell me where you are."

"At Ben's."

"The beach house?"

"Yeah. I drove up last night."

"What's going on?"

"Just shop talk."

She seemed to wait for more, but Max couldn't tell her the real reason for this visit with Ben Hafner, another of the Mossad's newest recruits. Fresh from an assassination attempt on his own life, Ben was also Liesl's brotherly best friend since their Harvard days together. It didn't matter that as Noland's domestic policy chief and Liesl's confidante throughout the hunt for the sonata code, Ben trusted her to hold state secrets to herself. The thing that had suddenly plunged Max and Ben into a nightlong furor of communications with their Mossad chief would remain off-limits to Liesl.

Max bridged his brief, half-truth answer to a more pleasant topic. "Even though I just told you not to come, everyone here anxiously awaits your arrival next week. You should see the bedroom I've prepared for you and Cade. Like an Old South B&B with all that potpourri stuff sitting around in little antique bowls. It's enough to make anyone break into that magnolia-speak of yours." And there it came again, finally. Liesl laughter.

"You've been on that magnolia kick ever since I've known you. Have I ever once swiped at your Yiddish?"

"So, what's to swipe?" he intoned in his best Tevye accent.

Liesl's laugh seemed to restore her somehow. "Max, we'll be there soon. It will be good to decompress with you in Israel before we leave for Nuremberg. And by the way, is your new friend coming too?"

Max stared at the fireball sunset spread over the horizon and wished he could see into tomorrow, to see if there would be something good to hold onto. Was it Erica? "Yes, she'll join us."

"I'm anxious to meet her."

"I am, too."

"What do you mean?"

"You don't know someone in just a few months." Max heard the back door of the house behind him open and close. He stood up and saw Ben wave him inside. It wasn't a take-your-time summons, and Max quickly returned the wave.

"Well does she—" Liesl began, but was cut short.

"Liesl, honey, I'm sorry but I've got to go. Call me when you and Cade are inbound."

"Okay, Max. I understand. Give my love to Big Ben and the family. I can't wait to see you all."

Max pocketed the phone and sprinted over a low dune toward the house. The sinking sun wasn't going gently into darkness. Like the spitfire finale of a fireworks display, it lit up the drab little house with an intensity that Max found wholly unsettling. The look on Ben's face did nothing to dispel the foreboding.

When the call ended, Liesl remained fixed to the spot, next to the hydrangeas her grandmother had tended so faithfully. Liesl reached over and ruffled the petals of a giant blue mophead, watching some flutter to the ground. After witnessing her mother's brief but torturous battle with cancer, Liesl had prayed that when it was time for Lottie to pass, God would take her peacefully home to him. And he had.

Watching the petals gather at her feet, Liesl wondered how long it would take for their color to fade once separated from their life source. Then Christ's words returned to her. "Apart from me you can do nothing." It had taken her too long to discover that.

A sudden clatter made her spin toward the playhouse, and she smiled at the perennial handyman who'd evidently just launched a new fix-up project. Henry had just dropped a stack of boards next to the child-size porch, and was pulling a tape measure from a clip on his belt. Liesl had recently noticed the rotting wood and knew it wouldn't be long before her father replaced it. Now, his only child observed him from across the yard. She marveled at the efficiency of him, at his determined stride, how he never carried more tools than he needed for a certain job, never spoke with more words than a telling required. His only excess now was his love for Liesl.

As she watched him work, she burned with the need to protect him. He'd suffered epic loss. She'd pleaded for God to breathe new life into her father and make him whole. But it had to start with him, with surrendering his stubborn conviction that he could repair himself as easily as a rotted porch.

He would learn soon enough that the Russian president Liesl's sonata code once saved from assassins had finally succumbed to them. The news would hit her father hard. He would look at her and wonder how far down their list she was, and nothing she could say would convince him that Gorev's killers had never heard of Tidewater Lane. Hadn't she already convinced herself of that? Hadn't she scolded herself for fretting over a wayward call to her studio that morning, over the motorist who'd followed her route through town? Yes. And that was that. There was no need to mention those incidents to anyone, even though Max's words still hung resonantly in the air: *If anything else surfaces anywhere in your hemisphere that doesn't look or sound right to you, you'll notify me, Ava, or the president himself.*

But none of them were here. They couldn't see how gently the light fell on the flower beds this afternoon. She pivoted to survey each one. They couldn't hear the familiar cadence of her father's sawing, or the birdsong high in the trees. They couldn't understand the . . .

Liesl sucked in her breath and stared toward the street. Slowly passing the house was a brown SUV with a roof rack.

"I followed her from the college to the marina, then the house," the man said into his phone. "She is in the back yard with her father. What's that?" Pause. "No. No sign of Kozlov or anyone else of interest. A couple of bikes parked in front, but Evgeny Kozlov isn't known to travel by bike." The man snickered to himself as he turned at the end of Tidewater Lane and headed toward the street behind the Bower home.

"Come again, comrade. Our connection is very poor." Pause. "No, sir. She has no idea I'm following her." Pause. "No, sir. I've made no contact with her." The man lied easily to his superiors. Why should they know he derived more pleasure than he should from trailing the beautiful Liesl Bower? Just because he wanted to hear her voice on the phone that morning, to listen to her breathing, why should they deny him that? His was a thankless job. The endless days of canvassing the street, changing up the cars he used, waiting for the signal to finally complete his assignment. On that day, he would find her and do more than listen to her breathe. He would watch the fright contort her exquisite face—so very close to his.

"You will leave Charleston now," his superior ordered. "I have changed my mind about the setting for Miss Bower's demise."

"What?"

"The Nuremberg stage will be a far better venue."

Chapter 8

$\mathcal{M}$ax removed his sandy shoes before entering the Hafner house. "What's up?" he asked Ben, now closing the door behind them and sliding the bolts into place.

"New satellite photos," Ben answered. "Come on."

Max followed him through the small kitchen where Anna Hafner was scooping ice cream for her two young daughters. She smiled weakly at her husband as he passed. Max watched as Ben nodded reassuringly toward his wife, whose tiny frame seemed not much bigger than her children's. She flicked a wavy lock of dark hair, as well as the smile, off her face.

From the moment Ben and Jeremy, Anna's brother, were gunned down by Ivan Volynski's people, she had retreated into a hiding place within her. Ben had confided to Max that it was a place even her husband couldn't enter. She had listened as Ben spoke what they both thought were his last words, through the FBI-planted microphone still attached to his bullet-pierced body as he lay sprawled outside an abandoned warehouse in Brooklyn. Her brother was already dead.

After slow, excruciating months of healing and therapy, Ben had left for his parents' homeland, Israel. Knowing the risks his undercover work to infiltrate Volynski's U.S. network might visit upon his wife and children, he'd sent them ahead to Tel Aviv, before his first clandestine meeting with

Jeremy Rubin's terrorist cell of Russian saboteurs, led by Volynski. Ben's later decision to offer his services to Israeli intelligence, specifically the Mossad, had knocked the wind from Anna and upended her jubilance over finally getting her husband back. It appeared to Max that she hadn't yet recovered. He knew Ben had to tread lightly around her.

In an upstairs room off-limits to everyone else in the family, Ben closed the door, turned out the lights, and flicked a few switches at a bank of communications equipment Max found antithetical to the Stradivarius he usually commanded.

"Moshe Singer uplinked this to everyone just minutes ago under flash code, and he wants immediate feedback." A grainy image appeared on a screen Ben lowered from the ceiling.

Singer, their immediate Mossad chief, was no excitable alarmist. Max knew that this had to be real and pressing. "You're looking at a Ural mountain range," Ben informed as he zoomed in on a high mountain plateau pocked and oddly barren for the region. At the top of a switchback trail snaking up from the valley floor was a line of old canvas-covered army trucks that looked like props from a World War II movie. At the front of the line, though, backed up to what appeared to be a broken-down mine shaft, was a late-model tractor-trailer rig with enough antennae on top to rival a NOAH weather station. Only Max didn't think they were gauging wind and humidity. "Singer doesn't like the looks of this."

"What does he think it is?" Max asked.

"He's not saying. Just wants to know if any of us have come across anything like it in that region."

Max shook his head. He'd been tasked with searching every available satellite image for signs of his father, whom Israel was eager to chat with. One of the country's most notorious moles, planted inside the Israeli Defense Department decades ago by Volynski, was ripe for interrogation. But Max had seen nothing with a visual footprint like this.

"There's no more mining in that area," Ben informed. "While you were on the phone with Liesl, I did a quick read-through on the region. By the way, is she okay?"

"I believe so. It's hard to tell with Liesl. She's got a backbone as rigid as that mountain range." He looked hard at the screen. "The ground around that mine entrance is pretty well chewed up. Lots of vehicular activity. And not all of it heavy trucks." He pointed to several small cars parked in the shade of a single stand of gnarled trees. Then he spotted a small cluster of what, from above, looked like flat disks on the ground, but the shadows they cast proved otherwise. "Look at this." He moved his finger just outside the shade of the trees. "Barrels."

"Of what?" Ben wondered aloud. Then he glanced at Max with a flash of amusement. "And by the way, just how does a violinist morph into a know-it-all spy?"

Ordinarily, Max would have zinged an apt reply, but his first thought was too sobering. "Genetics."

Ben's grin faded and he openly studied this fellow Jew who completed the other half of the notably "odd couple," or so their Mossad associates had dubbed them. The White House bureaucrat and the symphony hall fiddler. What could they possibly bring to the venerable brotherhood of Israeli intelligence? For starters, the sonata code that stopped the assassinations of two heads of state. Then there was the ferreting out and destruction of the plot's mastermind, Ivan Volynski, before he could cripple U.S. infrastructure, overthrow the Russian government, and prompt his Middle East accomplices to aim a few warheads at Israel. That's all.

Of course, Max and Ben both knew that the key player in those missions was missing from their team. But she would be there within the week, as unwilling a participant in such matters as she'd ever been. Yet the name Liesl Bower was still spoken with something close to reverence in the jagged world of Israeli spy craft.

"Oh really," Ben responded. "So you think the whole time you've been stroking genius out of that violin and making audiences swoon with the rhapsody of it all, somewhere inside you this dark little gene from your corrupt father has been secretly transforming you?"

Max thought that over. "Pretty much," he answered with no expression, then turned his full attention back to the screen. "So you should listen to me." He pointed again. "I think those are barrels. Stainless steel judging from the reflection off the tops. Probably chemicals." He lingered on that thought. "They're probably building a weapon of biological or chemical warfare."

Ben crimped his lips together and slapped his hand down on the table. "Max, don't go making hasty judgments like that as if you don't know any better."

"What else could it be?" Max replied calmly.

Ben looked back at the screen, but was silent.

"I mean, you haul a bunch of trucks, cars, barrels of something, and probably a mine-load of equipment that evidently these people are using to manufacture something they don't want anyone else to know about—or else they wouldn't be shoving it all inside an abandoned mine shaft in the middle of nowhere. So, what else could it be?"

"You idiot! Where is your hazmat suit?"

"In the truck, sir."

"Well go get it and put it on!"

"Sorry, sir." The man turned and ran back to his truck, one of four lined up and waiting to discharge their cargo. It was a stifling day in the Urals and all the drivers had complained about having to wear the suffocating suits. Young Vlad Potensky had suffered terribly during his last delivery, sweating so profusely he'd almost collapsed from dehydration before the physician on duty could pump him with fluids. Once the drivers were clear of the site and relieved of the barrels of deadly chemicals, they could strip off the suits and hide them in their trucks, according to strict instructions.

Vlad hated the job, but prized the money, an unheard-of amount for an uneducated laborer with little experience but driving everything from the big rigs to the small flatbeds used to haul chemicals and equipment from the mouth of the tunnel to the reinforced heart of the mountain. Vlad didn't know what they made inside the high-tech facility that looked more like an old James Bond movie set to him. And he didn't care.

His boss now approached the truck, his face an indelible scowl. "Now keep it on!" he barked, his eyes roving the zips and snaps of the white suit wrapped head to toe around Vlad, whose water bottle rested in a cup holder in front of him. He'd heard this would be the last delivery for a long time, though he would continue to receive a percentage of his salary. Earn money for doing nothing between jobs? Vlad wouldn't dream of breaking his contract of silence forced upon him when he signed on three years ago. He'd rather cut out his own tongue than lose that money.

He also wouldn't jeopardize his job by asking too many questions. He already knew that whatever they were building inside was about to be shipped out and the mountain temporarily sealed off. And he didn't need to ask where the mystery cargo was headed. He'd overheard one of the inside technicians ask the same question of a supervisor. In answer, the man had simply whistled a tune that Vlad recognized immediately.

"Yankee Doodle Dandy."

Chapter 9

*T*hough the president's cold had advanced to bronchitis over the weekend, he remained in the Oval Office that Monday afternoon, impervious to the fever and chills wracking his body. At that moment, little else mattered but the call he'd just taken from CIA Director Don Bragg. The Israeli Mossad, with the aid of enhanced satellite imaging, had positively identified known terrorists operating at an old mining site in the Ural Mountains of Russia. American undercover operatives immediately dispatched to a local village had confirmed unusual military-type transports to and from the site over several months. None of the locals would yield more information than that, their fears worn clearly on their faces.

It was readily apparent to the agents on the ground, however, that something was being manufactured or at least assembled deep inside the mountain. Though the area appeared to be swept clean of evidence, it had taken only one empty canister carelessly discarded in a nearby ravine—and the identity of one on-site terrorist—to ignite a firestorm in the bunkers of Israeli intelligence.

The terrorist was a Palestinian associated with Volynski's forces and possessing a near-legendary proficiency in escaping one Mossad dragnet after another. But it wasn't the terrorist that troubled Noland most. It was the lab report on the residue inside the canister. That report, now spread before Noland, was accompanied by a hastily supplied brief on the deadly nerve agent sarin. Odorless, colorless, delivered through warheads and other explosive devices, capable of death to thousands throughout the bomb site, outlawed by the Chemical Weapons Convention of 1993. Sarin was a weapon of mass destruction now in the hands of a terrorist once complicit in Ivan Volynski's attempt to annihilate Israel and launch serial domestic assaults on the United States. Most notably, though, satellite surveillance had detected a surge of activity at the Urals camp beginning last Thursday—the day Russian President Dimitri Gorev was assassinated.

Noland lifted his weary eyes from the reports and tracked a splinter of sunlight from the windows behind his desk to a spot on the presidential seal woven into the carpet before him. "What's happening?" he murmured to himself. "Who are these people and where are they shipping their poison?" His eyes lingered on the seal, reading *E pluribus unum* on the scroll tucked in the eagle's beak. *Out of many, one.* He alone held the nation's highest office. A mere human, sweating off a fever of 101 degrees while trying to compose a proper response to one or more weapons of mass destruction possibly inbound to the land of the free.

Could the Israelis be wrong about this? Overreacting? But they weren't known to be. They were, however, often unwilling to share intelligence. Why now? What else did they know?

The buzzer on his phone sounded. "Yes," he answered.

"Sir," his secretary began, "a diplomatic pouch has arrived from the Russian Embassy with an envelope inside tagged with instructions to deliver it only to you. It was marked *urgent.*"

Noland rested one elbow against the desk and rested his pounding head in his hand. "It was also marked *personal*, sir," she added.

"Bring it in, please," he told her, still thumbing through pages on the lethal effects of sarin on the human body. "I assume security has already swept it."

"Of course, sir. It's clean."

"Very well." He hung up and slumped back in his chair, resisting the urge to retire to the residence and the soft sheets of his four-poster bed. His wife would bring him chicken soup with his antibiotics and encourage him to forget, for just a while, that he was *Out of many, one.*

Rona Arant walked at her usual time-is-of-the-essence pace across the room and stood before the president, who leaned forward in his chair. "This one's a bit different, sir. Rather awkward writing." She extended the sealed, legal-size envelope to Noland's waiting hand. He noted the expensive, heavy-stock vanilla linen and glanced up at her. "Was anything else in the pouch?"

"No sir."

Noland stared at the unofficial-looking block handwriting on front of the envelope and wondered what diplomatic officer had let something like that slip by. "A courier made a special trip for this?" he asked.

"It seems that way, sir."

He nodded distractedly and sat back against the soft cushion of his chair, every muscle in his body crying out for analgesic relief. "Thank you, Rona. That's all. Oh, and would you bring me a couple of ibuprofen, please?"

"Right away, sir." She quickly returned to her station outside his door.

Noland looked back at the elegant, if oddly addressed, envelope. *Of personal interest to the President of the United States.* When he pulled the single, folded sheet of matching paper from the envelope, something fell out and landed in his lap. An old photograph. Noland picked it up, stared at the black-and-white image, and suddenly lurched forward. His hand trembled slightly as he locked on his father's stern face. He was seated on a park bench. In the distance were the Kremlin towers. Close beside F. Reginald Noland III, the late U.S. State Department's keeper of national secrets, was a small boy the president didn't recognize. Not at first. But something inside him began to stir. Yes, of course. It had to be. But who sent the photo?

He looked back at the single page, at the few words written in the same block handwriting . . . *Our papa and me.*

Below that was a date written in the same hand. Yesterday's date.

Chapter 10

Tally Greyson had slipped undetected through the porous membrane around the Anhinga Bay Spiritualist Camp too many times. Tonight, there would be no soft-footed retreat from the place she'd come to watch, from those who'd already claimed her mother and persistently cast their unearthly tentacles for the daughter. Once again, though, Tally would elude their security guards whose labored breath she could hear behind her, their feet thrashing against a tangled mat of dead palm fronds, their voices demanding that she stop.

How many had given chase? Two? Three? It didn't matter. She'd just cleared the palm thicket rimming the bay. Now, her sneakered feet had found their rhythm against a tidal shore which, a couple of hours earlier, had been under water. She glanced up at a moon as elusive as she was, and in its reluctant light, sprinted like an Olympian beyond the sound of her pursuers, hugging the curve of the bay until she rounded the far point and pumped hard toward home.

Not until she turned off the beach and crossed into a blind of palmetto bushes did Tally stop to look back and listen for advancing footfalls. Except for the gentle slosh of bay surf, the night was silent again. The path ahead was as familiar to her as all the other escape routes from the camp. She plunged down the sandy ruts twisting through a dense tropical woodland that was forbidding enough by day, with its rumored rattler nests. "Only a lunatic would go there at night," her friend Denise had declared. But Tally had found The Bog, as it was known locally, benign compared to what lurked inside the pleasantly landscaped reaches of the camp. Besides, she'd never encountered anything remotely resembling a snake pit in the cool, seaside glade she now navigated with ease, until it abruptly ended at the asphalt road to her house.

Before stepping into the glare of streetlights, she removed the hooded, tissue-thin black shell she'd worn to the camp that night, wadded it tightly, and shoved most of it inside the back pocket of her jeans, should any out-of-breath, sandy-shoed security guards be searching the streets for her. The one they'd chased could have been a *him* for all they knew. Tally's long brown hair had been tucked inside the hood, pulled snug around her face. Though she was twenty, her lean, straight-sided figure betrayed no womanly profile, especially in the charcoal haze of night.

Though she longed to bolt for the sanctum of her bedroom, Tally restrained herself to a casual stride, taking a full twenty minutes to reach the other half of Anhinga Bay. That's how this small Florida town in the north Keys was divided—into two halves that equaled far more than the whole of anything normal. Anhinga Bay was like a split atom whose fission rumbled along the fault line through town, a line separating the fenced colony of practicing mediums, seers, healers, and psychic readers . . . and everybody else. It had been that way since the 1800s.

The Greyson home—or *manor*, as Tally's mother preferred—wasn't hard for anyone to find. Situated on nearly an acre, not only was it the largest house in Anhinga Bay but it was the only one outside the camp draped with dozens of Bagua mirrors meant to deflect negative forces circulating about the property, or so Mona Greyson had explained to her only child, then sixteen. But the protective shield hadn't stopped there. Tally had watched in horror as her mother hung a boxful of Turkish evil eyes, nazars, top to bottom on a helpless fig tree near the street. "They're talismans, dear," her mother had said of the glassy concentric-circled "eyes" of blue and green. "They're meant to repel The Evil Eye by looking into it head-on."

Tally had sprung at that. "I didn't realize we were having a problem with that. In fact, I don't know anybody who ever has. Why do we have to be so . . . abnormal? And what happens if that ole evil eye gets crossed on its way down the driveway and can't make eye contact with your stupid tree. I guess we're doomed then, right?" She hadn't waited around for the full onslaught of her mother's scolding. Like always, she'd dashed for her room under the eaves of the soaring Victorian house.

It hadn't always been this way. They'd laughed easily with each other through Tally's childhood and early teens, relishing life in the Georgia mountains and exploring their natural wonders. They'd hiked the hills, camped beside creeks in the parks, and returned home with plans already made for their next excursion. Because Tally's dad was often away for extended periods of time, favoring the corporate-jet lifestyle of his CEO status, mother and daughter grew into a tight team, together fighting off the abandonment and finding comfort in each other. Even when her dad died of a sudden heart attack in Hong Kong, little changed in the way Tally and her mom lived their lives in the old Georgia farmhouse. But all of that had changed when Mona went to a spiritual retreat one weekend and encountered her first medium. From there, it was a swift slide into the occult.

Now, in the wash of streetlights, Tally could see the breeze-tossed eyes of the fig tree just ahead. She hated their mocking, their fraudulent stares. The only thing they deflected was her, every time she returned home.

Tally crossed the street and cut through the pines scattered down one side of the manicured grounds, her mother's valiant attempt to create her version of heaven on earth. As she cleared the tree line, the moon slipped from behind a bank of clouds, illuminating the gray stucco house. As often happened, Tally was struck anew by its grandeur, at the steep, asymmetrical roof that rambled over a promenade of gables, porches, and bays trimmed in gingerbread molding. In the five years they'd lived in the house, she'd never grown accustomed to its lavish form and scale. But it was the tower rising three stories on one side that had held the greatest allure. She'd wasted no time claiming the top room with its 360-degree view and privacy—sweet isolation from Mona Greyson's growing madness.

Inside the house, Tally could see that her mother had left lights on here and there. Of course, she hadn't known where her daughter slipped off to after dinner. She rarely knew. Tally no longer felt the need to give notice of her goings and comings. It was a sad fact that weighed heavily on her as she crossed in front of the carport and climbed the steps to the kitchen door.

There would probably be a slice of cake or pie left out for her. "Back home in Georgia," as Tally often said, mother and daughter used to bake together for whole days in the big country kitchen with the potbellied stove. Perhaps Mona's current baking habit was an attempt to salvage something from a better time with her daughter.

The house would be empty. Tally had just seen her mother's car parked inside the camp. This time it was the Thursday-night class on healing, something for which Mona Greyson believed she was gifted. On Tuesdays, Wednesdays, Fridays, and Sundays there were other classes, séances, gatherings, or volunteer services to keep her mother engaged in the work of the spirit world, but not Tally's. As her mother sank deeper into the occult, Tally understood that she truly lived alone.

Bypassing the peach cobbler on the counter, Tally grabbed a bag of chips and a can of root beer from the pantry and started up the stairs. A rapid ascent up three flights of steps four or five times a day had produced the strong legs Tally needed to flee trouble.

She opened the door at the top of the tower, closed it behind her, and plopped in the middle of her bed with her unhealthy snack. Since she'd returned home, her diet was just one more irritant that sent her mother into fits of admonishment. "Not good for me?" Tally had responded once. "When you sit out there at night in the woods with a bunch of crazy psychics waiting for some dead person to show up?"

Tally picked up the phone and speed-dialed her best, probably only, friend in this town. Denise Northcutt and her mother had arrived at the Greyson home with casserole in hand the day Tally and her mother moved in. The Northcutts lived just two doors down in a modest coquina-rock house surrounded by royal palms and lots of boys, all of them Denise's brothers. Her dad was the associate principal at the regional high school and a deacon at the local Baptist church.

Denise picked up on the first ring. "Hey, Tally. Tell me you didn't go there tonight."

"To the loony farm? Sure did."

"So what happened?"

"Nothing you want to hear about."

"Did they chase you again?"

"Of course they did. They must think it's the same thrill-seeking boy they've chased off before."

Denise laughed at that, then shifted to another topic. "Tally, when are you going back to school?"

"Oh, not that again."

"Yes, again. You can't be an architect with only two and half years of undergraduate work. They just won't let you."

"And I won't let my mother slide into the abyss with those who think it's perfectly okay to conjure up talking ghosts. Not if I can stop it."

"And if you can't?"

Tally was quiet. Then, "Look, Denise. Just to get inside that place, I've taken their classes, sat in on their séances, and heard the shrieking babble of people you wouldn't dream of bringing home for dinner. But there's even more that goes on late at night, things I don't think they want their daytime guests to encounter. That's why I have to go back and spy. They're about to suck the soul right out of my mom if I don't do something." She paused. "I'm not going anywhere until she's either free of them or dead. On second thought, though, even if she were dead, they'd still try to drag her back for a little chat at one of their spook shows."

"Tally!"

"Tell you what. You go back there with me tomorrow night and I'll prove a few things to you."

"Oh, I don't think so."

"I do. It's the only way you'll ever understand why I had to leave college and come home."

"Well, maybe it would . . ."

"That's good enough. Be here by dark. And uh . . . better wear running shoes."

Chapter 11

*T*hat Friday found the Bower household in a frenzy of preparations for Liesl and Cade's departure. They had gathered with Ian, Ava, and Henry the night before at their favorite Folly Beach crab shack, where the tables were covered with newspapers and the marsh waters lapped at the door. Friends of the owner, who was an avid fan of Liesl's, the little group had huddled over their salty feast in a private back room that teetered precariously on stilts driven into the creek bed. The well-fed evening had ended early.

At the kitchen table that morning, Ian said, "Hey look, when you get to Tel Aviv, tell that young Max fella that next time he needs a concert from someone in this household, well, I've been brushing up on my fiddle."

"Yeah, Pop," Cade answered, "I've been meaning to talk to you about that. Would you consider some time besides the crack of dawn to practice?"

Ian glanced between Liesl and Cade, who were downing a bagel-and-cream-cheese breakfast. "You two lovebirds need some special kind of quiet at that hour?" he asked, barely containing a grin.

"No, but Mrs. Fowler next door does." Cade winced at his own unintended implication, but Ian gave him no time to correct it.

"Well, I hardly think a ninety-year-old widow needs the same kind of quiet you're talking about."

Over Liesl's giggling, Cade protested, knowing it was futile. "I wasn't talking about it. You were. Now listen to me. You may think your, uh, version of bluegrass is the ideal way for everyone on this block to start their day. But Mrs. Fowler doesn't. Neither does Henry."

"Henry said that?" Ian looked genuinely hurt and Cade regretted the whole conversation. "I thought Henry liked my fiddling."

"We all do, Ian," Liesl jumped in. "Maybe you could just wait until a little later in the day to play for us."

"Well, now that's a perfectly reasonable thing to ask." Ian turned to Cade. "You should take a lesson in diplomacy from your wife."

"You're absolutely right, Pop. I apologize for the clumsy handling of my request."

Ian frowned. "What request was that?"

Cade moaned a sigh of surrender. "I forgot."

"That's okay, son. Happens to me all the time. But I'm glad we had this little talk. I've still got something to say, though. This is the serious part." He put down his coffee cup and focused intently on them. "It's about this trip. Now, I'm not much good at protecting anybody anymore, but God is. And me and him have had a talk. He's going with you to Israel and Germany, then back home to this old place that you think is safe from foreign-speaking hoodlums, even though recent history proves otherwise."

Cade knew his grandfather had been bitterly opposed to their traveling so soon after the Volynski ordeal in New York, though he hadn't voiced the full extent of those objections.

"Now God can do a respectable job of just about anything," Ian said. "But if you resist what he tells you to do, if you stand up when he tells you to lie down, or ignore any other warnings he gives you, you're going to get hurt. And if you don't survive, folks here will have to bury me right alongside you." Ian had to pause in a moment of emotion Cade had rarely seen.

Clearing his throat and swallowing hard, Ian continued. "I'm going to pray you through every moment. You listen for God to answer and do exactly what he tells you, you hear?"

Liesl wiped her eyes and reached across the table to grip Ian's hand. Cade logged his grandfather's advice but was eager to dispel the somber mood. "But if you're in your grave, how can you play the fiddle over ours?"

Chapter 12

Tally waited for Denise on the front porch, dressed in sneakers, long cargo pants, and a plain black T-shirt. The black hooded shell was tied around her waist. At dusk, Denise came bounding up the drive toward the front porch. Tally looked down the steps at her delicately framed friend with the silky blond hair tucked behind her ears. Hanging from one shoulder was a small tote bag in a bright pink plaid. "What's in the cute little bag?" Tally asked as Denise approached.

"Fruits and peanuts."

Tally squinted as if for a closer look at her friend. "We're not going to the zoo, Denise."

"They're for us. I thought we might want a snack."

"While running for our lives?" Tally teased, though there was sufficient reason to question what those who'd pursued her the night before might have done if they'd caught her.

"Don't be ridiculous. We're just going to spy a little. Aren't we?"

"Grow up, Denise. You're a junior in college. You should be committed to expanding your knowledge of the universe . . . at the esteemed University of the Spirit." Tally issued the name with a bitter flourish. "Give me that bag." Denise reluctantly handed it over and Tally dropped it inside the front hall, closed the door, and headed down the steps.

"Aren't you going to lock the door?" Denise asked, following her friend across the yard.

"With crazy mirrors and Turkish evil eyes hanging all over the place, who would want to break in?"

Tally grabbed Denise's arm and pulled her along the sidewalk. "Let's hurry. It's almost time."

"For what?"

Tally didn't answer.

Fifteen minutes later, they entered the woods that surrounded the fenced camp. Though the wide, drive-through gate to the Anhinga Bay Spiritualist Camp was usually open, a guardhouse there was manned most of the time. So a few years ago, Tally had used wire cutters to open her own private access to the grounds.

The girls hurried down the fence line along one side of the camp, picking their way through the underbrush. At one point, Denise was about to speak when Tally raised a hand for quiet, then whispered for her to stay put. Tally inched from under the cover of the trees toward a span of chain-link fence. Even in the dark, she had no trouble finding the loose flap of metal lattice she'd so cleverly disguised. She'd found a roll of pliable wire the gauge and color of the fence wire. When wound in the same pattern of the fence, the passageway was undetectable to a swiftly scanning eye. Closer scrutiny might uncover the entry, but not since Tally had fashioned it. It was always as she'd left it the time before.

Now, starting at the corner anchor post, she stepped off five strides and stopped. After a few minutes of unwinding the wire, she pulled back the flap and motioned for a hesitant Denise to hurry through. When both girls had passed through, Tally secured the flap again and they ran low and straight toward the maintenance shed that had become Tally's rallying point. In all her intrusions to the camp, she'd waited in the crook of the L-shaped metal building for the sense of an all clear before beginning her surveillance of this bizarre enclave. At first, her after-dark exploration had sprung from both curiosity and a bit of careless thrill.

But lately, as her mother became more entrenched—brainwashed, Tally believed—in the metaphysical order imposed behind the fence, Tally had, herself, become possessed by a desperate need to uncover and expose that world for what it was. "A bunch of theatrical fakes!" she'd once declared to her mother. "Why do you keep going back to those people?" she'd persisted.

Her mother's answer still stung. "Because nothing else matters. They're all I need."

Even so, Tally had tried to patch over that wound and listen for what she hadn't heard. Was it a silent scream? Tally believed it was, and so she'd pushed off into the dark of her mother's desperate obsession. If Mona Greyson didn't care for or need her daughter anymore, her daughter had to know why.

Now, with their backs pushed against the metal side of the shed, Denise was finally allowed to speak. Even in the lee of the shadows, away from the spotlight near the front of the building, Tally could see the bulging fright in Denise's eyes. "I want to go back," she whispered.

"We just got here and I haven't shown you anything yet."

"I don't want to see."

"Well, you've got to. So quit being such a baby and come on."

Before Denise could object again, Tally pulled her up and told her to be quiet and stay close. Only a twinge of regret crept over Tally as she crouched low at the corner of the shed and looked back at her nervous friend. She turned and laid a hand on Denise's shoulder. "Look, I'm sorry to be so rough. But I've discovered things about this place that you have to know. All you good Christian people think it's just hocus-pocus silliness going on in here. But I finally stumbled on some things I wasn't prepared for, things that made me realize there just might be something real about what they—at least some of them—do in here." Tally peeked around the corner. "Nobody's out there. Come on."

The camp covered nearly four hundred acres, vastly expanded since its founding days in the late 1800s. The oldest phase was a horseshoe-shaped colony of small bungalows fronting on a broad green with a small amphitheater in the center. At the head of the horseshoe, opposite the main gate, was the hotel. Tally and Denise now hid in a palm thicket just behind it. "So this is the famous hotel," Denise said.

"Yep. People from all over the world have been coming here for centuries. You've lived here longer than I have and never laid eyes on it? You need to get out more, Denise."

"I was always afraid of this place. Besides, my parents wouldn't let me anywhere near it. So what's so special about it?"

Tally looked at her irritably, a demeanor that surfaced too often lately. "Don't you know where you are?"

Denise shrugged her shoulders but remained fixed on Tally.

"There's only a couple other places like this in the whole country. According to my freshman history professor and the Internet, the psychics who live here are supposedly the best there are. All kinds of famous people come here to meet with these mediums." Tally waved a hand toward the rest of the compound. They all live in those little houses with shingles hanging outside that say what they're good at. You know, telling your future, or summoning an ancestor who'll tell you secrets from the other side. They talk through the mediums from places called the etheric planes. I don't think it's like heaven, not the Jesus kind, anyway. But I'm not sure."

"Have you seen the kinds of people who come here?" Denise asked wide-eyed.

"You mean besides my crazy mother?"

"Don't talk about your mom that way, Tally."

Tally eyed her solemnly. "You don't know her. She's changed into someone I don't even know." Tally looked down and wanted to cry, but wouldn't dare. She raised her head. "But to answer your question, people who look real normal come here all the time and stay in the hotel. And sometimes, Hollywood celebrities sneak in here like they don't want anybody to know. Mom says there's been a few congressmen, too. Now that's scary, don't you think?"

"Everything about this place is scary."

"You don't know anything yet. Come on." They slipped from the trees and made a dash for the closest bungalow, skirting around to the back. From there, Tally led the way to a house three doors up, pausing long enough to point toward the car parked at the front curb, then heading toward a large tree behind the house, Denise fast on her heels.

"That was your mom's car," Denise whispered when she caught up.

Tally nodded, then held a finger to her mouth, gesturing toward an open window where, drawing closer, they could hear the murmuring of voices inside. Stepping cautiously behind a large live oak tree whose limbs spread above the house, they hid themselves and listened, neither one moving. Two sets of eyes locked on the two people inside seated in high-backed chairs, facing each other, the room hushed in a yellow glow from unseen lamps. Mona Greyson sat like a porcelain doll clothed loosely in a pale blue sundress and yellow wrap slung haphazardly around her bare shoulders. Before her was an older woman dressed in a plain shirtwaist dress, as if she'd just returned from grocery shopping. No gypsy fortune-teller stereotypes here. In all her secret forays into the compound, Tally had never seen anyone who fit that description. They all looked so normal.

Just then, normal ended. Mona Greyson suddenly cried, "Daddy, don't!"

Tally flinched as she watched her mother's arms fly up from her sides as if shielding her body. "Don't do it again," she wailed, then slumped forward, the other woman catching her and rocking her gently.

Denise gripped Tally's arm, digging her nails into the flesh. Refusing to tear her eyes from her mother, Tally released her friend's fingers and patted her hand reassuringly. Tally had witnessed something similar another night, from another client of this particular medium who was rumored to be the matriarch of the colony. Tally hadn't known her mother would be the client this night.

The girls watched as Lesandra Bernardo calmed Mona, speaking softly, cooing over her. She made Mona lean back against the chair and rest. Then, Mrs. Bernardo resumed her straight-back position in her own chair and fell silent. Waiting. For something. After a moment, the slightest movement began in her torso, which rotated slowly, steadily, then stopped. The woman grabbed the arms of her chair and her head jerked upward. A man's bass voice erupted from inside her, coursing through her open mouth. "I didn't want to hurt you," it said.

"Yes, you did," Mona answered, her own voice seething. "You did what no father should do to his little girl!"

"Forgive me, Mona," the voice pleaded. "It's the only way you'll ever be free of me and those things I did to you."

"I won't forgive you. I want you to suffer like I do."

What had he done? Tally had never known her mother's father. He'd died when Tally was a baby. She couldn't bear to think the worst.

With a smothering guilt for barging into her mother's secret pain, Tally started to leave when Mona jumped from her seat and fled the room. Mrs. Bernardo didn't try to stop or follow her. She appeared fixed in one position. Seconds later, though, she sprang from her chair and hurried after her client. That's when Tally heard the car at the curb crank and pull away. With no thought of exposing herself, she ran from behind the tree and toward the street, watching the silver Lexus head toward the main gate. She felt like crumpling to the ground, surrendering herself to those who patrolled there. She wished she'd never asked Denise to come. She had no right to be here. Neither one of them did. But how could Tally have known what was coming, what wretched secret her mother had harbored for so many years?

Across the green, someone moved. Tally caught sight of the security guard. She lunged back into the dark and returned to Denise. "We have to run. Now." But Denise seemed too stunned to move.

"That man's voice—" she began in a strained whisper, seemingly unable to tear herself from the open window. She shuddered.

Tally had seen similar things happen, always from her hiding places. It was why she'd brought Denise here, though now she regretted it. "Probably an act," Tally lied. "I don't know. But I do know we've got to get out of here." Tally jerked against Denise's arm and forced her away.

Slipping house to house, scanning for the guard, the girls finally reached the back of the hotel and then the shed. When they got to the fence, Tally quickly unlaced the cording, opened the flap, and both girls slipped to the other side. Tally had just finished securing the flap again when she heard something. The faraway drone of an engine. She'd heard it before from her tucked-away hideouts in the compound. A small plane. Sometimes a helicopter. At different times, she'd seen them descend to the private airstrip behind the camp, always at night.

As the girls plunged back into the dark of the woods, something her mother once said returned to Tally, making her stop and turn toward the sound of the plane: "It's a powerful place, Tally," Mona Greyson had told her daughter. "And powerful men go there."

"What are you doing?" Denise asked. "Come on." Tally still heard bare fright in her voice.

"You know the way home, Denise. Can you get there by yourself?"

"What? Aren't you coming?"

Tally wondered how much more to tell her, how much her over-sheltered friend could take. "Listen. That plane. I have to see who's on it."

"Are you crazy?"

"Maybe. But I'm going back, this time all the way to the school."

Denise gaped at her. "You think Curt Vandoren is going to let you in there?"

"I'm not asking permission."

"This is nuts, Tally. You don't know anything about that place."

But Tally did know. After leaving the University of Miami to keep a closer eye on her mother, Tally had made it her business to know the compound and those who had lured others into their cosmic web.

Charismatic Curt Vandoren had swept into Anhinga Bay from nowhere, she was told, just eight years ago, moving into the quiet camp and setting up shop like just another medium. Only he quickly gained a following of people from around the world who began filling the hotel on weekends. Then he started the mass séances. They were spectacles that the camp old-timers protested. Vandoren had stirred their waters too many times, and they finally made him leave. But he didn't go far.

Either from spite or an irresistible land deal, he bought the property behind the camp, all the way to the bay, and built what he called the University of the Spirit. He brought in his own faculty who taught Vandoren's clairvoyant protégés about channeling spirit guides and the departed loved ones from the far reaches of the etheric planes. About paranormal contact between humans and the all-knowing others who've passed on to that other side. About psychic healing and counseling.

There was something else working there, though. Tally had overheard her mother confess suspicions to another patron of the camp, who, like Mona, was attending some of the few university classes offered to the public. Just home from Miami and needing a closer look at the school, Tally had joined her mother in those classes. It was during a break one day that Tally heard her mother admit sensing "an evil presence in this place."

The whine of the engine grew louder and Tally looked up. Through the trees, she now saw the blinking lights on the plane's wing tips. There wasn't much time. "Denise, you've got a whole family and lots of friends. I've got no one but my mom, and she's in trouble. I have to go back." She pointed the way through the woods. "Take this path and keep going. Pretty soon, you'll see the streetlights. Okay?"

"Okay," came the weak reply.

Without waiting for further objection from Denise, Tally spun around and ran hard toward the bay, just outside the camp's fence. She knew she'd abandoned her friend in a place that was frightening to her, and for that, she was sorry. But Tally was riding a runaway locomotive and didn't know how to get off, refused to get off while her mother was still on board.

Chapter 13

Near heedless, again, of her own safety, Tally sprinted toward the bay, her ear tuned to the incoming aircraft. Where the camp fence ended, a cement wall began, enclosing the campus of the University of the Spirit. It wasn't what she'd expected that first visit with her mother. No darkly draped rooms, incense, candles, pyramids, or crystals. Though hunkered low against the threat of hurricanes, the one-story concrete building drew light through expansive windows that pulled in waves of ocean light. Its marble floors were polished, its glazed stucco walls shining, its air almost astringent. There seemed to be a wellness about the place that Tally found contradictory to what transpired there.

"The University of the Spirit," Tally repeated the name to herself. "Like it takes a degree to know your own soul." But did Tally know hers?

She ran along the outside of the wall, sandwiched between solid concrete and a dense swath of slash pines. She glanced over the wall to see the school's asymmetrical roof that ran at odd angles. Another time and it might have engaged her eye for architectural lines, but not now. Her sights were set on the airstrip straight ahead. As she ran, she felt for the bulge in a pocket of her cargo pants. She'd sold one of her mountain bikes to afford the night-vision binoculars now tucked inside the pocket. The special optics were light and compact, but powerful enough to spy through camp-bungalow windows if she couldn't get close enough. They'd been particularly handy for monitoring her mother's bizarre séances in the far trees of the camp green.

Pulling the binoculars from her pocket, she looped their wide strap around her neck and clutched them tightly as she ran. She wanted to be ready as soon as the plane landed.

When she made the ninety-degree turn at the far end of the wall, she saw the runway lights across a stretch of sand and low brush. As though she'd been trained in military reconnaissance, she ran upright as far as she dared, then dropped to her belly and crawled to a mound of young palmettos not too far from the airstrip but outside the arc of the runway lights. As the plane circled overhead, she tucked herself entirely within the bushes to avoid a chance beam of light that might catch her. As the plane steadied its landing course, she parted the leafy fronds just enough to see out. When she trained her binoculars on the landing strip, her mouth fell open at the sight.

She'd been there once before to watch a plane land. Only Curt Vandoren, whose form she'd recognize anywhere, and one of his aides had met its passengers, three men she couldn't identify who were shuttled the short distance to the university campus in a stretch van.

That wasn't the scene before her now. Besides the passenger van and Vandoren's refrigerator-size presence, illuminated by the nearby lights and Tally's night-vision technology, there were two panel trucks and a small squad of armed men gathered near a tractor-trailer rig Tally had never seen anywhere near the camp or university. At that moment, she was especially grateful for the cover of dark and the palmettos, dense enough to hide a person from those who'd surely apprehend an unwanted observer. She was certain of that, though she wasn't sure why. She'd had no history with Curt Vandoren, except on one visit with her mother. He'd only spoken briefly to her when introduced, but curiously enough, had reached out to finger her hair in a way that made her recoil. He'd only laughed at her startled reaction and moved on.

Now, she focused on his ponderous form, dressed in a loose tunic over billowy pants. His silver hair shone brightly in the light, but his face hung darkly, its mouth grim, eyes lifted toward the plane just now clearing the treetops. The aircraft was bulkier than a passenger plane. It looked like a miniature version of the great cargo planes she'd watched take off from Homestead Air Reserve Base farther up the mainland. *What could they be hauling into this freaky little place?*

The plane landed smoothly and rolled slowly toward the welcoming party. Even before its wheels came to a complete rest, the armed men rushed forward to stand guard. When they raised their automatic weapons shoulder high, Tally's pulse spiked. *I really shouldn't be here*, she groaned inside, though she dared not move.

Now she could see how much larger the plane was than the one she'd spied on before, than others she'd seen from town on their ascent toward the university, the only place in this water-gorged region where a plane could land.

When the aircraft's engines shut down and chocks were placed behind the wheels, the side door of the plane opened and the stairs were lowered. Two men in fatigues descended the steps first, both with automatic weapons cradled in their arms. Barely breathing, Tally didn't move anything but the finger on the focus wheel of her binoculars.

At the foot of the steps, the two armed men were joined by several others already on the ground, all of them facing away from the plane in a 360-degree sweep that made Tally suck in a breath and hold it. They appeared to be waiting for someone else to deplane. Just then, from the open doorway above them, a muscular man in what looked like black running clothes emerged, took one step down, then turned toward the man following behind him. To Tally, the second man appeared much older and unsteady on his feet, so much so, the black-clad aide had to grip the man firmly and help him down the remaining steps. Someone else on board followed, carrying a wheelchair. Only when the older man was on the ground and settled into the chair did Curt Vandoren approach him and deliver a kiss to each side of his face.

Tally squinted hard at the man's features, but they were hooded by the brim of a safari hat. *That's an odd thing to wear at night*, she thought, then watched Vandoren commandeer the wheelchair and push it and its passenger toward the rear of the plane.

Moments later, another man descended the steps of the plane and Tally looked long and hard at him through the binoculars. There was something familiar about this face. She recalled a day two summers ago when she had accompanied her mother to the school. In a hallway outside one of her mother's classes, she had watched two men arguing with one of Curt Vandoren's aides. The three men hadn't noticed her as she was mostly hidden by a giant, potted schefflera. The last man down the steps of the plane was one of those three men, she believed. He'd been the shortest of the three, with a wide face, though his features just now were vague. He joined Vandoren and the man in the wheelchair, their voices now floating toward her on the wind off the bay. But she couldn't distinguish their words. Too many others spoke at the same time, some issuing orders, others responding. A tension seemed to build among those assembled nearest the plane. Then one in the group ran toward the cab of the tractor-trailer rig, and Tally heard its engine roar to life. Distracted by the truck now maneuvering toward the plane, Tally didn't notice when the big door at the rear of the aircraft yawned open. But now, she watched the truck back toward the opening and stop. Several other men jumped to open its cargo door and withdraw a long ramp.

Tally pressed the binoculars' eyecups harder against her face. She saw a team of people enter the back of the plane, and soon, they rolled a large wooden crate down the ramp onto the pavement. The man in the wheelchair propelled himself forward and laid a hand on one of the wide straps securing it. Vandoren joined him and the two spoke just to each other. Again, Tally strained to hear their words, but couldn't. The wind had picked up, out-voicing the two men and causing Tally considerably more distress. *If it blows any harder, it will flatten these palmettos and leave me exposed.*

She lowered the binoculars, tucking them inside her shirt, and was about to risk a slithering exit on her belly when shouts rose from the tarmac. Four men had harnessed themselves to the rectangular crate and were now pulling it up the ramp to the truck while four others pushed from behind. Vandoren and the man in the wheelchair watched the whole maneuver. Only when the crate was secured on board and the door lowered did the wheelchair move. Vandoren pushed it to a waiting van and helped the man inside. The others from the plane joined them, and the van headed for the school. The armed squad piled into the panel trucks and followed the tractor-trailer along the same route. Not until all four vehicles rumbled into the walled campus did Tally stir. Still inside the palmetto blind, she scanned the area with her binoculars, seeing no one from that strange pack left behind. Regardless, she crawled all the way to the piney woods before bolting up to a full run.

The binoculars tucked beneath her shirt, she retraced her path along the wall, a howling wind pushing from behind as if shooing her away. Something had stolen into her reserve of grit and self-confidence threatening to loot it bare. Despite her well-practiced defenses, she now ran scared, the trees swiping at her with low, spiked branches. A vine grabbed one ankle and almost brought her down, but she yanked free of it and stumbled forward. The woods closed in on her as she approached the divide between the university campus and the camp, where the wall met the chain-link fence. Suddenly visible, she stopped and peered into the dimly lit colony of psychics. Nothing stirred. Had the ghosts and their handlers all gone to sleep, as if such a normal thing were entirely within their paranormal grasp? But Tally knew better. And so she crept cautiously around the far reaches of a security light, its beacon harsh and repelling, and set her sights on home and her tower fortress.

She'd just found her stride again when something moved through the trees ahead. She stopped cold and listened. There was the outline of someone moving toward her. In the split second between immobile fear and flight, a voice spoke.

"Tally, don't run."

She didn't respond. She couldn't.

"Don't be afraid." The figure moved closer and Tally saw a face materialize in the gray wash of light. She knew this face.

"I watched you go there, Tally. You shouldn't have done that." Now, the figure dared to come closer, and Tally saw the thin, bent frame of the old man. *Mr. Fremont!* He was a sales clerk at the camp bookstore. What was he doing here?

"You have nothing to fear from me, child. Come quickly. You're in danger." He motioned for her to follow him.

Instead, Tally spun around and searched the long wall and woods behind her. Had someone followed her from the airstrip?

"This way," he urged, waving her on as he turned toward a side gate to the camp.

If she had been followed, she sensed no quicker retreat than to disappear inside the forbidding grounds of the camp. The old man stopped once to look back at her. "Now."

As she fell in step behind him, he said, "Stay close, and don't look back." Of course, that was the very thing she did—just in time to see two men stomping up the path from the airstrip. The old hand suddenly grabbed her arm and pulled her to the gate. He furiously worked the combination lock until it sprang open, then grabbed her again. "Hurry!" came his coarse whisper. He tucked his withered body into a hunched scurry which Tally mimicked all the way to an open shed behind one of the bungalows. They'd just dropped into the opaque shadows inside the dirt-floor shelter when running feet passed nearby and stopped.

Tally squeezed her eyes shut and listened to the labored breathing of her rescuer and to the clipped voices just beyond the fence. "Go straight to the road. I'll search the woods."

"Was it a man or a woman?" the other voice asked.

"Couldn't tell. Get going. You know what to do."

To me? Tally turned toward Mr. Fremont. She couldn't see his face, only hear him wheeze. Then he laid a calming hand on her shoulder, but said nothing. After a long, silent interval, he whispered, "Let's go."

They eased from their hiding place and looked around. Then he led her along a worn dirt path to a back corner of the compound, to a small, gray-shingle house nearly smothered in flowering vines whose colors faintly shimmered in the fan of Malibu lights lining the front walk.

A weathered picket fence enclosed the small front yard of the house where, she discovered, Spencer Fremont lived alone. He opened the wooden gate and ushered Tally toward a front door set deep on the porch. Tally might have commented on the American Craftsman charms of the little cottage, but her aesthetic senses had been eclipsed by the events of that night.

Tally trailed the man into his living room, then did a slow rotation, noting how sparsely furnished it was. There was only a small sofa and two matching chairs, a coffee table, and a bookcase against one wall. A worn hooked rug spread its faded colors over the wooden floor.

Spencer Fremont lingered at a front window before finally turning to Tally. "Please sit down. You're safe now."

Tally did as she was told, not understanding why she should trust this man. She'd only spoken to him once before when her mother had dragged her along to the camp bookstore. That was in the days before Mona Greyson fully submerged herself in the cosmic waters of the camp and Tally finally realized that she would have to enter those waters to retrieve the mother she'd lost to them.

Tally recalled that first introduction to Mr. Fremont. Against her mother's objection, Tally had worn the new cross necklace Denise had given her for Christmas to the store that day. She stood next to her mother as a clerk, a woman working alongside Mr. Fremont, busily rang up the stack of books Mona had brought to the counter. When the woman finally looked up to announce the total, she smiled at Mona then glanced at Tally, and the smile abruptly disappeared. The clerk had locked on the necklace and her disapproval was palpable. "Who is this?" the woman huffed, pointing to Tally. "And why is she wearing that?" That's when Spencer Fremont had stepped in.

"Rita, surely you've seen a cross before and most certainly will again," he chided amiably. The woman slid a bristling look his way and recovered her composure. She faked another smile at Mona, avoiding Tally altogether. She had been shocked at the clerk's reaction to the necklace. And Spencer Fremont knew it. He followed them into the parking lot, introduced himself, and, with Mona's permission, pulled Tally aside.

"Please forgive my coworker's thoughtless behavior. She's usually more gracious than that."

"She was rude," Tally sniffed. "Was she afraid?"

Mr. Fremont looked curiously at her. "Why would she be?"

Tally had learned enough during the few months she'd been going to church with Denise's family to answer the question. "A lot of people who don't know God are afraid of him. They just don't understand him."

"Do you?" he asked simply.

Tally thought hard about that one. "I'm trying to."

"Well, understand this," Mr. Fremont said. "You know things these people here don't. And they know things that are important for *you* to know."

Tally stared into his lined face, at the eyes that held hers so intensely.

What were those things? And . . . "Why do you say 'these people here'? she asked. "Aren't you one of them?"

But he wouldn't answer. Instead, he led her back to her mother and bowed slightly to them both, an out-of-date gesture, Tally thought, but one that seemed natural for this elderly and quietly composed man.

"Thank you for letting me talk to your daughter, Mrs. Greyson." He looked directly at Tally. "She's a perceptive young woman . . . who should be very careful." He ambled away without explanation, and Tally watched him return to the bookstore, stopping once to look back at her.

Now, Tally looked more closely about the man's living room, landing on the one thing that took her by surprise. A small wooden cross hung over the bookcase. She stared at it, remembering the question she'd asked him that day outside the store. She turned to confront him. "You aren't one of them, are you?" It was more a statement than a question.

He smiled faintly as he lowered himself into one of the overstuffed chairs. "These old legs aren't used to such strenuous walks—tracking foolhardy young women who sneak around in places where they shouldn't be."

Tally gaped at him. "You've been watching me?"

"Guarding you."

"Why? And why won't you answer my question?"

His gaze didn't waver, though his words were slow in coming. Finally, he gestured again for Tally to sit down. "We don't have long. Your mother will be looking for you."

"My mother rarely looks for me," Tally said, seating herself on the other chair whose seat cushion sagged. "I'm an adult who can take care of myself. She much prefers it that way. Besides, I told her I would spend the night with a friend."

"Ah, the young woman you brought with you tonight."

Tally balked again. "You saw us?"

He chuckled. "You aren't the consummate spies you think you are."

Tally noted the scolding tone and braced for more. But his next words fell more softly.

"Where is your cross, Tally?" he asked.

The question surprised her and her hand went to her neck, but she didn't answer. Then he asked another.

"Do you believe in Christ?"

Who is this man who asks me such things? As if he already knows I can't answer. I don't know the answer. A half lie would have to do. "Sure I do."

"Why *sure*, Tally? Not everybody does."

"Do you?"

He studied her a moment. "Light shines brightest against the dark."

Tally didn't understand.

"I had to witness the dark of this place to see him clearly. To understand who he was and why he had to come to us. To understand his warnings against the other powers."

"What powers?"

He smiled, not in a patronizing way, but as one who'd long awaited this moment. "Ever since that day in the store, Tally . . . ever since I first spotted you spying on this place, I've wanted to ask if it was just mere curiosity or if you were earnestly searching for something. Before I go any further, you must answer that." He drew back and waited.

Tally looked at the floor, perhaps *through* it as if the battlefield of her mind were laid out clearly on the underside. After a moment, she answered. "At first, I couldn't believe there were other people like my mom, especially a whole community of them. It was like going to a freak show watching my first séance out on the field. Then, without her knowing, I followed her to the woods where I saw things I didn't understand. Heard voices I wasn't sure were real. It scared me. I was scared for her." She looked down. "Since my dad died a few years ago, she's gone a little nuts.

No, a lot nuts. She sees things I don't. Hears things I don't. She craves all this heebie-jeebie stuff. That's why she closed up our farmhouse in Georgia to bring us here. I had to prove to her, somehow, that it was all fake. But the more I witnessed, the more I wondered if it was."

Spencer nodded, his understanding visible on his face. "And I followed my wife here. It was that or leave her, and I couldn't bear to do that." He repositioned himself on the sofa across from where Tally sat fidgeting with a loose thread on the upholstered arm of the chair, though her eyes were steady on his. "At first, she was just a dabbler in the occult practices here. In time, though, she became a licensed medium, discovering her clairvoyant gifts, she said, and wandering into transcendental fields where I couldn't go. Because, like you, I didn't believe in those forces. But that changed."

It wasn't what Tally expected. She'd hoped he'd be an ally, someone she might enlist in her efforts to drag her mother away from this place where frightening people hung their shingles with authority: *Spiritual counseling. Past life regression. Psychic healer. Connect with the departed. Channel a lost loved one.*

He must have seen her disappointment. "No, Tally, I'm not one of them. But because of what I was forced to see, I ran the other way. To the cross. Because I finally understood." He picked up a small book with a tattered cover and turned quickly through its pages until he landed on one. Slipping on a pair of glasses, he said, "From Ephesians, this is God's letter to us, Tally. Listen. 'For our struggle is not against flesh and blood, but against the rulers, against the authorities, against the powers of this dark world and against the spiritual forces of evil in the heavenly realms.'" He removed his glasses and eyed her quietly for a moment. "I read that to my wife, but she wouldn't listen and I couldn't make her. I can't make anybody listen, including you."

But Tally had listened, and now she resisted the urge to spring from the chair and flee. Not from Spencer Fremont and his message, but from her own miserable confusion.

"Why are you still here?" she asked.

"After Millie died, the counsel here agreed that even though I wasn't a follower, and certainly not a medium like the rest of them, they would honor my wife's long service to this community by letting me remain in our home. It's the only home I've known for fifteen years."

"But how could you go on pretending to be part of them? To work in their bookstore and guide others to teachings you don't believe in?"

"For the rare moment when I might keep someone—like an impressionable young woman—from falling into the abyss." He tilted his head to one side. "You see? One of those moments just came. Hopefully, something I've told you will hold you back from plunging in after your mother, even if you think you're just trying to save her. The others here would love to draw you in with them, Tally. That's why I watched after you those nights when you slipped into the camp. Why I followed you tonight."

"To the airstrip?"

"Yes, I wasn't quick enough to stop you."

Tally brushed past his concern for her. "Did you see the guns and that guy in the wheelchair?" She was almost breathless. "Did you see the crate?"

Spencer held up a calming hand. "I did. But you must forget that *you* did." He leaned forward. "Tally, Curt Vandoren is the epicenter of a black hole. You stay away from him and his place down there."

"But what's going on there?"

"I don't know. Right now, it's more important that you get home safely and never go back there. And stop your nocturnal spying on this camp." He wagged a finger in her direction and stood up. "You won't approve, but I'm calling your mother to come get you. You can't stay here, and it's too dangerous for you to go out there alone. Those men will soon circle back to look for you."

Tally shot up from her seat. "Well, they won't find me unless you haul Mona Greyson in here and give her another excuse to scream and yell at me. That might attract a little bit of attention." She outstepped him to the door. "You and I have a lot more to talk about, Mr. Fremont. Starting with that big box that must be real important to all those guys with guns. So I'll be back. You obviously know how to watch for me." She regretted her sarcasm only a little. The man had no right to stalk her. She wasn't entirely sure it was for her own good.

She opened the door and raced down the steps, leaving Mr. Fremont in silhouette against the open doorway. He was still there when she turned and tossed a compatriot's salute his way before slipping into the cover of the pines.

She was running on steam and sass because she had no other defenses. They'd served her adequately for many years. But tonight, she'd crossed a line in the sand, inside a clump of palmettos. No matter how inadequate those old defenses were now, she couldn't turn back. Her mom was about to disappear into that black hole.

Chapter 14

A week after the assassination of President Dimitri Gorev, Moscow still vented its outrage. The ever-expanding crowd of mourning protestors hadn't left their dug-in position in front of the Kremlin since news of the massacre, unaccountably delayed by hours. Some in the crowd simply wept while too many others shouted and hurled flaming bottles, their toxic indignation prompting the threat of curfew on the whole city.

Even at one in the morning, Evgeny Kozlov could hear the rumble many blocks away, crooking his way through a neighborhood too tired and defeated to raise much protest of its own. After all, some had noted callously, the president hadn't done anything for them.

From an alley, Evgeny approached the back of the bookstore where he and his informant and friend, Viktor Petrov, had dared convene only once before. The store's owner, indebted to Viktor for springing him from public-demonstration charges, had never detected surveillance of his shop, he'd assured Viktor. Still, Evgeny crept through the darkened alley, his hand on his gun and his eye on every doorway, his reflexes cocked and ready.

When he reached the door to the bookstore, he tapped a knuckle three times against its paint-bare wood. It opened immediately and the airless, blacked-out interior drew him inside. "Comrade," Viktor said, embracing his friend and kissing both Evgeny's cheeks. "It is too dangerous for you to be in the city. To be in this place." He lit a small candle in the back room where a musty inventory of books lining the walls further insulated the conversation. "They found you once not far away. They will find you again."

"Who did this thing, Viktor?" Evgeny charged, ignoring the warning.

"You know I cannot move too brazenly on this."

"You must have some idea."

"No different from your own. That Volynski's people believed Gorev ordered their leader's execution, and so repaid the president in kind."

Evgeny dropped into one of two wooden chairs and hunched his shoulders. "But Ivan died at *my* hands, not Gorev's. They killed the wrong man."

Viktor slowly pulled the other chair beneath his bulky frame before confronting his friend. "By killing Volynski, you saved Russia from a kind of death at the hands of the Americans. Why he ever thought they would not retaliate for terrorist attacks on their soil is incomprehensible. A mark of pure madness."

"Perhaps not."

"What do you mean?"

"It is up to an American president to launch a full-scale attack or bury his head in 'diplomatic sanctions.'"

"Travis Noland would have ridden the tip of the spear to the heart of Moscow," Viktor declared confidently.

Evgeny stared into the small flame. "I do not know what he would have done, only what I had to do. I do not regret it, only the slaughter I encountered on that country road." He thought a moment more. "It is curious to me that it took six months for Ivan's people to strike back in revenge."

After a long pause, Evgeny looked up and watched Viktor's face in the flickering light. "I have known you too long not to sense your apprehension right now. You suspect something. What is it?"

The older man shifted in his chair, which creaked beneath the strain. "Glinka has not been seen in two days."

Evgeny pulled himself up straight. "And . . ."

"Rather odd, you think? He is now our acting president until new elections in three months. Our nation is in turmoil over this atrocity. The world press looks on with drooling readiness to report our every move. And where is our leader in the midst of it all? Word has it that he is at his river dacha, choosing to prepare for his transition to the presidency in the privacy of his home. But my superiors refuse to confirm or deny that. Even more strange, we have been told to stand down in our usual security of a president's home, that Glinka prefers his own guards, whom we never trained and hardly know." Viktor shrugged. "Very odd, I say."

Evgeny's eyes bored deep into Viktor's, his mind zooming down new pathways. "Keep going. I sense there is more."

"Just one more thing. The morning before the assassination, someone taped a pamphlet to the post office door in Gorev's village, where he was headed. Someone wrote over it. It read: *A Memorial Concert for the Late Dimitri Gorev.*"

Evgeny's mind spun. "Someone announcing what was to come. A teaser. But for what purpose?" He looked back at the flame. "What kind of pamphlet was it?"

But Viktor was silent too long. Evgeny raised his head, his forehead creasing over his black eyebrows. "Viktor?"

"It was German. Announcing an upcoming concert at the Nuremberg Music Festival."

Evgeny stood up slowly, peering down at his friend. "A concert given by whom?" But he already knew, and the implications exploded like shrapnel in his brain.

Viktor stared up at him. "Calm down, Evgeny. You cannot let affection for that woman rule your better judgment."

"One more question." Evgeny placed both hands on his knees and bent eye level to Viktor. "Where is Glinka's dacha?"

Chapter 15

Arkady Glinka had never owned a dacha until Gorev appointed him prime minister. Afterwards, Glinka wasted no time in purchasing a country retreat like those owned by, or provided for, others in the Kremlin's upper echelon. Gorev had suggested a particular residence he knew to be available. Located farther up the Volga from Gorev's village, the rustic two-story dwelling was larger than a man with only an ex-wife and no children needed. But of utmost appeal to Glinka was its seclusion.

The home was perched in a dense hammock overlooking a backwoods branch of the Volga, accessible only by a winding, unpaved road, or by water, though nothing but a canoe or kayak could navigate the shoals and rapids along that stretch of river. The fishing harvest from these waters, however, was bountiful. But Glinka cared nothing about fishing.

The air sagged over the river that Saturday afternoon, laden with moisture and lethargy. Though sheathed in a hazy gauze, the summer sun pulsed with relentless heat. The old man shuffling along the road to the Glinka house removed his cap and lifted his arm to swipe at his damp forehead. The old homespun shirt was already sticking to his skin.

He carried a fishing pole, bucket, and knapsack as he scuffed his worn-out boots over the gravel lane. Nearby villagers had long claimed these backwaters as their private fishing grounds, until Glinka bought most of the river frontage and moved his small entourage into the isolated house on the point. A few from town had been caught sneaking onto the private riverbanks with their fly-fishing rods, but were promptly chased away by the guards.

Before reaching the gated drive to the Glinka house, the man veered into the trees near the river and wound his way along a timeworn footpath toward the point, where the confluence of currents promised the best catch. He knew the gate would be guarded more heavily now that Arkady Glinka was the Russian Federation's new president.

The man cautiously eyed the river, the woods, and the path behind and before him. What good fortune that no one appeared to be around. As he approached the fenced estate, he scanned the trees for security cameras, but saw none. Though electronic surveillance had never been detected around the house before, the old man knew it might appear at any time.

The man gripped his fishing rod tightly, threading it between trees that crowded more closely now, partially obscuring his view of the river. When he emerged into a small clearing beside a rapids, he stopped cold and his right hand shot inside the pocket of his pants. A uniformed guard stood on the bank before him, skipping stones across the water with one hand and tipping back a metal flask with the other. The fisherman was close enough to hear the slosh of liquid inside the container. Before he could retreat, though, the young guard turned a tipsy body toward him and slurred a warning, "Better stop right there, old peasant. They will shoot you dead."

Old? Evgeny Kozlov bristled slightly. His villager disguise had worked well, but it seemed nothing masked his age.

The guard skipped another rock and looked back at Evgeny. "But I tell you what. You go on and fish all you want to. I will just sit right here and watch you . . . me and my good friend." He hoisted the flask as if by introduction.

Evgeny remained silent, his hand still on the gun in his pocket, his eyes darting between the guard and the hillside that rose to the Glinka house.

"They will fire me anyway because, as they say, I am a disgrace to the force, sent down here to the river to sober up. But that will not happen." He lifted the flask again.

Evgeny couldn't believe the opportunity before him, already gauging the guard's size, the likely fit of his uniform on Evgeny's own body. If Glinka were here, there was a chance Evgeny could get in and out of the estate with as much intelligence as he could gather there, if not from the man himself, perhaps from his aides. By force, if necessary.

"You are right, young man. What is wrong with a little drink?" He paused. "Did Glinka send you down here?" Evgeny asked sympathetically, plying the man's inebriated brain.

The man laughed and shook his head. "Oh no. Comrade Glinka is off conferring with his ghosts." The man bent to pick up more stones, nearly losing his balance.

Ghosts? "What do you mean?" But even as he asked, Evgeny recalled long-ago rumors about Glinka's penchant for the occult. Nothing was ever confirmed, and soon the rumors faded.

The guard wagged a finger at Evgeny. "Ah ha! I know something you do not." He grinned with satisfaction. "That little place he goes to is a secret. Yes, it is. But this 'disgrace to the force' knows about it." The man squatted low to the ground and clumsily slid into a sitting position. "He and his friends go there to talk to dead people. Ha!" The guard slapped his thigh and chuckled lightly. "What do you say about that?" Now the man stretched into a full recline on the ground, gazing up at the trees, his hand still tight around the flask.

Evgeny knew he didn't have long before the man lost consciousness. "Have you been to that place?"

The man breathed deep and stretched again. "To America? Never. But he goes quite often. To Florida. The, uh . . . oh yes, the Keys." He removed his hat and placed it over his face. Evgeny was about to pursue that when the man suddenly sat up, his head cocked. He was clearly alarmed. "Do you hear that?"

Evgeny listened. A car approached from the top of the hill. The driveway ran within sight of that spot.

The man did his best to stand up, stumbling once before righting himself. As the car drew near, the guard looked squarely at Evgeny, a sobering transformation. "He's coming!"

"Who?" Evgeny asked. "You said Glinka was gone."

"The other one." The man kicked his flask into the bushes, then eyed Evgeny as if seeing him for the first time. "You better get out of here, old man. If he catches you here, he will shoot you!" Without further word, the guard scrambled up the hill into the cover of trees, a safe distance from the car descending the curving drive.

Evgeny dropped the fishing gear on the ground and followed the guard part way up the path, but where the man clambered away from the advancing car, Evgeny headed straight for it. Drawing his binoculars from the knapsack still strapped to his chest, he dropped to his belly and crawled through the underbrush, pushing toward a clear vantage point.

Just ahead of the car was the gate and what looked like a hastily assembled guardhouse, manned by two soldiers in the same uniform as the drunk now running away. One of the soldiers stepped away from the checkpoint to open the gate for the gray Mercedes sedan now approaching. Evgeny was just about twenty yards away.

As the car slowed at the gate, he trained his binoculars on its windows, which were all down. He could see two uniformed men in front and one plainclothes passenger in back, though not clearly. As the car exited the gate, its dark-tinted windows began to rise, front and back. Trained only on that back passenger, Evgeny squinted down hard as the window slowly closed.

He had only a couple of seconds. But it was all he needed. In the last instant, the face in the back seat turned toward the unobstructed light and Evgeny jerked at the sight.

Maxum Morozov!

Chapter 16

A strong headwind buffeted the yacht as it sailed toward the eastern horizon. The sooner it left U.S. waters the better. Inside the forward salon, three men gathered on creamy-yellow calfskin sofas. The sleek, glassy room was soundproof and routinely swept for listening devices, though none had ever been found. To the owner's knowledge, no one had ever suspected who lived aboard his ship.

According to its registry, the vessel belonged to a Dubai real estate magnate with holdings all over the world. But the real owner and full-time resident was the man now pouring black tea for his guests. When they'd been served, he settled back to sip his own brew laced with potent herbs and roots, a potion prescribed by Curt Vandoren, who now eyed his host with amusement.

"We should all be banished to such exile," Vandoren said, scanning the opulent salon clad in polished teak, crystal, and buttery leathers, all surrounded by a panoramic sweep of the ocean. It was an unfortunate comment that drew a scowl from the man who considered his ship a gilded prison and nothing more.

"I would gladly return with you tonight to your swampy little nest onshore and never see this ship again." Ivan Volynski gestured toward the empty wheelchair near the sofa. "Never again confine myself to such an indecency as that."

The man proclaimed dead just six months ago knew he wasn't fully alive today. Though he'd escaped the explosion that had killed his closest aides, there remained a lit fuse inside him. In the night roaming of his mind, when everyone slept but him, he still wondered at the prompting that afternoon of his "death." To stay in New York and search for the leak that had, just seconds earlier, aborted his plans for the Brooklyn Bridge. To bail from the helicopter at the last minute and send his aides on ahead to the ship. Wouldn't it have been easier to die with them? Without warning, with no time to suffer as he did now.

If he could, Ivan would leap to his feet and rush out on deck to inhale the ocean's empowering vapors, to feel them lift him, to assure him that all was well. But all was not. The man who'd narrowly escaped death would soon condemn others to that fate. So many innocents. Why did that only now disturb him?

Could those before him read his mind? Had the sentient mystic Curt Vandoren already seen an abscess growing inside the mastermind of Soviet Russia's resurrection?

Ivan regretted his visible brooding and quickly ushered himself back to higher ground. His subordinates weren't used to such displays of weakness in the man who would rule Russia. He glanced at the van Gogh painting above the sofa, at the bandaged ear of the painter in self-portrait. The artist had severed the ear in a fit of madness. Was Ivan mad too?

"Ivan, you will soon return to the motherland," Glinka offered, as if clearly reading the mind of his superior and wishing to allay his fears. "At this moment, there is a crate awaiting shipment to the Potomac and delivery upriver to the U.S. capital. President Travis Noland and his powerhouse will soon be extinguished."

Strangely, Ivan was unmoved.

That's when Vandoren leaned in. "Ivan, you are not listening to those who counsel you from beyond. Tonight, we will visit them again and you will see that everything they have led you to do will bear fruit."

Something inside Ivan quaked. Those words. A sudden memory. His grandmother holding his hand as they walked to the village church. Her sweet voice assuring him that God loved him better than anyone ever had. The priest speaking of bearing fruit for the Lord. Surely a weapon of mass destruction wasn't the kind of fruit he meant.

Who, or what, was this *Lord*? Was it not the voices of those Vandoren summoned from the other realm? The spirit guides who came to Ivan in dreams, in séances, their voices clear and compelling. Was it not the voice of Vladimir Lenin himself who'd called Ivan from obscurity to such heights? Ivan closed his eyes. Wasn't it?

He opened his eyes to see his companions studying him curiously.

Just then, Glinka slapped his thighs and stood up. Ivan saw it as restless frustration. He had to regain control. "Arkady, please sit down and give us your report." His voice, once again, resonated with authority. He was pleased to see the now-you're-talking relief rise to Glinka's face as he took his seat and faced Ivan.

"Please allow me to first establish what is known. The man you believed ordered your execution is dead. Who President Gorev sent to kill you is not clear, though I and others in our intelligence force strongly suspect it was our disenfranchised friend Evgeny Kozlov. Only the few of us, and those on this ship, know that he failed. Even President Noland acknowledged your death on national television." Glinka allowed the faintest smile. "He still believes that is true."

Ivan stiffened slightly. No one knew that he had already slipped an irresistible taunt to his half brother, a photograph of Noland Sr. with his illegitimate Russian son. Even now, Ivan relished the impact that barbed clue must have had. He would send another soon. No one would interfere with his march against the House of Noland.

"Our men were swift and effective in eliminating Gorev and escaping the hit site, though with only seconds to spare. An unidentified motorist came upon the massacre even as our men were fleeing the forest. However, it is still disconcerting that Noland was alerted so soon afterwards. His spies are too firmly entrenched in our soil. We will have to remedy that."

"Excuse me, Arkady," Vandoren interrupted. "The American authorities know that our saboteurs are still in place on their own soil, correct?"

"They do, though our people are on temporary stand-down." Glinka turned a satisfied gaze on Ivan. "Everything is on track. You should be well pleased, Ivan. As you directed me to, in the months leading up to Gorev's assassination, I have appointed as many of our people as I could to positions of influence in our government. In three months' time, an election will be held to replace Gorev with a new president. By that time, I will have surrounded myself with all the support I need to move officially into that office." He smiled triumphantly. "Then, you will return to Mother Russia, her savior back from the dead. Her resurrection!"

Words! *Savior. Resurrection.* His grandmother's hand on his. The cross behind the priest. *Stop this!* he commanded himself. *No more!*

Ivan struggled to stand. He had to get outside. Now.

"Are you all right?" Vandoren asked, as he moved to assist his friend.

"Yes," Ivan snapped. "Let me be. We'll continue this later." He regretted his tone but seemed incapable of altering his mood. He needed air.

Glinka reached for the wheelchair, but Ivan waved it away. "No. Just my walker."

Vandoren pushed open the outside door as two of the crew scrambled to assist. With a uniformed deckhand on either side of him, Ivan pushed the walker to the railing then dismissed them. Alone now, he gazed at iridescent waters that sparkled clean and pure. He inhaled their primal essence and willed it to restore him.

He felt those behind him watching, wondering if their "savior" had fallen hostage to this thing marauding through his body, what they believed to be rheumatoid arthritis. Would they discard him like soured milk? No more the future of Russia. Would they even martyr him? Certainly Glinka was capable. But what about Vandoren?

Ah, Curt Vandoren. Just as Czar Nicholas II had his Rasputin, Ivan Volynski was to enlist his own mystic healer, seer, channeler of Russian icons past to counsel and empower the new Soviet leader. Curt Vandoren salivated at the prospect of one day entering Ivan's royal courts as one anointed. He couldn't know that Ivan, himself, would never reach such courts. None of them knew. Only the German physician who had made the indisputable diagnosis.

Just before dawn on Sunday, from a private airfield in the Bahamas, the small jet lifted into the flight pattern back to Russia. Ivan's fleet of vessels and aircraft had served Arkady Glinka well. They had afforded him the stealth to slip in and out of countries undetected, leaving his Kremlin staff to explain the occasional absences with well-constructed scenarios. At this moment, he was reportedly ensconced at his river house attending the complexities of transitioning into the presidency. But that task had been rehearsed for so long, it required no such preparation. He and Ivan had been plotting this course for many years, ever since their neophyte days at the Kremlin, learning the lay of the political land and the slight-of-hand techniques for grabbing power. The attempt on Ivan's life in January had only accelerated their plans to replace Gorev, whom Ivan was certain had orchestrated the attempt.

But Glinka had never been so convinced. Volynski's coconspirators Vadim Fedorovsky and Pavel Andreyev, after their first attempt to as-sassinate Gorev, had been executed on Russian soil, in a Russian prison, under Russian law. Glinka believed that the by-the-book Gorev would have done no less with Ivan, and that he certainly wouldn't have opted for the fireball spectacle in the heart of New York City, even caught on film by the American press. But Ivan rejected Glinka's reasoning.

The new president of Russia, though interim for now, lifted a snifter of aged brandy to his lips as he gazed into the Caribbean skies just begin-ning to blush with day. He rested his head against the seat back and let the golden elixir burnish his thoughts. He smiled at the future, certain of his place in it. The voices Vandoren had summoned from the other side just hours ago had assured him he would take the election in three months. He would commandeer his homeland and its military, appoint a new prime minister to his former office, raise the hammer and sickle once again, take back Soviet lands, and deal with the American threat as never before. Even now, the crate lay in wait for its cruise up the Potomac and the last turn toward Washington.

It would all be done without Ivan.

Did he think I was just a wooden-headed puppet? Here to do his bidding and gladly scrape up the crumbs from his table? Did he think I would not seek out his doctor and learn the truth? A steward appeared to replenish the brandy, but Glinka lifted a dismissive hand. He needed a clear head, perfect vision. *Now, I will not have to end his dominion over me. Mr. Lou Gehrig's unfortunate illness should handle that for me.*

Glinka closed his eyes and summoned the voices through the visualization pathways Curt Vandoren had led him to discover, to let the mind of Arkady Glinka slip free of its earthly tethers and soar to the place vividly imagined for himself. A place of cool waters running swift and deep, surrounding a palace high on a hill with legions of servants and soldiers loyal unto him. In that place, he had always found assurance of his own powers. A god, that's what he was. Worthy of all he could conceive. Free to rule himself, and now his native land, with autonomy. Guided by the powers of the air, endorsed and coveted by them.

Not asleep, not awake, Glinka traversed an astral plane. Searching. Wandering. Always wandering. No anchor. Just flying.

Suddenly . . . *What is that?* Something ahead of him. A form, not like his own. A creature advancing, menacing, snarling. *Who are you?* Glinka called in his mind. *Get away from me! I command you!* But the form kept coming, its breath now curling toward him, smoldering, stinging. Creature-eyes fixed on him. Radiant. Unblinking. Watching. Coming closer.

No! Glinka suddenly lurched forward in his seat. His eyes sprang open, wild and darting. His own breath heaving now, sweat coursing through his thick hair and soaking his body. Words wouldn't form in his mind, only fear. His hands shaking, he reached for the brandy and gulped. The steward appeared again. "Are you all right, sir?" he asked.

Glinka tried to compose himself. "Yes," he answered too abruptly. "Another brandy." When the steward left, Glinka stared into the void beyond the window, and Vandoren's warning surfaced. He had once dared to quote the book of Ephesians to Glinka: "For our struggle is not against flesh and blood, but against the rulers, against the authorities, against the powers of this dark world and against the spiritual forces of evil in the heavenly realms."

Vandoren had closed the Christian Bible and returned it to the bookcase in his study at the University of the Spirit. "You see, Arkady, even this man Paul knew about the place we go, about the powers you and I, even Ivan, call upon. This apostle warns the followers of Jesus about the 'ruler of the kingdom of the air.' Our ruler, Arkady, the one who empowers us, who will lead you to power over nations and all their people. But understand that there is risk in such an allegiance. There are other forces in our ruler's kingdom who delight in reminding us who we belong to."

The skin of the aircraft did nothing to separate the Russian president from those threatening forces. But yes, he had willingly engaged them, and now he understood. They would follow him in whatever menacing form they chose. He must be vigilant. And obedient.

So be it.

Glinka lifted the glass and sniffed the swirling fruit of it. He had earned its pleasure and all others to come. Closing his eyes, he leaned back and was just drifting into sleep when the phone in his shirt pocket sounded, the phone only a privileged few were linked to. He noted the ID code and answered promptly. "How was the fishing this morning?" he asked, his pulse finally settling to normal.

"No fishing for me," said Maxum Morozov. "I had to leave."

"What?" Glinka strained to keep his voice down. Both pilots and the steward were Ivan's trusted staff, but there was no need to alarm them.

"Calm down, comrade. Like you, I do what I must."

"You were to stay at the river until I returned."

"I have gathered rather pressing information regarding our favorite musicians."

"That's over, Maxum. I warned you."

"No. I warned *you*. I will serve you and your new regime in whatever way I can, but I will not allow you to dictate to me. I will go and come according to my own agenda."

"Your agenda almost preempted the attack on Gorev. That stunt with the flyer nailed to the post office door in Gorev's village was insane."

Maxum responded instantly. "I told you, I did not do that! I do not know who did, but you should. One of your overzealous assassins, no doubt. You really should screen your killers more carefully, Arkady." He snickered.

"Just make certain that vengeance against your son does not poison your senses."

"And what poisons yours? That magician in Florida?" Maxum laughed loudly.

Glinka clenched his teeth. Now wasn't the time to wage his war with the aging Israeli statesman, no longer the valuable mole but a liability Glinka must eventually deal with . . . along with his son. Young Max had burrowed too deep, uncovered too much. He, too, would be eliminated. For now, though, Glinka must tread carefully.

"But you are exposed, Maxum. I cannot protect you in the open."

"I need none of your protection. I have my own resources."

He sensed where Maxum was headed and why. "I know your skills with forging any document you need, including passports," Glinka said, feeling a prickly dread for the damage Maxum could do. "But surely you will not attempt to reenter Israel."

"But surely I will."

Chapter 17

*L*iesl and Cade saw the familiar knot of people waiting for them at the end of the concourse. Their flight into Ben Gurion International near Tel Aviv had been delayed by several hours. Still, there was no deterring Ben and Max's welcoming party. Ben had assured her they would find amusement in the waiting hours. They certainly had.

As she grew closer, Liesl watched the guys hoist something over their heads. Teddy bears. One in a tuxedo, one in a sequined gown, each one bearing a flag that read *Shalom*. With them were Ben's wife, Anna, and, Liesl assumed, Max's new girlfriend, who waved and smiled as exuberantly as if she were old friends with the approaching visitors, though they had never met her.

Max rushed ahead of the others, his arms opening wide for Liesl. Though he tossed a hardy smile and greeting to Cade at the same time, it was obvious where his affections rested. He hugged Liesl to him. "So we're really going to do this, huh?" he spoke into her ear.

She gently pulled away and appraised him. Not much had changed. He was still slight of build, and the red hair still ruled the head, as fiery as his violin. But now, a foreign restraint had moved in and camped about the eyes, tugging at their corners and clouding their old radiant light. It disturbed her, but she wouldn't let him see.

"With everything we've got." She squeezed his shoulders once more, then turned to see Ben ambling forward. She had to fight the tears. It had been just six months since bullets ripped through his chest and neck. If not for the Kevlar vest, Volynski's marksmen would have killed him along with Anna's brother.

She moved quickly to close the distance between them and reached for her old friend, the tears she could no longer control running free. "It's about time you got here, old girl," he said as she lightly wrapped her arms around his still-mending body, noting how much weight he'd lost. But his voice still carried the same resonant strength she'd known since college. So many times, it seemed, that had been her only strength.

Swallowing hard against the bulge in her throat, she beamed at him. "I've missed you." He just squeezed her hand and pulled her toward Anna. "Look who I found," he told his wife, who then engulfed Liesl in a long-held embrace. Liesl had introduced the couple at Harvard and been named godmother to their two daughters.

"Where are the kids?" Liesl asked.

"In Haifa with Ben's cousin, but you'll see them tomorrow. She's driving them here to see you for a couple of hours in the morning."

Liesl's eyes strayed to the young woman standing just outside the circle of friends, obviously so comfortable with each other. She was watching Liesl intently, her face alight with what seemed like anticipation. Liesl was used to the open adoration of fans, but responding to it still made her feel uncomfortable and awkward. She hoped this was different. Maybe the girl was just curious about her? She was about to make a move in the girl's direction when Max came alongside, Cade in tow, and guided Liesl that way. "Time you met my lady," he beamed. The three approached Erica Bachman who was now smiling broadly.

"Erica, I want my friends here to meet the talented photographer all of Tel Aviv is buzzing about."

Liesl extended her hand and greeted the girl warmly. Cade did the same, both of them pleased that Max had finally found someone to invest himself with. After the debacle of Maxum Sr.'s scandalous treason, young Max had drifted even further into his isolationist lifestyle. Liesl hoped that the young woman before her now, with long blond hair falling about her shoulders and an engaging expression, might one day match Max's great capacity to love.

Then the girl suddenly gushed like a starry-eyed teen. "You don't know how excited I am to meet you both. Miss Bower, I'm just a huge fan of yours. You're so incredible!"

Cringing at what she'd hoped wouldn't be, Liesl responded as best she could. "Thank you, but please call me Liesl." She glanced at Max, who seemed as taken aback by the effusive display as Liesl. But he quickly rallied, wrapping his arm around Erica's shoulders and hugging her to him. Then, he abruptly prompted, "Well, everyone, are we ready to go?" Liesl caught his embarrassment. It seemed the girl had to. She fell into a bit of a pout as he led her away with no further comment. It had been an awkward introduction that Liesl hoped to overcome in some way.

Ben and Anna followed Max's car to his high-rise apartment overlooking the Mediterranean. The Saturday afternoon traffic flowed easily, and in the back seat, Liesl found herself in a near-slump against Cade's shoulder as he and Max chatted about Israeli politics. She'd managed only a few fitful naps during their all-night flight into the Tel Aviv time zone and now fought to focus on the conversation. She felt obliged to draw Erica into conversation, noting how the girl had fallen silent after leaving the airport. But instead, Liesl lost her battle against sleep and didn't awake until Max pulled into the parking garage beneath his building.

In a moment of total confusion, she lifted sluggishly from Cade's shoulder and commanded her brain to tell her where she was and why the girl in the front seat was looking so intently at her, again. She returned the girl's too-nice smile then looked away, letting Cade pull her resistant body from the back seat. Seconds later, Ben and Anna arrived and the whole party took the elevator to the fifteenth floor.

Walking into Max's apartment brought Liesl to full waking surprise. Unlike his signature look of practiced dishevelment—the unruly red hair topping a fond disregard for coordinated apparel—the apartment was sleek and polished. "You couldn't have done this," Liesl said with certainty. She spun in place surveying the meticulously ordered room of ultracontemporary furnishings, the sum of it floored in a plush-piled white carpet.

"Right. My mom did. I had no choice in the matter, but I kind of like how things actually go together."

"Unlike your clothes, sport," Ben shot as he headed down the hall rolling his and Anna's overnight bags. "We'll take this back bedroom if that's okay."

"It's yours," Max said. "I'm sleeping on the sofa and giving the master to our honeymooners." He motioned for Cade to follow with their luggage.

That left Liesl alone with Erica. "May I get something for you to drink?" the young woman offered.

It was welcomed. "Something very cold, please," Liesl said. As she followed Erica to the kitchen, Liesl stopped to admire a wall gallery of photographs, all stunning. They were studies of light and shadow cast over the land, architecture, and the creviced faces of the elderly. She turned to look at Erica, already busy filling glasses with ice. "Erica, did you take these?" She tried to conceal her surprise, if it were true, but was struck by a stark disconnect between the fluttery young woman she'd just met and the one whose mature and soulful eye had captured these images.

"Yes, they're mine." Erica emerged from the kitchen and handed Liesl a tall icy glass. "I hope you like ginger ale. I guess I should have asked first. Sorry."

"It's fine, thank you. But your photography, Erica, it's amazing. I'm so impressed by your talent." Was she gushing? As Erica had?

But the girl didn't seem embarrassed by the attention. In fact, there was something hard and impervious on her face as she perused her own work. Liesl dared to linger on that face now. It was handsome, not pretty, with a pointed nose, wide cheekbones, and squared chin. As sharply composed as one of her photographs. But when the face turned toward Liesl, the expression grew soft and compliant.

How does she do that? Liesl was growing more intrigued by this girl.

"Okay, time to cook," Max announced as he and Cade returned to the living room. He came up between Liesl and Erica and gave both a squeeze around their waists, whispering conspiratorially to them. "Since I have no idea how to do that, you two must take charge." Then he looked soberly at Liesl. "Oh wait. What am I thinking? The classical pianist with hands insured by Lloyd's of London can't even pour cereal. You're on your own, Erica."

"I'll do it," chimed Anna.

Moments later, they were all in the kitchen, grateful that it was big enough to contain them and their convoluted efforts to prepare sea bass. Erica seemed to unfold into something close to delight in the midst of the banter and camaraderie, often nuzzling Max's neck and drawing his obvious pleasure in that. She even managed to pull off a near-perfect roasted red pepper sauce for the fish, relishing the gratuitous compliments. By the time Erica left that night for her own apartment downstairs, they had all gathered her to themselves and given Max their blessings.

The two couples and Max now lounged on the terrace overlooking a slumbering sea, its surf rhythmically breathing in and out, exerting its lunar pull against Liesl. They were talking about anything but Ben's and Max's enlistment in the Mossad, which Liesl knew never to discuss in front of Anna. Ben's wife was still reeling from his surprise enrollment into yet another clandestine pursuit.

At this moment, though, Liesl could focus on nothing but the prospect of sleep. Until a phone sounded somewhere inside. A certain phone deep in Liesl's bag, its coded pattern of beeps drilling into the peaceful night. Liesl jerked forward, glancing first at her husband, then Max. He'd been the last to access her CIA-assigned phone, just hours after President Noland had. Barely nine days ago.

The beeps demanded she come immediately. "Stay here," she told them, scanning their anxious faces before she rushed inside. She closed the bedroom door behind her, regretfully acknowledging that despite the wedding ring on her finger, there remained an insular chamber in her life where forces set in motion long ago still prevailed against her and her alone. In the seconds before she retrieved the phone, she cast an urgent prayer. *But, Lord, you command all things and all places, even that chamber. Lead me through it.*

She answered with a hesitant "Yes?"

"Liesl, this is Ava."

Ava. Friend first, CIA agent second. Or was it the other way around? Which was she now?

"Listen to me, Liesl. There's no need to be alarmed, as I know you probably are. So calm down. I called your phone because I needed to hear your voice and know you were safe at Max's by now. That's true, right?"

"Yes, but there's more, isn't there?"

"I have news of a development that I need to speak with Max about."

"Tell me first, Ava. Please."

The agent hesitated. Then, "I just took a call from Kozlov."

Liesl barely breathed. "Go on."

"There are details of his report—"

"Report? Does he work for you now?" She meant the greater sovereignty of the CIA.

"He offers what he chooses, when he chooses."

Liesl understood. Her former nemesis and unlikely advocate had declared himself a man without a country, and certainly without allegiance to those who might hang him. So why does he offer anything at all? Liesl suspected the answer, though she hardly knew what to do with it. After once threatening her life, the man had risked his own to save her from an assassin. He'd risked capture to protect her, to befriend her. He'd briefly allowed her behind the barriers he'd erected around his troubled soul, and now she mattered to him. If he dared initiate contact with Ava, it was probably because of Liesl.

As if Ava had sensed the dread, she said, "It's best that you bring Max in now. Most of what I have to report is for him."

Moments later, Max sat next to Liesl as Ava issued her news through the speaker. "Just hours ago, Evgeny Kozlov saw and positively identified Maxum Morozov riding in the back seat of a car outside Moscow."

Liesl watched Max's fingers flex once then ball into fists. "Where?"

"Liesl, I'm afraid this is where you must leave us."

"But—" Liesl began her objection.

"The rest is classified," Ava headed her off. "Max's work for Mossad is part of the system, so to speak. And I can see those eyes flashing now, Liesl. You resent being left out after all you've endured, but—"

"But President Noland asked for my help if Evgeny made contact with us. What am I supposed to do?"

"The president has already been notified of Evgeny's call. Now, I really need to speak privately with Max. Please understand."

Liesl did. "But one more question, Ava. I need to know. Is Evgeny here in Tel Aviv?"

There was a long pause before Ava answered. "I'm sure of it."

"Max, your father was spotted leaving Arkady Glinka's river house," Ava finally answered. "It seems to confirm your suspicions."

Alone in his bedroom with the door closed, Max gazed at the night-blackened sea. Though he couldn't see it, he knew it was on the move, like his father, driven by treacherous currents running just below the surface.

"My suspicions that there remain two occupied collars on the late Ivan Volynski's long leash? That because his pet mole Morozov now comes down from his Urals hiding place and risks capture to consult with Glinka, we might assume them both complicit in Gorev's murder?" He waited for no response. "Allow me to explore this a moment, Ava. With Ivan's generals Fedorovsky and Andreyev gone, the mantel of insurrection falls on the mastermind's childhood friend and avenger, the extraterrestrial-communing Arkady Glinka. The assassination of Gorev is just his first salvo. It is not only revenge for what he believes was Gorev's order to kill Ivan, but more critically, it is the all-systems-go for Ivan's strategy to overtake the government. Gorev out, Glinka in." Max sniffed. "No doubt, Glinka has already celebrated the victory with the dead Ivan in a reunion of the two in some smoky séance somewhere. I venture to say it was—"

"I must stop you there, Max. There is something else you should know."

Max waited.

"President Noland has received what he believes to be a message from Ivan Volynski, a recent message, which suggests he's still alive."

Max didn't stir, but his mind leapt to one implication in particular. Liesl. If the man who twice had ordered her death were still alive, what would it take to protect her now? And why should he consider that before the more obvious: that Ivan Volynski still ruled. That a confirmed-alive Morozov and a confirmed-active WMD had both recently departed the Ural Mountains bound for where? The back yard of Ivan's hated half brother? But that hadn't been Max's first thoughts. It had been Liesl. It was always Liesl. Would he ever learn to love another as much as her?

"Max, are you there?"

"Of course, Ava. Tell me what the message said." His mind whirled in two separate chambers of thought, simultaneously. Liesl's safety, and the rest of the world.

"It was a photograph of Noland's father with a young Ivan. The accompanying message was simply, *Our papa and me*. It was dated less than a week ago."

Max grew hopeful. "Can you be sure it was Ivan's handwriting? Someone else could have sent it as a perverse but timely joke. Ivan himself could have postdated it with instructions to deliver it should something happen to him. Who knows the real source?" Still, Max knew they couldn't ignore it altogether.

"We're working on that," Ava responded. "In the meantime, I suggest you talk Liesl into canceling your upcoming performances."

Max chuckled. "Sure. Right after I reverse the rotation of the earth."

"I understand. I can hear her insist that Volynski, if he's alive, can get at her anywhere, anytime he wants, as he's already proven. And she's right. But why make it easier for him?"

"You and I think that way. Liesl doesn't. And won't, I can guarantee it. But I'll try again."

"It's not just Liesl I'm worried about. Maxum is out there too and he knows it was his son who literally dug up the evidence against him. You and Liesl would be twin targets, wide open on that stage."

"No, Ava. He's had a year and a half to come down out of those mountains and do anything he wanted to me. I believe he's the only reason I haven't been a target like Liesl has. Maybe out of some belated sense of fatherhood. He probably knows, though, that if anything were to happen to her, it would—" He stopped himself. Ava Mullins had no right to know that such a thing would mean a kind of death for him, too. He covered himself without missing hardly a beat. "It would hurt us all."

"Still, you must both be alert and cautious at all times."

"I suggest we concentrate on finding Ivan if it's true he's alive. We already have a fairly positive ID from the cop in Florida that it was him with Glinka in that speeding stop just two years ago. That would be a good place to look."

"There's an FBI undercover team on its way there now. But there's something I don't get. The whole world watched Ivan's chopper explode in New York and heard Noland declare him dead and gone. If he's alive, we've given him the perfect cover. If everyone thinks he's dead, then no one will hunt him. He can move about invisibly. So why would he deliberately blow his cover by sending that teaser to the president?"

Max thought about that, about the peculiar strain of sadism that sometimes runs between blood kin, father to son, scorned brother to anointed brother. Then he answered, "To jab with a needle that no one can prove exists."

Ava hesitated only a moment. "Then we must prove it does."

Chapter 18

Tally was awakened that Saturday morning by the tinkling of wind chimes hanging from the knob of her bedroom door. It's what they were supposed to do when anyone attempted entry to her tower domain. The slightest turn of the knob from either side of the door set off the alert.

"It's just me, Tally," Mona Greyson called.

Tally knew it shouldn't be anyone else. Just the two of them lived in the house. That was the reason for the chimes. It was just the two of them . . . in a house with lots of outside doors and climber-friendly balconies. Regardless of what she'd told Denise about not locking the front door, the kind of person who would break into a house draped with evil eyes and ghostly mirrors was the kind of person Tally feared most. It was another reason she'd claimed the farthest reaches of the house for her room.

Tally rose from her covers and swung her legs over the side of the bed. "Come in," she answered, gratefully acknowledging her mother's customary habit of announcing herself before entering.

"I hope I didn't wake you," Mona said, crossing the small room to sit next to Tally on the bed.

"That's okay. I was going biking early this morning anyway. Better get going." Tally made a move to get up, but her mom laid a firm hand on her arm. "Not just yet. I need to talk to you."

Dread rose in Tally's chest as she settled back on the bed. "It won't take long, will it?"

"As long as it takes." Mona examined her daughter's face. "I saw you sneak into the house last night. You said you were staying at Denise's. What happened?"

Another good lie would end the inquisition. But that was getting harder to do. As much as she'd resisted the things she heard at Denise's church, they'd begun to make sense to her, even appeal to her. Maybe like Mr. Fremont, watching someone you love lose themselves in the dark made you want to run to the light. Was God that light? Maybe, maybe not.

She drew a long breath. "We both got busy with other things." No need to say more than she had to. Besides, it was the truth. Too busy stalking through the woods to indulge in silly sleepovers as if they were still children. She smiled pleasantly at her mom.

"So where were you last night?"

The smile vanished. *That's going to be harder.* "Well, uh, we just went out for a walk and Denise went straight home."

Mona looked down and fingered the old pink chenille robe tied snugly about her slim waist. "Tally, a friend of mine at the camp called this morning. She told me she was pretty sure she saw two girls slipping around there last night. That one of them might have been you."

Tally didn't dare make eye contact with her mother. Nor did she say anything, though that was as good as a confession, she knew.

"Tally, look at me."

When she did, Tally saw a glimmer of fear in her mother's eyes.

"Did you follow me?"

Tally could answer truthfully. "No, Mom." She had known her mom was somewhere in the camp but hadn't gone there to find her. It had just happened that way.

"Then why were you there?"

A loaded question. Tally and her irritating conscience were trapped. She glanced at the muddy sneakers she'd tossed in the corner last night. "Just wanted to show Denise what it was like." Another truth. She turned innocent eyes on her mom.

"And what did you see?"

This is getting worse. "Nothing much."

Mona turned fully toward her daughter. "Did you see me?"

Tally couldn't escape her mom's piercing brown eyes. She found herself nodding quietly, unable to shut out the cries she'd heard from the open window of Lesandra Bernardo's house. Her mother's tormented pleas.

"Did you hear me, Tally?" Now the brown eyes filled with tears.

Tally swallowed hard and tried to look away but couldn't. Again, she nodded, then began to sob, quietly at first, then uncontrollably.

Mona wrapped both arms around Tally and clung to her. "I'm so sorry," she moaned, her own tears spilling onto Tally's cheek.

But Tally suddenly pulled away. "Don't go there ever again, Mom. Something bad happens there."

But Mona only shook her head and looked away. "You don't understand. Something bad already happened, when I was a child."

Tally dared to ask. "Was it your dad? Did he do something to you?" Tally did and did not want to hear the answer to that.

But Mona suddenly drew herself up straight and wiped away her tears. She pulled the robe tightly across herself again and stared into space.

"Mom? Are you all right?"

She could see her mom's mouth working, speaking silent words. Her delicate hands rose to her cheeks, now flushed and quivering. Then she calmed, laid her hands back in her lap and turned to Tally. "I'm trying desperately to be all right. Miss Bernardo is helping me."

Go ahead and ask, Tally told herself. "Was that really your dad's voice we heard?"

Mona turned on her daughter in something close to terror. She sprang to her feet and looked down with hard, accusing eyes. "Don't you ever ask me something like that again. Don't you ever follow me again. And never—ever!—talk about this to me or *anyone* else." Her voice didn't match her eyes. The fiery words drowned in the liquefying eyes that, for an instant, pleaded for help. Then the instant passed.

Mona rushed from the room leaving her daughter in a puddle of hurt and confusion. What had just happened? Tally wondered. What had she done but ask honest questions? She looked out over the tops of fruit trees growing near the house. Mango, lime, tangerine, grapefruit. All so lush and thriving. Why not the people who lived here? She mourned for her mother, for the loss of her. What had happened to the exuberant woman who'd taught Tally to roller-skate and fly kites, who'd taken her for long walks in the country around their Georgia home and taught her how to grow a vegetable garden. Who had filled Tally's head with reverence for the creator of all living things. And who was that, exactly?

With an irresistible need to feel something pure and cleansing against her, Tally went straight to one of the tall windows surrounding her room and opened it wide. Then another window and another until a whirlwind of crosscurrents fresh off the Atlantic swept through the room like the fanning of wings, soft and feathery against her skin. She inhaled them to the depths of her and lifted her face to the touch. As if by pure reflex, without forethought or calculation, she closed her eyes, opened her mouth . . . and prayed. *Is that you? You'll have to tell me because I don't know. Are you the one true god? Not one of the voices I hear at the camp?* Tally opened her eyes and looked into a bright morning sky fluffed with cotton-ball clouds. Another gust caught the sheer curtains at one window and swirled them gently about her. *The people at Denise's church say you are the creator. If that's true, then you know me and my mom pretty well, don't you? Will you help us? I don't know how you're going to do that. But I'll be watching.*

Chapter 19

*I*an O'Brien bounded up the steps as fast as his seventy-four years would allow. It was early Sunday morning but there would be no church service for him and Henry Bower today. The Lord would understand, Ian reasoned as he paused outside Henry's door. The house on Tidewater Lane was quiet. With Mr. and Mrs. Cade O'Brien in Israel, the two men had rattled aimlessly about the old house the day before, until Ian had left to join Ava for an early dinner at her place. The carriage-house apartment she'd rented after transplanting herself to Charleston was a short walk from Tidewater Lane. Ian had arrived early, too early and unannounced.

He hadn't intended to eavesdrop on her phone call after letting himself in, and later regretted the compulsion to snoop through notes she'd left on her desk. But the sum of what he'd discovered had sent him headlong into a tailspin. He'd lain awake most of the night trying to decide what to do about it. If he questioned her, Ava, the bulldog federal agent, would only evade, which she was well trained to do. There was only one option.

He rapped twice on the closed door and called, "Henry, if you're not already awake, you'd better pretend you are because I'm coming in."

But as he reached for the doorknob, it turned and the door opened. Standing there in a pair of ragged pajamas, Henry squinted irritably at

Ian. "What's the matter with you? It's just six o'clock. We don't leave for church for two hours."

"We're not going to church. Now get dressed and meet me in the kitchen. And bring your charter book with you. We've got a slew of cancellations to make. Now hurry."

As Ian clomped back down the stairs, Henry called, "Could you do just a tad more explaining?"

Without turning around, Ian waved him on. "As soon as you get down here. And if you want to burn those pajamas you got on, it's okay with me. But do it later. There's someplace we got to go."

He didn't have to look back up the stairs at his friend and fishing partner. Ian could picture the man's scowl clearly. That would change instantly, though, as soon as Ian used just one word of explanation—Liesl.

Before heading back to the kitchen, where he'd already started the coffee, he stopped briefly in his room for the map. Cade and Liesl had insisted he take the recently passed Lottie Bower's main floor bedroom. The climb from the basement apartment he'd been living in or to a top-floor bedroom was too taxing for his arthritic knees.

He'd just returned to the kitchen when Henry appeared in the doorway, a plaid bathrobe slung loosely over his lanky frame, his face filled with something unlike his earlier irritation. It was dread, as if he already suspected.

Ian jumped right to it. "Our girl's in trouble."

Henry's eyes blazed but Ian gave him no time to respond. "Now you just sit right down and hear me out before you go shootin' off in every direction at once." Ian pulled two chairs from around the kitchen table, lingering only a second on Liesl's initials she'd carved on top with a fish hook at age eight. Henry hadn't missed the stolen glance, though. When Ian looked back at him, his eyes were fixed on the childish scrawl. But they soon snapped to attention on Ian.

"You'd better tell it to me straight, Ian," Henry said, stiffly lowering himself to the chair beside Ian, who was now spreading the map over the table.

"I'm going to." Ian feared he was about to unleash the tempest holing up inside Henry Bower for too long. The man had struggled to suppress it ever since resurfacing into his daughter's life. After a gunman had opened fire on Liesl six months ago, just a few steps from her front door, it had taken every warning the O'Brien men, the CIA, and the FBI could issue to keep her father from charging after her and the shadowy Russian who'd whisked her from death. What had finally contained him, though, was his mother's final days, feverishly reaching for him. That and the assurance of everyone on Liesl's case that Henry's intervention would only jeopardize their efforts to find and protect her.

But this was different.

"I got to Ava's early last night thinking I'd help her cook. I don't ever do this and don't really know why I did last night, but I just went on inside without knocking. She obviously didn't hear me come in because she kept talking to someone on the phone in her study. You know, it's down that little hallway behind the kitchen."

Henry nodded impatiently. "Get to it, Ian," he urged.

"Well, I was about to announce myself when I heard the phrase, 'If Ivan Volynski is alive.'"

Henry looked dumbstruck. "That monster didn't die?" His face reddened.

Ian raised a "hold on" hand. "I didn't dare budge, only listen, though whoever was on the other end was doing most of the talking. But I heard enough, and here's the convoluted sum of it: Ava and this person, probably another agent, think Volynski just might have avoided that chopper explosion in New York. And if so, Liesl and the younger Max Morozov might still be at risk, or so Ava thinks. Evidently Max's father is also alive and well, and perhaps coming after his son. Ava's worried about the concerts he and Liesl are giving these next two weeks. And—"

"We've got to get Liesl home!"

Ian shook his head. "So she can be shot at right here? Again? Now listen. There's more. Twice I heard Ava mention 'the weapon.' Just snatches about it. She said, 'if the weapon is inbound.' Then she said the president knows about 'the weapon' and that there's some kind of FBI investigative team heading to 'the camp.'"

"Well that really narrows things down," Henry snapped.

"I'm not finished. Stick with me here. I heard her say that Volynski had been spotted in the Keys about two years ago. Got to mean Florida. She listened a long while, didn't say anything else I could make sense of, then she ended the call. So I hurried back outside the front door, then knocked like I was just arriving. I should be ashamed, but there's no time for that right now . . . because of what else I discovered." Ian took a labored breath. "After dinner, I excused myself to the bathroom next to her study. While she was washing dishes, I stepped inside the door and did a quick survey of her desk. On a notepad next to her phone was the reason we're not going to church this morning. It said *Anhinga Bay Spiritualist Camp.*" Ian reached over and jabbed a finger down on the map. "I've fished Anhinga Bay a hundred times. Nobody knows it better than I do, and certainly not some FBI type who's never even been there!" He jabbed again. "That's where we're headed."

"To do what?"

"That's the camp she was talking about! It's got to be. And everybody around those parts knows about the psychic folks who live there. People say you don't want to mess with them. But we're going to. Something's going on down there and, directly or indirectly, it's tied to whoever's been gunning for Liesl."

"Then let's go!" Henry fairly leapt from the table, but paused a moment. "My old car won't make it that far."

"Don't need a car. We're taking the boat. Just a couple of clueless fishermen with a hankering to get their fortunes told. Anything to get us inside. Now go get your gear. I'm already packed."

A couple of hours later, *Exodus II* motored from Charleston Harbor into Wapoo Cut and the Intracoastal Waterway beyond. They were headed south to the Florida Keys with enough provisions for a week. Ian had left Ava a voice message telling her that he and Henry had decided to take off for a few days to fish on their own. He'd call her later. It was the truth and Ian was content with it. Of course, she wouldn't approve of what they fished for. She believed terrorists belonged on government radar, not Ian O'Brien's.

While Henry drove, Ian read a long computer printout on spiritualism and the Anhinga Bay Spiritualist Camp. "You know, Henry, it would be real easy to dismiss the folks at that camp as just misfit weirdos. Plenty of people do and I've been guilty of it myself. But there's more to it than that."

Henry slid a wary glance at him. "Don't tell me you buy into that stuff."

"Palm reading, fortune-telling, tarot cards, crystals? No. And no doubt there's plenty of carnival phonies peddling those kinds of tin-can thrills. But there's something else out there that's real enough for God to warn us away."

Henry nodded slowly and a bemused grin spread over his weathered face. "That's right. You and God talk a lot."

"Got that right. That's why you and I are hauling our puny selves to Florida right now. When he says go, I go."

"I thought it was because of Liesl."

"Well, she's his child, too."

Henry cut hard eyes at Ian. "You just read your fairy tales and let me drive the boat."

"It's where you're driving us that you need to know more about, so listen up." Ian returned to the damp pages in his hand, to the text that was so disturbing to him. "This camp doesn't allow all that carnival stuff. It says here that only 'licensed mediums of the highest integrity' are allowed to practice there."

"What kind of test do you think they have to pass to get that license?" Henry snickered.

Ian ignored the taunt, though he was glad to see Henry's mood lift even slightly. "They don't even allow hypnosis. Although they talk a lot about the trances these clairvoyants go into while they're summoning up the dead and communicating with other beings in the spirit world, which they call the etheric planes." Ian read on silently a moment. "Ever hear of ectoplasm?"

"I don't recall the subject ever coming up in my circle of drunks and homeless bums." The grin had now faded from Henry's face.

Ian looked up at the man he'd known so short a time. Yet Ian had seen the depths of tragedy in his haggard face, in the brutal scorn he still inflicted upon himself. Ian took the man to church with him, talked to him, tried to break through all the locked chambers surrounding the heart of this ravaged soul, but seemed no closer today than when Henry first returned to Tidewater Lane. Every morning since, Ian wondered if they would find Henry gone again. Ian closed his eyes and uttered yet another silent prayer for the man now hunkered over the wheel of the boat, trying to stay the course on a turbulent sea-lane.

Ian ended his prayer and kept reading, for both their sakes. "It says here that ectoplasm is something like smoke or a hazy aura that rises off the body of a medium when a spirit—or spirit guide—makes contact. This spirit from another plane can use the medium's body to materialize or convey a message, speaking through the medium."

He looked up to see Henry's probing eyes on him. "What's the matter?" Ian asked.

"You think these powers are real?"

Ian didn't know the intent of the question, but answered as clearly as he could. "I believe that some people who pursue these forces—and may sometimes receive certain powers from them—think it's for the good of mankind. That they are helping others find peace or direction in their lives. That the forces are godly."

"So again, what do you think?"

"That they're dead wrong. That the forces are real, all right, but they're not from God."

Henry stared quietly ahead. After a long while, he asked. "Ian, you ever kill anybody?"

Ian studied Henry's sharp profile and the severe set of his face. "No," Ian replied warily, fearing what was to come.

Without looking at him, Henry said, "There's not much difference between killing and causing a death. I've done both." His mouth pinched hard against itself. "And I did it all by myself." He paused. "I've taken a man's head in my hands and snapped the neck bone like a dry twig. I got drunk and let a spear gun get away from me, then watched my aunt bleed to death. No force anywhere in the universe could stop her blood. So it doesn't matter much to me what powers might be out there, what they can or can't do, or who they come from. God or Satan. I've got no use for either one of them."

Ian lowered the pages onto his lap and folded his hands on top of them. At that moment, there were no words to speak.

Chapter 20

Spencer Fremont left by the side gate to the camp early that Sunday morning and hurried along the trail to the University of the Spirit. The fewer people who saw him leave the better. Though Curt Vandoren had alienated most everyone in the camp with his flamboyance and arrogance, Spencer had found him just another hurting human, but with powers that both repelled and intrigued the benevolent widower.

A squall line had mounted along the eastern horizon and was advancing toward shore. By the time Spencer reached the main gate to the university, pellets of cold rain began to fall. He entered his employee code and the heavy wrought-iron gate hummed mechanically. The handle turned easily in his hands and he pushed against it, wasting no time getting to shelter. A different code was required to enter the shining glass lobby, which was empty at this hour. From there, he entered a short hallway that ended at the school's library. Long before classes began at the University of the Spirit, Curt Vandoren recruited Spencer to work part-time. Anhinga Bay's celebrity medium had been impressed by the older man's competence and efficiency in his work at the camp bookstore. The fact that Spencer didn't participate in the metaphysical disciplines of the camp, having entered its tightly knit community on his wife's coattails, didn't seem to bother Vandoren. It still didn't, and he'd given Spencer more and more responsibilities about campus, even encouraging him to leave the camp and work solely for the university.

But Spencer was content with his dual allegiance to camp and university, though it wasn't an allegiance to their missions, but to the possible rescue of those who wandered innocently into either. Camp residents had always considered this amiable old clerk as harmless in his subtle rejection of their ways, and they had even grown affectionate toward him. But they didn't know it was Spencer Fremont who'd led more than one medium and client out of their dark journeys into the spirit world, after that world had turned on them and threated to devour their minds. It had been Spencer who'd met secretly with at least three camp practitioners over the years, teaching them God's truths from his Word and helping them find their way. After each left the camp, no one, to Spencer's knowledge, suspected he'd had a hand in their defection. Under the camp's very nose, he'd quietly launched a counterattack against the "powers of the air" that spiraled about the whole of Anhinga Bay, masquerading as benevolent and nurturing, but whose ferocious appetites would eventually claim the souls of all but God's own. Spencer was certain of this.

The man who'd failed to extract his own wife from those clutches had determined that surely someone would listen to the truth. And so, he had reported each day to the bookstore, pausing in prayer before entering and asking for God's protection against enemy forces and those who channeled them.

The day Curt Vandoren approached him about organizing the university library, Spencer believed that God himself had opened that door. For what purpose, he wasn't sure, not then. Was it to expand his reach to those who sought Vandoren's teachings? Or something else? He would know in time.

Spencer began his service to the university in its library, but was soon tasked with ordering books and supplies for classroom use. He would occasionally man the reception desk and even do some gardening, bringing starter plants he'd rooted at home to the bare beds scattered about the small campus. It's not that he took pride in the school or was grateful for the extra paycheck, which he didn't need. He'd believed all along that there was a particular reason why God had placed him there. Each time he'd arrived on campus, he hoped for a glimpse of that reason. Now, he was certain it had something to do with what he and Tally had seen at the airstrip two nights ago.

Spencer unlocked the library and walked in, sniffing the familiar musk of old books, the sterility of the new. He hung his damp umbrella on a coat hook behind the door and headed for his desk to check the work schedule that day, specifically who was on duty and when. Because his job of ordering books often meant receiving and inspecting the shipment, he'd been cleared for access to the small loading dock and warehouse at the far end of the building nearest the service road . . . and the airstrip.

Because it was Sunday, Spencer didn't expect to see anyone in shipping-and-receiving, no one to halt his inspection of the warehouse where surely they'd stored the large wooden crate he'd seen transferred from the plane to the tractor-trailer rig Friday night. But the schedule did show a few employees on duty about the building. He scanned the hallways for them now as he left the library and headed for the warehouse, where he entered yet another code at the door and, before pushing it open, took one more cautious look down the empty hall behind him.

Vandoren was a perpetual presence at the university, except on Sundays. After teaching classes, conducting workshops, holding séances, and giving private audience to patrons—most of them wealthy—who flew in from all over the country, Vandoren adhered to strict seclusion on Sundays. He lived in a small but lavish bayfront home just outside the walls of the campus. A housekeeper and cook staffed the home six days a week. But Vandoren admitted no one to his isolated residence nights or Sundays when he rarely left his home.

That's why the sound of his voice gave Spencer a start when he swung open the warehouse door. But it was too late to retreat. He'd been seen, and not only by Vandoren. It seems the armed guards he'd watched Friday night had never left the premises. Now, three of them turned aggressively toward him.

"Stop!" Vandoren shouted at the men, then turned with obvious displeasure at Spencer's unexpected intrusion. "Spencer, why are you here?" he barked.

Spencer had never heard the man speak so gruffly to anyone. And now, it seemed Vandoren instantly regretted his tone. His scowl slid away and the practiced smile Spencer was used to seeing quickly surfaced, an amazing transformation. "I'm sorry, but you startled us." Suspicion clung to Vandoren's eyes. "But why are you here?"

Spencer's heartbeat pumped hard toward an answer, and it had better be good, he feared. Even as he willed himself to stop shaking, he risked a glance behind Vandoren at the object of such security. The crate. About the size and shape of a refrigerator on its side. Then he deliberately shifted his focus toward a plastic-wrapped stack of books, as if he'd been merely trying to locate it. His eyes flitting back to Vandoren, Spencer replied, "I'm sorry, sir. I just wanted to gather more healing workbooks for Classroom B." He nodded toward the stack of books. "They're running low in there." It was the truth, though he hadn't planned to restock that room until tomorrow.

Vandoren's smile grew generous as he stepped toward Spencer, one fleshy arm outstretched. "Perhaps you can collect what you need another time." He offered no explanation for the unusual presence of the guards or his own attendance on a Sunday, and certainly not for the most recent addition to the warehouse inventory. He seemed to silently forbid any such inquiries from his subordinate, even one for whom he'd openly admitted his fondness.

"I'll do that, sir. Excuse me." Spencer closed the door behind him and returned to the library, but there would be no more work for him that day. He soon heard the rumble of a truck behind the building. Searching out the tractor-trailer he and Tally had seen had been next on his agenda that day. But now, it called to him. He dared to slip into the darkened office of a coworker with a window facing that direction. Without turning on the light, he eased toward the window and peered through the blinds. The rig was backing into the warehouse. Spencer was certain of its payload. Though he wondered why the crate he'd watched transferred from the plane to the truck Friday night had been moved to the warehouse and now, it appeared, back to the truck. If it were just books, why the guards? Why Vandoren's appearance here on a Sunday? And who, besides the camouflage-wearing guards, were the two men who'd arrived on the plane? One in a wheelchair. Spencer had never gotten close enough to recognize either one. He assumed they were back on the plane when he watched it depart yesterday afternoon. But who had arrived by helicopter just before daybreak this morning? Spencer had heard its incoming rotors as he dressed.

A sudden footfall down the hall sent Spencer scrambling to the door to listen. Someone passed close by and stopped. Spencer heard the rattle of keys and the door to the supply room open, the footsteps retreating inside. He slipped from the room and back inside his own office seconds before he heard the storeroom door close firmly and the footsteps approach his office door, the keys still rattling.

"You're here early for a Sunday, Spencer," said Danny Otis, one of two custodians who tended the facility. Setting a plastic bucket on the floor, the young man slouched against the doorframe and leaned the handle of a mop against his chest. "I'm used to having this place all to myself on Sunday mornings, but, hey, glad you're here." He glanced toward the door to the warehouse and his expression grew conspiratorial. "It's been a little dicey here the last couple of days, know what I mean?" He inclined his head toward the warehouse and cut his eyes to that side.

Spencer didn't respond. He often didn't whenever Danny's habitually seamless chatter began. The man liked to talk more than work, an ethic which didn't sit well with Spencer, except now. He willed the man to share as much as he knew about the crate in the warehouse.

"I mean, without much warning, all classes were canceled yesterday. Imagine that." Danny looked at Spencer like he might shed some light on the situation, which Spencer wouldn't do even if he could. So Danny kept going. "There was nobody here but those soldier types who proceeded to wander all over this place like they were looking for someone to attack at any moment, and those two foreign guys who stayed holed up in Vandoren's house 'til they all flew out of here yesterday. And today? Well, we don't ever see the boss here on Sunday. But here he comes flying back in that whirligig before the sun's even up and heads straight here." Danny shook his head. "And man, he's on edge about something. I don't know." His gaze wandered back down the hall.

"Have you seen the crate in the warehouse, Danny?" Spencer asked, cutting to the one thing he wanted most to know.

"Oh, so you've seen it too, huh. And you lived to tell about it?" He chuckled. "Boss nearly took my head off when he caught me peeking under the tarp they were keeping over it." But there was no covering on it just now, Spencer noted, its bare-wood case unmarked. "You and me's probably the only ones around here who's seen it." He stared at the floor, a curious expression on his face.

"Do you know what's in it?" Spencer asked.

Danny looked up at him. "Naw." He thought a minute. "But probably some big deal statue or something that costs a million dollars, for all those guards he's got on it. Maybe it's one of them fertility gods or some kind of are-tih-fact." He pronounced the word as one who's just learned to say it. "Boss is always flying off to some jungle or island tribe and bringing back weird stuff. Just something else for me to keep clean down there."

That surprised Spencer. "You mean at his house? Do you work there too?"

"You bet I do. He pays me good, too. But he tells me to keep my mouth shut about what I see in that place." Danny snorted. "Like I can do that. Right?" He laughed too loudly, and Spencer cringed, hoping it wouldn't bring attention from the warehouse. Still, he kept prodding.

"So what do you see?"

Danny looked toward the ceiling. "Well, let me see. There's the jade Buddha and the big blue evil eye from someplace like Turkey, I think. There's a big crystal pyramid he keeps touching and getting fingerprints all over that I have to wipe off." He looked around the room at Spencer's bookshelves. "Boss has lots of old books. I mean really old with yellow pages and gold lettering. Real gold, too. They're in his library, off course. Along with the egg."

Spencer cocked his head. "Egg?"

"You know, one of those fancy ones with all the jewels and stuff on it?"

Spencer thought a moment. "A Fabergé?"

Danny squinted at him. "Hey, I know that word. Isn't it some kind of perfume? I think that's what my ex-wife used to squirt on herself sometimes."

Not wishing to detail the evolution of Fabergé-the-royal-jeweler's name into a line of cosmetics, Spencer said, "It's also a collection of enameled and jeweled eggs created for Russian czars. And Vandoren has such a thing?" Though Spencer knew there were many reproductions.

"Guess so. It's got some kind of alarm system on the case it's in. That's one thing he won't let me touch with my Windex." He paused. "Did you say Russian?"

"Yes, why?"

More to himself than Spencer, Danny said, "I'll bet that's what those guys were."

"What guys?" But Spencer knew.

"Came in on the plane a couple nights ago. Stayed with the boss. There were two of them, but I never saw them up close, especially the one in the wheelchair. They stayed in their rooms while I was there, and wouldn't let me clean inside. But I heard them talking like those guys in . . . what's it called? Oh yeah, *The Hunt for Red October*. Oh man, I loved that movie." He nodded to himself. "Yeah, Russian. That's what they were."

Thoughts scrambled for traction in Spencer's mind. An alarm system? Does Vandoren own an original Fabergé egg? What if he does? What does that have to do with the crate? Unless there's another treasure inside it. Something much bigger than a Fabergé egg. Or a whole crate of them. That would account for the security. And maybe the visitors. Russian art dealers personally guaranteeing the delivery. Yeah, that's it. But how could Vandoren afford such things?

Too many questions made his head spin, his body suddenly fatigued. He watched Danny pick up his bucket and grab the mop handle. "Thanks for talking to me, Danny." He really meant it. The hapless custodian had provided a reasonable and far more palatable explanation for the matter. Spencer would share it with Tally and hopefully halt her perilous midnight surveillances.

But Spencer had one more question. "Danny, while you were at Mr. Vandoren's house on Saturday, what did he talk to these Russians about?"

Danny shrugged. "I was just there about an hour. The boss made me leave right after I cleaned up a bit, so I didn't hear much. Mostly about the boat the wheelchair guy owns. Big yacht he keeps somewhere close by. That's where he and the other guy were headed Saturday afternoon. The boss, too. They all met a chopper somewhere down the coast. Same one that brought the boss back here, I guess. I don't live in that kind of world, so I don't know about those things."

"That's all you overheard them talk about?"

"Yep. Well, better get these bathrooms spit shined." He took a step and stopped. "By the way, you be on the lookout when you go back to the camp."

"Why is that?"

"I hear from some of the camp guards that they got 'em a night prowler out there. The boss is real upset about whoever's been snooping around in the woods near us."

Spencer's mouth went dry. "Any idea who it is?"

"They think it's a girl."

Chapter 21

*A*fter spending Sunday morning with Ben and Anna's children, Liesl and Max left for rehearsals at the Mann Center in downtown Tel Aviv, home of the Israel Philharmonic. The two were giving a sold-out benefit performance at the indoor-outdoor facility Monday night. On Thursday, they—along with Cade, Erica, Ben, and Anna—were scheduled to leave with the entire orchestra for the Nuremberg Music Festival that weekend.

"I've got a wonderful idea, Liesl," Max said as they climbed into his little car. As soon as they were buckled inside, they automatically looked to their right and nodded resignedly at the two men in the car beside them—their plainclothes police escort dispatched early that morning, compliments of the Israeli government at the request of the FBI and CIA. And the White House.

Ignoring the constant reminder of their vulnerability, as declared by those who watched over them, Liesl and Max refocused on each other with only subliminal acknowledgment of their questionable need for protection. Max was no more inclined to it than Liesl, who'd wholeheartedly rebuffed the notion of canceling their concerts and "cowering in some fetal mode of surrender," she'd asserted.

He met her somber eyes. "Okay, those guys aren't really there, and we're just a couple of anonymous musicians off for a gig with the band. Got it? So, as I was saying, here's an idea." He backed slowly from his assigned parking space beneath his condo building. "Let's all leave a couple of days early and fly to Berlin first, since Cade and Erica have never been there. It's just a shuttle flight down to Nuremberg. Or we can drive from Berlin with plenty of time to spare. What do you say?"

As they pulled into the street, Liesl watched the Sunday drivers dart as erratically as they did at rush hour and thought of Berlin. "Cade should see the memorial. Everyone should."

"The Memorial to the Murdered Jews of Europe. That's exactly what I want Erica to experience. She has a strange kind of denial going on about what took place during the war. It's unspoken, but there all the same. I sense it and don't understand it from a fellow Jew." Liesl watched him drop quickly into himself, as he often did. At those times, she'd always given him sanctuary inside his thoughts. And always, as now, he'd finally surface with a fresh impenetrable veneer . . . and a so-what smile, which he now turned on her.

"I'd like that," she agreed. "What a preamble to a concert by the Israel Philharmonic . . . in the heart of Germany."

Max turned to her and she caught a glimpse of something wary about him. "What's the matter?" she asked.

He turned a corner not far from their destination and proceeded at his usual glacier speed until he stopped for a traffic light. "Just can't get the post office flyer off my mind. I mean, why would someone about to commit murder announce it on the town square?"

But Liesl was no longer listening. It was the shape of the head, the angle of the parked car across the intersection, the abrupt surfacing of something—someone—that both repelled and attracted for reasons she couldn't explain. Evgeny Kozlov.

"Are you hearing me?" Max asked.

"Look there," she said, pointing to a small dark sedan hunched oddly against the far side of the street.

She watched him study the man inside the car. When the light changed, Max swerved to the curb and stopped. Without looking at her, his gaze unwavering on the little car, he said calmly, "I want you to stay here with the doors locked." She watched him reach inside the light windbreaker he wore and feel for something at his waist. Finally, he turned to her. "Tell me that you will, Liesl. Tell me now."

She nodded slightly but said nothing. There were too many conflicts raging inside her, inside the man watching her from across the street. The man who'd hunted her down to kill her, who'd later risked his life to save her. Which was he this day?

Before opening the door, Max punched in a quick call to the police escort just pulling in behind his car. He issued a standby directive to them and asked that they remain in their car with full attention on Liesl.

Now turning from her, Max looked squarely at the driver in the small sedan across the street and raised a surrendering gesture with both hands. Then slowly, he stepped from the car and stood still, his hands dangling at his sides, clearly free of what Liesl knew to be a gun in his waistband. Surely Evgeny knew it too, she guessed. Why was he just waiting there?

Max moved steadily, confidently across the street, waiting now and then for a car to pass. Liesl watched the distance between the two men close. When Max reached the car, he stopped and waited. The man at the wheel hadn't moved since Liesl first sighted him. But now he did. She watched him lean toward the passenger door and open it.

"The last time I saw you, you were running from me through the airport in this city," Evgeny said after Max settled into the passenger seat and closed the door. "Besides myself, I never knew anyone to drop from sight as quickly as you did that day. I was impressed."

Max noted the gaunt severity of the man's face. His was the pallor of one who'd lived too long without light. "Well, I can't tell you what that means to me," Max bristled. "Maybe another time, though. Right now, we've got some talking to do. Let's start with this: Thank you for saving Liesl's life in Charleston. Why did you do it?"

A placid smile rose on the thin lips. "I owed her." The smile vanished.

"But the better question is, why are you parading her around in your father's sights? Quite possibly Ivan's?"

"So you heard."

"Ava told me about the photo your president received. Perhaps I failed my mission that day on the East River. Perhaps not. We will see. Meanwhile, why do you think a couple of impotent cops trailing you is all the protection you both need?" Evgeny looked toward the unmarked car parked behind Max's. "What did I save her from in Charleston? A danger that is still there."

Max knew it was true. But it was also true that Liesl was vulnerable anywhere. "She won't hide under an armored blanket, Evgeny. You know that, don't you? Because you know her." Max said something else he knew to be true. "And like me . . . you love her."

Evgeny rounded on Max with flashing eyes. But at once, the eyes paled and turned away. Toward Liesl. For a silent moment, the two men watched her sitting alone in the car across the street, her face in shadow but the sunlight catching a strand of golden hair. Max wondered how much more pathetic he and the lone-wolf Russian could be.

"Forgive me, Evgeny. I spoke out of place."

Evgeny flipped a hand of dismissal. "We have much more to discuss. I know of your search for your father, for the sordid truths about our new president and the link between the two. Tell me what you have uncovered."

Evgeny's long, deep tentacles into Russian intelligence, his well-documented turn against those who would overthrow the government and endanger his homeland, and his extraordinary covert skills all made him an invaluable asset to the U.S. government and to Israel. That's why Ava Mullins and the Mossad had already given Max clearance to share such things with Evgeny Kozlov, should the occasion arise. Such as now.

So began Max's brief review of Arkady Glinka's secret life in the occult, of his and Volynski's yet-undetermined connection with the Anhinga Bay Spiritualist Camp, and most critically, of the recent detection of suspicious activity in and around a suspected weapons factory deep inside a Ural mountain. When he finished, Evgeny continued to stare at Max's car and the sedan still parked behind it, the muscles of his jaw working, grinding as if hashing his options.

Finally, he looked back at Max. "You have done well. But what you do not know is that the 'suspicious activity' you speak of is not at all suspicious. It is a certainty. A chemical weapon left Russia days ago on a private plane, its destination yet unknown. The bomb contains sarin. Colorless, odorless, a nerve agent capable of massive death.

"How can you be sure?"

"I don't question your sources. You don't question mine. As long as they keep us both alive—and her—we must act on them." His eyes strayed back to Max's car. "Look."

Max turned to see the passenger door open and Liesl emerge. The two security officers sprang from their car and approached her, but she waved them off and strode purposefully across the road. Max flung open his door and jumped out. "Liesl, go back!" But she kept coming until she stood before him with her eyes on Evgeny.

"I'm tired of waiting to see what international incident you two are hatching inside this car." She smiled tightly at Max and pulled him with her into the back seat.

Evgeny made no move to turn around until she and Max had closed the door, then he faced her squarely, his eyes piercing through some membrane that seemed to separate the bilious spy from every other living being, Max observed. Except Liesl. Now, he wondered at the change.

She didn't have to say a word, only look at Evgeny with the knowing eyes that smoldered with disarming compassion. His tired old face relaxed and his hand reached palm up for hers. She gave it fully to him, leaning forward and closing her other hand over his, locking him in something secret and hidden from Max, who could only guess at the times the two had known together. The rampage and reconciliation, the haunting and the peace forged between them during those days in New York.

She released Evgeny's hand and sat back. "Only six months ago, Evgeny, I thought I would never see you again. That you would finally be free of me." She smiled thinly. "Yet here you are again. Why?"

Evgeny looked toward Max then back at Liesl. He shrugged. "Because you remain an impetuous child dashing into harm's way."

"What should I do?" she probed. "Surrender to people I can't see? Can't talk to or even place on a map? Maybe they're here, or back in Charleston. Or maybe they don't exist at all."

She looked at Max. "Right now, you and I are late for a rehearsal. Cade is on his way here to join us." She looked out the window. "The sun isn't hiding behind clouds today, and neither will I." She turned back to Evgeny. "I believe that the dangerous things you and Max discuss, those classified things I'm not supposed to know, matter greatly. But so do the things that aren't so dark and classified, like playing the music that lifts us higher than that. Can't we just do that, Evgeny? Can't we just play the music?"

Max thought he'd never seen more yearning hope in a human face than what shone in Liesl's that moment. He longed for such hope. Why would it not come to him? Was her God its composer?

Evgeny straightened before them. With an unwavering eye on the two officers watching him from outside their car, he finally replied. "Go and play it, Liesl. You and Max. Wherever it takes you. And leave me to what I do best."

Liesl stared at his profile, at the eyes now refusing to meet hers.

"Go now," Evgeny commanded them both, and turned fully around in his seat, both hands back on the wheel. Silent.

Max hovered by the open back door as Liesl slid across the seat to exit the car. Then she paused and spoke one last time to Evgeny. "Will I see you again?"

With only a trace of sarcasm, he spoke into the windshield. "You always do."

Chapter 22

*A*s Cade, Ben, and Anna were led to their seats inside Mann Auditorium, Cade noticed his phone light up inside his coat pocket. Risking a peek at the caller, he grinned at the bushy beard filling the tiny screen but dared not answer the summons. Once they were seated, though, he bent over the silenced instrument and tapped out a quick text: *Concert starting. Talk later.*

Slipping the phone into his pocket, he calculated the time in Charleston. It would be noon on that Monday. At that hour, his grandfather and Henry were either nosing the *Exodus II* back into the harbor after a half-day charter. Or O'Brien Charters was headlong into the Gulf Stream with all-day customers tracking wahoo, tuna, maybe a trophy marlin. Cade glanced about the auditorium and smiled to himself at the memory of Ian O'Brien's last visit to a major concert hall. It had been Avery Fisher Hall in New York a year and a half ago. As clearly as if his grandfather were sitting beside him now, Cade could see him stuffed into a dress shirt barely containing his thick, whiskered neck, his hooked forefinger tugging at the starched and bedeviling constraint. But when Liesl had emerged from the wings and took her place on stage, resplendent in an emerald green gown, both O'Brien men had lost all concept of discomfort—and in Cade's case, alarm over what had delayed her entrance into the spotlight that night. Now, recalling what that delay had been, the smile vanished from his face.

Where is he? Cade wondered as he scanned the audience, now settled and waiting for Liesl Bower and Max Morozov to appear on stage. Cade was certain that Evgeny Kozlov was there somewhere. Inside, outside. Disguised, most certainly. He would have to be if those he guarded her against were present. Max Morozov's elusive father. Ivan Volynski, alive or not, because his faithful followers might kill more than their own president out of vengeance. The pretend-postman who carried fake mail and a real gun in his pouch. And all the shadowed ones who'd harassed Liesl with dead-air phone calls and stalkings. They would know and recognize the Russian turncoat who'd forsaken his duty to their cause, in part for the sake of the young woman Cade O'Brien had married.

Cade had come to grips with the hovering threats to his wife, resolving to protect her as best he could. But he knew the insufficiency of that, and that God would have to remain her greatest defender. He'd also reconciled himself to the Russian spy's singular devotion to the preservation of Liesl Bower. If Kozlov was in love with Cade's wife, so were others. He'd read it in the unmasked eyes of Max Morozov. Cade also knew that love to be as innocent as Liesl's returned affections. He'd long forbidden jealousy to take root in him, but couldn't help savoring Liesl's every valiant effort to assure him how crazy in love she was with him and him only. Just like the lyrics of a song, he thought.

Cade turned to see Ben watching him closely. The former White House staffer and expat leaned toward Cade and whispered. "Spotted him yet?" Cade shook his head. "You won't," Ben assured him. "But the others are plain to see." Ben's eyes roamed side to side. Cade had already counted at least ten of Tel Aviv's finest, both in and out of uniform, at the ready to defend the pair about to perform.

And that time came.

The lights dimmed and the curtain rose on the Israel Philharmonic. To a crescendo of applause, Liesl entered from the left, the sequins on her pale blue gown catching the lights and star-dusting her entrance to center stage. Max and his violin approached from the right wing, his tux neat and crisp, unlike the errant thatch of red on his head. They were a study in contrasts until they began to play. Only then did Cade relax and let the melding of these great artists wash over him, soothing his fears and lifting him to a higher place, as always happened when Liesl performed. But his cautious eyes never stopped roving the theater.

Taking her seat at the concert grand, Liesl allowed the briefest dart of the eye toward Cade and an almost imperceptible nod of the head. All was well, he interpreted from the gesture. For now.

He leaned back and propped his elbows on the armrests. There would be music in Tel Aviv, he mused, and fish in Charleston. He smiled to himself, picturing the two intrepid fishermen of O'Brien Charters just heading back from sea, their ice lockers full of fat catch. They'd collect their pay, hose down the boat, then head home to a peaceful evening on Tidewater Lane. At least some things were predictable.

Heavy seas off Florida's east coast tossed *Exodus II* through white-foam troughs as Ian struggled to maintain a southerly course. Henry had grabbed the binoculars to track a waterspout just reported by an outgoing tanker over the marine radio. "Yeah, I see it," he told Ian. "Kind of dancing around out there."

"Well, keep an eye on it. I sure don't like the looks of these skies. We may have to pull in at Ft. Lauderdale."

"I say we keep going. We should hit the Keys well before nightfall."

"We might hit more than that if this weather doesn't let up. We get blown off course in a storm and we could pile up on a jetty."

Henry lowered the binoculars and looked ahead. "Skies along the south horizon seem to be lifting." He looked at Ian with determination clamped hard about his mouth. "We're running against time, not the weather."

Ian caught his eye. "I understand. This was my idea, remember?"

Henry nodded and resumed his watch on the waterspout. It had taken a clear path north, moving off behind them, its funnel swilling the Atlantic and spitting it back. Ian struggled with what to do. Henry Bower was close to igniting. His daughter, who seemed to be his only reason to persist in this life, was back on the endangered list, and reason was running in short supply inside the desperate mind of her father. But Ian knew the sea as Henry never had. The old charter captain had tangled with it too many times to ignore its warnings to back off and head for shore. Is that what it was telling him now?

For another hour, Ian listened only to the sea and the wind, not the entreaties of a father on a mission to save his child. What good would he be trapped in the belly of the ocean?

Soon, though, the dead gray of the seas to the south and east took on a metallic glint. Something had flung a spritz of light across the waves, a cloud-swaddled sun straining to be seen. Ian took the signal as an all clear. He confirmed it with NOAA, who reported the storm wall finally moving out to sea. *Exodus II* and its skippers soon cleared the battering swells, throttled up, and sailed confidently into the last leg of the journey.

Henry had just taken a turn at the wheel when Ian's phone rang. He grabbed it instantly. "Cade? Is everything okay there?"

"Everything's fine, Pop. No incidents to report. But you should have heard the uproar at the end of the performance. The applause was deafening. Max and my girl hung a few stars in the heavens tonight, or so this crowd thinks."

"How about that Russian fellow?"

Cade didn't answer right away. "What do you mean, Pop?"

"You know what I mean. Did Kozlov show up? 'Cause when he does, there's always trouble."

Cade hesitated again and Ian read it for what it was. Withholding. Before Cade could muster a reply, Ian said, "You think I don't know what's going on, and that I'm better off not knowing. Wrong on both counts."

"Pop, now calm down. I'm not trying to keep anything from you. Everything here is going fine. If it weren't, I'd tell you."

"Okay, son. But don't you take your eyes off Liesl. And the rest of us will do what we have to do." He squeezed his eyes shut and groaned. *Why did I have to say something like that?*

"And just what is that?" The wind picked up and sent a hard blast of salt spray against the windshield beside Ian. "You still on the boat, Pop?"

"Yeah. Well, I need to go now, so—"

"Hold on, Pop. What did you mean by doing what you have to do?"

"All I mean is, Henry and I are doing what we do best. Fishing." That ended the call.

Making better time than expected, *Exodus II* pulled into Anhinga Bay about six that evening. The oblong basin was ringed by Norfolk Island pines and coconut palms, the waters deep and sapphire from end to end. A few dwellings broke the tree line around the shore. Still not sure what he was looking for, Ian's gaze swept them quickly then focused on the marina straight ahead. He'd visited it many times over the years. It had once thrived on the fishing trade, but a newer, larger facility a mile south had left the Anhinga marina teetering on old age and under use, or so it appeared from the few boats tied up at its sagging docks. "I'm going to find Chet," Ian said as Henry tied down the boat and prepared to hook up shore power. "Catch up when you can."

Ian had known the dockmaster, Chet Blanchard, only casually, enough to swap fraternal greetings and a few fish tales. Now, however, Ian was casting for as much information as he could harvest, from as many sources as he could find. Fishing, he'd told Cade. Something was going on in this quirky little place and he and Henry weren't leaving until they'd landed on it.

He spotted Chet bent over a box of Styrofoam cups at the back of the marina store. "Don't throw your back out lifting those things," Ian called.

A slick-bald man in a denim shirt and shorts straightened in a hurry, a smile already on his face. "I knew that voice instantly." He came around the counter with his hand extended. "Ian O'Brien. Where you been, man?"

Ian took Chet's hand and pumped it. "Charleston. Moved there with my grandson. You remember Cade?"

"Sure do. Puked a lot, as I recall."

Ian laughed. "That's why he's a magazine editor now." Then he remembered his mission and allowed no more extraneous news. They were here to uncover information, not give it away. A low profile was best. Just a couple of fishermen with a hankering to get their fortunes told. Wasn't that what he'd told Henry? Better stick to it.

"So what brings you back?"

Careful, Ian warned himself. "I just wanted to show my South Carolina buddy there what a real fish looked like." He gestured toward Henry, who was just entering the door.

With introductions and harmless banter out of the way, Ian started pumping for information. "Say, Chet, what do you know about this spirit camp down the road?"

"The spooks?"

"Yeah, I guess."

Chet shrugged. "Been there a long time. Mind their own business. Even got a university now."

"A what?"

"A guy named Vandoren built it a couple of years ago behind the camp. Classes on how to talk to ghosts." Chuck raised one hand. "I swear it. And folks come from all over to learn how to do that. The hotels in town are lovin' it."

Ivan Volynski was around here two years ago! Ian suddenly remembered that snatch of data from the conversation he'd overheard at Ava's house, and a laser beam just shot from Volynski to Vandoren. Ian turned to see if Henry had made the same connection. He had.

"So tell us more about this Vandoren fella," Henry urged, though his eyes drilled into Ian. "What's his first name?"

"Curt," Chet answered, then cocked a half grin at Ian. "Say, you two aren't into that funny stuff, are you?"

"Naw, just curious," Ian replied.

"Well, come on out here." Chet led them through the door of the little store and onto the fuel dock. "See that red-tile roof through the trees there?" Ian and Henry turned that way. A steep slope of terra cotta stood in relief against the chartreuse fronds of a palm thicket. "That's Vandoren's house. Pretty fancy place, I hear. Not like those little dried-up bungalows the camp mediums live in." Chet shook his head but barely paused for breath. Ian knew to stay quiet and just listen. "There seems to be more money in training spooks than being one." He chuckled at his own wit.

"Notice any unusual activity around here lately?" Henry asked.

"Are you kidding? How many of *your* neighbors carry on with dead people? Everything about this place is unusual. Plain weird. Now, if you're talking *new*, well, there's that big séance they've been advertising. I think that's going to happen tomorrow night. So you guys are just in time for Halloween." He laughed some more. "Go on up there and take a look," Chet added. "And get you some dinner at the camp hotel." He looked over at *Exodus II*. "Probably not much of a galley on that tug, right, Ian? Or a cook." He clapped Ian's shoulder.

"How far a walk is it from here?"

"Couple miles. But if you want, you can use my bikes. They're behind the store."

"Bikes?" Ian frowned.

"Yeah, sure. Keep 'em as long as you're here."

Ian had just one more question. "How big are the seats?"

Chapter 23

Ian and Henry showered on board, changed into clean clothes, and peddled off toward the Anhinga Bay Spiritualist Camp. Surprisingly, Ian immediately took to the rusty old cruising bike with the fat tires and, best of all, a broad-beam seat. The memory of how he'd suffered on the painfully narrow seat of Ava's rental bike was still fresh. "Now this is the way man was intended to sit on a bike," he declared to Henry as they rode. "Or else God would have made us a lot different in the crotch area."

It didn't take long to reach the camp, which spread between the marina and the little town of Anhinga Bay. Chet had told them the front gate was usually open until just after dark, but that a guard would stop them anyway.

It was a simple entrance with cement columns on either side of a wide, asphalt driveway. A small sign drilled into one column declared the name of the camp. Just inside was the guardhouse.

"Hold up here," Ian told Henry, and they stopped their bikes short of the gate. "There's something I have to do, so bear with me." Ian bowed his head and began to pray silently.

But Henry interrupted him. "Nothing doing. No secrets. If you've got something to say to him, do it where I can hear." It was as honest a request as Ian had ever heard from him. So once more, Ian bowed his head.

"Lord, I know you're here," he began in a hushed voice. "Make Henry know it, too." He paused, his eyes still closed. "We don't know what to expect in there, but I believe you brought us here for a reason. So lead us to it, and protect us as we go. Amen."

Henry frowned at him. "That's all?"

"Well, how much praying do you want?"

"I didn't ask for any. But I expected you'd come up with more than that." Henry pushed off, leaving an exasperated Ian to sputter a reply.

"I don't trouble the Lord for more than I need at the time," he called.

Ian caught up with Henry, and the two stopped at the guardhouse where a friendly young man in knee-length shorts and a camp T-shirt greeted them.

"Welcome to Anhinga Bay, gentlemen. How can we help you?"

Ian and Henry had already agreed to present themselves as honestly as possible: just a couple of fishermen tourists with a keen interest in the history and culture of the camp. No lie there. No need to expound on their motives either.

"My friend and I are touring the area and would gratefully appreciate a chance to explore the camp and learn as much as we can about its history and its residents," Henry said as if he'd practiced every syllable before a mirror. Ian found himself staring at him as if he'd never heard him speak before.

"Of course you can," the young man replied with an accommodating air. "You might want to start at the camp bookstore for some background on us." He pointed across a grassy commons to a cluster of buildings. "And maybe grab some dinner at the hotel next door. Where are you staying?"

Henry avoided the question by asking one of his own. "Is Vandoren's university also open to visitors?"

The young man's demeanor caved slightly. "The camp and the University of the Spirit are entirely separate entities." Henry and Ian hadn't understood that. "You'll have to inquire at their front office about a tour." It was a cordial reply, but not a willing one.

"And how would we get there?" Henry persisted.

Patiently, the young man pointed out the road that ran along the camp's fenced property and ended at the place where Henry and Ian most desired access. "Now, please come in and enjoy your stay with us," the guard resumed his official welcome. "Feel free to roam about. I won't be closing the gate tonight until nine."

Ian and Henry rode into the camp and stopped to get their bearings from the map the guard had given them. The broad commons was ringed by thirty or more one-story cottages, all neatly kept and fairly uniform in design, most with screened front porches and picket fences. In the front yards of those nearest, Ian and Henry saw shingles that advertised such services as *spiritual readings*, *healing*, and *past life regression*.

"Let's head for the hotel first," Ian said. "I'm hungry." Henry readily agreed.

It was a simple, three-story facility of beige stucco with a broad front porch dotted with rocking chairs and pots of bright flowers. At one end, the porch flared into a gazebo where two couples were lounging in high-backed wicker chairs. They were talking quietly while sipping wine and dipping into a tray of appetizers on a small round table. Two or three single people sat alone reading or listening to iPods.

Once inside, Henry and Ian were greeted by a yellow and green bird who sang the Alabama fight song and ended with a clearly enunciated "Roll tide!"

"Oh don't mind him," said the hostess who approached them. She was a comely woman in her late forties with a cascade of chestnut hair falling over a delicate, ivory-lace blouse cinched neatly about her small waist. "The contractor who renovated our guest rooms taught that to him and we can't get him to switch allegiance to the Gators for anything." The woman spread her peach-glossed lips into an engaging smile. "Will you be dining with us?" she asked, grabbing a couple of menus.

When Henry didn't answer, Ian replied, "Yes, ma'am," then glanced over at his friend. *Well, would you look at that. I believe he's smitten.* As they followed the woman to a table, Ian leaned toward him. "Pick up your lower jaw and put it back where it belongs. We've got work to do."

The hostess led them to one of several tables at the front window. At the next table, a young couple sat waiting for their meal and watching a man throw a Frisbee to his dog on the commons.

"This place will be humming like a hive by tomorrow afternoon," the woman informed as she placed their menus on the table before them. "Will you be attending the mass séance?"

Henry looked blankly at Ian, who hadn't expected a confrontation with the paranormal so soon upon their arrival, if at all. Though they had come as sleuths focused only on uncovering anything relevant to Volynski, Ian also knew they were entering waters more dangerous than anything the Atlantic could hurl at them.

Henry believed that mediums and their claims to summon the dead were, in his words, full of malarkey. Ian knew that was often true. Frauds and fools would gather about a séance table, after an exchange of currency. The trickery was real, the voice of dead Aunt Ethel wasn't. But some mediums possessed real preternatural powers, the kind God warned his people about. Sometimes those who wandered into a séance for either cheap thrills or a genuine desire to contact a dead relative suddenly found themselves in the grip of a spirit who was neither an amusement nor a departed loved one—but a very real and demonic presence, one of Satan's own.

Ian knew he should have spent more time warning Henry about such things. Even knowing his companion's resistance to spiritual matters, Ian should have anticipated such a moment as this and better prepared his buddy for what Ian knew on a too-personal level. His own sister had plunged into the occult as a teenager, subjecting herself to a medium in whose Key West home a group of young people indulged in such pagan practices as divination and necromancy, summoning spirits of the dead and communing with them. Only after one of those teens committed suicide did Ian's sister flee the group, but she never escaped the spirit world's demonic hold on her. She later forfeited her sanity and spent the rest of her life in an institution.

Ian peered into Henry's questioning eyes for an instant more, then answered the woman. "No, we won't be going to that, but thanks for telling us about it. We would like to visit that fellow at the University of the

Spirit, though. What's his name? Vandoren? Just to get another perspective on what you all practice here."

The woman looked thoughtful. "You'll find lots of information at our camp bookstore." She pointed next door. "Ask for Spencer Fremont. Real nice guy. He'll help you." She perked up again. "By the way, the meatloaf tonight is outstanding." She smiled and returned to her station at the door.

Just then, the young man at the next table leaned over. "Forgive me for overhearing, but it appears you haven't been to the camp before."

"Correct," Henry answered. "You?"

"First time for us, too. So you haven't been to the school either, or know anything about it?"

"Nope," Henry answered.

Ian mused at the mercurial nature of conversation with Henry. The guy at the guardhouse got more information than he needed. This poor man had nothing to work with.

"What do you know about this Vandoren fellow?" Ian asked the man. The fisherman was casting about wherever he could.

The young woman's eyes flitted instantly to the man's face as he spoke, "Not much. Are you a, uh, spiritualist like the others here?"

"No, just a couple of curious fishermen. What brings you here?"

"The same. Curiosity." He glanced at his companion. Ian didn't notice wedding rings on either.

"You going to this séance tomorrow?" Ian asked him.

A waitress arrived with two plates of food for the couple. "Probably," the man answered and turned back to focus on his meal.

Ian noticed two women enter the restaurant, then heard the hostess greet them affectionately. "Mona. Tally. Come give me hugs." Ian and Henry both turned to see the new arrivals gathered into a group embrace. Like the hostess, one of the women was in her midforties, slim, with a powdery, doll-like face.

"I promised my daughter a home-cooked meal. From your kitchen, not mine." The woman laughed skittishly and wrapped an arm about the younger woman's shoulders. But this one wasn't laughing. Her sullen face offered no light, no permission to draw closer. Dressed in black running shorts and a plain white polo shirt, she held herself like an athlete, square-stanced and sure of her strength. But the eyes weren't so sure. They darted too quickly about the room, searching, appraising. And just then, they came to rest on Ian. Embarrassed for staring, he turned away and wondered if she'd grown up in this environment. No, he *worried* about it. His sister had been about the same age when she left for Key West.

"Sad girl," Henry said without turning to look at her again. "I had one of those."

Ian studied his friend's sharp-nosed profile as he gazed out the window. "And I caused it," Henry added stiffly.

"But you repaired it. So stop slamming yourself against meat hooks and move on, my friend. Liesl adores you."

Henry casually stole another look at the girl. "There's a tempest brewing in that one. I know the look."

Ian was about to turn back for another glance at her when the hostess steered her and her mother to the next table. Taking their seats, the girl sat facing Ian, her eyes steady on him. "Hello," he said warmly to both women.

The mother gushed a smile at him and Henry, who now offered his own semblance of greeting, which was barely a nod.

"You must be visitors," the mother said. "Welcome to the camp. Are you here for the séance?"

"Didn't know about it until we arrived this evening," Ian allowed, noticing the young couple on the other side turn their heads slightly toward them.

"Are you staying at the hotel?" the woman asked.

"A little too nosey, Mom," the girl interjected without looking up from the menu she'd hastily buried her nose in.

Ian observed the pinched young face, then answered the woman, who seemed to ignore her daughter's comment. "No. We've got a boat at the marina." He caught a visual jab from Henry. *Oh, yeah, we're supposed to be spies.* That meant covert, not loose-lipped, and that was going to be real hard for him. "But say," he continued, "maybe you could tell us about this university place and Curt Vandoren." *Just wade right in*, he resolved.

The woman looked kindly at him. "What would you like to know?"

For starters, is he plotting murder with Ivan Volynski? But what he said was, "We were told people come to his place from around the world."

"That's true," the woman said. "By the way, I'm Mona Greyson and this is my daughter, Tally." The girl lifted a wobbly smile and looked back at the menu.

It just occurred to Ian that he and Henry hadn't thought about aliases. That was in the category of bold-faced lies, which Ian found distasteful. If this was indeed Volynski territory, though, *O'Brien* might not flag anyone's attention, but *Bower* sure would. Ian hoped first names would suffice.

"I'm Ian and this is Henry." He hurried past the surname omissions. "Now, about Vandoren . . ."

"I take classes there myself," Mona said, "and yes, ironically, people travel great distances to come here and learn about the spirit world hovering just beyond their fingertips."

Tally looked at her mother with unveiled disdain. Her mother returned a scolding glance at her.

Ian tried to ignore the fleeting yet awkward exchange and cast on to the next question. "Well, uh, ever get anybody here from, say . . . Russia?"

The question dangled in a silent void for too many seconds. Then the woman answered. "Well, let me see. Maybe one or two." She appeared only mildly surprised by the question.

But there was nothing mild about her daughter's reaction. The head shot up from the menu and the eyes bore down on Ian. He'd struck something. "Do you remember anyone?" he asked Tally directly. Her retreat from him was just as swift, and Ian saw something he hadn't before. *She's afraid.*

"No," Tally answered him, then looked at her mother. "I just want a hamburger and that's all."

And that was all Ian would get from her, for now. Somehow he had to pursue this young woman. There was something there. He sensed it. In a colony of mediums, he reminded himself, sensing anything could be dangerous.

After a while, the couple on the other side rose to go. They both nodded courteously toward Ian and Henry. "Hope you enjoy your stay," the man offered, and they left.

A shuttle bus pulled up across the street and began dispensing others now headed for the hotel. The mother and daughter beside them appeared to have drawn a curtain on further communication with the old fishermen.

"Ian, leave those people alone," Henry said. "Let's just eat our meatloaf and get over to the bookstore before it closes."

Chapter 24

The camp bookstore, like the hotel, boasted no architectural person-
ality, just function. As with many South Florida structures, its squat
profile offered little resistance, therefore more resilience to hurricane-force
winds. Its unadorned cement block walls had been painted a pale green to
complement the small facility's only saving attribute: an encircling profu-
sion of hibiscus, ixora, elephant ear, and swayback palms.

It was after eight when Ian and Henry entered the store. Though the
sign on the door indicated normal closing time of six, the place was full of
people. The two men cruised slowly past what to them was a baffling assortment of books and pamphlets, overhearing snatches of conversations
from customers, mostly about their past visits to the camp and expecta-
tions for tomorrow night's big event. "Henry, who did that hostess tell us
to ask for in here?"

"Guy named Fremont, I think."

"That's me," came a cheerful voice beside them. They turned to see an
older gentleman with a pleasant smile and an armload of books. "Spencer
Fremont. Sorry I can't shake your hand, but how may I help you?" He was
hunched around the shoulders and light of frame, but having no trouble
with the weight in his arms.

"Well, it's real nice to meet you, Spencer," Ian chirped. "My friend and

I are looking for something like a for-dummies handbook on, uh, what you do here."

A twinkle rose in the clerk's eyes. "But you're not sure what that is, correct?"

Both men nodded. "Sort of," Henry allowed.

"Perfectly all right. Follow me."

From a rack near the check-out desk, Spencer selected two small volumes and handed both to Henry. Ian had been distracted by the two women just entering the bookstore, Mona and Tally Greyson. When Ian turned back to the clerk, he saw the man's eyes also on the pair, then Mr. Fremont looked quickly back at Henry and tapped the spine of one book. "That's a complete overview of spiritualism, which the camp's residents and mediums practice. The other is a guide to the individual services offered at the camp."

Something about his wording made Ian curious. "Do you . . . I mean, are you also a resident?"

The man smiled hesitantly. "Yes."

Ian waited for more but had to press for it. "So, are you a medium?"

"No."

Henry went straight to what Ian was fishing for. "Do you believe what they do?"

The man was clearly taken aback and glanced around him with what Ian interpreted as caution. Though it wasn't an answer, the clerk responded softly, "They're good friends and neighbors." He looked away, seeming to hunt for something, or someone. "Please excuse me. If you need further help, just lift your hand. My assistant or I will be happy to help." It was polite but perfunctory.

Ian and Henry watched the man hurry off toward the front door where Mona Greyson had just left her daughter standing alone. Ian was surprised to see Tally and Spencer Fremont drop into quick conversation, their heads slightly inclined toward each other. Though every impulse told him he wouldn't be welcome, Ian headed straight for them. As he drew close, though, the two stepped just outside the door. Ian followed, painfully aware that he was about to make a nuisance of himself. But something about the word *Russian* had given Tally Greyson a start and Ian would bludgeon on until he knew what it was.

When he opened the door and approached, Tally and Spencer snuffed out their conversation and stared at him. "Excuse me for interrupting," Ian began, slowly stroking his beard to mask his awkwardness. "Young lady, I'm afraid I did or said something I shouldn't have at dinner, and I want to apologize." He was feeling his way along a narrow limb, uncertain if it would hold. "I'm not sure what it was, but you seemed a bit startled when I asked if any Russians ever visited here. I was just curious why."

Then it happened again. This time with Spencer Fremont, who suddenly turned wide, searching eyes on Ian, his mouth falling slightly ajar.

I've struck a vein, Ian thought. But before he could pursue it, Tally's head jerked upward at the sound of a small plane approaching the camp. Spencer instantly did the same. But after searching the skies, now turning night shades of cobalt and lavender, he refocused on the two people before him.

Why had an incoming plane so completely snared their attention? Ian wondered. And what was that? The old man and girl had just met each other's eyes before resuming their watch on the sky. Something unspoken had just passed between them. Ian was certain of it. Now, he looked back to see the blinking red and green lights emerge from the hazy distance and the profile of a private jet materialize. He was surprised to see it drop in altitude as it neared the camp.

"Is there a place to land around here?" Ian asked.

"At the university," Spencer answered without looking at him.

"You're kidding. Vandoren's got a landing strip?"

Tally remained silent and fixed on the plane. Spencer seemed too preoccupied to entertain any more of Ian's questions. "I must get back to my post," he told them, but his gaze held Ian's a few moments more. There was a question in it and Ian wished the man would ask it. But he returned to his duties without more than a courteous nod to Ian. Tally also excused herself and followed Spencer into the store.

When he told Henry about the plane and the reaction it had caused, they decided to have a look at the landing strip. They paid for the materials

Spencer had selected for them and left the store. Back on their bikes, they approached the camp gate and slowed. Ian wondered how to proceed toward the university at this late hour without drawing an inquiry from the guard, but the young man wasn't there.

They turned onto the road that ran alongside the camp. Where the fence ended and a wall began, they stopped to peer into the darkness. There appeared to be another gate ahead, but they weren't anxious to openly approach it. They looked about for an alternate route toward the bay, having learned that the university campus skirted many acres along the waterfront. Henry got off his bike and retrieved a flashlight from his pocket. It was a low beam he aimed into the surrounding woods. "There's some kind of trail through there," he told Ian. "I'm going in. You'd better wait here."

"Why's that?" Ian objected.

"Because you're old . . . and slow," Henry answered without expression. "Now let's get these bikes off the road, then you hide yourself. If you need me, do some kind of birdcall or something. I'll know it's you."

"Well, that's just brilliant," Ian growled. "I'll just stay right here and take my blood pressure while you're gone. Maybe check my pulse." But even as he fumed at being left behind, he knew the history of the man now slinking off into the woods, the one who'd crawled through sinkhole woods to watchdog after his daughter. Ian had heard the tales of the runaway father declared dead on a Mexican beach, then returned to shadow Liesl through her long career, mastering disguises, running midnight patrols past her home, confronting Russian spies who broke into her house. And she never knew, not until the day she found him at the island off Charleston Harbor, finally at the end of himself. He'd lived too hard in the wilds, undercover and fiercely protective. Just like now. *So let him go*, Ian told himself.

He pulled his bike into the trees with Henry's, about ten yards off the road to the university, and waited almost twenty minutes in the night shadows of a huge live oak. The moon peeped now and then from behind the clouds but nothing moved or sounded about him. He could only guess at what Henry would find near the bay, surely something as big as a landing strip. He was wondering why Vandoren needed one. Most visitors to the Keys flew into Miami or one of the regional airports in the Keys and drove to their destinations. Why the privacy? Unless there were those who wished to arrive in secret. Ian's mind was rummaging around that notion when he heard a sound behind him, someone approaching. He crouched at the foot of the tree and peered around it. A figure too dim to see clearly in the waning light tread cautiously through the woods to the right of Ian, who hardly breathed as it passed. But as it did, the moon slipped into the open and illuminated the face of Spencer Fremont. Ian was startled. Had the man followed them? Why? Was he now trailing Henry? There'd be no birdcall. Ian would have to go after him.

He gave the man a cautious lead then stepped from behind the tree when someone else entered the woods. Two people, too close behind him. There would be no more hiding. They were on him before he could retreat. He turned fully to face them, the glow of moonlight just enough for recognition.

What? It was the young couple from the hotel café. "Sir?" the young man said as he and the woman approached. "What are you doing here?"

Ian relaxed, ignoring the question, and looked around him. Like Henry, Spencer Fremont had disappeared into the dark, leaving no sound in his wake. "Well, I'll tell you one thing. There are entirely too many people in these woods tonight." He eyed the couple suspiciously. "Why are *you* here?"

As Ian had, the man ignored the question. Instead, he said, "Sir, we need to ask you a few questions."

The wording sounded official. "And you came all the way out here to do that?" He carefully looked them up and down.

The woman finally responded by reaching into her pants pocket and producing a badge. The man did likewise. "We're FBI, sir," she said. "And we're quite serious about those questions. Would you mind coming with us?"

Ian gaped at first, then clarity dawned. "Oh, you're the FBI team she was talking about."

The man cocked his head. "Excuse me?"

"I thought you'd need some help," Ian explained. "That's why my buddy and I are here. So just hold onto your questions and let's wait 'til he gets back. If we're lucky, we'll snag that clerk fellow on his way out of here, too." Ian shook his head in dismay. "Yep, the woods are full tonight."

"Sir, I don't think you understand."

"No, son. *You* don't understand. The man probably crawling on his belly down there spying on that plane that just landed is Liesl Bower's dad." He assumed that revelation would help explain things. He was wrong.

"We really do need you to come with us," the young man insisted.

"And I really can't do that right now." He turned slightly to look for any sign of Henry, who should have returned by now. Ian looked back at the two agents. "But I will do a birdcall for you."

The two confounded agents stared at him as if he were teetering on senility, or worse.

Just then, Ian ripped into a shrill, fluttering whistle that brought an instant response.

"I'm here!" a strained voice called. "I was just kidding about the bird—" Henry's words fell away as he rounded a clump of bushes and saw the young couple with Ian. "Ian, you okay?" he asked with urgent undertones, moving quicker now.

Ian was about to answer when Spencer Fremont flanked the same bushes and followed in Henry's footsteps as if they'd set out together. Ian raised his hands in exasperation, scanning all the faces before him. "Next time, let's all just get together in a conference call. That might be easier than traipsing through the woods in the dark trying to find each other." He looked at Henry but gestured toward the young couple. "Henry, these young folks are the FBI team I heard Ava talk about. I think we know why they're here. But what about you, Mr. Fremont?"

"Well, I—" Spencer began but was cut off by one of the agents now square on Ian.

"Ava who?" the young man asked pointedly.

Ian wondered if it was wise to answer that. Well, maybe partly. "Spiky hairdo, feisty as all get out, and too old to be carrying on like she does. Know her?"

After a moment, a broad grin erupted on the young man's face. "You're Ian O'Brien!"

This is like a foreign movie, Ian thought. You think you know what's happening, but not really. "How'd you figure that out?" he asked the man.

"Never mind," the agent answered. "We've got more serious issues here." He glanced toward the university campus. "And we need to get out of here. There's a guard detail due to head this way pretty soon."

"You can come to my house," came a voice from behind the agents.

All five heads jerked toward the sound as Tally Greyson stepped through the trees. "I wish you could see how silly this looks." She approached slowly, her arms folded in front of her. Ian was struck by how unmovable her face seemed, like granite in the moonlight. "At least get off the streets and out of the woods, and find a place to figure out what you're going to do about this."

The two FBI agents rounded on Tally. "Just what are you referring to, and what is your connection here?"

"Oh, for Pete's sake," Tally groaned. "Can we just call it like it is? Obviously, there's something weird going on at Vandoren's place that's got the FBI and these nice old men poking around where they don't belong. We're each worried about it for different reasons, it seems. So come on with me and let's try to figure it out. My mom's spending the night with her shrink-medium at the camp." Tally turned and waved them all to follow her, then stopped.

"By the way, you don't want to be anywhere near my mom tomorrow night."

Chapter 25

*I*van took the call on the stern deck of the yacht, where his assistants had just lifted him from his wheelchair into a chaise lounge. The grip of his right hand had grown so weak, it was of little use to him now. The phone rested in his left hand and his head against the reclined cushion. "Where are you?" he asked of the caller.

"Inbound. I should land about noon Berlin time."

"And you are anxious to be done with this."

"After months of tracking her through New York, Charleston, and now Tel Aviv, just waiting for your signal? Yes, I am ready. But I will miss the, uh, stimulation of watching her."

Ivan looked into the blanket of midnight and felt it threaten to suffocate. His breathing had grown more labored in recent weeks despite the ocean forcing its primal steam into his afflicted lungs. He thought of Liesl Bower. Why should she breathe so easily, or at all? Had she not toppled his faithful generals? Sent his prized mole into hiding? Destroyed his long-laid plans to assassinate those who stood in his way of reclaiming Russia?

"But now it is time," Ivan assured his loyal comrade. "Just take the shot when you can. I prefer the concert stage in front of her adoring fans. But if you must, do it sooner." He ended the call with no pleasantries. The assassin Felix Shevcik wasn't a pleasant man. Only necessary.

Ivan tried to relax but the disease wouldn't let him. He attempted to stretch but his muscles yanked him into painful submission, as few things in the life of Ivan Volynski had ever done.

Still clutched in his hand, the phone sounded again. He noted the code name on the screen and hesitated. Maxum Morozov, the elusive mole, once gone to ground, but now surfacing with new vision, yet old wounds that still festered. Ivan hadn't spoken to the man since he'd fled Israel, though Ivan's orders to him had been relayed at regular intervals. He was much too valuable to relinquish into permanent obscurity. His knowledge of the Middle East political minefield alone would serve the new Russia admirably. But there was one problem. His son.

Maxum had been ordered to track his son's movements through the Israeli intelligence field, to siphon what he could from observations, intercepted phone calls and e-mails. Once the brilliant Israeli mole, Maxum was poised like no other to do that job. But his vitriolic relationship with his son had dangled a barb in the midst of the assignment. Ivan couldn't be sure the father's need for vengeance wouldn't override his orders.

"I have been expecting your call," Ivan answered.

"It is good to hear your voice, sir. I trust you are feeling better."

Ivan grimaced. How long before they all knew his condition? He ignored the inquiry. "Are you being careful?" he asked instead.

"Of course."

"And are you yet in Germany?"

"I soon will be."

Ivan had thought it best that Maxum Morozov knew nothing of Felix Shevcik or his plans for Liesl Bower. "Be warned, Maxum, that what you do with your son is not entirely personal. It could affect us all."

"But it won't. And it's best you don't trouble yourself with it. There are far greater things that demand your attention right now."

Ivan dragged as much breath into his lungs as he could, trying to conceal the sound of that effort. He closed his eyes and wandered carelessly into reflection. "Do you know what sarin does to the body, Maxum?"

"Yes. It is the vilest of nerve agents."

"So you know what we are about to unleash on this nation's capital?"

"Yes," Maxum answered. "It will take only seconds for symptoms to appear. Then, the blurred vision, drooling, loss of bodily functions. They will struggle to breathe. Convulsions. Paralysis. And death."

Ivan looked down at his own body. How clever he'd been to prescribe almost exactly the same torture for the House of Noland as Ivan now suffered. The neurological disease known as ALS, or Lou Gehrig's disease, weakened the muscles, slurred the speech, shut down breathing, paralyzed, killed. And now his father's anointed son would know it too, along with as many of the American Congress as would inhale the air one fine morning as they hurried to work with their Starbucks in hand. They wouldn't see it coming, or smell it. No time for the antidotes. No one would know what had stricken them. But Noland would know *who* had done it. Ivan would make sure of that.

And now there was another matter. "Maxum, there is something else I want you to do. Someone else you must find."

"Evgeny Kozlov?"

Ivan was pleased. "For six months, we have failed to track him down. He strikes at us then disappears." He'd already given Felix Shevcik the same orders. Again, there was no reason to dilute the man's efforts with knowledge that he shared the assignment with another.

"Yes. Find him and remove him."

"I understand, sir. And now, I must board my flight."

"I will expect to hear of your successes. And very soon."

When the call ended, Ivan paged for assistance. The damp night air had dropped like plastic sheeting on him. He needed oxygen. He needed the voices to assure him that when the oxygen no longer mattered, he would travel to the other side to join them. And he would do it by his own hand. He touched the bulge at the waistband of his pants, felt the stainless steel barrel that would deliver him when he, not the disease—and certainly not Arkady Glinka—commanded.

Chapter 26

That Monday night in the old Victorian house, its open windows yawning in salty drafts off the bay, Tally drew an improbable web around herself: the intersecting paths of two strange fishermen who'd wandered in off the sea, a couple of FBI agents, and Spencer Fremont, the old man who'd somehow deposited himself at the center of her odd little life. *Little* because there was no place to expand, caught on this spit of land surrounded by wild seas and even wilder people. Tally wondered how many daughters lived with mothers like hers, a woman who preferred the company of those Tally considered half dead. Half in this world, half in some sulfurous afterlife.

"Your mother is staying where?" the young female FBI agent asked as they all grabbed a seat around the kitchen table. Her name was Meg Thomlin. Her partner was Randy Jakes. Their IDs said so.

"With her favorite person in the whole world, Lesandra Bernardo." Tally dragged out each syllable with a flourish. "She takes Mom to visit dead people who've hurt her, then lets her jerk their chains, so to speak. It's supposed to give her some kind of relief. Make her feel like she's gotten in her licks and now she can heal. But she doesn't. She comes back worse than ever. Selfish, dazed, and even further from reality."

All five of Tally's guests stared at her as if trying to formulate something uplifting to say. They felt sorry for her. She could see that plainly, and silently scolded herself for allowing it. "That's enough of that." She wished them to move on. A plane had landed at the university that night. What was on it? "Mr. Fremont, what did you and, uh . . ." She pointed to the younger of the two fishermen.

"I'm Henry Bower, Tally. And this is my friend, Ian O'Brien." Then he said something Tally thought very strange. "I used to be dead. But there is a pathway back. Maybe my friend and I can help your mom find it."

That seemed to take his friend by surprise, too. But soon, everybody hurried back to business. "What did you see tonight, Mr. Fremont?"

"When the plane landed, about six men got out and drove into the campus. No one was there to meet them. And no one came back to the plane. That's all." He looked straight at the two agents. "Now, you want to tell us why you're here, and what you think is going on back there?"

"We have reason to believe someone we're looking for might be associated with Vandoren," Agent Jakes said, looking at Mr. O'Brien like he might know who that person was. "I'm afraid we can't give more answer than that. We will, however, have to ask the questions, starting with you, Mr. Fremont. What have you observed about Vandoren and his university that sent you into those woods tonight?"

For the next few minutes, Mr. Fremont described his part-time job there and the crate he and Tally had seen off-loaded from a plane three nights ago. He told them about seeing Vandoren in the warehouse and the armed men guarding the crate. Mr. Spencer assumed it was more rare art, he said, the kind Vandoren liked to collect.

"Yet, you still went to see about the plane," Agent Thomlin stated as if cross-examining a witness.

"Just a hunch," Mr. Fremont allowed.

Agent Thomlin turned to the two fishermen. "And you went, too. Why?"

Mr. O'Brien stroked his beard, then answered. "Maybe we should talk privately." The agents considered the old man carefully, then both nodded agreement.

Agent Jakes asked Mr. Fremont, "Sir, can you get inside that warehouse tomorrow morning?"

"I can't leave the store until afternoon. But we're closing early to prepare for the séance. It's not my day to work at the university, but I'll think of some excuse to go. Maybe five o'clock?"

Agent Jakes frowned. "No sooner?" Mr. Fremont shook his head. "Okay. We'll wait for your report before Agent Thomlin and I proceed."

"Proceed at what?" Tally asked. "Are you going to raid the place? What do you think is in that crate anyway?"

The agents now turned their attention on Tally, deflecting her questions. "You never told us why you were watching the airstrip with Mr. Fremont last Friday night."

"He followed me there," she corrected, then looked around the table. "Mom takes classes there. I heard her tell somebody once that she sensed an evil presence in that place. I could tell how much it frightened her. So I went looking for it."

They all stared at her for an awkward moment, but it was Ian O'Brien who reached across the table and picked up her hand, cushioning it inside his gentle grip and smiling at her with something that made her grow still and quiet. "Tally, none of us are equipped to battle evil all by ourselves. You give that job to God and ask him to protect you and your mom. I'm going to talk to him about that and I know he'll see to it."

Tally felt as if everyone else in the room had disappeared but this old man. Then she recalled her prayer in her room with all the windows open wide and the wind rushing through like brooms trying to sweep away her mother's madness. She'd asked God to help her. Had he sent this old man? She gazed at the sun-worn face before her, at the gray and tangled beard, but in the eyes she saw hope.

The others began to stir, and Ian released her. She slid a self-conscious glance around the table, but found oddly consoling eyes upon her. Who were all these people? How did they wind up in her life?

Shortly before midnight, the group left Tally alone, only after Agent Thomlin's offer to stay with her was rejected, though politely. "I'll meet you behind the old stables on the north edge of the commons at dark tomorrow night," Tally told them. "And ignore that mass spectacle every-one's been pumping up. That's tourist stuff. I'll take you to see Vandoren's private show."

As soon as Ian and Henry left the house, the agents took them aside. "Mr. O'Brien," Agent Jakes began, "you and Mr. Bower obviously know things you shouldn't, or you wouldn't be here. I don't know how you acquired that information, but I think it's best that you tell me what you know about this situation and exactly why you're here."

Ian nodded. "That's a real efficient way to begin, son. So I'll do the same and tell you right up front that we're tired of this man's daughter being shot at." He cocked his head toward Henry. "When she married my grandson, that made her my daughter, too. As for what we know—that you don't think we should—don't think for a second that Agent Ava Mullins slipped any classified information to me. I just overheard a phone conversation in her home when she didn't know I was around, then found a note on her desk."

"And just what did you overhear and read, sir?" Agent Thomlin asked.

Ian saw no reason to continue this evasive nonsense. They were the FBI team Ava had sent. They already knew more than he and Henry. It was time to pool resources and get on with it. "That Ivan Volynski might still be alive. That he was spotted down here a couple years ago and might be connected to Vandoren. We also know there's an uproar over some kind of weapon that the president knows about. And now we know that Vandoren's got some mysterious crate in his warehouse. I'm standing here looking at you two well-scrubbed young folks and my rickety old friend here and wondering when someone's going to send in the troops."

"Now hold on, Mr. O'Brien," Agent Thomlin cautioned. "First of all, you don't charge into something you know nothing about. We're here to investigate, that's all. If Volynski's anywhere near, we want to keep him happy about that and not scare him off before we can apprehend him. As for the crate, it might be a real pretty vase like Mr. Fremont suggests.

We'll wait for his report tomorrow night, then let our Miami bureau tell us what to do."

She was right, Ian had to admit. But he glanced at Henry and read a completely different reaction. The warrior-father's eyes bore down on the agents, and the man of few words found some. "If sending a fragile old man in there to poke around—after he gets off work—is your idea of uncovering a monster like Volynski, you go ahead. I've got something else to do."

"I should remind you, Mr. Bower," Agent Jakes said, "that interfering with the duties of federal agents can get you into trouble."

"Old Mr. Fremont is no federal anything," Henry countered, "and I don't see the two of you doing much to help him. He looked at the ground and drew a weary breath. "Look, I'm sorry. I don't mean to be a jerk. I just want to expedite this thing. Let me go in there tomorrow morning, just a curious newcomer interested in classes. I've got a few reconnaissance skills."

Ian almost sputtered confirmation of that, but caught himself in time. It wouldn't do for the FBI to start digging into the exhumed life of Henry Bower, whom the Mexican government had declared dead, even buried. Or trace his former life on the underside of polite society, where he honed the skills he later used to watch over his daughter. So Ian said nothing, only nodded agreement with Henry, all the while wondering what percolated in that hard and scarred head.

The agents seemed to appraise Henry with fresh eyes. "Sir," Agent Jakes said after a few moments, "We need to report all this to our bureau tonight. Perhaps you should return to your boat. We'll talk about this in the morning." He raised a cautioning hand. "I can't emphasize enough to you, Mr. Bower, that you are to do nothing further until we talk again."

"He's right, Henry," Ian quickly agreed. "We're both bone tired and not much good for anything else tonight." He paused before one last query for the agents, running a few fingers through his beard. "Say, uh, I guess that report will make its way back to Ava, right?"

"I'm sure it will, sir," Agent Thomlin answered, the faintest glint of amusement on her face.

"Right away?"

"Tonight, sir. We're working tandem with the CIA on this."

Ian sighed. "I don't suppose you could skip the part about us being here."

"Not a chance," the agent said flatly.

"Okay then," Ian drawled absently while raking through the likely consequences of Ava's anger with him. Then he thought of something else. "But tell her I found a bike that doesn't hurt. She'll understand."

Chapter 27

*W*hen the plane landed in Berlin that Tuesday morning, Max led Liesl, Cade, Erica, Ben, and Anna through the airport to baggage claim, where the German extension of Israeli and American security waited for them. Though danger to certain members of the traveling party was merely potential—Ivan Volynski's survival was still unsubstantiated and Max's father had only been glimpsed by Evgeny Kozlov—the Mossad was taking no chances with the lives of two of its agents, one of them still recovering from attempted assassination. Nor was the American government willing to let Liesl Bower and her new husband dangle out there where too many uncertainties could galvanize quickly into real-time danger.

Two black Suburbans pulled up at the curb nearest baggage claim and loaded everyone and their luggage, including the guards. "Everyone comfy?" Max chirped inside the lead car, buckling himself in and slipping an arm around Erica's shoulders. Liesl watched her discreetly, pleased with the apparent affection she displayed for Max.

Satisfied with his companions' affirmative responses, Max added, "Good, because we've got two jam-packed days ahead in this amazing city." He gazed admiringly at the passing sights. "Erica, you'll probably wear that camera out on this trip."

"I plan to," she said, patting the canvas bag at her side. "But tell me something. Are you sure your friend doesn't mind six people crashing in his apartment while he's away?"

Liesl watched something almost subliminal pass between Max and Ben. She knew what it was. Max had confided to her the true nature of their accommodations for the next two days. It was a German safe house near the Brandenburg Gate.

They soon passed beside the colossal arch through which Hitler once goose-stepped his proud military, where the Communists later walled off half of Berlin, and where President Ronald Reagan immortalized his demand of Soviet General Secretary Mikhail Gorbachev to tear down the wall. Just two years later, the Russian leader did just that. To celebrate the historic fall of the wall, Leonard Bernstein conducted an international orchestra and chorus performing Beethoven's Ninth Symphony on site at the Brandenburg Gate. In the famous *Ode to Joy* chorus of the performance, the word *joy* was replaced with *freedom*. That particular footnote to musical history had always captivated Max, just as this city had. But Liesl knew that the focal point of its allure for her friend was coming up ahead, down the Ebertstrasse to a place of both shame and honor—the Holocaust Museum, dedicated in 2005 and officially known as the Memorial to the Murdered Jews of Europe. She hadn't even bothered to describe it to Cade. He would have to absorb its visceral impact as she had—alone, without words. She had been there twice during concert tours, but never with Max. She wasn't prepared for what was coming when they returned to the site that afternoon. For now, they would pass by the memorial on the way to the apartment.

Since leaving the airport, Max, whose solo concert tours had brought him here many times, had entertained them with colorful snippets about the landmarks along the way. Liesl heard the sizzle of his eagerness to show this favored city to those who hadn't been there—Erica, Cade, Ben, and Anna. But as the driver approached a break in the buildings, Max fell silent at first sight of the memorial. That open space in the midst of downtown Berlin was over four acres of plain coffin-like concrete slabs, unmarked symbols of the millions killed in the Nazi carnage.

"We'll come back here later today." He smiled and said nothing more until they rounded a corner south of the memorial and headed toward Friedrichstrasse, a major thoroughfare through the city. A couple of blocks short of it, the driver pulled into an alley and stopped before a closed garage. He entered a code into his phone and the door opened.

Everyone dispensed into an express elevator that took them to the top of the ten-story building and opened onto a small vestibule with only two doors fronting on it. One to an emergency stairwell, the other to the penthouse apartment they now entered. Liesl wondered at the luxury of this safe house. Over the past two years, she'd been ensconced in two different ones, a farmhouse well beyond the Washington Beltway and a New York high-rise. When would it ever be safe to just go home?

She looked over the fine furnishings and rugs, the spacious rooms, but noted how unusually small the windows were, each one covered with blinds. She turned to Ben, who nodded approval. "This will do what we want it to."

"And what is that?" Anna asked, running a hand over a velvet settee. But her expression seemed to hold the answer. Surely Ben had told Anna where they were, as Liesl had told Cade. Only Erica remained. Why should it be such a secret from her that they were staying in an official protective nest? But that was Max's business, to tell her or not.

An hour later, they'd unpacked, helped themselves to a generously stocked refrigerator, and plotted their tour that day. As requested by those who guarded them, the six-pack group was split into two and four. Ben and Anna volunteered to sightsee on their own, since that would include a visit to one of Anna's elderly uncles, who'd recently moved from Israel back to his native Germany.

As they parted ways, Erica took a call and excused herself from the remaining foursome. That gave Max time to explain his reluctance to trouble Erica with knowledge that she was staying in a safe house. He explained to Liesl and Cade that she was already unnerved by the constant presence of the guards. "She's a timid soul who likes her privacy," he maintained. "Like me, I guess. Maybe that's why we get along so well."

Erica rejoined them and they left on foot, heading south to "what every American male is first drawn to in Berlin," Max said. "Checkpoint Charlie." Cade had to agree.

But when they arrived at the notorious gateway through the Berlin Wall, where American and Soviet tanks once squared off during the Cold War, they were affronted by the carnival antics of those assigned to portray American soldiers manning the small checkpoint booth. Yes, it was a replica, and Allied control over the site had long expired. But brave people had died here trying to escape Communist East Berlin.

"Those guys don't understand," Cade said, observing three young men in mock-up U.S. Army uniforms. "They're too young to remember or relate to what happened here."

"And too utterly stupid," Max growled. "Look at them clowning with their fake guns and senseless grins. Like Auschwitz guards at a mass burial, only their guns were real . . . and still smoking. These idiots don't know there was often little difference between Nazis and Soviets. They were both—"

Liesl reached over and gripped Max's arm then patted it gently, aborting his tirade. He turned to face her and Cade. "I'm sorry." He looked back at the little booth and the careless actors. "I didn't exist when this place was real. But the things that happened here could have been yesterday. Maybe even today." He shot a knowing glance at Liesl, and she understood it clearly. The two of them had battled a Soviet-brand evil and neither one was certain it had vaporized in a helicopter over the East River.

When Max turned back to Erica, she was studying him closely, silently. Liesl watched her look away when Max drew near her. Perhaps Erica also was too young, too untouched by a dangerous world to appreciate the things that tugged so hard against Max Morozov, the son.

Chapter 28

Tuesday's dawn was a couple of hours away when Henry slid from the stern of *Exodus II* into the water. *Like I said,* he silently reminded the young FBI agents, who most certainly still slumbered, *I'm not waiting for that old store clerk to get off work.*

Stroking silently toward the distant shore, he didn't fear anything beneath him, though he packed a knife and revolver in a waterproof pouch strapped around his waist. There were also wire snips he'd helped himself to from an open shed by the marina store.

In the dark, he couldn't see the red tile roof of Vandoren's house, but he'd taken his bearings the day before, as soon as the dockmaster had pointed the place out to him. Now, he glided through the calm, colorless waters, remembering the nights he would swim the tidal creek behind the cabin in Charleston, fearless of what creatures had roamed in from the sea and might overtake him. Usually on those nights, he was too numbed by drink and hopelessness to care. Tonight though, all his senses flared on high alert.

When he drew close to shore, he crouched in shallow water and waited. No movement, no sound. He wished the moon to make an appearance and light his surroundings. He thought of Ian and smirked. The old man would probably just pray for moonlight and his god would provide. But seconds later, the moon did appear and Henry's head jerked toward the heavens. *Coincidence.*

Still, he could now see that the house was two stories with a main level terrace and a smaller upstairs balcony. The broad leaves of banana trees swept back and forth in the breeze, blocking Henry's view of the home's interiors. He would have to move closer, at a different angle.

Cautiously emerging from the water, he adjusted the pack at his waist and hurried into the dense foliage surrounding the house, hoping not to trip any alarms along the way. The undergrowth rustled with his approach and he stopped every few feet to listen, alert for anyone who might have already detected his steady advance on the house. But still nothing. No wires, no spotlights, and evidently no motion detectors. This was a confident man who lived well and fearlessly in his hidden world, Henry mused. *Not so hidden anymore.*

Within fifteen feet of the back terrace, he hunkered low to observe. Only one light shone in the house, a floor lamp that cast a soft glow over what Henry guessed to be the living room. Though dimly lit, Henry saw large paintings in bold colors on the walls. A glassy pyramid rose from a tall pedestal near a sofa. But no sign of life. Henry noticed a couple of open windows and the slightest stirring of movement in the house. He waited and listened. Moments later, a noise like a wind chime, like crystal shattering, rang out inside the house. The ring tone of a phone. A man's voice answered immediately.

"Is it ready?" the voice asked. And that was all. A moment later, a figure crossed the lit room and another light came on, this one revealing an adjacent kitchen. Henry hovered motionless and watched. It had to be Vandoren. If he'd waited for better information from the FBI or that store clerk, he might now positively identify the man. But he hadn't been willing to wait any longer.

The size of him surprised Henry, who envisioned him a small wizard like the legendary Merlin of Arthurian tales. But this man filled the window with his unfit bulk, his silver hair curled against the back of his neck. He wore a blousy white shirt and Henry caught the glint of gold on his fingers and around one beefy wrist. The light in the kitchen went out but

Henry didn't move. Seconds later, he heard a door open and close, the scuff of shoes along pavement, the sound receding. Henry waited a few seconds more before daring to follow, catching no sense of anyone else around him.

He'd worn a lightweight black diving suit and fins, now shedding the latter at the shoreline. His feet padded noiselessly in dive shoes thin enough to feel the scrabble of shells and natural debris along a flagstone path, its wandering traced by low Malibu lights. For all the years, nothing had diminished his hearing. Just ahead, he detected the rhythmic, deep-sinus breathing of a body exerting itself, syncopated with the heavy footfall. It sounded like the dragging of sandaled feet, surely Vandoren's. At one point, though, the dragging and breathing halted in one spot and Henry had to draw up short before tumbling upon the man. Soon, though, the pursuit resumed.

Henry was led through a wild subtropic tangle to emerge into a dangerously open yard lit by a spotlight at the back corner of the university. While the man wasted no time clearing the open yard, Henry had to hug the rim of it, stepping carefully through a buffer of Norfolk Island pines that ran along the shore.

When the figure disappeared around the corner, Henry had no choice but to follow. He'd have to tuck his head and run, the thought of praying no one would see him only a passing notion. He'd never found such things to work. Never really tried. Why now? Then again, why not now? Was Liesl not worth the effort?

Before sprinting from cover, he formed a semblance of a prayer. *If you're really there, please get me where I need to go without anyone seeing. Then show me what's going on here, for Liesl's sake.* He didn't wait another second before plunging into the arc of the spotlight and crouch-running to the building where he paused and peered around the corner. Even before he got there, he could hear voices in that direction. Now, he saw an open warehouse door and a tractor-trailer rig backed inside, its driver still at the wheel. But the trailer was too far inside to see what cargo was being loaded or unloaded. The blousy figure Henry had followed from the house now entered the warehouse through a small, adjacent door and closed it behind him. The level of voices inside the warehouse rose at that point. Someone shouted, "Where's the hydraulic?"

Several voices responded at once, then the one voice came again. "Well get it! The three of you are not going to lift that thing without it. Are you crazy?" A pause. "No. The sooner we ship it, the better. I never wanted it here. I didn't have a choice."

What is it? But Henry knew he could go no farther without being seen. He scanned the back of the building for an entrance but saw none. No, this was the best vantage point for now. He would wait and watch. But no sooner had he retrained his sights on the truck than he heard other voices, from the opposite corner of the building. Growing louder, at least two people speaking Spanish. The guards making their rounds, Henry guessed. He had nowhere to go. There was no time to retrace his flight across the open yard, and if he did, would they shoot? The warehouse and its populace were in one direction, and the voices continued to rise in the other. They were bantering with each other, both speaking at once, unsuspecting of an intruder lurking around the next corner.

He did the only thing left to do, one more time. Without taking his eyes from the path of the approaching voices, he prayed, *God, please help me.* That was all.

Flattened against the building, his hand firmly on the gun at his waist, he waited for the inevitable. And there came the first man rounding the corner, his image full in the spotlight on that side. But as he cleared the building, instead of looking down the length of it toward Henry, he suddenly rounded on his companion behind him, yet unseen by Henry. There was a dispute unfolding, the first man's arms now flailing in the direction of the other man. And then, as quickly as they'd arrived, they were gone, retreating the way they'd come, still disputing something of apparent significance. Had one accused the other of not adequately checking a locked entrance? It didn't matter. Henry was already fleeing the spotlight, headed for the cover of the trees with no small jolt surging inside him. He should have been in the guy's gunsight by now. All he had to do was turn Henry's way. What stopped him?

Henry remembered the prayer. *Couldn't be.* But he'd think on that later.

He had to scout a safer vantage point, and then he saw it. Straight ahead, a small tributary off the bay ran close to the opposite end of the warehouse. Henry was going swimming again. Still inside the tree line, he reached the deep-cut waterway prepared to slip into the water when he realized there was a wide sloping bank on each side. On the side nearest the building, the bank seemed to have caved in at one point, leaving a narrow, muddy ledge just below ground level. Crawling through the black mud, it didn't take him long to reach a point about thirty yards or less from the front of the truck, where the driver seemed to be awaiting orders.

His head barely above the bank, Henry could see between one side of the truck and the frame of the doorway as a great deal of back-and-forth scurrying took place inside. To his amazement, they were all dressed in white coveralls, some with headgear, some without. And then he knew. They were hazardous-material suits.

Just then, one of the white suits emerged from the warehouse and approached the cab of the truck. A very large white suit, the headgear now pulled away to reveal long gray hair curling about the neck of the man Henry had followed.

"Curt!" someone called from inside, and the man hurried back to the warehouse.

There was no doubt now. It was Curt Vandoren, and he was either receiving or shipping something that probably had nothing to do with talking to ghosts or adding a new vase to his living room.

What have you got in there, big man? Henry watched Vandoren return to the truck cab. Henry couldn't hear his orders, but when he'd finished giving them, he slapped the side of the door and the truck cranked to life. As Vandoren stepped aside, a loud clang was heard at the back of the truck. No doubt the doors closing. And then the massive vehicle began to move. Henry ducked as it headed straight for him, headlights blazing, then turned wide toward the exit drive. When the back of it cleared the building, there wasn't enough light for Henry to see the license plate, and there were no other markings on the truck. But he could see clearly inside the warehouse now, though it appeared to be empty, at least from that angle. The wide floor was clear and only a wall of small, stacked cardboard boxes was visible.

But Curt Vandoren was front and center, and moving Henry's way. He lifted one hand to an ear as he stopped just short of the bank to which Henry clung, his muscles tight and threatening to cramp at any moment.

"It's on its way," Vandoren said into his phone. "They'd better be ready for it, because it's not coming back here." Pause. "Yes, it's still sealed tight and sitting level. No accidents. What's that?" Pause. "Our man's riding in the cab. He'll stay with it all the way." A long pause, then Henry heard the name clearly.

"Ivan, stop worrying. This end's clear. But listen to me. Don't ever ask me to do something like this again. I won't take this kind of risk."

It was all Henry could do to keep from grabbing the man and pulling him into the muck, pounding his soft, wretched body until he spilled all that he knew.

Where is Ivan? Who has he sent after my child? And what's in that truck?

Henry seethed without sound, without movement until the man ended the call and returned to the warehouse. Another vehicle approached, a van now pulling up to face the open doorway. A man got out and went inside. Henry finally allowed himself a stretch and a new position, just in time. The van driver reappeared with his arms full of hazmat suits, stacked and wrapped in individual clear bags, evidently unused. The man tossed them into the back of the van, leaving the door open, then retrieved another load. Four suits? Five? But soon to be one less.

The voices retreated and the warehouse grew still. It was now or not at all. Henry scrambled over the top of the bank and first crawled then sprinted toward the van, grabbed one of the bags, a pair of work gloves, and a piece of paper lying nearby, then raced back to the ditch. He dropped onto the muddy shelf and resumed his watch. But still, no one there. He waited another ten minutes. No one. It was time to go.

He reached the bay in no time, but didn't dare to return for the swim fins he'd left in the brush behind Vandoren's house. Besides, he couldn't swim the bay with the evidence he'd confiscated. So he set off running along the shore, in and out of finger inlets and eddies, tripping over drift-wood and sinking into washouts. The black veil over the eastern horizon began to lift. It would soon be light enough for anyone to see him thrashing along the wild shoreline toward the marina, muddied, frantic, and carrying a most unusual package.

Henry navigated the entire shoreline of the small bay, finally reaching the marina with the first rays of morning . . . and the arrival of a white Jeep just pulling into the parking lot. He immediately recognized the two people that climbed from the front seats and turned to stare at him.

As Henry hurried toward them, he noticed Agent Jakes's right hand move slowly inside his windbreaker. *Leave the gun alone*, Henry silently ordered. "It's me," he called in a hushed voice, then cast his first look back toward Vandoren's house. It was possible for someone there with a pair of binoculars to clearly see what Henry carried. Had he been spotted?

"Henry?" Agent Jakes responded, both hands now planted on his hips.

But Henry didn't answer. By the time he reached them, both agents were slack-jawed at what dangled from his now gloved hand. He dropped the thick, clear-plastic bag containing one hazmat suit onto the dock, then pulled off the gloves and the diving suit, leaving them alongside the bag, which the agents now bent to visually inspect.

"Henry, what have you done?" Agent Jakes asked.

"What I had to. You got a plastic bag in your car?"

"Yeah."

"Put this evidence inside it and keep it in your car. We'll talk there."

It didn't take long to tell the tale of his night's sojourn. When he finished, the agents seemed too excited over the suit to fret about how it was obtained. They didn't even bother to chastise or warn Henry again.

"It looks like it hasn't been worn," Agent Thomlin said. "We'll send it to the lab in Miami for testing." She frowned. "But it might come back clean."

"So you'd better pack something else I found near that van along with the suit," Henry said, pulling a single, folded sheet of orange paper from the pouch at his waist. "This ought to trip a few alarms." He held up the sheet and read, "'Emergency Treatment for Exposure to SARIN.'"

Chapter 29

*T*hey didn't stay long at Checkpoint Charlie. The sun was dropping and the place Max had promised to take them to was a long walk from there, though closer to their apartment.

By the time they arrived at the Holocaust Memorial, the sea of concrete boxes was already etched in deep shadows. As the architect intended, the ground beneath the cement stelae undulated, causing the visitor unsteady steps. The vast maze of symbolic coffins was designed to disorient those who navigated through it.

Max turned to his companions. "Ben and Anna will arrive later, as their guards intended." He grimaced. "I'm afraid we're at the mercies of those who only wish to help us, by separating us." He glanced up at the surrounding buildings that overlooked the chilling acreage. "Better be on our way."

Liesl watched as Cade followed Max's line of sight to all the windows overlooking their little party. "It's okay," Liesl told him, slipping her arm around him and resting her head against his shoulder. The feel of him, the scent of him remained intoxicating to her. She wondered if she'd ever loved this much before.

Cade looked down at her upturned face. "But let's take no chances." He glanced around them and urged her along. The four entered the memorial and soon found themselves at odds with the intersecting paths that offered no direction, only choices. During the Holocaust, choices led to survival or death. Flee at the first sign of Nazi domination or remain with hope that the plague would soon pass.

From a shop across the street from the memorial, Felix Shevcik delighted at the sight of Liesl Bower, but not at her entourage. He recalled all the times he'd found her alone in Charleston. *Ivan was a fool to wait.* Felix wouldn't wait for the concert if he could get a bead on her earlier.

He watched the foursome turn into the labyrinth of concrete slabs, groaning over the unpredictable turns his prey would now take. He must be patient. And vigilante. His was the luxury of anonymity, unlike the man just now appearing in Felix's sights.

Is that who I think it is? Felix almost pressed his square face to the glass of the storefront for a clearer look. *It is. What good fortune. Liesl Bower and Evgeny Kozlov in the same afternoon!*

Felix watched the defrocked and fugitive Russian agent trail cautiously behind Liesl. Did she know he was there? Did her bodyguards not see him? Would they know him if they did? It was doubtful. But Felix had once trained under the legendary KGB agent who would most certainly recognize his former student. Felix had changed little since those years, his powerful bulk showing no flab along his low-to-the-ground frame. He was a solid cube.

As tantalizing as a double tap was, though, Kozlov's presence complicated things for Felix. He would have to be careful. To just keep watch for now.

After a meandering hike through the memorial, during which few words were spoken, Max suggested they proceed underground to the information center. A long staircase dropped them into a catacomb museum where those who'd died came vividly to life again.

Liesl and Cade scanned long walls of photographs, home movies, handwritten letters, family documents, biographies, and other texts tracking the methodical extermination of a people. Max and Erica headed in a different direction, but after a while, they came alongside again. "Follow me," Max urged, and led them all into a display room Liesl and Cade hadn't yet seen.

The hallway was darkened down the middle with only spots of light trained on small video screens set into the walls here and there. "This way," Max said.

Near the end of the hallway, he stopped and the three of them gathered around him, their guards close by.

Max pressed a button on the wall and activated a particular video. In seconds, a grainy film began to run. Children squealed loudly as a young woman bearing a large white cake with flaming candles on top entered the room. She set the cake on a low table in the midst of the children and hugged one little girl warmly, saying something to her in a language Liesl recognized as Polish. The whole room full of people burst into song. Some hugged, some danced. Then the video ended.

"The woman with the cake was my great-aunt Bethel," Max said dryly, his eyes fixed on the screen. "She was my mother's aunt who lived in Warsaw, who didn't follow the rest of the family to Russia. Her little girl was six that day." He pointed to the screen. "Aunt Bethel, her husband, and two children died a year later at Auschwitz."

An audible gasp rose from Erica, but she spoke no words. Liesl, too, was taken by surprise, but somehow, the truth of what Max had just told them unfolded naturally in a place of horrors such as this. As Max turned back to the video and ran it once again, Liesl saw that Cade's attention didn't return to the screen, but remained on Max. When the video ended the second time, Cade laid a hand on Max's back and quietly ushered him away.

As they walked from the hall, Max gathered himself together again and offered, "There's controversy among the Germans about this place being here. Many would rather forget what their ancestors did." He smirked. "But wouldn't we all like to forget the sins of our fathers?"

"Every day, Max, Berliners walk through the grounds above us," Cade observed. "For some, it's probably just a shortcut through town. But it's still a reminder of what people, of any nationality, are capable of doing to each other. And could do again."

Abruptly, Erica turned and walked away. Max excused himself and followed her. Liesl saw one of the guards shadow the two of them.

Felix watched Evgeny Kozlov hover about the entrance to the underground museum, blocking access to the target. This wasn't supposed to happen. The guards wouldn't have recognized Felix, allowing him to draw close to Liesl without suspicion. But Kozlov posed a real barrier. He'd know Felix in a second.

What's this? Felix squinted to focus more clearly at the young woman just emerging from the stairway at the entrance. It was young Max's girlfriend, and he was in hot pursuit. Until . . .

What was that? A signal between the two? It couldn't be. Max and Kozlov? What's going on here?

"Erica, wait!" Max called as he caught up with her at the base of the steps. "What's the matter?"

She paused and stepped aside for those coming down the steps, then turned to confront Max. "I don't feel well. It's only a headache. I'd rather go back to the apartment, alone. No guards, if you don't mind." Her voice was firm, almost demanding.

Max was startled. "Are you upset by what I just showed you?"

She hesitated. "A little, but I'm mostly just sick. I'll be fine, though. Go back with the others. Please."

Max looked around. "But it's not safe for you to be out here alone."

"No, it's you and Liesl who need protection, not me. So please don't send anyone after me." She turned and ran up the stairs. Puzzled by what seemed bitter words, Max pursued her.

They had just surfaced to ground level when she turned toward him again. "Please, Max!" The voice was angry now. "Just let me go back. I'll be okay. The guards know who I am. They'll let me in the apartment." She managed an apologetic smile and hurried away. It was then Max spotted Evgeny Kozlov nearby, signaling his intention to follow her. Sending Evgeny after an already distraught young woman was the last thing Max wanted. He met the Russian's questioning eye and held up one hand in a stand-down gesture. Max was fairly surprised to see Evgeny nod and retreat slowly into the shadows again. But then, it wasn't Erica he'd come to protect.

Max, too, retreated, letting her go and hoping she remembered the way back, certain she'd call if she didn't. He blamed himself. He hadn't realized the depth of her sensitivities to his kind of world.

Pure instinct hurled Felix headlong into rush-hour pedestrian traffic along the sidewalk, heading east after the girl. It was the same instinct he'd relied on for too many years to question it now. No, she wasn't the target, but he'd find Liesl Bower again soon. The itinerary of a celebrity wasn't hard to follow. He found himself struggling, though, to catch up with the girl who'd just shifted into turbo walk, head down, sure of where she was going and wasting not a moment getting there.

A few blocks before the apartment they called a safe house, which Felix found laughable for the ease with which he'd found it, the girl ducked into a small, leafy park. He paused at the entrance to it and watched her exit onto a sidewalk a half block away. Racing to the corner she'd just turned, he suddenly lurched to a halt. At the curb just ahead of him, she'd stopped at a small navy-blue sedan. She now flung open the passenger door and crawled inside. The door closed and Felix knew he had no means to follow, but the car didn't move.

From the back of it, Felix could only see the dark profile of a man turned to face the girl. As Felix hung back behind shrubbery at the edge of the park, he watched the two in the car talk, their attention often drifting to those who passed by them. Moments later, the girl got out and resumed her hurried pace along the sidewalk. But not before Felix saw her slip something inside the bag slung over her shoulder. It appeared to be a packet of some sort.

Desperate to identify the driver, Felix was about to risk stepping into the open when, during a lull in the traffic, the car pulled from the curb, did an immediate U-turn, and headed Felix's way, the driver's side now facing him. Even partially hidden behind leafy branches, he had no trouble recognizing the man at the wheel.

Maxum Morozov!

Chapter 30

Travis Noland had barely launched Tuesday's seamless agenda when his secretary appeared at the open door, a large envelope in her hand. The president only glanced her way, then back at the documents awaiting his signature. When he didn't hear anything from her, he looked back. "Rona?"

Only when she raised the envelope for his attention did the chill set in. She approached his desk and laid the envelope squarely before him. A diplomatic pouch from the Russian Embassy. There was no need to feign indifference with Rona Arant. She'd served too long beside him in the trenches, including this one. "I'll be at my desk, sir." She hesitated only a moment for a response, which didn't come. "I'll hold your calls," she added, then left, closing the door behind her.

He stared down at the envelope marked like the other one: *Of personal interest to the President of the United States.* The same handwriting, same elegant stationery. Drawing a long, stabilizing breath, he broke the seal and withdrew one folded page, its edges sharp as he opened it and read:

> *It will come like a terrible swift sword,*
> *trampling out your vintage. Your temple.*
> *Hallelujah to the other son, so ingloriously born.*
> *His truth marches on.*

The president read it once more then laid it calmly on his desk and rose. Moving to the window behind him, he looked toward the Capitol, though he couldn't see the sun-washed dome, the majestic mount. The *temple!*

How many presidents before had declared war? How many fought an enemy they couldn't find? Travis Noland pounded a fist into his open palm. *But God willing, we will!*

The president returned to his desk and grabbed the phone. "Rona, get Salabane and Bragg in here immediately. And tell them to—"

"Sir, Director Salabane just arrived. He's waiting to see you."

"Send him in. But I need Bragg, too."

FBI Director Rick Salabane wasted no time reaching the president. Closing the door firmly behind him, he approached Noland, now seated at the desk. "Sir, we have just received reliable intelligence regarding Ivan Volynski."

The president couldn't mask his surprise, but rebounded quickly. "Go ahead, Rick."

For the next few minutes, the director related the reconnaissance efforts of Henry Bower and the name of the person he'd overheard Vandoren address by phone. *Ivan.*

The president felt strangely relieved for even scant confirmation related to the cryptic messages he'd already received. He chose to withhold news of the most recent one until Salabane was finished.

"Our agents have sent the hazmat suit to Miami for testing, and we're tracking surveillance cameras for a tractor-trailer rig leaving the vicinity about five this morning. Only problem is, Anhinga Bay doesn't have a camera. We're having to estimate departure time, speed, and direction—north or south, no other way to head from there—and try to catch up with the rig at the next available camera. But we've got no license number and not much of a description. We do have every weigh station in and outside of the Keys ordered to inspect every rig."

"You believe it's a bomb?"

"Our agents down there sure do, sir."

"What's happening with Vandoren?"

Salabane shook his head. "It's best we just hover and watch him right now. I know that's hard, but we can't afford to send in the troops and run him off. He's our pathway to Ivan, who could be anywhere on the planet with his finger on the trigger. No, for now we just watch Vandoren. He'll make a move soon, I'm sure."

The president squinted at a spot on the ceiling, then at Salabane. "And Henry Bower got close enough to hear him call Ivan's name," he repeated.

"That's right, sir. It seems Bower exhibited more initiative than our agents." Noland heard the irritation.

"But Liesl's not theirs," Noland reminded him, then stood up. "Regarding that, I want her and Max Morozov on immediate lockdown, wherever they are. They'll scream and kick, but do it. Tell them it's only temporary."

The president pulled the envelope he'd received that morning from his drawer. "Now, there's something you need to see." The president handed over the single page of . . . what? Rambling verse? The babble of a fool? No. Travis Noland knew exactly what it was. His phantom brother's declaration of war.

Chapter 31

After watching Erica wind her way out of the Holocaust memorial, Max returned to the others still in the museum below ground.

"Is she all right?" Liesl asked when he approached.

"Oh, sure. She's not feeling well, I guess. All this was too much for her." He noticed Cade looking curiously at him. "Anything wrong?" Max asked him.

"How much does she know about you? What you and Ben do?"

Max shook his head. "Nothing. She thinks all the guards are for us celebrities." He laughed faintly.

"Why do you ask?" Liesl asked her husband, her arm locked through his.

Cade seemed to weigh his words, then opt for a simple. "Just curious."

Max was about to press him on that when one of the guards clamped a firm hand on his shoulder and urged him aside.

"Sir, we have to leave now. I just got orders to move you and Miss Bower to cover immediately."

"What's going on?" Max demanded with alarm.

"I'm not at liberty to say right now, sir. Just come with us. There's a car waiting."

Max turned to see the other guard speaking with Liesl. He saw the same shock in her face as she turned it toward Cade first, then Max. He motioned for her to comply.

Bypassing the elevator from the museum, the guards ushered them up the stairs and made them wait inside the door until an all-clear signal came from someone outside. The same car and driver that had whisked them from the airport now waited in the street, its engine running, an agent stationed outside the vehicle.

When they arrived at the apartment, Ben and Anna were already there. Erica was not. "Either one of you seen Erica?" Max asked tightly. His annoyance at her behavior had turned to fear for her being out there alone, especially now, though he still didn't know the cause for this dash to safety.

Ben motioned for Max to follow him into his and Anna's bedroom at the end of the hall. "What's going on?" Max asked once they were alone, but his ear was tuned to the front door. Surely she'd return soon.

"It's looking more like a WMD loose in the States, coming out of that little hole in the Keys, they think. They also 'think' they've traced a still-breathing Ivan there." Ben frowned. "Too much half information for my taste, but the feds are all over it now. Ava too. I just got off the phone with her." Ben rubbed his forehead. "You won't believe who uncovered all that."

Max waited, in no mood to entertain a guess.

"Liesl's dad," Ben said straightaway.

"What!" Max reacted too loudly.

Ben hushed him, then added. "And Cade's grandfather."

Seconds later, a knock came at the door, and Max was sure who it was. "You might as well explain it to her," he sighed. "She'll know soon enough."

Ben opened the door to find Liesl standing with her arms folded, her expression ironclad. "This is going to end," she said. "You're both too big for a secret clubhouse. Now tell me what's happening?"

Ben gathered her, Anna, and Cade into the bedroom and closed the door. The guards didn't need to hear it all. Ben and Max unfolded the gist of the last twenty-four hours in the Florida Keys, ending with the surprise intervention of two familiar fishermen.

Liesl and Cade reacted as expected. Drop-mouthed and unbelieving.

"Dad?" Liesl cried. "Ian?" Both hands flew to her face, as if she suddenly had to support her head. "How did they . . . What did they . . ."

Cade stopped her with a steady grip on her arm, then turned squarely on Ben. "Are they hurt?" his tone demanded. Max had not heard that from him before.

"No," Ben said.

"Are they in danger?" Cade asked, still focused hard on Ben.

"Not if they pull out of there and let the FBI do their work."

Cade openly searched Ben's face. After a moment, he said, "They're not going anywhere. I don't know what led them to that particular place, but my guess is they're on a mission to save Liesl. And probably you, too, Max."

Max looked curiously at him. "How do you know that?"

"No one knows my grandfather like I do." He looked deep into Liesl's eyes. "And Henry Bower would leap into hell itself to save his daughter." He looked between Ben and Max. "They're bloodhounds, both of them. And nobody's getting them off the scent."

Liesl moved toward the window and looked out. Max watched her head bow slightly and knew she was praying. He wondered at the change that had come over her, this drawing close to a god whom Max had always considered remote.

A door slammed in the living room.

Max jumped as if jerked from sleep. *Erica!*

"Excuse me," he uttered and left the room, the door open. She was crossing toward the kitchen when he emerged from the hall. She stopped and seemed to cautiously judge his expression, then peered around him, looking surprised at those gathered in the bedroom behind him. He scrambled for an excuse, knowing he couldn't share the recent conversation with her. She would have to know they were on lockdown, though. What would that do to her? Send her packing?

"Erica, there's been a development in this, uh, perceived threat to Liesl's safety, and perhaps mine. I can't share the details with you, and I know this whole security thing has upset you, even sent you running away this afternoon."

She raised a small hand. "No, Max. I told you I just didn't feel well. I even stopped on the way here to buy aspirin." She fished a new bottle from her bag and held it up as if he might require evidence. "Just a headache, though."

Max tried to read her, but couldn't. He wondered if he ever had, accurately. Or only what he'd wanted to read.

"What are you all doing?" she asked directly.

"Discussing what to do next."

"About what?"

Max shook his head. There was no point in soft-footing it. "We have to remain here under guard for a while. Maybe a day or so."

"Why?"

"You deserve to know that, Erica, but I can't tell you."

"There seems to be a lot of things you can't tell me."

He watched her closely, but didn't respond.

"You can't tell me what you do at night when you're not teaching lessons or rehearsing. You can't tell me where you go sometimes on weekends, or why Ben Hafner leaves you texts at odd hours of the night. You can't—"

"Wait a minute." Something sparked inside him. "How would you know that?"

She answered without so much thought. "You showed me a photo he sent from the beach one time, then got up to check on dinner. I shouldn't have, I guess, but I was just scrolling through when I noticed the times of other texts."

Max was dumbfounded. Was the Mossad's new recruit really so stupid as to leave his phone in someone else's hands. But he couldn't remember doing it. When did that happen? But look at her. She's so innocent. Aggravated, but innocent.

"Erica, if you'd like to leave, I'll arrange it. None of this concerns you. I'm so sorry I dragged you into it."

As if something inside her tripped a switch, her mood suddenly and unexpectedly brightened. She moved quickly toward him and wrapped her arms around his neck, then kissed him gently. "I don't want to leave," she purred. "I just want you to be as truthful with me as you can." She kissed him again, this time with unabashed longing.

There was a stirring at the doorway to the back bedroom, and Erica released Max, who found himself slightly teetering. Smiling impishly, she said, "I'll make sandwiches for everyone." But as she turned toward the kitchen, Max caught her hand.

"I'm serious about you going home," he said. "It might be best for your safety."

But she stood her ground. Arching one eyebrow, she asked, "Pastrami or roast beef?"

After a light dinner that night, no one was in the mood for much conversation. Liesl and Cade retired early and shut their bedroom door. Anna and Ben lingered a bit with Max while Erica took a shower.

Max wanted to show Ben the latest photos from the mine site in the Urals, these sent by Mossad to Max's computer that afternoon. He hurried back to the bedroom he shared with one of the guards to retrieve it from under his bed. He reached for the handle of his briefcase, but no handle was there. He'd stored the case flat on the floor with the handle facing out. The case was still there, but reversed, and the handle now faced the wall.

Chapter 32

*I*van wheeled himself onto the forward deck, resisting his crew's efforts to help him. More than anyone else, they knew the rapid acceleration of the disease. One hand now useless, escalating weakness in all the limbs, weight loss. Each day, the tremors, twitching, and drooling grew worse, the breathing more ragged. There was trouble swallowing, occasional choking. Only his German physician administered professional care, sending prescriptions, medical-supply orders, and instructions for Ivan's care to the two stewards who tended his needs. They would make port often enough to restock, though Ivan never went ashore, never appeared on deck until they'd returned to sea.

Since Travis Noland's televised admission of his half brother's terrorist plot to sabotage American infrastructure, energy plants, communications networks, and national landmarks, the media had saturated too many airways and newspapers with Ivan's photograph to risk recognition. Though the world believed he'd perished in flames high over the East River, the world also loved a resurrection story. Might he and Elvis share in that fascination? Would it take just one sighting by an observant dockhand at some remote Caribbean atoll to ignite a hunt for him? Or just a couple of messages sent by diplomatic pouch to the White House? Ivan chuckled to himself at the thought of Noland bearing down on those words, reading them from every angle, dissecting their meaning. It wouldn't be hard. Ivan hadn't wanted him to labor over them. Surely by now, the lord of the Oval Office had grasped the urgency of finding his resurrected kinsman with the *terrible swift sword.*

A V-formation of pelicans off the starboard side caught Ivan's attention. Migrating whites, he guessed, as he watched the two choreographed columns angle away from their leader, who was certain of their destination. Ivan's own troops had once been so trusting, lining up behind him on their way to a glorious touchdown in the new Russia. But now? Did he dare look behind to see if anyone was still there?

He watched the great birds leave him in their wake, alone in a wheelchair, wiping spittle from his chin. He'd once been the point of the V, his wings sturdy and sure. He looked down at the limp and twitching arms and legs. No, no one followed now. He knew that.

He lifted the phone in his hand, swiped and tapped the screen a few times and listened as a series of beeps signaled contact with Russian air space. At ten o'clock that Tuesday morning off the south Florida coast, it was six PM in Moscow. *Glinka has enjoyed his first cognac of the evening,* Ivan mused. *Toasting himself for the victory to come. In less than three months, he will take the election and rule Russia . . . with no intention whatsoever of relinquishing his office to a dying man.* Though Glinka pretended not to know the diagnosis, Ivan was certain he did. That it was incurable and fatal. Ivan also was certain that Glinka wouldn't wait long for the disease to take its natural course.

"Yes, comrade," Arkady Glinka answered. "How are you feeling today?"

But surely your man on board has already reported that. Ivan knew that one of his crew had been persuaded—handsomely, no doubt—to keep Glinka informed of Ivan's condition, because if the roles were reversed, that's exactly what Ivan would do. He just wasn't sure which of his loyals had turned.

"Very well," Ivan lied, then went straight to the point of the call. "The shipment is en route and on schedule."

"Excellent. And Curt?"

"He will join me later tonight. We depart together in a few days. It will be a long journey back to Russia. I trust your campaign is going well." Ivan knew there was little need for Glinka to campaign for the seat he already held, even if interim. He was a skilled politician and had amassed all the support he needed to overwhelm the polls. Ivan's own youth movement had played a critical part in rallying the country in the wake of Gorev's assassination. The secret core of that formidable collegiate force had long been in Ivan's pocket. If anyone believed he was still at the point of the V-formation, it was the heady young subversives drunk on the promise of a Soviet resurrection. Ivan smiled at the thought of them. They would lead the revolution, the trusting flock. Not Glinka. Ivan would see to that.

He already had.

Chapter 33

Spencer Fremont had no choice but to leave his post at the store and hurry straight to the university. He'd never received orders from the FBI before. It felt strange to be intrinsic to national security, if that's what this was. Agents Jakes and Thomlin weren't telling, but two agents had suddenly become six that morning, the reinforcements newly arrived from the Miami bureau.

Spencer had just opened the store and turned on the lights when Jakes and a fellow agent, whose name Spencer didn't catch, entered. Alone in the store, they had explained to Spencer that certain evidence had been gathered during the night and it was imperative that he proceed immediately to the university. He was to check the warehouse and gather as much intelligence as he could regarding the departure of the tractor-trailer rig just before daybreak that morning. All without drawing undue attention from Curt Vandoren, in particular.

With the influx of camp visitors bound for the séance that night, Spencer found a good many of them in the university lobby that morning. Two of Vandoren's front-desk personnel were busy answering questions about classes when Spencer slipped through the crowd and headed down the hallway to the library. He was grateful he'd avoided the usual small talk with one administrative assistant or another, since he'd be compelled to explain why he was here on an unscheduled day. He knew Vandoren didn't care when he worked, though, as long as the work was done.

Once inside the library, Spencer hurried to the window and looked out. The tractor-trailer rig he'd seen on Sunday was, indeed, gone. He hadn't noted anything about its markings or license plate. Now, he hurried back to the hallway and peered toward the lobby. With the convenient distraction of visitors milling about, he went straight to the warehouse and entered his code, already clear on his excuse for being there. Like before, he only wished to restock workbooks to the classrooms.

He opened the door and stopped to listen. There was no one there, and no crate. It didn't take long to give the open space a thorough once-over, finding nothing unusual to report to the anxious agents waiting for him outside the camp gate. He was supposed to meet them there as soon as possible. They were nervous about something, Spencer knew. And it was clear they all didn't agree on sending a civilian to do their investigative work. He'd overheard them discuss it, one of them insisting that the "least resistant path was best." That meant sending someone who belonged there and would raise no suspicions, sound no alarms. Spencer had waited meekly for them to decide his fate. Mild-mannered store clerk to super spy in a single bound. A divine alignment of circumstances had brought him to this point. Just like the clear direction God had given him about his role in tonight's séance. Not the tourist event on the commons, but the one deep in the woods.

He couldn't fret about that now. He had to figure a way to get information about the truck, maybe from the receptionists, though he doubted anyone on staff would know about something as off-radar as Vandoren's late-night activities. Still, he would try to gather whatever he could.

As he headed back to the door, he heard someone enter the code on the other side. He held his breath, prepared to deliver a practiced alibi when Danny Otis pushed open the door and hailed him with a bright, "Hey there, Mr. Fremont!"

The cringe inside Spencer must have traveled to his face. "What's the matter?" Danny asked, his voice still booming.

"You just startled me, Danny. That's all."

"Whatcha doing here?"

As Spencer considered how best to answer that, Danny went to a closet on the other side and pulled out a telescoping pole with an oval brush on the end. He didn't seem to be waiting for an answer, so Spencer kept quiet.

"Those high paddle fans are a bear to clean," Danny said, closing the closet door and returning to Spencer. "But I rigged this old pool-cleaning pole with a loop brush. Pretty smart, huh?"

"Indeed! I'm impressed with the things you know." This was his chance. "By the way, do you know what happened to the truck that was parked out back?"

"Naw. I heard it leave early this morning. Didn't know they were going to ship that big thing out of here. I thought it was going to be something else for me to dust down at the house. Guess not. Don't know where it went."

Spencer was disappointed. "Well, uh, say, who's truck was that anyway? I never saw it around here before."

"Don't know that either. None of my business." He looked a bit sideways at Spencer as if maybe it wasn't his either. "But now Mr. Vandoren, he's my business, you know, since he pays me to keep his house. And now he tells me he's leaving for a while and won't be needing me. Heck of a note, I say. I need that money."

"Where's he going?" Spencer pressed.

"Don't know."

"Leaving by chopper again?"

"Not this time. By boat, after the séance tonight. Friends of his, he says."

Tonight? That was too soon. For what, he wasn't sure, but he worried that news wouldn't sit well with the FBI. "You don't know how long he'll be gone?"

"Nope," Danny said as he steadied the long pole and reached for the door. "Now, I got to get back to work. Unless you need a hand with anything." He looked expectantly at Spencer. "You come in here for something?"

"Oh, uh, yeah. A box of those séance manuals for tonight, but I can get them. We're going to display them in the store for Mr. Vandoren." He thought again about the man leaving by boat. "Uh, Danny, just curious. Where would Mr. Vandoren meet that boat?" *Better give him a good reason for asking.* "I might need to catch up with him after the séance. You know, take him something for his trip." He winced inside at such a weak excuse. But Danny didn't seem to notice.

"The marina," he called over his shoulder as he left, closing the door behind him.

Spencer grabbed a small box of the manuals and closed up the warehouse. Minutes later, he left the university, choosing not to engage anyone else in questioning. He feared he'd pushed the limit with Danny. After the FBI cleared out of Anhinga Bay, Spencer would have to remain. This was his home and Curt Vandoren his employer and neighbor. Spencer didn't know if the man had done anything wrong or not. Maybe the agents were on the wrong trail. Still, he hurried to meet them with his news.

The cabin of *Exodus II* was too crowded for Ian's comfort. Agent Jakes was decent company, but his fellow agent, Jim Stetz, was wound so tight he moved and talked in squeaks, Ian observed to Henry. They'd been camped with the two agents since Spencer Fremont had returned from his mission that morning and reported Vandoren would leave by boat that night.

Besides Jakes and Stetz, Ian had occasionally entertained a few more federal agents who'd wandered into the marina dressed like fishermen with nothing else to do but observe the catch coming in from some of the half-day charters—all the while, watching for Curt Vandoren's ride out of there. It would be after the séance, Spencer Fremont had reported, but the agents couldn't be sure Vandoren wouldn't slip out sooner.

"And you're sure he's going to meet Volynski?" Ian asked those assembled in his boat's cabin.

Agent Stetz sprang at him. "Mr. O'Brien, I must ask you to refrain from speaking that name too loosely or loudly. These windows are open and nobody else on these docks needs to know our business."

Ian studied him calmly. "Well, that's a reasonable request. Now, I've got one for you. Finish that tuna sandwich I made for you and down some of those Twinkies. They'll sweeten you up a bit." He smiled kindly at the middle-aged man and turned to wipe down the galley counter.

A few moments later, Agent Jakes was at his side. "You're right, Mr. O'Brien," he said in a hushed voice. "We suspect Volynski is in the Keys somewhere, and that Vandoren might be meeting him tonight. If that bomb is on its way, we think the two of them will be, as well."

Ian nodded, thinking ahead. "So you'll need to plant a GPS tracker on his boat, won't you?"

Agent Jakes looked pleasantly surprised. "That's exactly right, Mr. O'Brien."

"But how will you know which boat it is? By the time you watch him board, it'll be too late."

"That's why we're here, sir. To watch for the most likely vessel."

Ian shook his head. "Wrong. It'll be the *unlikely* one."

"How do you mean?"

"Well, by *likely*, you probably mean something high-end like Vandoren's house and that fancy university with its own airstrip, right?"

Jakes answered hesitantly. "Yeah."

"It's obvious that Vandoren has money. But if he's looking to slip out of here unnoticed, he won't do the obvious." Ian pulled a curtain back over the galley window. "You look out there. See anything high-end?"

Agent Jakes obliged, scanning the nearby slips lining the main dock. "No, sir," he admitted.

"Right. Just a bunch of workhorse tubs and a sprinkling of cruisers and sailboats not much spryer than I am. This isn't resort country. Never has been." He pulled the curtain back over the window. "Now, if it's okay with you and your friend, I'm going to find Henry and see what we can come up with."

But Ian didn't wait for approval. Seconds later, he was on the dock and hailing Henry, who'd just stepped from the marina store carrying a small grocery bag. Chet Blanchard followed him out.

As Ian approached, Henry drilled him with a warning glare, which Ian took to mean, *don't say too much.*

"Mornin', Chet," Ian began. "How's the fishing today? Got many boats coming in?"

Henry aggressively cleared his throat, the glare still intact. "I was just answering Chet's questions about all our visitors this morning. I told him how we'd met them at the camp last night and invited them to hang out with us here at the boat until the séance started tonight."

Ian understood. That was the story Henry had concocted and Ian had better stick to it, though it was terribly rehearsed.

"We don't get a lot of traffic here," Chet answered sadly. "You know that, Ian. Mostly the locals and a few travelers in for fuel. The new marina down the coast took my business."

Ian swept a hand before him. "But you're making it on the locals, right?"

"Yep. It's enough."

"Any business from the mediums?"

"Are you kidding? Those pasty-white hermits?"

No time like now. "How about Vandoren? Does he keep a boat here?"

Henry nodded silent approval.

"No. I never see him out here."

Ian went slack. He was running low on questions.

"Except when his buddies over there come to visit," Chet added.

Ian and Henry suddenly inflated. "Buddies?" Henry asked.

"An older couple. Live down the coast and come up about once a year for classes. They'll take Mr. Vandoren out in the boat for a short cruise sometimes. It's the only time I ever see him down here."

"Which boat is theirs?" Ian asked.

Chet pointed to an old cruiser tied up at a slip closer to shore. "Came in this morning," Chet said. "I saw them walk off toward the university."

"I guess they're staying for the séance tonight," Ian probed.

"Yep. Then pulling out for a night cruise home, they said."

Ian and Henry glanced at each other. "Well, Chet, nice talking with you," Henry said. "We'd better get these sodas back to our guests."

Just before dark that evening, Jim Stetz and a fellow agent boarded the cruiser and affixed a tiny GPS device inside a cabinet where life vests were stored. Instead of returning to *Exodus II*, though, they walked to the camp, crossed the commons where an expectant crowd was gathering, and hid themselves behind the stables at the north edge of the woods. Ian followed them.

Chapter 34

Go back, Mr. O'Brien," Agent Stetz said. "This is no place for you."

"Because I'm not wearing a gun and a badge like you are, Mr. Stetz? Neither one of them will do you one bit of good against the kind of trouble that visits these woods."

In the near dark, Ian could see the man roll his eyes. "Go back, sir," Stetz repeated with more grit this time.

"Let me tell you something, son. You may think you know the occupational hazards of your job, but I don't think you're prepared for this one." Ian looked behind them. "And you see that young lady coming this way?" The agent looked where Ian pointed. "I can't stop her from going into those woods either. She's come to watch over her mom. You've come to keep an eye on Vandoren. But guess who's got his eye on you both?"

"Let me guess," Agent Stetz chuckled. "Jesus." In the moonlight, Ian could see the spread of the man's patronizing smile.

"Well, I sure hope he does, but that's not who I meant."

Stetz's smug expression faded.

Before Ian could explain, Tally whistled to them, motioning them toward a path on the other end of the abandoned stables. Ian saw someone coming up behind her and recognized the silhouette of the old man with the hunched shoulders. Spencer and Ian had come to a reckoning earlier in the day.

"Spencer, there are a few things I need to know before tonight," Ian had told him. "Let's start with what's going to happen in those woods. What are we walking into?"

As if beginning a lesson, Spencer answered, "About three times a year, Vandoren gathers a select few for what he calls a private audience with the spirits. He always schedules one of his private séances to coincide with the big one the camp stages out on the commons." He gestured to the grassy field in the center of the camp, where folding chairs were now grouped in lots of small circles. "Vandoren doesn't take to the annual mass séance, even though he started them when he was still part of the camp. He calls it the circus of fools, and delights in leading his more, uh, gifted clients in spiritual battle against the camp 'frauds,' which he insists they are."

"Are they?"

"Some. But most are genuine in their attempts. Only a few are successful, though, in connecting with the other side."

"And you've seen this done?"

"Oh yes." He peered intently at Ian. "Your God is my God, Ian. We both know his warnings about certain forces loose in this world, about the dangers of initiating contact with them. That's what my wife did and it cost us our happiness and her life."

"So you stayed behind to run interference for God? Is that it? Does that include Tally and her mom?"

"That's my biggest job right now."

"What can we do to keep mother and daughter away from Vandoren?"

"It's not Vandoren we need to worry about. It's the ones he and Lesandra Bernardo have already led Mona Greyson to. And now they want her daughter."

Just like they wanted my sister, Ian thought. He would tell Spencer that story another time.

"Sometimes it's just one spirit," Spencer continued. "One contact with the other side, then the haunting begins, the penetration into the soul. It's very real. And unpredictable. We can only pray a shield of protection over Tally and do battle for Mona's rescue."

Now, Ian was glad to see Spencer at Tally's side as they waited for

Ian and the two agents to catch up. Henry had agreed to stay behind at the marina with agents Jakes and Thomlin. Two of the reinforcements sent from the Miami bureau were already at sea awaiting Vandoren's departure. They'd hastily arranged the use of a local trawler to run sweep behind him that night. Satellite tracking to the GPS would make it easier to trail from a discreet distance.

When Ian and the agents drew near, Tally raised a cautioning hand. "It's not far. No talking, and stay close."

Agent Stetz released a huge sigh. "Listen, Miss Greyson, I don't know whose idea it was for any of you to be here, but I want you to go back and let us do our job."

"And just what job is that?" Spencer asked flatly.

But Stetz ignored him. "Stay here!" he rasped with authority.

The three gave the agents a reasonable head start, then followed. The trail snaked through a piney wood then dropped into a glade from which a tendril of smoke now rose. At first sight of the campfire, Tally, Ian, and Spencer came to a halt. Ian noticed the heads bobbing a few paces in front of them also stop. Agent Stetz moved sideways into the trees that ringed the glade and looked back at those who'd ignored his orders. His face was striped by moonlight shadows through the trees, but it was obvious he was an angry man. Albeit a quiet one. His fellow agent had moved to a flank position on the other side of the glade.

There was no sound but the crackling of the small fire and the occasional scuffing of Vandoren's feet as he paced the circle around the fire. Seated there were three women and four men. It was hard for Ian to tell their ages from this distance, but he squinted down for as clear a view of Mona Greyson as possible. She sat next to another woman, whom Spencer had already advised would be Lesandra Bernardo.

The five observers settled into the night shadows, all eyes on the glade. Ian couldn't distinguish all of Vandoren's words as he paced, but detected the repetition, the cadence of one relentlessly imploring someone to "come." It was the only accented word of volume, and there was no doubt in Ian's mind of the nature of that summons. Only then did he fear they'd all ventured too close.

Suddenly a man in the circle raised both arms and called to someone. The name was Sheila. Vandoren rushed forward and placed both hands on the man's shoulders as he continued to call into the dark above him. Then came a woman's voice in answer. Vandoren pulled the man from his seat and stood before him. The voice spoke again, in a foreign tongue that Ian couldn't identify. For several minutes, the man's and woman's voices vibrated in the darkness, their messages to each other lost on those who listened from their hiding place. Ian was now seriously questioning his judgment in being there, in condoning the presence of the others. Could he have stopped Tally from coming, though? Would he have let her venture here alone? Of course not.

Though Ian had prayed fervently for God's watch over them that night, he repeated the prayer again. *Oh God, be here now! Protect this child! Protect us all!*

It was then that Vandoren turned so the firelight caught him full in the face, and Ian saw why he'd been led to urgent prayer. The woman's voice came from Vandoren.

Was it real? Ian believed it was. Just then, a hand gripped his arm. Tally had reached for him, but her gaze was hot on the figure just rising from a chair in the circle. Mona Greyson stood facing the fire, her head tilted upward, arms limp at her sides. Vandoren's attention turned to her as he helped the man back into the chair, his and the woman's voice now silent.

As Vandoren moved slowly toward her mother, Tally's grip on Ian grew tighter. He finally released her hand and wrapped his arm snugly about her shoulders. He bent and whispered in her ear. "We need to get you out of here."

But she shook her head and pulled away from him, never taking her eyes off her mom, whose arms now lifted with the smoke, her hands fluttering gracefully above her head. Just as Vandoren reached her, she cried, "Raja, come!"

Spencer spun toward Tally. Ian heard him ask her, "Your grandfather?"

Tally just shook her head, her face a mask of confusion, her eyes wide with fear.

"Spirit Raja, come! Come now!"

Tally put a hand to her mouth and leaned forward. Ian was certain they should leave. He reached for her, but she stepped farther away. Spencer nodded toward Ian in something like unspoken agreement and moved next to her, placing his own arm about her. She didn't resist this time. Ian was surprised at how calm Spencer was, as if he'd known all along what to expect.

But Agent Stetz obviously had not. Ian turned to see the man sweating profusely, his mouth open, eyes unblinking on the transformations before him.

Then Mona cried out. "Raja! Make my father burn!" Her body swooned to one side but Vandoren caught her and held her close to him. Then he spoke.

"I am Raja." The voice from Vandoren's mouth came softly, soothingly. "Do not fear your father. I will not let him hurt you anymore."

"Don't let him come near me again," Mona cried, her voice pitched and pleading like a child's. She began to rock herself. "No! No! Bad daddy!" she cried as her rocking grew feverish. Vandoren kept his grip on her shoulders, finally slowing her to a standstill. Just as she seemed to relax, though, he jerked her hard, and a different voice bellowed from his mouth. "You belong to us all! Say it!" Vandoren slapped her across the face.

Mona began to sob.

"Say it!" the voice demanded and Vandoren shook her violently.

The childish voice obeyed, "Yes, I will always—"

"Let her go!" Tally suddenly screamed and surged forward on a dead run toward her mother. "Get away from her, you monster!"

Ian and Spencer rushed to catch her, but she closed the distance to the fire in seconds and lunged like a feral cat at the ponderous man still holding her mother as if she were a rag doll. He released Mona to fend off her daughter, who all but leapt on his back. He grabbed Tally by the wrist and flung her dangerously close to the fire, but she righted herself instantly and stepped clear of the flames. No one else in the circle moved, Ian observed in the second before he and Spencer raced between the chairs reaching for Tally. But before they got to her, a blur of a figure hurled itself at Vandoren and tackled him to the ground.

Agent Stetz, quickly assisted by his partner, made quick work of sub-duing Vandoren and ordering all the other séance participants to leave. All fled but Mona, who offered no comfort to her daughter. Instead, she pushed her way past Ian and Spencer and stepped over the feet of the prostrate Vandoren still pinned to the ground by the agents. As she passed in front of Ian, though, he saw something he didn't like in her eyes. They were searing and locked on Tally.

No more the rag doll, the sobbing child, Mona Greyson had crossed over to something else entirely. She was just inches from her daughter's face when the voice returned. Vandoren's voice. Raja's voice. Now howl-ing profanities from the contorted mouth of Mona Greyson.

Spencer didn't waste a second. In one lightning move, the frail old man lunged between mother and daughter, grabbed Tally by the arm, and yanked her out of the woman's reach. "In the name of Jesus, get behind us, Satan!" he cried, and pulled Tally away. Ian was a split second behind him, kicking chairs aside as the two men made their escape with the dis-traught young woman, who had offered no more resistance.

Moments later, though, she suddenly stopped and turned around. "It's a demon!" she cried, looking back toward the fire.

"Yes," Spencer replied. "That wasn't your mother. You have to forgive her. She needs help."

Now Ian looked back through the trees, worried about those he'd left behind. "Spencer, take her away from here and stay with her. I'm going back."

"No, Ian!"

"Just go." He was panting hard now. "And send someone to help us."

When Ian reached the still-burning fire, he found Vandoren seated in a chair, his hands and feet cuffed. Agent Stetz paced a short distance away, a phone to his ear. Ian guessed he was alerting those in an offshore boat waiting to follow Vandoren that night. The unexpected violence and the need to protect Mona Greyson and her daughter had obviously pre-empted that plan. It was Mona Greyson that Ian most wanted to help now. But she wasn't there.

Ignoring the agent standing guard over Vandoren, Ian stood squarely in front of the restrained man and demanded, "Where's Mona?" He got only a sneer in response.

"Maybe there's some demon running around inside you who speaks English and can interpret the meaning of what I just said. It's real simple. Where is Mona Greyson?"

"Who are you?" Vandoren growled, in his own voice.

"Don't say anything else to him," Agent Stetz instructed Ian, stepping up beside him. "He'll get an earful from the feds. They're on their way now and they're very anxious to talk to the witch doctor here about the meaning of capital crime." Ian saw the path Stetz was taking and why. Since this night hadn't gone according to plan and there was a boat with a GPS on it that wasn't going to lead anybody to Volynski, someone would have to scare his—and the bomb's—location out of Vandoren. Ian was happy to oblige.

"Oh, you mean he'll get to choose between the chair and the needle? I don't think Florida hangs 'em anymore, do they?"

Stetz cast a let's-not-overdo-it glance toward Ian, but it was Vandoren who spoke up. "What do you mean 'capital crime'?"

"Try attempted assassination of a U.S. president, collaboration with a foreign enemy to transport and detonate a weapon of mass destruction inside the U.S., and other crimes against the state."

Even in the glow of the fire, Ian watched Vandoren go pale. The man was in shock.

They heard a thrashing through the trees and saw two beams of light strafe the glade. Agents Thomlin and Jakes rushed in, weapons drawn. After quickly appraising the situation, they holstered their guns. Some from the mass séance on the commons had begun to drift toward them, curious at the distant sounds coming from the woods. "We need to contain this immediately," Agent Jakes snapped. There's a patrol car waiting to take him to the nearest holding cell. We'll head that way." He pointed away from the commons.

Vandoren struggled to get up. "I'm not going anywhere. You've got no right and no evidence to hold me for anything."

Agent Stetz jumped on that. "Oh, I think a certain tractor-trailer rig that left your warehouse early this morning will provide all the evidence we need."

Disbelief swept over Vandoren's face. His body slumped as though the full weight of his collusion, like an anvil, had just dropped on his head. It didn't take long, though, before he straightened defiantly. "I demand to see my lawyer."

"We can arrange that," Agent Stetz said. "But here's your choice. You can sit around with all your rights to legal counsel and let innocent people die, or . . . you can help us stop that bomb now and maybe they won't strap you to a chair and fry you."

Vandoren said nothing more as they led him away. But hours later, he told them plenty.

"It seems the big mystic hadn't exactly been a willing host to a WMD," Agent Jakes later informed Ian. "His lawyer advised him to cooperate in locating the thing."

Chapter 35

$\mathcal{M}$ona Greyson had fled all the way to the bay before Ian and the sheriff's deputies found her. They'd tracked her after finding a shred of her clothing caught in a bramble not far from the now doused fire. The agents had dispatched two of the three deputies reporting to the scene to find the tormented woman before she harmed herself or her daughter. They were almost too late.

Arms bleeding, her face and hands smeared with mud, Mona was knee-deep into the bay waters when the deputy lunged for her and dragged her back onto the beach, her writhing body and flying fists almost more than the two men could contain. The deputy had to cuff her hands and feet for her own protection until help arrived. She was incoherent except for one phrase uttered repeatedly between wild and frightened cries. "Raja, you lied! You lied!"

Tally had allowed Spencer to lead her to his cottage on the camp property where he ushered her to the sofa and covered her with a warm blanket. She was trembling and crying, exhausted from the ordeal. But moments later, she threw the blanket aside, insisting she had to find her mother. Before she reached the door, though, Spencer caught her arm and gently pulled her to him. "You've had a terrible fright, my child," he said, folding her into his arms. "Let the authorities and Ian take care of your mother for now." He gently led her back to the sofa. "We'll go to her soon enough." He paused. "You've seen your mom in a condition you've never seen before, right?"

"Yes," came a small, weak voice, not the one Spencer was used to hearing from her. "What happened to her?" Tally asked, clutching the blanket tightly around her, as if it were a shield.

Ian looked into the eyes of a young woman and saw the innocent fright of a child. "Tally, do you remember the first time we met? At the store when my coworker responded so rudely to your wearing the cross necklace?"

"Yeah."

"When I took you aside, I told you that those in the camp knew things that were important for you to know."

"And you never told me what they were."

"I think you know now," Spencer replied gently.

Tally stared at him as if watching the answer materialize on his face.

"Just like I told you about myself, that because of what I was forced to see in my wife and others like her, I had to run the other way—to the cross. Because finally, I understood what God meant when he said that our struggle is not against flesh and blood but against evil forces in the heavenly realm. Tally, you just witnessed those forces and how they can overtake someone like your mom, even using her voice to say things that she, in her own right mind, would never have said, especially to you. But she opened herself willingly to them. At first, I believe, it was to find and persecute the father who'd abused her, maybe raped her. To find some emotional relief from that trauma. But she didn't know who was on the other side. That it wasn't her father, but someone far more evil."

As tears slid down her cheeks, Tally replied, "At my house last night, Mr. O'Brien said he was going to ask God to protect me and Mom. Why didn't God do that?"

"I believe he just saved you both from greater harm, Tally. We're going to help your mom find her way back from a very dark place. And if you'll let him, God will build a new life for both of you."

It wasn't long before Spencer received word that Mona Greyson had been found and taken to the regional hospital. She'd been sedated and would be held over for psychiatric evaluation. Before he took Tally to see her mother, he excused himself long enough to make a quick phone call.

When they arrived at the hospital, another car was just pulling up at the curb. Denise Northcutt jumped from the back seat and rushed to hug Tally. "Mr. Fremont called us, Tally. You're going home with me tonight, after you visit your mom." Denise's parents climbed from the car and started for Tally.

She looked up at Spencer, then threw both arms around his neck. "Thank you for caring what happened to me and my mom," she whispered. "You're part of us now, do you know that?" she asked with wide, teary eyes.

"Perhaps I am," he answered with mild surprise, and the small entourage filed into the hospital.

Chapter 36

*J*ust after midnight, President Noland lifted from his pillow to take the call. FBI Director Rick Salabane had been cleared through to the residence, where the president had just drifted to sleep.

"Sir, we've located Ivan Volynski."

The news snatched the president from bed. "Where?" He was up and moving.

"On a yacht off the north Keys. We have the coordinates."

"And the bomb?"

"Nothing on that yet, sir." Salabane detailed the events leading up to the arrest and interrogation of Vandoren earlier that night. "What we have so far from him is this: Volynski arranged for the truck to transport the bomb from Anhinga Bay to a ship on the Miami River. Vandoren doesn't know which one or when it's departing. Our teams are scrambling now to gather surveillance camera footage of the river docks and any trucks making deliveries early this morning. We've calculated the travel time to the Miami River," Salabane continued, "and the likelihood that the bomb was off-loaded immediately. But sir, at this point, we have to consider a wide-scale evacuation. We don't know the stability of that weapon or the vessel receiving it. Or if the bomb's still sitting in the heart of Miami."

The president's mood grew darker. "What if surveillance tapes show the transfer to a boat that, by this time, has already left port?"

"Homeland Security is already on it. The Coast Guard will soon dispatch boarding teams to search every cargo ship that's left Miami since early this morning. There's one thing we do know, sir, if Vandoren's confession is reliable. We know where the weapon is headed."

Noland knew it, too. His brother's last message had made it clear. "It's coming here."

"Straight up the Potomac, sir."

Now in the living room, the president gazed out over the city, the seat of government, the bane of "the son so ingloriously born." What had Ivan just done to destroy his brother's "temple"?

"Sir?" Salabane prodded after too many silent moments.

Noland glanced at the grandfather clock beside him. "Listen to me, Rick. There will be no deployment of any kind to Ivan's boat. Not yet. No communication with it, no risk he'll spot any ship or aircraft the least bit suspicious to him. No hint whatsoever that we see him. Understood?"

"But sir, we need to—"

"Those are my orders, Rick. Now, I'll be in my office in thirty minutes. Get here as soon as you can."

By four that morning, the president's secretary—fetched by Secret Service from her Georgetown apartment—had dispatched Vice President George Sievers and the White House press secretary to the Oval Office. There was much to prepare for the coming hours.

They arrived just moments after Rick Salabane. After a hasty briefing and a round of objections, all three now stood before the president, who was seated at his desk busily stuffing files and one brown envelope into a metal briefcase.

"George, you're on standby only so don't be eyeing this chair yet," the president cracked with a half grin. Turning to Salabane, he said. "They're waiting for the three of you in the situation room. Better get going."

"Sir, again, I must strongly advise against this," the vice president protested. "It's far too dangerous."

Snapping his briefcase closed, the president stood to leave. "Until we locate that bomb, I'll do what I have to do."

The first smudge of morning appeared on the eastern sky as Marine One lifted off the south lawn of the White House with Travis Noland on board. From Andrews Air Force Base, he would fly to U.S. Coast Guard Station Miami Beach and the cutter that would take him to his brother.

The lights of the city receding beneath him, Noland cradled the briefcase in his lap, hoping that its contents would hold a madman at bay. Long enough.

Chapter 37

Ivan was up early Wednesday morning for his usual breakfast of smoked salmon, hard-boiled eggs, and chilled mango, whose sweet nectar always soothed him. The rising sun had cast a pavé setting of diamonds over the surface of a gentle sea and kindled a memory incongruent to the sparkling lights before him. Ivan set down his fork and sat back.

He'd been twelve when his mother took him with her to a temporary cleaning job on the Black Sea near Gelendzhik. The American embassy in Moscow had hired her to clean a seaside dacha for one of its high officials, a middle-aged man from Boston who'd often taken his family for vacations at the house high above the rocky shoreline. Galina Volynski and Ivan had spent the week before the family's arrival scrubbing and scouring the old stone house until, to them, it shone. But the man and his wife didn't think so. Soon after they arrived, the woman complained so bitterly that her husband refused to pay Galina. Ivan and his mother were ordered to leave the following morning.

At first light, though, Ivan saw the man leave by the back door with a fishing pole and tackle box. No one else in the house was up. The young boy followed him down a steep switchback path to the water where nothing stirred at that hour but the hunched pines that rooted along the windy shore. The man headed for a half circle of aluminum chairs gathered about a campfire site, no doubt where he and his young sons had spent time together, and probably planned to do so again. Maybe even that night. But when the man dropped heavily into one of the chairs and busied himself with the fishing line and bait, Ivan Volynski changed the family's plans for the evening.

He'd never slit a man's throat before. It would have gone easier if the knife he'd grabbed from the butcher's block in the kitchen had been sharper. But it had done the job, silently and completely. Not one more American would insult his mother, his country, or him without retribution. They would all pay and keep on paying.

"Sir, was the breakfast not to your liking?" the steward asked, coming up beside Ivan and noting the little-touched food.

"No, the food was very good, but you may take it away now."

After the steward had cleared the table, Ivan rolled himself to the railing and looked down into the placid waters. He felt for the handle of the small revolver in the pocket of the light fishing vest he wore. Like the one the American embassy official had worn that morning by the Black Sea.

Ivan's thoughts churned to a halt when the phone in another pocket vibrated. So many pockets, so many complicated instruments. The knife had been so simple.

There you are, he thought, looking down at the ID on the encrypted phone. "Good evening to you, Arkady."

"Yes, it is a good evening here in Russia. It would be better if I could reach the others, though. Curt does not answer. Maxum does not answer."

"But here am I. I hope you are well, your defenses in place. It will be soon now."

"We are prepared for the full onslaught of American outrage. Their seat of government is about to become a very unhealthy place to be."

"Coupled with what our friends in the desert have planned for Israel, Mr. Noland won't know who or where to strike first. "Yes, Arkady, this is indeed a fine evening for us both. Now tell me about my young ones moving into position."

Even before Gorev's assassination, Arkady Glinka had quietly moved

Ivan's people, like players on a chessboard, into positions of power and influence. As interim president, Glinka had further solidified the ranks with the youth he and Ivan both knew to be the future of the new Russia. They were ready and eager to snatch their country from its lethargy and run with it like Olympian torchbearers to the summit. By the time Glinka took the polls as official president of Russia, he and Ivan calculated, Israel and Washington would be reeling from attack, especially from the legion of saboteurs still inside its own borders. And Russia and its allies would command the summit.

For the next few minutes, Glinka reported two new cabinet appointments he had made, replacements for those whom he was convinced were of no further service to their country. He outlined plans to introduce new amendments to the constitution, once he was permanently installed, that would accommodate the territorial expansion of a new Russia. A new energy consortium was underfoot with China and allies in the Middle East. There were issues, though, on the domestic front. The demands and demonstrations of the lower classes had become a nuisance.

But something of more import needled Glinka just now. "Why isn't Curt returning my calls?"

Ivan smiled toward the eastern horizon, now a bright azure. "You forget what took place in the camp last night, Arkady. Our friend is sleeping off the strain of his all-night decadence." Ivan laughed.

"Decadence? Have you fallen away from us, Ivan?"

"You mean from yours and Curt's netherworld? Those who lie beyond the thin membrane that surrounds us all?" He laughed in a low, condescending tone.

But Glinka didn't pursue this. Instead, he asked abruptly, "How are you feeling, Ivan?"

Ivan was ready for the question, knowing that Glinka would secretly welcome a bad report. Why would he want to share his upcoming throne with anyone else?

"I am robust and have decided to live forever, Arkady."

The conversation had ended amiably enough, though Ivan was certain he'd never had a dead reckoning on the soul of Arkady Glinka.

Again, the phone vibrated in his hand and he answered immediately. "What is your news?"

"It is afternoon here, comrade," Maxum Morozov began, "and they remain under guard in their safe house. Do you know why?"

Ivan didn't, but he immediately thought of Felix and hoped he hadn't shown himself to the wrong people. But Felix Shevcik was known to only one operative in Berlin—Evgeny Kozlov, whom Felix also hunted. Could Evgeny have spotted him first and ordered his coveted Liesl under lock and key? Ivan bitterly recalled the Russian traitor's daring rescue of the woman from Ivan's assassin, right at the front door of her old Charleston home.

"Tell me more," Ivan said.

"I have uncovered nothing. Nor has my source, other than what they're calling a heightened alert. It falls suspiciously close to the transport of our package to Washington, wouldn't you say?"

Ivan agreed, but saw no possible connection. "Coincidence," he concluded. And then he remembered his last message to Noland. That was it. The man had panicked enough to order Liesl Bower out of the path of his living, fire-breathing half brother. Ivan laughed with abandon, until his breath caught and he suddenly fought for air.

"Sir?" Maxum's concerned voice sounded in the phone, now dropped in Ivan's lap. An aide rushing to his side picked up the phone and wordlessly ended the call.

Chapter 38

*E*rica had to get out of the apartment. Maxum would be waiting. She opened her bedroom door enough to see the others gathered in the living room, the tension in the room palpable. Max and Ben had been holed up most of the day behind doors, their phones and computers red-hot. Something was going on and no one was talking about it. But Max's father would know.

Maxum Morozov was her employer. She'd profited handsomely from their liaison so far, though the money didn't matter as much now. She'd been hired to watch Max the son from as close as she could get, to report his comings and goings, his contacts, his phone and e-mail messages. She hadn't counted on falling in love with him, or him with her, if that's what it was. He'd certainly grilled her hard enough about the computer she'd carelessly left in the wrong position under his bed. She'd confessed her use of it immediately, but only to shop online for photographic supplies. Because she hadn't brought her own computer, she'd told him, she didn't think he'd mind her borrowing his. Of course, she'd found it locked. It'd taken a few hours for Max to regain his good spirits with her.

Now, he'd been walled away in another room with nothing forthcoming about what had snared his and Ben's full attention for most of the day.

With an affected breeziness, she bounded into the living room and announced, "I'm going out to take photos and get some groceries. I think we're all tired of cold cuts."

"Not a good idea," Max responded instantly. He and Ben had momentarily returned to the fold.

"No one out there is interested in me," she insisted. "It's you gifted ones everyone is protecting." She offered a brief smile. "I'll come right back, I promise."

Max looked oddly toward Ben, then picked up his phone. As he punched in a number, he told Erica, "I'm sorry, but only with an escort. I'm calling one now. Hold on." He talked briefly with someone and hung up. "He'll meet you in front of the building and bring you back. You stay with him, please. I'm sorry, Erica. I can't take chances with any of us."

She tried to conceal her irritation, her options flying through her mind. "Okay, but how long will it take him to get down there?"

"He's already there."

She tried to mask her disappointment.

When Max cleared it with the guards to let her leave, Erica took the elevator just to the second floor, then switched to the stairs, in case anyone had their eye on the elevator doors in the lobby. When she reached the ground floor, instead of following orders to exit through the front and meet the escort, whoever it was, she slipped out the back door and raced from the building, anxiously looking over her shoulder until she'd cleared the area.

She was now on the main boulevard of Friedrichstrasse, but not for long. She turned quickly into a small hostel with a back entrance emptying into an alley, which she navigated for several blocks before finding Maxum's car parked behind a small bank. She quickly climbed inside.

"Well?" she asked. "Why are we under lock and key?"

He shook his head. "My contact isn't worried about the alert. In fact, he laughed at the notion that they felt the need for greater protection. Why that amuses him, I don't know. Regardless, stay on your job and take this." He handed her another large envelope. "Add these to the other documents and guard them with your last breath."

She frowned at him. "That's not amusing."

"It wasn't meant to be."

When she left the car, the envelope inside her bag, she hurried away to snap a few pictures, should anyone wish to see what she'd been doing, and to find a grocery store along the commercial glut of Friedrichstrasse. Before she reached the boulevard, though, a man caught up with her on the sidewalk and called her name. She stopped and whirled around. He was short and squared with a nose of like dimensions, and she was certain she'd never seen him before. Though all her instincts told her to run, he moved swiftly in front of her to block what he must have sensed coming. "I think you should follow me inside here for just a moment," he said with no expression. "I only want to talk with you." He gestured toward a little deli whose window was covered with a handwritten listing of its meats and cheeses. With his hand firmly at her back, she found herself herded into the restaurant and toward a small table near the rear.

Her thoughts racing, her practiced eyes sizing up her surroundings, she slowly lowered herself to the table.

"Don't be afraid of me. I'm here to offer my help."

"Who are you?" she demanded bluntly.

"The name is unimportant. It is our jobs we should discuss." He winked in a way that seemed almost comical.

"Don't try to hide what you are," he told her. "Or who. Because I know."

"You know what?"

"That you've been meeting with Maxum Morozov. I checked my sources and discovered you and I work for the same people, for the same objectives. Though your skills are far less impressive than mine." He chuckled. "But I will teach you if you let me." His gaze moved over her body, resting in places it shouldn't.

She was certain she could outrun this idiot, though not his weaponry. But she had her own. Beneath the table, she slipped her hand toward her thigh and the slim holster strapped to it. It was time to go.

"As you say, we both have our jobs," she said icily. "If you'll excuse me now, I'd like to return to mine." She rose steadily and never looked at him again as she strode confidently from the deli, furious with herself for not detecting this man, for letting him follow her to Maxum.

Maxum. Who was he really? She hadn't cared so much when he unrolled the wad of bills and placed them in her hand. She'd never heard of him or his son. The father had preferred it that way, reading her for what she was. An independent spy with no allegiances. Until the last few months with Max.

She never looked back as she left the deli, dismissing the arrogant boor as extraneous, just another cog in whatever elaborate network it was that Maxum was involved in. She only knew the Russian government was at the center of it. That the recent assassination of its president somehow figured into it. It was high stakes and very lucrative. She didn't need to know much more than her immediate assignment—to watch Max. So far, she'd detected nothing threatening to his person, certainly not from his own father. She knew they were estranged and that Max rarely spoke of him. But despite the overlay of Russian espionage, she'd believed her assignment was only of personal interest to Max's father.

Before returning to the apartment, she stopped for a bag of groceries. She couldn't return without her cover for leaving. But as she now approached the apartment, she saw another man who made her pause, staring hotly at her from the front entrance to the building. This one was tall with a thin face and slick hair. He, too, knew her name.

"Erica, where have you been?"

The escort, she guessed. "Where have *you* been?" she snapped, feigning irritation with him. "You were supposed to meet me in back."

He looked oddly at her. "It seems there has been unfortunate miscommunication." He kept staring at her. "I regret that. You'd better hurry upstairs." His face remained rigid, unsmiling. She turned once before entering the building to find him still watching her.

"The president just left the White House on some sudden and undisclosed mission, leaving the VP on standby should Noland fail to return," Ben announced quietly, dropping his phone into his pocket.

"He did what?" Max struggled to cut the volume on his shock. They were closed up in their makeshift command center down the hall. Erica had returned with food for dinner and, for now, the others were all distracted with cooking. But Max knew the level of restlessness was rising, and not just in Erica.

"That's all we're being told for now," Ben replied, opening his laptop. "But there's also this." He flipped to a reconnaissance file and turned it toward Max. "Looks like that Urals mine is heating up again."

Max studied the photos. "But maybe now we've identified the pipeline they're using to deliver those things."

Ben mulled that over awhile. "Think there'll be a concert on Friday?" he asked, abruptly shifting focus.

Max shrugged and looked toward the closed door. "You know her as well as I do. An executive order might hold her here a couple of days. But it would take Hitler's army to keep Liesl Bower off that stage."

"No doubt there are mystics at the Anhinga Bay Spiritualist Camp who might warn you that the ghosts of that army won't be far from where the two of you are headed.

"Hitler's rallying grounds," Max mused. "I remember watching the old newsreels of him standing on that high platform, booming his ferocious rhetoric to thousands of cheering Jew haters."

"Are you ready to stand there and play your violin in front of his ghost?"

Max smiled and looked Ben straight in the eye. "I'm not afraid of ghosts."

Chapter 39

Ian had spoken to Ava only once since she'd discovered him in the Keys, and only on Agent Jakes's secure phone, which he'd just brought to Ian again. "Call for you, Mr. O'Brien." The agent barely suppressed a grin as he boarded *Exodus II*. Ian had returned to the boat and an anxious Henry, awaiting more news of the previous evening's—and this early morning's—unfolding drama. In the meantime, Henry had been on the phone with Liesl for almost an hour, and reported to Ian that she'd assured him all was well in Berlin, though Henry had sensed there was something she wasn't telling him.

Now he watched as Ian reluctantly approached Agent Jakes. "Uh oh. My head's back on the chopping block, right?"

"Afraid so, sir."

Ian expelled a wobbly breath. "Okay, hand it over." He reached for the phone and immediately shifted tone. "Hey there, sweet lady. How are things in Charleston this afternoon?"

"Cut it out, Ian. You're in enough trouble without adding mockery to your list of offenses—eavesdropping on my conversation and sneaking around my desk."

"I did not sneak. That note was lying right there on top of your desk for anyone to see. I just had to turn it around a bit so I could read it clearly."

"You're unbelievable and—"

"Well hold on now. Who just went traipsing all over New York last January with a Russian spy? You see, if you think certain information is important enough, you don't rightly care who leads you to it, do you?" He kept barreling. "So maybe it's okay if a couple of geezers with not one Uzi between 'em came down here to get more of that information." He had to stop for breath. "There was just something about mailmen shooting at Liesl that didn't sit too well, you know?"

Ava was quiet.

"You there?" Ian asked.

"I'm here. Where are you?"

"At the boat."

"Where's Henry?"

"Here with me, We're headed home early in the morning.."

"That's why I'm calling. For whatever good it does, I'm telling you you've got to stay where you are at least for the next twenty-four hours."

"How so?"

"I can't tell you any more than that, but the last place I want you two is offshore in any direction."

"What about flying?"

"Excuse me?"

"Henry and I thought we might take in that concert Friday night."

"In Nuremberg?" Ava blurted with surprise.

"Well, unless they've moved it to Pigeon Forge."

Ava sighed. "You just can't leave the boat in Florida and fly off to Nuremberg at the last minute. What you *can* do, though, is stay put for the next day or so, then cast off for Charleston." She paused. "I miss seeing your scruffy old face around here."

"Oh yeah? Well, wait till you see the scruffy old bike I'm bringing home."

Chapter 40

Long before dawn that Thursday, two Sentinel-class Coast Guard cutters left Miami cruising south to a point barely ten miles off Key Largo. The coordinates were sure, the target vessel sighted earlier by overhead reconnaissance, and radar contact maintained to the second. It was forty-two nautical miles away and stationary.

At 154 feet, the Sentinel-class was the newest in the Coast Guard fleet. It was fast and formidable with a 25 mm autocannon and four .50-caliber machine guns anchored topside. Running hard with a tailwind that overcast night, the cutters together carried four officers, forty crew, and one U.S. president.

At three nautical miles distance from Ivan Volynski's yacht, both cutters went into darken-ship mode, with all exterior and interior lights doused. Navigation was facilitated by infrared scanners on the ship's mast, their night-vision images displayed on a screen on the bridge.

At one nautical mile out, both cutters came to a stop. At the stern of one vessel, six crewmen outfitted with night-vision goggles, bulletproof vests, .40-caliber side arms, and M16s prepared to board a twenty-two-foot Zodiac off the launch ramp.

With night-vision binoculars, President Noland watched the operation from the bridge of the other cutter.

In full blackout, the rigid-hulled inflatable eased its way to the yacht, which displayed the requisite number of anchor lights but only a few interior lights. It was almost two in the morning.

The sea slapped hard at the small interception boat as it approached, but it was the only sound from the boarding party.

Ivan had awakened with a sharp pain in his back. Turning slowly in his bed, he opened his eyes and focused on the dim blue lights running at floor level throughout his stateroom, housed in the forward section of the upper deck. The lights were meant to keep his travel paths lit at all times, but he found their soft glow and color strangely ethereal. It seemed all of life now bore some twilight unearthliness, except when real-time pain jerked him back to reality.

He had trouble lifting his head from the pillow, the neck muscles beginning to lose their grip. With most of the crew asleep, he refused to call for help. There would be enough of that in time. He struggled to sit up in bed and look out, but the night fell densely against the windows, two of which were partially open. He preferred to sleep in ocean breezes, not the mechanically chilled ones from the vents.

He reached for the heating pad, positioned it beneath the back spasms, and turned it on. When he finally settled down again, he thought of Vandoren and the voyage they would take the next day. They would follow in the distant wake of the cargo ship as far as Charleston, where he would dare to disembark long enough to see for himself the house on Tidewater Lane—a house unlike any he and his mother had ever lived in, or gone hungry in. Once they left Charleston Harbor and were safely at sea again, the device he planned to leave at the doorstep of the house would lift it from its foundations and deposit it piece by splintered piece over the Holy City. That is what they called Charleston, wasn't it? He laughed to himself. After Felix eliminated Liesl Bower and Ivan destroyed the family home, what did holiness have to do with anything?

That made him think of his pet spiritual guru who wished to infuse the new Kremlin with his mystic powers. As Ivan pondered the eventuality of that, Glinka's complaint echoed. *Why isn't Vandoren returning my calls?* Now Ivan wondered the same thing. He didn't care if Vandoren was still recuperating from a night of psychic phenomena or not, Ivan needed to talk to him. Finally pulling himself up against the cushioned headboard, he punched in Vandoren's secure number and waited. After a long interval, he ended the call and stared into the blackness beyond the window. He'd begun to wonder if installing a flamboyant medium such as Curt Vandoren in the new regime was wise. If it was to be billed as the people's revolution, would the people stand for the same radical indulgences as Czar Nicholas II had allowed himself?

Who would the new president be anyway?

Not Glinka. Ivan would see to that. He'd long favored one of the young ones in his camp. There were several fine candidates from which to choose. But as long as Glinka was in power, even as interim president, those young ones must not know they were even in the running. But Ivan would place his choice in office, within the year, if he had that long.

The heating pad was beginning to comfort him even as his irritation with Vandoren grew. Ivan would call again in a moment, but first, his mind's eye caught sight of the cargo ship plowing north with its secret container. That image pleased him, erasing any doubts of his scheme to kill off an entire government. He lifted his phone again and punched in the code for the cargo ship's captain, who answered immediately. *Curt Vandoren will have to be retrained to this level of attention if he's coming with me to Russia.* "Your voyage is going smoothly?" Ivan asked the captain.

"Yes, sir. We're approaching the South Carolina coast."

Ivan smiled. *How timely.*

"We should reach the Potomac sometime tomorrow afternoon."

"And your friends at the boatyard?"

"They're already there and waiting for us, sir. As planned, we'll off-load downriver from Washington and deliver it by truck."

"Monday morning rush hour," Ivan confirmed.

"Yes, sir. Within a block of the Capitol. Don't worry. Your plan is etched deeply in our heads. We've practiced this many times to your satisfaction."

"Yes, I know. But I must be sure the same personnel I've met and trained remain loyal."

"Sir, you handpicked the driver. You can have no doubts about him. He knows exactly where to park the truck and you know his skills with the bomb."

"I would hate to lose him."

"Delayed detonation allows him over an hour to flee the area. His escape route to the heliport is charted and I spoke with your pilot this morning. The chopper is primed and ready. All is well. Please don't trouble yourself further, sir. Let us do our jobs."

Ivan inhaled with some effort, and exhaled slowly. It was a labored rhythm that could either pain or steady him. Right now, he was at peace.

"The balance of your payment awaits you, along with your country's enduring gratitude, comrade."

"Thank you, sir."

When the call ended, Ivan started to phone Vandoren again, but decided against it. His words to the man would have to be scolding, and Ivan wished not to dispel the peace he now felt. *Let him sleep. He will be here soon enough in the morning.*

Ivan slipped back under the covers, his frail body relaxed and ready for sleep, but his mind still churned. What if the driver was held up in rush hour traffic? He would carry oxygen, but using it would signal his prior knowledge of the attack. Who would just happen to have an oxygen mask in his everyday belongings? And what about the pilot? If he were somehow detained, he and the driver both would be casualties. Ivan hated to lose two good men. It would be service to their country, though, and their names would be bronzed somewhere in the new Russia. Ivan would see to it.

What was that? A sound, a slap of seawater against . . . what? He halted his breathing to listen. The ponderous boat barely rocked, but now, through the open window, he heard the rush of wind over water, and yes, another hard clap against something. *Against your own boat, old woman!* He admonished himself for his jittery fears and closed his eyes.

He was beginning to drift when his eyes suddenly sprang open. Somewhere a voice had shouted. Now, feet pounded the hallway, advancing on his stateroom. He wrenched himself from the covers and reached for the handgun on his night table. But the door to his room burst open and two men in heavy armor crossed the room before he could force his weakened hands around the grip of the gun.

"Drop it!" both men shouted at him, one of them virtually on top of him before he could utter a sound, the man's hands searching him, his knees boring into Ivan's chest, expelling what little air he'd accumulated in his lungs. As he gasped for breath, the other man quickly cuffed Ivan's wrists and pulled him harshly from bed, eliciting a sharp cry from him. He slumped to the floor, but their rough hands hauled him back to his feet. One of them must have noticed the wheelchair in the room.

"He can't walk," one man shouted. Together, they lifted Ivan by his shoulders and legs and carried him into an adjoining study where they sat him upright in an executive desk chair and tied him to it.

He screamed at them, "Who are you? What do you want?"

"United States Coast Guard," one of them reported, his gun aimed at Ivan's chest. "Are you Ivan Volynski?"

Ivan refused to answer. But the man pulled a photograph from his pocket and held it up, then showed it to his buddy. Looking back at Ivan, the man said, "It looks like you are. So I suggest you sit calmly and wait."

"For what?" Ivan demanded angrily, but got no response. Something outside his windows halted the indignant tirade he was about to launch. An unmistakable sound, the thrashing rotors of an inbound helicopter. Now it was on him, hovering over his ship, its searchlights arcing through his windows, exposing him. Ivan squinted in the glare of the arrogant light.

Who did this? How could they know where I was?

Then Glinka's voice returned to him, again. *Why isn't Vandoren returning my calls?*

And Ivan knew.

From the moment he'd left the White House, Noland had struggled to contain his fury. The massive dragnet to locate the bomb was ongoing. Every moment that passed without finding it was agony. Still, he believed he'd triumphed over his rage. Until now.

With no shots fired, the boarding team had surprised the sleeping crew and subdued the two bridge personnel on watch. Hours earlier, after federal authorities had informed Vandoren of the capital-offense nature of his crimes, he'd displayed a pitiable desperation to reduce the sentence by cooperating in every way conceivable. That meant spilling as much information as he knew, which included the number of Ivan's crew and the layout of his yacht. With that, the boarding team had gone straight to crew quarters and Ivan's stateroom.

The cutter that had dispatched the team now idled along the yacht's port side. Once all three levels of the ship had been thoroughly searched and secured, its entire crew accounted for and restrained, the second cutter eased up to the starboard side. Its own Zodiak was launched from the stern ramp and cruised cautiously toward the yacht, its path bathed in light from the vigilant chopper. Like the first boarding party, the six men on the Zodiak wore bulletproof vests.

Once a boarding ladder was secured to the yacht's gunwale, three men armed with assault weapons scrambled up and over the side, followed by Travis Noland, whose footing was as sure and swift as his soldiers'. Two more men followed him.

"Where is he?" the president demanded the moment he stepped foot on deck.

"This way, sir." Blended with the two Coast Guard boarding teams were three Secret Service agents. A shield of men and weaponry surrounded the president as he was led to the forward stateroom on the upper deck.

Strapped to a chair in the middle of the room, Volynski was hurling insults and threats on those guarding him when the president entered the room.

At first sight of him, Ivan flinched as if struck, his words chopped off, his shock profound. Then something inside him shifted. The open mouth slowly closed and spread into a malicious curl. The eyes flared and burned like coals. "Well, look who came down from his throne." Now the eyes fairly danced. "How worthy I must be of his presence." Ivan looked pointedly toward the windows and the ferocious beat of the chopper. "And you brought your toys with you."

But the president heard past the verbal swagger. Devastation sounded just below the surface.

Travis Noland glanced around the room. A walker stood in one corner. He turned toward the open door to the bedroom and spotted the wheelchair, then back at Ivan.

"What's wrong with you, Ivan?"

"Said one caring brother to another." Ivan sneered, squirming against his restraints.

Noland turned to one of the guards. "Loosen the straps."

"Don't pity me!" Ivan snapped.

"You pity yourself," Noland returned. "Is that what this is about? The poor, illegitimate son who spent his whole life hating the father who rejected him and the brother who had everything he didn't? Is that why you kill?"

"I won't dignify that with an answer."

"Dignify?" The president charged. "What do you know about dignity? You've tried three times to kill a woman who just stumbled onto the name of your little mole. You killed two men just doing their jobs at the Supreme Court. Did you know that the little boy who was injured in that blast died? And guess what? He didn't have a father either. Just a mom who loved him. A mom like yours."

"Then you pity them, not me."

Noland looked into the seething face and tried to understand that level of hate. But there was something more urgent for him to know.

"Where's the bomb?"

The mouth curled again as the face relaxed. Ivan looked at him with unmasked contempt. "You'll know soon enough."

Noland's mind spun with options for breaching this human barricade. How long did he have before this man murdered again? This time thousands.

Noland straightened. "We will soon return to Washington, and you will go with us. Right to the seat of government. The *temple*, as you wrote in your last cowardly message to me. If we don't find the bomb in time, you'll know what it's like to die at your own hands."

Ivan erupted in laughter, long and loud. "It doesn't matter to me if I die here or there. The symptoms of Lou Gehrig's disease and a good saturation of sarin are almost the same." He laughed with acidic victory. "Clever of me, wasn't it? Now you and I, the anointed son and the bastard, will share the same fate. Finally."

Noland swallowed hard and glanced at his watch. It had come to this. He gestured toward one of his Secret Service agents who nodded understanding, retrieved a small folder from his backpack, and handed it to the president.

"Anointed?" he asked calmly. "Is that what you thought I was?"

Ivan didn't respond.

Noland took a few photographs from the folder and approached Ivan. He held up one for the man to see. "Recognize the man in this picture?"

Ivan refused to look at it.

"Are you afraid?"

Though the eyes blazed defiantly, they soon turned to the old photograph.

"It's our father," Noland said, "in bed with someone who wasn't my mother, although it was her bed, too. You see, she was visiting her sister out of town and I was supposed to be asleep. But I heard the noises from my parents' bedroom. When I cracked open the door and saw what was happening, I hurried to get my camera. I was just nine."

"Stupid child," Ivan snapped.

"I guess I was, because he heard the click of the camera and saw me before I could run." The president held up another photo. "It took three surgeries to repair my leg, and I still had to wear that cast for almost a year."

Ivan only glanced at him, then looked away.

"My father threw his anointed son down the steps." He waited a moment to compose himself, offering an apologetic glance at the others in the room, then kept going. "My mother warned me not to tell a soul, that he'd be in jail and we'd be destitute. So she and I learned to lie about our injuries. All of them."

Ivan's expression didn't change, but he remained silent for several moments. Then, "And that story is supposed to move me to tears? To feel sorry for you? How pathetic."

"You're right, Ivan. It is pathetic. You and I carry pathetic wounds. Just like this woman." The president lifted the last photograph and forced Ivan to look at it. "See the young boy in her lap? Cute kid. Blond hair and chunky little cheeks, like you had in that picture you sent me." Noland leaned close to Ivan's impassive face. "That's the boy you killed!"

Ivan stiffened and pulled away from him.

"Where's the bomb, Ivan?" the president demanded again, his patience at an end.

But Ivan turned to the window and stared as if listening for voices. A bead of sweat trickled down the side of his nose and still he waited, for something. Then he began to cough and gasp for breath. He inclined his head toward his bedroom and rasped, "My medicine. Please."

Please? The president nodded toward one of the officers.

"Where is it?" the officer asked Ivan.

"My bathroom. In the shaving kit. A pill bottle marked Guaifenesin." The officer retrieved the medicine and returned with a bottled water.

"Untie me?" Ivan ventured, his gaze falling oddly on the president.

"No," Noland answered firmly. "Help him," he told the officer.

"There's only one pill in here," the officer told Ivan.

"That's all I need."

The president noticed he wasn't coughing anymore.

"I'm going to drop it into your mouth," the officer said, lifting the pill.

Ivan looked once at the president, then at the ceiling. "Hallelujah to the other son." He opened his mouth wide.

"No!" Noland yelled, suddenly understanding. But the pill had already fallen into Ivan's mouth. It took only seconds for the cyanide to kill him.

Chapter 41

Shortly before the president returned to the White House, a Coast Guard helicopter swooped low over a cargo ship off Cape Hatteras. Within the hour, a cutter engaged the ship head-on, ordering it to stop. When it didn't, the cutter fired across the ship's bow as two 45-foot CG response boats came screaming over the waves, each taking a flank position on either side of the huge ship. The helicopter returned and lowered a boarding team onto the deck of the tossing ship. Reinforcements from the cutter boarded minutes later.

They found the bomb beneath a false bottom to the ship. It was still crated and contained. A bomb crew, hastily dispatched to the cutter before it left port, boarded the cargo ship and dismantled the weapon. The entire crew was arrested.

Word of the president's daring raid on Ivan's yacht reached Max and Ben mid morning in Berlin.

"So Volynski's really dead," Ben said as the two men poured over the rest of the bulletin from Mossad. "This time, there's no doubt about it. It's been confirmed by the president himself."

Max was still scanning the report. "So that day on the East River, according to interrogation of Curt Vandoren, Volynski changed his mind about leaving New York and got out of the helicopter just before it took off." Max read on, paraphrasing the official script. "The heliport guard was so distracted by the NYPD assault on the tugboat about to take down the Brooklyn Bridge, he didn't see Ivan leave the chopper and climb back into the car. And he sure wasn't watching the car after that chopper exploded right in front of him."

Ben, too, was buried in the report. "I don't see any mention of Arkady Glinka."

"You won't until the Americans are pretty sure of what they're dealing with. They can't afford to cast hear-say incriminations against the sitting president of Russia by a guy like Vandoren. Evgeny spotting Maxum Morozov leaving Glinka's dacha doesn't prove anything. Even though it screams collusion to me. If my father was hinged to Volynski, so was Glinka."

Just then, another communiqué streamed online to Max's laptop. "Okay, here we go. The White House says we can step down the guard over Liesl and a certain fiddle player from Israel. Seems like Noland would like us to keep our concert date in Nuremberg."

"Then let's get out of here."

"He's dead?" Liesl asked in disbelief. Max had led her and Cade outside the apartment to unfold as much of the CIA/Mossad report as they were cleared to know. Mainly that the man who'd worked hardest to eliminate Liesl Bower had just ended his own life.

"We leave for Nuremberg this afternoon," Max announced with unabashed relief as the three now strolled away from the apartment building.

"You don't think it's too soon to just run outside and play?" Cade asked. Liesl saw the apprehension in his face. "Could there be remnants of Volynski's network still operating?"

Max looked into the trees overhead as they passed near a deli whose menu was handwritten in the window. "I'm certain that, as remnants go, we'll never account for them all. Who knows the scope of his reach or the number of minds he's infected. But how many of them care a whit about a couple of musicians?" Max was in no mood to belabor the possibility that between his father and Glinka, the likelihood of a remnant was probably worth fretting over. But would he, and Liesl, continue to live their lives in such a fret?

Max breathed long and deep. "It's a clean-start day for us. Let's not muddy it with lingering fears and uncertainties." He stopped to read the menu then clapped Cade heartily on the back. "I would like to linger, instead, over a hot pastrami sandwich."

Liesl saw beneath the mask. She'd known Max too long to miss it. Something brewed dark and thick beneath the light in his face. There was no doubt in her mind that he, indeed, concerned himself with Ivan's remnant, particularly his father. She knew he always would. The man had long impaired his son in ways few could detect. But Liesl was one who could.

"What about the others at the apartment?" Cade asked.

"About this time, Ben is probably sitting Anna and Erica down and informing them that there's no longer any need to smother under the security blanket. Of course, in private, he'll divulge a bit more to Anna, who knows of the man who tried to assassinate her husband and why."

"And Erica?" Liesl asked.

"She can't know any of this," Max said. "Ben will be adequately vague about lifting security and why."

"And the two of you?" Liesl ventured.

Max shrugged. "I don't know where we're headed. She's a hard one to know, and I don't give her much encouragement, I'm afraid. She's probably better off without me."

"Okay, I think it's time for pastrami," Cade announced with a wink at Liesl.

"Thanks for tossing a lifeline," Max said as they headed into the deli.

Across the street, Felix Shevcik watched Liesl Bower disappear into the deli with her husband and the violinist. Surely they'd leave for Nuremberg soon. The concert was Friday night. Outdoors. Surrounded by the dark. Thousands of cheering fans to muffle the shots.

Chapter 42

They were to stay at a country estate outside Nuremberg. A wealthy music patron and friend of Max's had offered it to him and his guests for the festival. The man's family dated back to the late seventeen hundreds in that region of Bavaria. They'd been bankers until Hitler's Nuremberg Laws wrested their German citizenship from them and then, for most of the family, their lives. Franz Bernhoff had picked up his family's trampled banner and carried it back to Nuremberg, where he reinstated the family name and grew a thriving medical practice. Now retired, he could fill his days with music.

After flying from Berlin late Thursday afternoon, Max, Liesl, Cade, and the rest of their entourage were met by two German police officers, still charged with protecting the celebrity musicians. They left Nuremberg airport and headed first to the city. Max had suggested they visit the performance site "before the ghosts are chased away by the crowds."

"Those ghosts will never leave," Ben had insisted.

Heading south from the airport, their driver, one of the officers, skirted the eleventh-century Imperial Castle rising high above Old Town, and veered southeast to the historic Zeppelinfeld rally grounds of the Nazi Party. Parking the van near the entrance, the driver and his fellow officer got out and quickly scanned the area, then returned for their charges.

After a short walk, the group entered the grounds and stopped to listen. The orchestra's stage crew had already set up close by. Though the final rehearsal was scheduled for the following morning, a few musicians had arrived to absorb the natural vibes of the place and tune them to their instruments.

But quickly, the familiar sounds died away, at least to Max's ear. He had now turned to find that one spot, that portal where it seemed that the ultimate evil had funneled its powers onto the man who used to stand in that place. Silently, Max drifted away from the others and made his way to the high platform, up the crumbling concrete grandstand at the base of the soaring wall once topped by a giant swastika. Now turning to mount the speaker's platform, he looked down at his friends and saw the quiet understanding in their raised faces. In all but Erica's. She had already strayed from the group and drifted across the field.

Max watched her a moment, but couldn't linger on the mystery of her. The ghostly thundering of allegiant shouts from two hundred thousand people drowned out everything else. He wondered if anyone else could hear them, or sense their spirits returning just now to life forms as palpable as if they'd never left this place. Max looked out over the vast parade ground, now choked with weeds and deteriorated buildings, and saw the tight legions of goose-stepping troops and the attendant throngs of citizenry jabbing the night with stiff-armed salutes to the Führer.

Now, the lone Jew, the gentle violinist, shuddered involuntarily at the nearness of the voices. At that one voice shouting murderous hatred from the place where Max now stood.

How many times such a portal to evil had opened through the ages, in different lands, to different rulers and those who schemed to be. How many times had they gone mad from the touch of it. Max closed his eyes and thought about the things he knew of Ivan Volynski and Arkady Glinka, about their willing reach through that portal into another realm where they were mere pawns in the hands of forces beyond their control, beyond even their comprehension, yet forces they gladly embraced for what such powers could do for them. And just what did those powers do for them? Volynski was dead of his own volition. But Glinka was sure to become the next president of Russia. Would the forces follow him there? Then what?

Max had stood there too long. The others had strolled off to explore the haunting acreage now used for car races, rock concerts, and campgrounds. Would that quiet the voices? Max didn't think so. Perhaps something else would, though.

Tomorrow night, descendants of the Holocaust dead would gather at the spot where Hitler had emerged from the portal, feverish with murderous contempt for an entire race of people. The collective voice of the Israel Philharmonic would raise from this very den of anti-Semitic fury. Could that voice defy the powers of the portal? Could anything?

Finally climbing down from the platform, Max saw Liesl and Cade waving him over. They were reading the interpretive signage posted about the grounds. Ben and Anna were nearby. But Erica was in the distance, a phone to her ear. His eye steady on her, Max approached the others.

"You okay?" Liesl asked him.

"Sure I am." He looked back at the place he'd just left, then across the field at Erica. "Is there a problem with her?" He didn't want to talk about the oppressive weight he felt descend on him each time he visited these grounds.

Liesl looked toward the girl. "She just said there were calls to return. Something about impatient customers waiting for their photographs. Does she stay busy with that?"

"Not really. Most of the display photos I've seen were taken years ago. Now, it's mostly bridal portraits, but not many of those." He kept watching Erica. "I'm not sure how she pays her bills. We don't discuss those things."

"Does she have family?" Ben asked.

Max shrugged. "All I know is her parents are dead. She's estranged from a brother in New York. And that's all she's ever mentioned. Well, here she comes. I hope everything's okay with the cat. That's all she's got in Tel Aviv. And me, I guess. Lucky girl."

"Okay, this happy little conversation has come to an end," Anna declared firmly, yet compassionately looping her arm around Max's. "It'll be dark soon, and we still need to find this house in the hills, right? So let's go."

"And when the quiet one speaks," Ben teased his wife, "we must all listen and obey." He glanced at the sky. "But she's right. Night's coming." He looked pointedly at Max. "My buddy here tells me he isn't afraid of ghosts. But I think he is. And I know I am."

An hour later, the group headed out of the city toward rolling farmland and forests so dense, they appeared deep blue from the road. As the sun cast its last rays of the day, their German driver followed his GPS toward a closed gate, stopped, and punched in an entrance code. A hush fell over the car as someone spoke through an intercom at the gate.

"Max, is that you?"

"It is, Franz, and my guests."

"Splendid. Come in. We are waiting."

The gates opened and the van lumbered onto a narrow, blacktop road that wound into a deep wood, drawing comment from Erica, who'd been notably withdrawn for the last couple of days. "If Hansel and Gretel come charging out of those woods with a witch on their tail, please let's not stop to pick them up."

It took a moment to register that Erica had offered a droll respite from her gloomy mood. Everyone but Max rewarded her for it, laughing gratefully with her. With a weak smile, Max turned away to study the roadway ahead. It was now opening onto rolling fields only partially tended. Erica's mood had been of less and less interest to Max as the concert hour approached. He couldn't let her drain the emotional energy he would need for the performance, so he chose to distance himself from her and concentrate on his good fortune in friends, those with him in this car, and the old man waiting to greet them, if feebly.

At eighty-two, Franz had survived two strokes and a heart attack. But his spirit remained valiant, reinforced each day, he'd said, by music. The home was often filled by friends who came to play for him and by invited guests to the small chamber concerts he gave inside the palatial home. And there it was now, settled on a hilltop overlooking ridge upon ridge of countryside. It was built of stone and dark timbers, the land around it stretching into meadows of wild flowers.

"Oh, look!" Liesl exclaimed with awe. "It's like a Romance painting of some absurdly beautiful landscape."

Max looked at her with open affection, then checked himself before anyone else might notice. He would love her forever, he was sure. But something had begun to turn in him. He'd finally come to realize that it wasn't the love he used to feel, when he would imagine her in his arms. It had matured beyond that. Platonic? He cringed at the clinical and antiseptic word. But he had no other to substitute. She was a friend whose attachment to him defied description.

He turned from admiring Liesl to catch Erica's hooded eyes. How long had she been watching him watch Liesl? Just now, it didn't matter. He smiled pleasantly at her and turned away.

When they pulled up at the handsome manor, Franz was there on his walker to greet them. An attendant stood nearby. When everyone poured from the vehicle, there was an almost exhaustive round of introductions and mutually admiring chatter. Max preferred to listen to it, like music. He was feeling so strange, like emotions long turbulent inside him were beginning to ebb into something like a monotonous flow. Or was it mere resignation? Why fight what you can't change. Or, perhaps he was simply numb.

That night after dinner and a couple of early *gute nacht*s from Ben and Anna, everyone else retired to the octagonal music room of the house where Franz had installed a grand piano and an assortment of instruments. It was a small concert hall where most of Nuremberg's gifted had performed over the years. A massive, carved walnut cabinet was filled with music for solo and ensemble performers.

While Cade, Erica, and their host settled into leather wingbacks, Liesl and Max launched into an impromptu recital that took them from Beethoven and Mendelssohn to Gershwin and Copland.

When the music that evening reached an end and all were ready for sleep, Franz took Max aside as the others were led upstairs by one of the housekeepers. The old man who played no instrument himself, but had a voracious passion for the music, laid a hand on the piano and stroked it as if it were a beloved pet. "Max, tomorrow night must come from someplace I'm afraid you've not visited lately."

Max didn't understand, not at first.

"The music of your countrymen, and especially that which flows from your own violin, will fall flat and perish in pity if you don't guard your hearts. If you don't go to that place."

Slowly shaking his head, Max insisted he didn't know what that meant. But he did know. He just didn't want to hear it.

"The place is forgiveness," Franz continued. "Your music will never know the power it should unless you go to that place and bring some of it back with you." His faded eyes held fast to Max, who turned his own eyes away.

"Look at me, Max." The feeble hand wavered toward the piano and the violin propped beside it. Max obeyed. "In that audience will be the sons and daughters of those who executed our people. And they're coming to hear you play because they no longer care that you're Jewish. They want to rid themselves of the bondage of what happened. Especially the young ones. Why do you think Hitler's exalted parade grounds lie in ruins while the Holocaust Museum in the heart of this country's capital is meticulously tended? They've moved on, Max, and so must you. Free yourself. Forgive them. And one more."

Max knew what was coming.

"He doesn't deserve it, but you must forgive your father. And then, young Max . . . then your music will soar."

Chapter 43

*B*y midday Thursday, Travis Noland had returned to the Oval Office. So far, the media had not sniffed out the president's sudden pre-dawn departure.

"Shelton, we've got another bomb on the way. At least, that's the chatter."

"From the Urals factory?" Shelton Myers asked. The president's long-time friend and confidante from their earlier State Department days had been called to the White House along with CIA Director Don Bragg, who would arrive shortly. It was Shelton Myers who had advised Noland in the aftermath of discovering that Ivan Volynski was his half brother.

"That's right." The president handed him a copy of intelligence reports citing probable transfer of another weapon from the factory dug into the side of a mountain. The satellite image of the remote wilderness site hadn't shown it ringed by cameras and trip-wire explosives. It had taken a sure-footed CIA surveillance team to detect the invisible security shield.

"How can I help?" Shelton asked.

"I'm about to place a call to Arkady Glinka. I want you and Don to listen in. It's my duty to give Glinka notice that we just intercepted a Russian-made WMD headed for Washington. And that the man who ordered it is good and dead . . . this time. But it's my intent to do a bit of probing. We know Ivan and Glinka were linked. We have the patrolman's positive ID of the two together when he stopped them in the Keys. And Tally Greyson is pretty sure it was Glinka she saw at Vandoren's place the night they unloaded that bomb from the plane. You and I believe Glinka is complicit in President Gorev's murder. But coincidence, "pretty sure," and gut feeling isn't evidence of Glinka's guilt or association with Ivan's operation."

"Then we need proof and we need it quickly," Shelton said. "The State Department already knows he's headlong into taking, perhaps even rigging, that election. He'll be permanently enthroned in just over two months."

The president nodded agreement. "But the bigger race is finding that second bomb."

Moments after CIA Director Don Bragg arrived in the Oval Office and received his briefing from the president, Rona Arant buzzed her boss's desk. "I have President Glinka for you, sir. Remember that it's almost ten PM there."

"Put him through." Noland picked up the handset and tapped the "speaker" button. "Mr. President, thank you for taking my call so late at night."

"I trust that it is most important."

Noland expected the man's usual discourteous tone no matter the time of day. There was no point in attempting formal cordialities. "I am advising you, President Glinka, that earlier today, we intercepted a cargo ship off our Atlantic coast which was carrying a chemical weapon of mass destruction. The bomb was en route to Washington, where we believe it would have been detonated sometime in the coming days." With no sound from the other end, Noland proceeded. "We have confirmed intelligence reports that place the manufacture of the bomb inside Russia. The Ural Mountains, to be specific."

Still nothing on the Moscow end. Then, with indignity, "Are you suggesting the Russian Federation just launched an attack on your capital?"

"No, Mr. President, I am not. We have proof that the bomb was ordered by, shipped to, and received by . . . Ivan Volynski."

After a long pause, Glinka erupted in a quick burst of laughter. "I hope you did not call me at this hour to play a prank. You know that Volynski is dead. You even announced it on television. A sad thing to happen . . . to your brother."

Noland ignored the provocation and waited, but nothing more was forthcoming. Shouldn't Glinka be assuring the U.S. president that the Russian government had nothing whatsoever to do with the bomb? An innocent man would.

Now it was time for Noland to drop his own bomb and see how the pieces fell. "It is no prank. Before dawn this morning, I boarded Ivan Volynski's boat off the Florida Keys and spoke with him myself. He told me many things." It was true, though nothing about Arkady Glinka.

All Noland heard through the receiver was the sudden intake of breath, then nothing more. He watched the transfixed expressions on the faces opposite him. Shelton nodded his head in approval of the conversation so far.

Finally, Glinka cleared his throat and spoke, his voice tight. "So now you have your brother in an interrogation room somewhere pumping information from a desperate man who'll say anything to save himself."

Noland didn't miss the obvious omission. "You surprise me, President Glinka. I would have thought your first, and natural, reaction would be shock at the news that Volynski was alive. Were you not surprised to hear that?"

"Do not test me! Save that for your deranged brother!"

"I can't do that. Ivan killed himself. I watched him do it."

Now Noland was afraid Glinka might really melt down and hang up before the most urgent matter was approached. "But there is something more critical to discuss right now. We have reports of a second bomb exiting that Urals factory, but we don't know where, or to whom, it is headed. I expect your government to track that bomb before our countries are forced into an unfortunate confrontation. And I expect that factory to be located and destroyed. There will be no compromise on this, President Glinka."

The line went dead.

Chapter 44

Arkady Glinka wasn't going to wait for officers to come arrest him. He didn't know what Ivan had confessed to, if anything, or who he'd implicated. Soon after Noland's call, Glinka evaded his security guards and fled his Moscow apartment. It didn't matter what appointments he would miss the following day or the ones afterward. He would hide out and wait to see if Noland was bluffing. Glinka's staff would cover for him. They were practiced at it.

He couldn't go to his dacha. It was known. So now, alone in his personal car, he was driving hard to the home of a former mistress in a small town southeast of Moscow. She would be glad to see him. She'd take him in and shelter him until his staff signaled an all clear. They were all Ivan's people, recruited by him to help the new president of Russia prepare for revolution, and for Ivan's arrival.

Even now, fleeing wild through a panic, Glinka welcomed the relief of Ivan's death, if he was indeed dead. But as much as he disliked the American president, Glinka believed the man was incapable of such a preposterous lie. Ivan would have died soon enough, Glinka was sure. But the inconvenience of waiting for it had been removed by Ivan's own hand.

So after all the years of planning and scheming, after all the dreams of glory, you killed yourself. How did you do it, Ivan?

If he hadn't been in such a hurry, Glinka would have pulled over and channeled himself into the other plane, letting his visualization skills take him to his special place, beyond the hazards of being an earthbound mortal. But he would survive this, he knew. He would take the election and defy Noland to come at him with anything resembling proof. What could that possibly be?

He reached for his phone and called Maxum.

"Yes," the man answered.

Glinka relayed everything about Noland's call, then, "This doesn't change anything, but you'd better be careful. I'm calling back the weapon. It's not the time, now. They're watching for it."

"They must have discovered the first bomb through Ivan, but how did they find him?" Maxum asked. It sounded to Glinka like the man had been running. "And where is Vandoren?"

Just then, Glinka fit a major piece to the puzzle. Vandoren wasn't answering his phone because he'd been apprehended. Ivan had been next. And Glinka? They still had no proof. Add the word of a suicidal madman to that of a spook, as the unenlightened called Vandoren, and you still have nothing to hang charges on, American or Russian. Besides, they would have to find him first.

"Another question," Maxum said. "Why is Felix Shevcik trailing Liesl Bower?"

"How did you know?"

"Someone working for me was approached by him. He wanted her to work with him."

"Her?"

"Yes."

"Shevcik would enjoy that, I am sure. Ivan knew of his perversions with women, but brought him in anyway. The man's there to kill the piano player. Leave him alone and let him do his job. He doesn't need to know about Ivan. But tell your girl to watch herself." Glinka laughed. Maxum didn't.

"I must go," Maxum said.

"Where are you?"

"Nuremberg."

Chapter 45

*E*vgeny had arrived in Nuremberg just ahead of Liesl. He'd taken a room near the Nazi Party Rally Grounds and watched as she had strolled there with Cade and the others. He didn't mind hovering in the shadows. He'd spent his whole life there. That he felt the need to remain there even after Volynski's death troubled him.

Ava had delivered the news immediately after Travis Noland had left Volynski's ship. Evgeny wished he could have witnessed that confrontation, wished to be there when Volynski breathed his last in the testifying presence of others. Evgeny still struggled with how he missed seeing Volynski slip away from the lift-off of that helicopter on the East River. He'd seen the driver clearly as he sped from the horrific scene, but Evgeny had been so certain the man was alone in the car, he hadn't focused hard on the back seat where Ivan hid.

The search for Volynski was over. And the threat? Ava hadn't been overly convincing in suggesting there was no more need for his watch over Liesl. He'd considered suspending it, but a tiny burr had lodged against him and he couldn't shake it loose. It was an insignificant little incident, but one that made no sense. And if it didn't make sense to Evgeny, he was inherently helpless to discard it. Why had Erica Bachman slipped away from him the day before? He'd seen through her flippant accusation that he'd not met her where he was supposed to. But he was certain that Max had not miscommunicated with either one of them. It had been a guise. She'd been told to meet him in front, yet she'd left through the back entrance. Why?

This afternoon at the rally grounds, he'd watched her distance herself from the others, a phone to her ear for an extended time. She'd shown no interest in the historic place, read no signage. The professional photographer had taken no pictures, as the amateurs around her had.

They'd left the grounds as they'd arrived, with police escorts. Ava had told him that would continue throughout their international travel. It was customary, she'd insisted. Liesl was still a celebrity and a guest of Germany.

But Evgeny had phoned Viktor in Moscow. "See what you can find on Erica Bachman," Evgeny had told him. "She is Max Morozov's new girlfriend. A photographer, late twenties, blond at the moment, attractive."

"Who do you *think* she is?" Viktor asked.

"A person of great interest to me right now."

"I need more than that."

"But I do not have it. Check aliases and whatever you have on free agents. There may be nothing there at all. I hope not."

"I will do what I can. Meanwhile, Evgeny, watch yourself."

The sun was barely up the next morning when Viktor's call reached Evgeny. He was walking to the rally grounds where Liesl, Max, and the orchestra would arrive for rehearsals in a couple of hours. If anyone was scouting for the best gunnery position overlooking the concert stage, Evgeny wanted to know it.

"Yes," he answered expectantly.

"First, I have nothing on Erica Bachman, but I will keep searching. You should know this, though—Arkady Glinka left Moscow in the middle of the night, skipping out on a full schedule of meetings today. The official advisory from his staff is 'an urgent family matter and he will return shortly.' Word has it, though, that he left immediately after a phone call from Travis Noland. Do you know anything about that?"

Evgeny knew then that Ava Mullins hadn't told him everything. "No, but I will find out. Keep after the Bachman girl."

He entered the grounds and stopped to take in the Zeppelinfeld, the vast square field where Ferdinand Graf von Zeppelin landed one of his bizarre airships in 1909. Evgeny looked up at the imposing grandstand, now in ruin. He remembered the clips of American soldiers blowing the giant swastika off the top in 1945. In his mind's eye, he could see Hitler railing from the speaker's platform. The concert stage had been erected directly below and slightly to one side of Hitler's rostrum. Evgeny wondered at the notion of Jewish musicians commanding a Nazi parade ground.

The wind swept in from the field, turning his attention to the thirty-four cement towers built at regular intervals into the spectator stands lining three sides of the grounds. They were bathroom facilities, now closed, encased in choking vines and weeds.

Before rehearsal began that morning, he would survey the entire grounds, then find the best vantage point for observing any suspicious visitors to the field. Who that could be was unclear. So, too, was his mission beyond this day. Volynski's death had sounded a knell for his own life. When the need to protect Liesl extinguished itself, what then? What good would he be?

Watching the man walking toward him, Felix Shevcik was glad he'd risen early and settled into position. He scolded himself for not anticipating that Evgeny Kozlov would remain vigilante over Liesl Bower, and would also rise early for work. But here he was, just steps away. He would look over the squat, cement tower and see no difference from all the others. He wouldn't see the hacked lock on the door beneath the wild vines, nor the weaponry assembled before the high, narrow window overlooking the concert stage. Felix was certain of this. What he wasn't sure of at this moment was the prospect of escaping the night's hit with the likes of Kozlov patrolling the grounds. Hadn't the man taught Felix every trick of surveillance and pursuit? And surely, if Kozlov had risked capture to be here, others must also be on watch.

Felix wondered if it wouldn't be wiser to take Liesl Bower early. Ivan would be disappointed. His preference was to pop her during the concert. He wanted the world to watch. Felix should prepare his boss for a possible change of plans. He would place that call after Kozlov was a safe distance away. The hole Felix had cut in the old window and the echo inside the empty concrete chamber demanded his silence for now.

When Kozlov was almost halfway around the field, Felix punched in Ivan's encrypted code and put the phone to his ear. There was no answer, only a series of faint beeps Felix had not heard before on Ivan's phone. But the man was half a world away, cruising under the Florida sun and anticipating news of tonight's success. Cell transmission might, understandably, be fraught with interference. Felix pocketed the phone. He would try again after a while. A van had just pulled inside the grounds and the first of the orchestra stage crew emerged, dragging coils of cables behind them. His watch had begun. He awaited the Bower woman and a bead on Evgeny's location. Perhaps he could take them both down seconds apart. Now or later.

Chapter 46

Franz's kitchen staff served a light breakfast in the sunroom, which overlooked a gentle scrolling of lavender mountain ridges. A pair of broad-winged birds cavorted in pastel skies.

"We moved the breakfast table out here years ago," Franz said. "I couldn't bear to look at walls when all this was going on outside. We even stripped away the heavy drapes my late wife had installed at every window in the house. Now, nothing separates me from . . . the things that soar." He looked directly at Max, then turned to the others and swept a hand over the table. "Now, refresh yourselves. The fruits, the breads, the eggs and yogurt—all fresh from our own grounds."

Throughout the meal, Max glanced repeatedly at Erica, who'd retired to her room the night before without so much as a peck on the cheek for him. He knew their relationship had withered dramatically over the last days, though he didn't understand it. Conjecture, assumptions, and innuendos didn't replace a solid answer.

Later, after profuse compliments and thanksgiving to their host, they wandered separately from the sunroom, preparing for different agendas that morning. Ben and Anna wanted to shop the antique stores in town. Cade would accompany Liesl and Max to rehearsal. But Erica hadn't yet voiced her intentions. Max caught up with her at the foot of the grand staircase.

"Erica, would you like to walk with me before I have to leave?"

She looked apprehensive, her eyes searching his. But an instant later, her clouded face suddenly brightened. Now it was open, and she was eager to join him. It was a transformation he'd observed too often. As they left the house and headed for a path into the nearby meadow, he wondered at what triggered the seismic shifts in her.

"You've been so withdrawn the last few days," he said. "Are you sure the clueless male that I am hasn't committed some colossal insult?"

She looked up at him and smiled. It seemed genuine. "Not at all. I've just been, uh, preoccupied with a few ornery clients back home." She looked away.

"Add to that a bunch of annoying bodyguards, quarantine conditions in Berlin, and a tour guide hauling you down to the catacombs of Holocaust atrocities. No wonder you've run the other way."

She grabbed his arm and stopped walking. "If I'd wanted to run, I wouldn't be here now." She slid her arms around his waist and pulled him to her. Her kiss was sweet and soft, but brief. When she pulled away she seemed flustered. She started to speak, then clamped her mouth tight.

"Okay, this is going to stop. Something's up with you. Up, then down, then up again. You're making me dizzy. Tell me what's going on with us. Please."

Then he watched it happen again. It was like a sheet of ice sliding over her face, weighing the eyes into narrow slits and the mouth into a hard line.

"What is that?" Max exclaimed, pointing at her face. "That thing you do like flipping a switch. This person one second, and polar opposite the next. Who's in there now? Have I met you before?" He didn't mean to lose all composure, but oddly enough, it seemed to have little effect on her.

"No, you don't know me. You don't really want to."

"What's that supposed to mean?"

But she shook off the question and started back toward the house.

"Erica, please wait. Talk to me!"

But she kept walking. Over her shoulder, she called, "I'm going with you this morning."

The whole way into town, Liesl felt the hard chill between Max and Erica. She hoped it would thaw before Max had to perform that evening. Then she shamed herself for thinking of the concert first. She should try to mediate between them, perhaps. Perhaps not. Neither one invited intervention just now, their faces set like plaster.

"Max, tell me about the program tonight," Cade piped brightly.

That's right, Liesl thought, catching his intent. *Create a diversion.*

It took a few moments, but Max's face finally relaxed into familiar lines, Liesl was glad to see. Her friend glanced at her and smiled. It was the old Max. Impish, passionate, and enormously gifted at overriding his pain. "A tribute to a couple of guys Germany's real proud of," he answered. "We'll begin with Beethoven's *Triple Concerto*—Liesl at the piano, me on my outrageously expensive fiddle, a cellist, and full orchestra. Then comes Bach. The orchestra will dazzle us with a *Brandenburg Concerto* before Liesl returns to the stage to hog all the spotlight for herself. You *do* know what she's playing tonight."

Cade grinned, but barely. "And high time, I think." He looked reflective. "No one in that audience, though, will know it was the piece that prevented a world war. But nearly cost me a wife." He nodded slowly. "It's time she chased off its demons."

Liesl fought the tears and lost. Blinking them away, she landed on Erica's clearly confused expression. *Oh no.* They'd spoken of things no one else should know. Classified things once vital to national security, even though the crisis had passed. How easy it had been to slip. She met Max's eyes, now wide with the sudden realization of what he and Cade had done. They all looked at Erica, but said nothing more about Tchaikovsky's *Grand Sonata in G Major*, and certainly not the code once embedded in it.

Now it was Liesl's turn to distract. "Erica, I hope you won't be bored with the rehearsal. Are you sure you wouldn't rather take pictures in Old Town?"

"I'm sure," she answered. "I'll get some good stuff from the rally grounds today." She smiled politely and looked out the window, offering nothing more.

They soon pulled up behind the bus now discharging members of the orchestra and their instruments. The conductor had promised a short rehearsal, for which Liesl was glad. She needed a long rest before the concert and the rigorous sonata, which she would rehearse alone at the estate. As she climbed from the van, she looked into a solid blue sky and was grateful for no threat of rain, especially after glimpsing the stage. The concert grand was now in place, a Gibraltar-size instrument. Perhaps she should have studied the piccolo. How convenient that would have been.

It didn't take long for the first notes of the *Triple Concerto* to lift from the stage. For the next two hours, the musicians polished their performances, working out the kinks of performing on the portable stage and adjusting to the occasional gusts of wind over the open field. But spotters about the grounds assured the conductor that the sound quality and visibility were favorable.

When the rehearsal ended, Liesl gathered her music and helped cover the piano. Max invited Cade to the stage where he was introduced to the other musicians. Liesl heard her husband's reporter instincts engage and the questions fly. He asked about their lives outside the orchestra and how they blended their music with professions that actually paid the bills, like dentistry and teaching.

Later, she took the steps to the ground and went off in search of the stage manager. She'd noticed a squeak in the piano bench that wasn't at all in tune with the music. She'd just rounded the side of one of the orchestra vans when Erica approached her, camera in hand.

"Hi Liesl," the girl said, her mood noticeably lighter. "Why don't you slip away for a breather? Come with me down to the lake." She pointed through the trees. "I'd love to photograph you against the sparkle of the water. The light's just right at the moment."

The girl's voice carried an almost singsong lilt, and Liesl welcomed the change in tone. She looked toward Cade, who seemed not to notice that she'd left the stage. He was deep in conversation with a man demonstrating his tuba. Max had his back to them, busily tuning his violin. It would be okay. She'd be right back.

"Will you come?" Erica asked buoyantly.

Liesl shrugged and glanced around her. "Escape the bodyguards? I can do that."

The two women walked at a brisk clip toward the far trees. "It's called Dutzendteich Lake," Erica informed. "On the other side is the unfinished congress building Hitler had built. He modeled it after the Colosseum in Rome. I guess he fancied himself the head of a new Roman-like empire."

"It could happen again," Liesl observed.

Without checking her pace, Erica's full attention snapped toward Liesl. "Why do you say that?"

The reason was obvious to Liesl, though she couldn't tell Erica why. A man named Ivan Volynski had penetrated the defenses that a post-WWII world had erected against another Hitler. Liesl had watched it happen, felt the heat of its force and its fangs at her heels. She'd seen those defenses against such a person fail, and the desperate attempts to patch them. She wasn't sure they'd hold back all the Volynskis to come.

Just then, Liesl remembered Evgeny Kozlov's refrain from his visit to her dressing room that night at Avery Fisher Hall. *Never stop watching them.* She glanced about her and wondered how far away, or how close, he was at this moment. There was never any way of knowing for sure. His was an elusive shadow.

"Hitler wasn't the last of his breed," Liesl answered simply. But that was enough on the subject. She didn't wish to taint the morning and this brief respite. She changed direction. "What will you do with your photographs from this trip?"

But Erica ignored the question. "Liesl, I don't want to talk about my photographs right now. I want to know why you all have to keep so many secrets from me. I'm practically held prisoner in Berlin, and all Max tells me is there are threats against your life, possibly his. I think there's more to it than that. Why won't anyone tell me what's going on?"

They were in the trees now, the shadows deep and concealing. Liesl stopped. "You're right. There is more to it." Liesl gauged the set of the girl's face. Was it childish pique at being left out of the clique? Or did she feel at risk by her association with them? Certainly she was and Liesl regretted that Max had brought his new friend along.

"I'm sorry if that brief quarantine in Berlin frightened you."

"Oh, I'm not afraid," Erica insisted. "And I'm not blind. I know Max and Ben are involved in some kind of intelligence work for Israel. I know you were at the center of something pretty awful a couple of years ago and again just six months ago. And now, it seems, something is still out there. But nobody trusts me enough to talk about any of it." The voice went cold. "There is the slightest chance I might have been of help."

Besides the sudden twist in tone and the letting of information Erica Bachman should not have known, the thing that struck Liesl most about that tirade was the tense of those last few words . . . *might have been* of help. As if the "something" still out there were over and done. And what could she possibly have done to help?

"I'm afraid I've said too much," Erica allowed. "I'm sorry. I didn't mean to ruin our time together." She touched Liesl's arm, tugged slightly, and encouraged her to keep going.

Though her first impulse was to retreat, she resumed her place at Erica's side and looked toward the water, which had grown bluer in the mid-morning light. Erica was quiet as they picked their way through the trees. When they emerged onto a sunlit path along the water, the girl stopped and looked around them. "There are a few high boulders a little farther down. Like the ones in Central Park, you know." She smiled hesitantly at Liesl. "If you climbed up on one with the water behind you, I could get a great shot for your publicity manager."

That sounded reasonable to Liesl, who was anxious to sidestep her mis-givings about this girl. She was just impetuous and boldly drawn, like a van Gogh portrait. The notion swiped at Liesl. *Why would I think of him? The artist with whom Ivan Volynski seemed to identify. Ben had told her of the man's fascination with van Gogh's self-portrait, with the bandaged nub of an ear he'd lopped off his own head.* Was this her mind on overload with too many barbed bytes of her own fractured history, randomly sorted and irrelevantly linked? She believed it was.

"How far down?" Liesl asked. "I need to get back."

"Just a little ways. Let's hurry."

But soon, Erica left the sunny path and headed back into the trees. "I thought the rocks were near the lake," Liesl said.

"There's a better place in here," she pointed farther into the woods. "The dappled light through the trees will make a more dramatic shot."

Liesl knew she'd been gone too long. Cade would be searching for her by now, and she'd left her phone—*both* phones—in her music bag. She'd seen Evgeny prowl the grounds earlier, though she hadn't noticed him as she was leaving. "Erica, I'm sorry, we'll take pictures another time. I have to go now."

"The boulders are right there," Erica said, pointing. "Just a couple of shots. Go on, climb up. But you might want to take off your shoes. They look slick on the bottom."

Liesl sighed heavily and kicked off her sandals. "Five minutes tops," she told Erica firmly. "That's all the time I've got."

Liesl hiked her long, filmy skirt and bunched it around her knees. She climbed steadily, finding her footholds. When she reached the top, she turned to face Erica. But Erica wasn't there. Someone else was. A man Liesl had never seen before had just emerged from the woods. He walked slowly toward her and stopped.

"Hello, Liesl. I'm Maxum Morozov."

Chapter 47

Felix watched Liesl Bower and Erica Bachman slip away from the field. *Where are they going? Alone.* He checked Kozlov's position again. During the rehearsal, the man had concealed himself at the far end of the grandstand bulwark, visible to few but Felix, who'd visually tracked him from the moment he'd arrived at the grounds that morning. It gave Felix great pleasure to outwit his formidable teacher, now foe. But had the great Kozlov taken his eyes off the Bower woman too long? What was he doing? The one he'd come to watch over had disappeared right under his nose and the veteran spy had missed it. Felix could hardly contain his delight at watching that happen. *You old fool. You've lost your skills. You don't even know where she is. Too bad for you. What an opportunity for me.*

To pursue the women, he couldn't leave through the door he'd entered in the dark that morning. Instead, he gathered his weapons, lowered himself through a back window of the tower, and dropped to the ground. Perhaps he should try his boss once more before bearing down on the target. He crossed behind the far spectator stands and merged into the indigo depths of the woods, only then stopping to phone Ivan once more. Again, there was no answer, only the same barely audible beeps. This time, he waited to see if they might convert to an open line, but nothing more happened. He ended the call and wound his way toward the lake.

Evgeny had just ended a phone call that had distracted him too long from his vigil over Liesl. Now he was desperate to locate her. He raced from his hideout behind broken columns at one end of the long grandstand, down the cement strata of stairs toward the concert stage below. His hasty descent must have caught Max's eye. The violinist now turned to face Evgeny, who waved him off the stage.

Max put down the violin he'd been tuning and headed down the portable steps to the ground.

"Where's Liesl?" Evgeny called at a half run toward Max.

Max turned to look around him. "I don't know." Evgeny watched the young man's slim body straighten to attention. "What's the matter?" The voice echoed alarm.

"Where's Cade?"

Max pointed behind him. "Up on the stage. What's wrong?"

"Come with me." Evgeny led Max a short distance from the rest of the musicians, who were securing the last of the instruments and packing up music.

Evgeny's report was swift and blunt. "My contact in Moscow did a check on your girlfriend. She is a freelance spy. She works for whoever will pay her." Viktor had finally searched the right files.

Max stepped backward and nearly stumbled, but Evgeny kept charging. "And the one paying her right now is your father."

The color drained from Max's stricken face.

"Where is she?" Evgeny pressed.

"Erica?"

"No. Liesl!"

Max seemed to have lost all bearings, then suddenly, he spun toward the stage. "Cade!" he hollered.

"Right here," Cade called, approaching the edge of the stage. It must have been the sight of Max and Evgeny together and the looks on their faces that made Cade leap from the stage and run toward them. Max quickly repeated the news to him, then asked, "Where is Liesl? And

Erica?" All three men pivoted in every direction, but could see neither woman.

Evgeny's phone beeped. He stepped away and took the call. A near breathless Ava Mullins told him, "One of the phones we took from Volynski's boat just received a call. Our people broke through the encryption. The signal came from where you are! Somebody there is trying to reach him!"

Evgeny's thoughts raced. "Make them think they have," he told her. "Return the call and get somebody to fake the voice."

"That's risky. We could lose the lead."

"We could lose Liesl! And Max!" Evgeny briefed her on Erica and who she was working for.

While he was still speaking to Ava, Max called to him from a huddle of musicians, one of them pointing toward the far trees. "The lake!"

Liesl recoiled at the name. *Maxum Morozov!* She stared at the man as if he were an apparition.

He moved closer to the boulders Liesl had just climbed. Perched on top, she was trapped. "Erica!" she called.

"Quiet," Maxum ordered. "Be still." He looked away and nodded. Erica stepped from the other side of the rocks and stood before Liesl.

"I'm really sorry," Erica offered weakly, her eyes drifting toward the ground.

Liesl struggled to make sense of what was happening. "What have you done?" she cried to Erica.

"She did what I told her to do," Maxum answered, cautiously searching the woods around them, then turned back to Liesl. He was oddly composed. "She's been watching Max for me."

What?

"Ivan is dead," he said, "but another has already risen to take his place. And his eye is on my son."

Liesl stared at the man. Max had once described his father's imposing stature and strength. But the man before her now was slumped, his face hollowed. Liesl had heard of his cruel and violent temper. What was this she heard now? A different kind of voice saying . . . *my son.*

"But I will not show myself to Max. You must carry something to him for me. Hand deliver it with great care. Erica has it, but she and I must disappear now."

Liesl turned to her. "It was all an act," she accused Erica. "You knew what was happening. And Max meant nothing to you." Liesl felt outrage rise up like bile to her throat. "He loved you. Both of you!" Her eyes darted between the two. "And you both betrayed him!"

"Keep your voice down and listen," Maxum ordered gruffly. "We don't have time for this. You and Max are in danger from—"

"From me," came the voice.

A man approached from behind Maxum, a man holding a gun with a long silencer attached.

"That's him!" Erica cried to Maxum, who whirled around too late. Liesl watched him reach inside the pocket of his jacket.

"Stop!" the man ordered Maxum. "Take your hand off the gun."

It was then that Liesl attempted to leap from the boulder.

"You!" the man called, turning his weapon on her. "Sit down!"

Turning back to Maxum, he said, "It sounds to me like you've switched sides, old man. I thought you and Glinka were a team. He'll be sad to hear about this."

"Felix Shevcik," Maxum snarled the name, showing his empty hands to the man. "Ivan's little sicko."

But the man just laughed. "Not this time, I'm afraid." He turned leering eyes on Liesl. "I should have taken the lovely Miss Bower long before now, when I had the chance, and the privacy to relish the pleasure." He glanced back at Maxum and shrugged. "But Ivan said wait, and he's the boss."

"Not anymore," Maxum said evenly, one hand signaling something to Erica. "He's dead."

Felix laughed again. "Still the trained liar."

"When was the last time you spoke to him?" Maxum prodded.

Felix didn't respond at first, then, "Don't mess with me. I have work to do." But as he raised his gun, a phone somewhere on him vibrated and he hesitated. For just a couple of seconds, he seemed distracted and unsure of what to do, the gun swaying just a bit. But it was all the time Maxum needed. He reached for his gun, dropped to the ground, and took the shot. But even the distracted Felix was faster. He pumped two bullets into Maxum. Then turned the gun on Liesl. Before he could fire, though, three shots rang out. His body jerked violently, and he crumpled to the ground, twisted and still.

The gun still in his hand, Evgeny dashed toward the body. Only after confirming that Felix was dead, did he turn his attention to Liesl. He climbed up the boulder and reached for her hand. "Come down. It's all over." But she couldn't move.

"I, I can't," she stammered. Then she heard a loud thrashing through the trees and looked past Evgeny. Cade burst through ahead of Max and raced for her. Evgeny stepped aside as Cade scrambled toward Liesl and lifted her to him. As he did, she saw Max drop suddenly to the ground. "Please put me down," she asked Cade, finally summoning her strength. She grabbed his and Evgeny's arms and let them help her off the slick rocks, then rushed to Max.

He'd just stripped the shirt from his body and pressed it into the hole in his father's chest. But Maxum Morozov reached for his son's bloodied hand and pulled it away. "It's okay," he whispered. "This is better." The gurgling in his mouth produced a stream of bright red blood.

"We'll get you to a hospital, Dad. You'll be just fine." Max looked frantically toward Cade, but Erica was already punching in an emergency call.

"No, Max," came the fading whisper. "No heroics for me. Now listen . . ." He tried to raise his head. "Erica . . ."

Max rounded on the girl as she came up and knelt beside him, his eyes piercing hers. "Go away! I don't want to see—"

"No," Maxum wheezed. "She's not the enemy. It's Glinka." He waved a hand toward Erica, who jumped up to retrieve her bag. When she returned, she pulled a large envelope from inside and handed it to Max.

"Evidence against Glinka." Maxum strained for the words. "Proof he ordered . . . " A spasm cut his breath. ". . . ordered Gorev's murder." He shook his head. "Legitimate proof . . . not my forgeries." He managed a blood-stained smile.

"Dad, don't talk. The ambulance will be here in seconds."

Maxum reached for his son's hand again. This time he held on to it. "I had to come. To see you." Another smile. "You're a fine musician." He nodded slightly. "I'm very proud of . . ." His body lurched in a spasm. He gasped once, and that was all.

"Dad! Dad!" Max cradled his father and mourned from somewhere deep and untapped for too long.

Liesl slid close and laid her hand on his back. "He came to warn us."

They sat quietly on the ground next to the body until they heard the sirens. Only then did they turn to see Erica watching them from a distance.

But Evgeny was gone.

Chapter 48

Max and Liesl refused to cancel the concert. With Cade, they returned to the Bernhoff estate and a fitful nap for all three. Erica had slipped away after the police questioning. No one knew where she'd gone.

When Max awoke that afternoon, he experienced just a trace of peace. Was it relief? Closure? The treacherous journey of Maxum Morozov finally at an end? He didn't know, only that there was a welling up of hope for something undefined.

He eased from his bedroom, passed the closed door to Liesl and Cade's room and slipped out of the house without even a servant observing. The path he and Erica had taken that morning lay ahead. He felt a warm breeze stir against him and he laid a hand over what had been his bare and bloodied chest just hours ago. His father's blood—tainted yet poured out in a final act of caring. But was it enough to wash away the wound scabbed over many times in the soul of Max Morozov?

He stepped up his pace and moved into the open meadow, crossing it without a thought for who might lurk just beyond. Until he heard a rustle in the grass behind him and turned.

"Can we talk?" Erica called to him.

Why not? he thought. She was dead to him, as well. He didn't answer but waited for her to reach him.

"It won't take long," she said. "I'm flying home in a few hours."

"I'm not sure Israel needs another spy walking its streets." He wished to extinguish his anger but couldn't.

"My home is Berlin. It always has been. And I'm not a Jew."

He ran a hand through his hair and laughed dryly. "You're just one illusion after another. I'll bet your name isn't Erica Bachman either."

"It's Erica. You don't need to know the rest."

"Of course not. Why should I care?" But he did. Why was he acting so childish?

"Max, I hired on for a job. Your father was just another employer who paid well. I was to stay close to you for maybe a year, he said. Until he could be sure you weren't at risk." She stepped closer. "I didn't know the man we killed was after Liesl."

"*We* killed?"

"Three shots. Two from Kozlov, one from me." She slid the long skirt up her leg, exposing the holstered gun above her knee. "They'll run ballistics on all three bullets in the guy, but won't find a match off Evgeny's. I hear he's too good for that. All the police know is that Liesl and I were followed and your father tried to protect us. He fired and missed. My shot connected. So did someone else's, though I didn't know who the guy was, I told them. If they identify Felix, they'll assume the fourth shooter was another hit man like him. They'd be right about that, wouldn't they?"

"You've got this all figured out, don't you? So now, you go back to Berlin a victim and a hero."

She glanced at the ground then back at him. "My family's short on heroes."

"But not liars."

She eyed him steadily. "No, not liars." She put both hands on her hips and looked over the meadow. When she turned back to him, he saw a steely resolve in her face. "I didn't have a headache that day at the Holocaust Memorial. Not only was Maxum waiting for me, but I just couldn't bear to stay there . . . because my grandfather was an SS guard who gunned down some of those Jews." She looked away and he could see the clenching of her jaw. "He was at Auschwitz. My other grandfather was a physician at Treblinka. They told their families they were keeping the prisoners safe from those who wanted to hurt them. Imagine." She swiped at her eyes, then turned them on him. "So how could I watch your great-aunt Bethel with all the laughing children, knowing it might have been my grandfather who exterminated them?" She looked at the ground and raised a hand to her chin, pushing hard against it. "How could I do that?"

Max remained as still as she, until finally, she turned abruptly toward him. "I have to go," she said. "I'm sorry for all the lies." She held his eyes a moment longer, then ran across the field and turned down the driveway. Max didn't stop her.

Chapter 49

By the concert hour that night, news of the shooting at Dutzendteich Lake had ricocheted throughout Germany and over the oceans, fired by the international celebrity of Liesl and Max. The media had not yet pieced together the backgrounds of those killed, but it was coming. Max was certain of that. Once the subterranean notoriety of the dead was dragged into the light, it would be a clear path to the roles he and Liesl had played through it all.

The orchestra and its solo performers for the evening had been sequestered in a building near the entrance to the rally grounds. The Nuremberg police had required it when crowds of people started showing up at the gates many hours before the concert. After local television first reported an assault on Liesl Bower and the shooting death of Max Morozov's father, a wave of shock and regret rumbled through Nuremberg, drawing its citizens—even Berliners and others from nearby towns—to the place where the two musicians had insisted they would still perform. The number of supporters had swelled to an unwieldy throng. It was then that Franz Bernhoff and a hastily gathered team of corporate sponsors opened the gates to the concert for all to come in, ticket or no ticket, reimbursing those who'd already paid.

"I have never seen such an outpouring of compassion in this town,"

Franz had declared to the anxious orchestra managers. "My fellow music patrons and I must do all we can to honor that."

The seating, already in place before the stage, was hastily multiplied, but it still wasn't enough for the masses who poured through the gates. Many had brought blankets to spread on the ground, and some their own chairs. By the time the sun set and the field lights came on, the Zeppelinfeld audience throbbed with anticipation, as if waiting to exhale.

When the musicians' buses finally pulled up to the gate and stopped, some in the expectant audience rose. Then others. Finally, all. In tuxedoes and long black gowns, the orchestra emerged from the buses with Max and Liesl absorbed within it, almost indistinguishable from the other musicians. For tonight, the soloists had declined the customary featured-artist treatment, no moving about in their own bubble of stardom.

As they all filed through the main gate, a thunderous applause broke out inside the arena, stopping the musicians cold. They gaped at the sight. They'd been told the audience had grown rapidly, but they weren't prepared for this. Max and Liesl were so startled by the enormity and apparent spontaneity of the audience, they had to be prompted to keep up with the others now advancing toward the stage. Liesl stole glances at Cade, on the front row next to Ben and Anna. The go-for-it set of her husband's handsome face transmitted strength to her.

The applause continued until everyone had mounted the steps and moved into position. Max and Liesl remained partially hidden behind the bass section. Knowing the scarcity of printed programs for the unexpected surge in the crowd, the conductor would announce each piece. In passable German, he prefaced the first introduction with this: "The appearance of the Israel Philharmonic on these grounds would have been historic enough. But what you have done here tonight surpasses even that. On behalf of all our musicians, we thank you for this unprecedented display of support."

When Max and Liesl finally stepped forward, the applause was so explosive, it sent a tremor through the metal undergirding of the stage. They took their positions in front of the orchestra, pausing long enough to smile and bow with gratitude. But Max felt like kneeling before them, to beg their forgiveness. He'd done nothing to deserve such affection, such solidarity with him. Solidarity with what? The wreckage and shame of his family? His fugitive father who'd met such a vile end. The scourge of the Holocaust that refused to relieve him of its curse, its possessive hold on him. *These people know none of this! And I can't tell them. I can only play what they've come to hear.* And that was reason enough to take up his violin and escape into the music. A cellist from the orchestra joined Max and Liesl, and the conductor announced Beethoven's *Triple Concerto*, a favorite of German audiences.

The strings of the orchestra opened with the familiar five-note theme of the concerto, to which the remaining instruments added their timbre. Poised and ready, the three musicians in front took their cue and joined the powerful piece. And the night began.

At that moment in a small town southeast of Moscow, law enforcement officers of the Investigative Committee of Russia surrounded the elegant residence of a socialite known long ago for her liaison with President Arkady Glinka. The house was dark and still until the officers broke down the front door and waved flashlights on a room-by-room search. They found Glinka in bed with the woman, too inebriated to effectively wield the handgun he grabbed from the nightstand—or to resist arrest for the murder of Dimitri Gorev.

News of the arrest was immediately relayed to President Noland, now seated with FBI Director Rick Salabane in the Oval Office. It was midday in Washington. "I am frankly surprised at the speed at which your Russian counterparts moved on this, Rick."

"That packet of documents Max Morozov took from his father was undeniably genuine," Salabane reported. "Ironic that it came from a master forger. Our Russian friends tell me they'd had their suspicions about Glinka, but no evidence of his hand in Gorev's assassination. The bigger job for them now is rounding up the rest of Ivan's people, some of them still in power."

"But Ivan obviously didn't consider Glinka one of his people any longer, or he wouldn't have ordered Maxum to gather such proof." Noland paused. "Now, I want to shift to another matter, something I want you to tend to right away. Everything you've got on Max Morozov, the son, and Liesl Bower is to be pushed as far down a classified crack as you can get it. I've ordered the same with the CIA, the national security team, and everybody else who interfaced with those two during this whole Russian debacle. The Israeli prime minister joins me in this and is issuing the same orders in his country. I don't want any reporter picking up even the faintest whiff of how embedded Max and Liesl were in all this.

"That goes for Evgeny Kozlov, too," the president added with emphasis. "Short of a presidential pardon, I want him off the radar and buried out of reach in those same files. He didn't set out to serve our national interests, but I don't know many who've helped avert greater disaster for our country."

"Yes, sir. I'll see to it."

"And hurry. The media bloodhounds are circling."

At the conclusion of the *Triple Concerto* and lengthy applause, Liesl, Max and the cellist returned to their seats at the back of the stage and waited for the orchestra to complete two of Bach's *Brandenburg Concerti*. It pleased them all to summon two of Germany's finest composers on such a remarkable night, though when the program was selected months ago, no one could have known the turn of events that would draw so many of the composers' countrymen together for this concert.

Liesl gazed at Max's profile, chiseled in something immovable. She'd never seen him so rigid. Even his playing of the sometimes melancholy *Triple Concerto* had lacked his usual eloquence, like he was playing just to reach the end. Liesl squeezed her eyes closed. *He hurts, Lord. Lift him.*

High in the Ural Mountains, a Russian military unit moved quietly into place around the entrance to what used to be a mine shaft. Their orders had reached them just hours before they launched the raid. In the dark, they counted down to the moment of surprise, then simultaneously stormed two small barracks and the gateway to the weapons factory. Accompanied by a hazmat team, they entered the underground facility and were grateful to find so few on duty inside.

Later, the unit commander phoned his assessment to Moscow authorities: three crated weapons ready for shipment. Two more in process and enough weapons-grade chemical and biological materials to disable much of the country. There was no doubt which one.

"Sir," the commander reported to his superior, "there was an American flag taped to each crate."

"Shut it down."

When the conductor motioned to her, Liesl rose from her seat, feeling Max's hand lightly grip hers and squeeze. Without looking down at him, she squeezed it back then wound her way through the orchestra to the concert grand. It was time. She bowed and looked into the first row of seats where Cade beamed with something close to victory.

This would be the first time she had publicly performed Tchaikovsky's *Grand Sonata* since her Harvard music professor Schell Devoe buried a code in a fateful copy of it.

Now, Cade's words returned to her: *It's time she chased off its demons.* The sonata had been the grappling hook that had dragged her, and later Max, into something they were still trying to escape. Was it finally time?

She longed to hold her husband and whisper her adoration. *But look at his face. He knows.*

Now seated, her hands poised over the keys, she drew a full breath and braced for the purging to come. It was a strenuous piece whose opening was indeed grand, a powerful march. Soon, there was nothing but Liesl and the music. She was enveloped by it, swept into its pounding stride, her fingers striking like steel, as if she had to keep pace or she wouldn't survive.

Then the march stopped. Her fingers relaxed, and the music turned lyrical. Now she could dance over the keyboard. She was free.

It was early afternoon in Anhinga Bay when Spencer Fremont drove Mona Greyson home from the hospital. Her daughter, Tally, sat in the back seat of the car, quiet and oddly content, it seemed. As soon as they turned in at the old Victorian home, Mona asked him to stop. She stared at the "For Sale by Owner" realty sign freshly inserted into the sandy soil.

Mona twisted in her seat to face Tally. "Already?"

"We agreed, Mom."

"But so soon?"

"We can't stay here any longer. Even your doctors said so. And Mr. Fremont knows it, too."

Mona looked at Spencer. "I'm hoping you'll seriously consider our offer to move with us. Tally's never had anyone like a grandfather around." She looked squarely into his kind face. "And she's right. You're part of us now. We sort of belong together . . . in some way."

He turned in his seat. "Certainly I'll come for good, long visits. But for now, I believe I'm where God intends for me to serve him best . . . for reasons that must be obvious to you by now."

Tally persevered. "I understand, but when you do come, you're going to love the Georgia mountains," Tally said, her tone buoyant, "especially the valley where we live. I'll take you in the four-wheeler right up to the top where you can see Tallulah Falls and the gorge, and then—"

"Tally," her mother interrupted, "slow down, girl. You're almost out of breath."

Spencer watched Tally in the rearview mirror, her face alight as he'd never seen it before.

"I know, Mom. But we're going home."

Sweeping toward the conclusion of the *Grand Sonata*, Liesl felt the thrumming of her heart in beat with the music. She was one with the elation Tchaikovsky must have intended for the players of his artistry. The elixir of relief streamed warm and sweet all the way to every finger, until she lifted them all from the keys, and rose from the piano.

The audience leapt to their feet with an uproar of praise. But Liesl looked only at Cade, with clear confirmation. The demons were gone.

The finale of the program had been saved for Max and the full orchestra in another Tchaikovsky piece, the formidable *Violin Concerto in D Major.* Liesl passed him as he came forward, and he smiled, but absently. He was hurting worse than she'd realized.

The virtuoso violinist, to the untrained ear, played brilliantly throughout the long piece. But to Liesl, Max Morozov had not inhabited his music that night. He simply wasn't there.

And then it happened.

At the end of the concerto, Max bowed low before his audience's applause, but his mind was in torment. All these people had come to share his grief and he'd hidden it from them. He couldn't let them leave yet.

How could he have known early this morning what he was about to do now . . . and why? What had prompted him then, even before the first shot rang out in the woods by the lake? He'd asked a sound technician to secretly wire a certain spot should the moment arise. And now it had.

In the midst of the applause that showed no sign of slowing, he looked once at Liesl, then gave a prearranged signal to the conductor. To everyone else's surprise, including Liesl's and the orchestra's, he hurried down the stage steps, turned to the empty grandstand behind, and began his climb. The audience abruptly ceased its applause and watched in obvious bewilderment as Max reached a point near the top.

Now, he approached the speaker's platform high above the crowd and turned into it, tracing Hitler's footsteps, one at a time, all the way to the place of hate.

As he raised his violin and began John Williams's haunting theme to *Schindler's List,* he heard some in the crowd nearest him gasp, surely at the images of the Holocaust that the music summoned. As the wrenching solo soared high over the field, many in the audience wept openly. But at the end of the piece, he transitioned seamlessly into something that caused others to clasp their hands in prayer. It was the powerful *Via Dolorosa.* Now, the bow struck feverishly against the instrument, sounding every step of Christ's march to the hill outside Jerusalem.

He played on as if the survival of every person there depended on the hope now lifting from the music. In his hands, the violin wailed and mourned. And then it forgave.

Chapter 50

FOUR MONTHS LATER

Exodus II left Charleston Harbor early that morning with a payload of customers angling for yellowfin tuna, dolphin, and whatever else might take their bait. The seas drifted lazily and the offshore run went smoothly.

Ian and Henry had added the latest fish-finder to the boat, and so far, it had paid off. Word had spread about the old sea captains' knack for hauling in impressive catches, and business was brisk. They'd even hired on a new man to ease the workload.

With three crew and four customers on board, the boat plied its way toward the offshore harvest until Henry finally slowed the engines and showed Ian the sonar signature of a school that looked promising. It wasn't one of their usual honey holes, but the computer images from below were too good to pass up.

All four customers dropped their lines near the stern and waited. It wasn't long before the first tuna bit, then another. Soon, though, an ominous shadow appeared off the bow. Ian spotted it first and called to Henry, who was still at the helm.

"We've got us a tiger shark out here. Better move on."

At the other end of the boat, though, the fishermen were still pulling in their catch and didn't want to go anywhere.

"That shark will chase the other fish away," Ian told them. "And besides, you don't want something like that in the water when you're leaning toward it trying to gaff your catch. You could lose an arm that way."

"Hey, I've never seen a shark in the wild before," one customer said, putting down his rod and heading straight for the bow. Another customer followed him. They were giddy as kids when they first spotted the dorsal fin about twenty feet off the starboard side.

"We're just going to leave that thing right there and find us another spot," Ian informed them. "So come on and—"

A gun blast sounded above them, the magnum round finding its mark on the shark's head. One of the customers at the bow screamed and the other dropped flat on the deck with his hands over his head.

Ian spun toward the bridge and saw his new crewman standing on top aiming for another shot. "Evgeny! Stop!"

Looking down at the terrified fishermen, Evgeny Kozlov apparently didn't understand their alarm.

"Come down here, son," Ian ordered, but gently. He still wasn't comfortable with the new hire.

Ian helped the customer who was lying frozen to the deck back to his feet and tried to calm the others as Henry cranked the engines and eased from the spot. Leaving them all with something to eat and drink, Ian guided Evgeny to the cabin for a little chat.

"I'm not sure how you do it in Russia," Ian began, "but we use hooks. We don't blow holes in fish, even a mean one, unless it's attached to your leg." He shook his head slightly. "Now I know you've been used to a different sort of lifestyle, and that a gun has solved lots of problems for you in the past." Ian noticed the corners of the man's mouth begin to twitch. "But I sure do hope that's all over now. Liesl and Ava seem to think so." He looked his new crewman straight in the eye. "What do *you* think?"

Evgeny smiled. "Can I borrow a hook?"

That same morning, Liesl and Cade took their coffee to the porch rockers overlooking Tidewater Lane. The air was laced with cool vapors off the harbor and the leaves fluttered in shades of autumn.

"Was that Max on the phone earlier?" Cade asked.

"Yes. He wanted us to know he's decided to pay a visit to Berlin."

"You mean to a certain photographer?"

Liesl nodded. "Erica invited him to come to a gallery opening for her work. And get this, most of the photographs are night shots from the Nuremberg concert."

Cade was surprised. "I thought she'd left town that afternoon."

"It seems she did a U-turn at the airport and came back. I think Max is anxious to see her, even though they've got a lot of reckoning to do with each other."

A brilliant gold leaf spun loose from one of the maples and blew onto the porch near Liesl. She picked it up and twirled it between her fingers. "Look at the light in this leaf. It flames brightest just before it falls away and dies. Too bad it couldn't find that light earlier and enjoy it longer, before it was time to go."

Cade pulled his wife's hand to his chest and held it close. "Is this the kind of hormone-induced introspection I can expect for the next seven months?"

"I'm sure of it." She smiled and patted her abdomen.

After Cade left for work, Liesl strolled into the garden and stopped in front of the playhouse. She could see them all there again, the day they celebrated the last nail driven into the little structure. Her mom and grandmother, her dad, and the little girl he'd called Punkin. She was someone different then, before the clawing things reached for her. Before all the dappled years of wandering in and out of the light, not knowing the difference.

She ran a hand back over her abdomen and the promise of new life inside it. Liesl would teach her child the difference between dark and light. She would do it long before the autumn.

Praise for *The Sound of Red Returning*

"The pop-pop-pop of surprise resolutions at the end makes a fine coda."
—**PUBLISHERS WEEKLY**

"Political intrigue, suspense, and just enough romance to keep readers guessing and interested. Well-defined secondary characters add that extra zing to the plot."
—**RT BOOK REVIEWS**

"Intrigue and suspense come together in an incredible story of love and betrayal, commitment and courage, power and danger . . . and a God who controls it all. Sue Duffy is a wonderfully gifted writer."
—**STEVE BROWN**, founder and president of
Key Life and host of Steve Brown Etc.

"Sue Duffy has mixed the mayhem of political intrigue with the melody of romance."
—**DICK BOHRER**, author, editor, and former journalism professor

Praise for *Red Dawn Rising*

"Sue Duffy writes with the authority and keen eye for detail of a journalist and with the flair for drama of a true storyteller."
—**JERRY BELLUNE**, chairman and former editor, *Lexington County Chronicle*

"The delicious quandary any Sue Duffy fan faces is whether to linger over every well-placed word or rush on to see what happens next. In *Red Dawn Rising*, Duffy creates a threatening world in which her all-too-human characters must survive. That they wrestle with God and their own painful histories makes it even more satisfying."
—**AÏDA ROGERS**, writer, editor of *State of the Heart:*
South Carolina Writers on the Places They Love

"Sue Duffy just gets better and better. Like the proverbial potato chip, a curious nibble at one of her books is the precursor to an all-out binge. Each tantalizing chapter invites her readers to neglect responsibilities and forgo sleep until they consume every last one in a satisfying, self-indulgent gorge of adventure and intrigue—lightly salted with romance."
—**LORI HATCHER**, author, blogger, and editor of
Reach Out, Columbia magazine

"The second book in the Red Returning trilogy continues the political intrigue and suspense that is so impelling in the first book. Sue Duffy has given us another fast-paced, suspenseful, and thought-provoking story of espionage, courage, and redemption."
—**SUE HARDIN**, South Carolina state leader for the Church Library Ministry